LINDSTROM'S PROGRESS

Volume Two of the Lindstrom Trilogy

A Stonewood Imprint

JOHN MOSS

Published by Iguana Books
720 Bathurst Street, Suite 303
Toronto, Ontario, Canada
M5S 2R4

Front cover image: "Univers-elle ou Larmes d'or" by Anne Marie Zylberman, 2006, commonly and erroneously attributed to Gustaf Klimt.

Front cover design: Ruth Dwight Designs

A Stonewood Imprint

Library and Archives Canada Cataloguing in Publication

Moss, John, 1940-, author

Lindstrom's progress/ John Moss.

Issued in print and electronic formats.

ISBN 978-1-77180-280-2 (softcover).--ISBN 978-1-77180-281-9 (EPUB).--ISBN 978-1-77180-282-6 (Kindle)

I. Title.
PS8576.O7863L572018 C813'.6 C2018-904094-7
C2018-904095-5

This is an original print edition of *Lindstrom's Progress*.

for Beverley because I love her

1 THE KRESSLER

HARRY LINDSTROM GAZED OUT A WINDOW ON THE SIXTH floor of the Kressler Hotel, searching for his reflection in the sheer glass wall of the office tower across Königstrasse. The sun setting behind the hotel surrounded the ornate façade of the Kressler in flames. Blinded by the illusion, Harry looked to the skyline beyond, which was pale and cool as the darkness of evening rose from the oldest part of Vienna and spread over the city. On the horizon, a moving circle of lights outlined the gigantic Ferris wheel in Prater Park as it came to a ponderous halt. The haunting tremulations of a zither resonated inside his skull.

Forget the theme music, Harry. You should be thinking about murder.

The voice was familiar, of course. He turned and scanned the room. As he expected, she wasn't there. He switched on a table lamp with a burgundy shade weighted with crystal pendants before returning to the window and pressing his forehead against the pane. The flames were subsiding. The Ferris wheel began moving again. Self-consciously, he raised his hand over his head as if waving and located his reflection, highlighted in a burgundy glow.

Well done, said the voice. *You've found yourself. But remember why we're here, Harry. She'll be downstairs by now.*

Harry was in no hurry. Madalena Strauss had kept him waiting three days.

He expected a plea for civility but heard only silence.

His gaze shifted to movement in the glass wall as a door opened onto a poorly lit balcony. Three people—a man, a woman, and a small boy—stepped out and stood against the ornate stone balustrade. It took a moment for Harry to realize that they were a reflection from the balcony next to his own.

The man seemed to look across the abyss at Harry watching him, then he turned and helped the woman clamber up onto the balustrade and lifted the boy and climbed up himself, with the toddler between them, holding their hands. The floor of the balcony above pressed low so that by reaching up with their free hands it provided the adults stability.

Again, the man looked directly at Harry's reflection. Then he turned to the woman, she looked down at the boy, and still holding hands, the three of them stepped into the air.

Harry gasped for breath, drowning, his mind reeling. He turned from the window, eyes groping for something, a colour, a texture, the brocade wallpaper, gilt-edged mirrors, the grotesque chandelier, something to grasp and take hold and draw him back into the everyday world. Time passed, and he heard honking; more time, then the ululation of sirens.

He looked out again, straight ahead. The light behind the reflected balcony was filled with movement. The balcony door opened and a very large man stepped out into the open. The man put his hand across his brow to shield his eyes and stared in the direction of Harry's reflection. He flicked a lit cigarette into the air, cocked his thumb and index finger and jerked his hand upward as an imaginary handgun exploded. Was he miming his contempt for death? Or passing judgment on murder—for the child had been murdered, whatever had driven his parents to end their own lives. Was it an existential gesture aimed at an absent God? Or was he aiming at Harry?

Before Harry could think how to respond, the large man receded back into the hotel room next to his and shut the door behind him.

Harry leaned against the window and looked down. Königstrasse was bustling with colours and people. One small area of the sidewalk was cordoned off. Otherwise, a springtime evening in the Opera district of old Vienna was in full swing.

The Riesenrad Ferris wheel stopped and started again. The zither in his head resumed its unsettling cadence. He listened for his wife's voice, wondering if she heard it too. She often spoke in his mind. They carried on conversations. While he knew she was dead, she was as real to him as his own sense of himself.

"Karen." He whispered her name. They had watched old movies together. They had watched *The Third Man* many times. The penetrating urgency of the music, the menacing play of distended shadows in a war-ruined city, seemed the perfect correlatives for what he was feeling now.

Don't confuse feeling with thinking, Harry.

I'm thinking about a movie.

And what should you be thinking?

About the boy. About the primal absurdity of arbitrary death. Instead, I'm thinking about music and shadows.

Maybe that's all there is, Harry. Music and shadows.

Don't, Karen.

I was a professor of cultural theory. That's how I think, she said.

Harry's struggle to avoid confrontation with what he'd observed was interrupted by a loud thumping. A key turned in the lock and his door burst open.

The large man from the balcony next door, the fat man who had turned his fingers and fist into a gun, strode over to Harry.

"Can I help you?" said Harry, standing firm. He could think of nothing more appropriate to say.

Staying close by the door, a hotel porter exuded smug condescension. So the intruder must be someone with authority, a cop or a gangster.

"You see nothing," the fat man said in oddly inflected English.

"Not very much."

"No, Mr. Lindstrom." The man looked out the window, sidling close enough that Harry had to back away. "You see nothing from here."

Less an inflection than grammatical distortion. Not German. Russian, perhaps?

"Perhaps you are right," said Harry.

"Good evening, then." The fat man turned and left abruptly. The porter, having stepped to the side, followed after him.

He knows your name, Harry.

Harry moved close to the window and looked down. After a few minutes, his portly intruder walked past the stained patch of sidewalk where a uniformed officer was removing the yellow tape that had sequestered the death scene. Within moments, pedestrians began passing over the pavement oblivious to the stains or the drama they recalled.

Vienna is like that, Harry thought. So many European cities are like that. Their bloody histories, small horrors and unspeakable suffering, absorbed into the pavement, the architecture, the atmosphere that in themselves speak of imperial grandeur. A North American city is simple, by comparison. It grows organically. Or, like Detroit, it grows and decays. Wars are fought elsewhere. Triumphal marches are through alien gates.

There was another knock on his door, this time deferential.

"I'm sorry, sir," said the same porter as if the incident of moments ago had never occurred. "There is a lady to see you."

"Send her up."

"I wasn't sure."

"No," said Harry. He let his thought hang in the air. "It's all right. I'll meet her downstairs. Ten minutes."

He could have just called.

Or she could, he thought.

Exactly ten minutes later Harry stepped off the elevator. Wearing jeans, a button-down shirt open at the neck and the nubuck sports jacket he had picked up while working a case on the Swedish island of Gotland the previous winter, he displayed the nonchalant elegance expected of guests at the Kressler. Being forty-three and fit, Harry was comfortable with his personal style. He did not dress for the setting. He assumed any setting he encountered would accommodate the way he dressed. In this, he betrayed not arrogance or sartorial insensitivity but confidence held over from his days as an academic that the mind made the man and clothing was an agreeable vanity.

He hadn't given much thought to how he was dressed at the moment. It would have been the nubuck jacket with jeans or his shabbily-genteel Armani blazer with jeans. Either, with brown Cole Haan shoes and no tie.

He wandered around until he spotted the only woman seated alone. She was ensconced in a splendid, intimate, decadent parlour panelled in dark wood, with an illuminated glass ceiling, formal furnishings, lots of floral prints and red brocade, no windows but wall sconces, an ornate chandelier, and table lamps ablaze with plum-red shades.

Your lady friend is posing over coffee and biscuits, Harry. She looks rather louche. Don't you love the word louche. *If she weren't a cop I'd take her for a desperately successful actress or a very expensive escort.*

Harry tried to ignore Karen's caustic congeniality. His mind was still crowded with images of smashed bodies on the pavement outside. These were intercut with grisly memories he tried to suppress of his family's destruction by water.

The woman looked up but didn't rise when he approached.

"Harry Lindstrom," he offered, holding out his hand. She nodded.

He sat down facing her. A waiter brought fresh coffee and hot milk. A second cup and saucer were already in place. There were sufficient biscuits for two.

"That was an unpleasant business outside," the woman offered as a conversational gambit, allowing herself a disinterested grimace approaching disdain.

"Apparently," said Harry with as much nonchalance as he could muster. Experience had taught him the best way to deal with the intolerable was to function as normally as possible.

"They jumped from the roof. It is fortunate no one was under them."

"From the roof?" He was not surprised by the distortion of facts, but he marvelled that the fat man could have taken control so quickly. "Quite fortunate," he agreed. He didn't associate good fortune with death.

"They were foreigners."

"Really?" Harry wondered why the qualification was relevant.

"Canadians. Like yourself, Mr. Lindstrom."

"Call me Harry."

"Call me Madalena if you wish."

Madalena Strauss sat tall in a high-backed chair. Her tumultuous hair spread away from her head in an arresting display of copper red waves. She looked around the room with a proprietary air. She was Viennese. This was her world. And then she looked back at Harry.

"Thank you for coming."

"It was difficult to refuse, Ms. Strauss."

"Are you attracted to murder, Mr. Lindstrom?"

"When the case is unusual, yes. And of course to Vienna and to being well paid."

"But, as you explained, not in advance. Not until after the case is resolved to our mutual satisfaction." Her composure seemed to waver but only for an instant.

"You find it awkward to think of yourself as a *case*?"

"My ex-fiancé's death is a *case*. I am simply the killer."

Harry's guts were still roiling in his struggle to erase the images of carnage outside, a scene he had not witnessed although the details were embedded like shrapnel in his mind. He wasn't surprised that Madalena Strauss proclaimed herself a killer. He had found the notion irresistible when she contacted him at home in Toronto. She wanted Harry to establish her guilt, not prove her innocence. He was intrigued from the start to know whether she had actually killed someone, or was something else going on, something more grievous than murder?

He gazed across the table, scanning her face, looking for emotion. She was very attractive, especially in the indirect lighting of the Kressler, but cool, poised, and predatory like a prize cat musing about vulnerable prey. "You said your *ex*-fiancé. Was the *ex* a posthumous designation?"

She smiled. He wasn't sure if she didn't understand the question or if she was amused by his cavalier attention to nuance.

Her smile lingered. "We were, you would say, *dis*-engaged when I shot him."

"You shot him?"

"Yes.'

"And the police refuse to charge you?"

"I am police."

"You shot him with your service weapon?"

"Yes."

"You told me on the phone you had no choice. Wouldn't that make your crime manslaughter, not murder?"

"The extenuating circumstances were personal. I intended to kill Dietmar Henning and I did. It was a premeditated execution."

"To which you confessed?"

"Absolutely. I stretched my neck on the guillotine block. But the blade didn't fall."

Harry shuddered, while appreciating her flair for the dramatic.

"Do they still use the guillotine in Austria?" he asked.

"Not since 1950. Capital punishment is no longer legal—although sometimes desirable. Before the Third Reich, we sometimes hanged people. Now we use extreme confinement and allow the guilty an interminably tedious lifetime to die from the inside out."

"Something you desire for yourself, it seems."

"I confessed. My confession was summarily dismissed."

"You offered proof?"

"My word and my knowledge of the circumstances. But three of my fellow officers swore an affidavit that I was with them the night of the shooting."

"And you weren't?"

"No. They are lying."

"What about fingerprints or DNA?"

"At the scene? Of course, we had been lovers."

"Other fingerprints?"

"None."

"The murder took place at his apartment?"

"His flat, yes. Beside the Danube Canal. He was shot on his balcony. I pushed his body over, went down the elevator, and dragged him to the water."

"No witnesses?"

"It was three in the morning."

"And your buddies claimed you were with them at that hour?"

"A late party, yes. They are not my *buddies*. My colleagues."

"What about ballistics?"

"A bullet embedded in his heart. I am a good shot, especially close up. But someone exchanged it for an untraceable slug of the same calibre. Another passed through his skull and was never retrieved. I fired three times. The first into the air to get his attention."

"Which I'm sure you did. And no one heard the shots?"

"It seems they did not."

"The police checked?"

"So they say."

"It appears there's a conspiracy to keep you out of prison."

"That is it, exactly."

"What about the media, the politicians, the police higher-ups, didn't they want a conviction?"

"As it turned out, my ex-fiancé was a very bad man. No one grieved for him, no one demanded justice. My claims were dismissed as the hysteria of an anguished lover. My bosses insisted I take some time off with full pay."

"And did you?"

"In Austria, if you are told to take time, you take time."

Harry was not familiar with the finer details of Austrian life. He spoke only a few words of German. He didn't know the legal system. His understanding of Austria and Vienna came from a brief visit over a decade previously and a couple of hours doing a Google chain where, following reference to reference, he wound up on the site he'd started from.

When he had at first demurred in the telephone conversation after their initial email exchange, Madalena Strauss insisted that most Austrians spoke English and that she could guide him through the intricacies of Austrian law; he would probably know more about Vienna, after his research, than people who had lived there all their lives.

"Ms. Strauss, you feel this Dieter Henning—"

"Dietmar."

"If you feel he deserved to die, if you are still convinced that his execution, as you call it, was justified—"

"A necessity, I had no choice."

"And you've tried to explain your reasons?"

"To the authorities? No, they are not relevant."

"The authorities or your reasons?"

She offered a wry smile with pursed lips that told him nothing.

"What I'm trying to get at is why you insist on being convicted for a crime no one wants to charge you with. Why not just walk away?"

"You do not walk away from murder, Mr. Lindstrom. If there was a moral imperative to kill Dietmar, there is an equally moral imperative to pay for having done so."

Harry was uneasy with facile equations, especially in relation to morality. Whatever her reasons for murdering the man, her task was apparently incomplete until she was jailed for the crime. Why? Retribution, expiation, atonement? She didn't seem like a woman in search of forgiveness.

"So you are here, Harry, to do the right thing. Yes?"

She called you Harry! That's a good start.

To what, he wondered.

Karen was Harry's conscience as well as his confidante.

He listened to the bustle of waiters, the ringing of crystal, the resonant clink of bone china. He was waiting. Not for Madalena Strauss. He knew Karen had more to say.

There's a pattern, here. Last winter, Birgitta Ghiberti wanted you to prove her son was a serial killer. This gorgeous creature wants you to prove she's the killer. In both cases you start out knowing who-done-it. Or think you do.

You're a cultural theorist. You know it's never as simple as that.

Was, Harry. I'm dead. And you're a philosopher. You love the confusion.

Was a philosopher.

Once one, always one.

It's something you do, not something you are.

Wittgenstein said that before you did.

He might have. Anyway, it's not the confusion that attracts me, it's the complexity—an existential challenge to explore the innumerable unknowns between the initial premise and what seems a foregone conclusion. You know where you're going but not how to get there.

You're being pretentious, Harry.

And you're being sesquipedalian.

That literally means "a foot and a half long." You're being sesquipedalian, saying I am.

He sat back and observed Madalena Strauss observing him. With a shock he realized it was not Karen who had distracted him from the images of death on the pavement outside but this woman sipping coffee like an autoerotic experience. With her red hair burning rampant in the pointillist light from the sconces and chandelier, with her tailored clothing and rakish demeanour, and with her piercing green eyes and petulant lips, he thought she must be the most sensual being he had ever encountered.

"From the roof," he reiterated, trying to get his bearings. "Are you sure?"

"The Canadians? Yes, from the roof." She gazed into his eyes with unnerving intimacy. "You will help me, Harry. My colleagues in Stockholm and Toronto told me you are very good at what you do."

"I am," he said. He worked more effectively by projecting confidence. He had learned that from Chief Inspector Gamache and Hercule Poirot. "You need someone discreet to find out why you have not been arrested," he said. "Canadians are renowned for discretion."

"Good!"

"Superintendent Miranda Quin? Inspector Hannah Arnason?" She nodded affirmation. For the time being, it was enough to know how she had found him.

Miranda's a fan, Harry. I doubt Hannah Arnason is. You slept with them both.

Not with Hannah; it was never consummated. Miranda was a very long time ago.

Measurable in months, not years.

"It is beyond my scope to investigate the police," he said.

"But not the crime."

"And I have no desire to prove an innocent woman guilty."

"I assure you, I am not innocent."

One way or another, I have no doubt.

A passing waiter refreshed their cups, pouring espresso and steaming milk simultaneously with an elegant flourish, and then slipped back into his place as a fixture in a milieu redolent of honourable servitude and Edwardian decadence.

Habsburg decadence, Harry.

He gazed around the room, taking in the ornate plasterwork, the dark wood panelling, the brocade curtains, and so much upholstery it seemed like an explosion of colour from his Aunt Beth Lindstrom's living room. An overlay of Regency, Victorian, Edwardian with not much of more recent vintage.

Federal, not Regency, Harry. And she was your great aunt.

Arguments with Karen continued to be a lovely diversion. They had resumed within months of her death, perhaps initiated, accommodated, encouraged, because her body had never been recovered from the Anishnabe River where the Devil's Cauldron had devoured their children, spit Harry out as a pathetic survivor, and ground Karen into detritus or secreted her battered corpse under muskeg downriver. The full impact of her death was not quite as apprehensible as those of Matt and Lucy, whose ashes were mingled in a rural cemetery near where the family had lived.

His mind swarmed with unruly details. Karen had distracted him from the woman opposite and her puzzling dilemma. He drew himself into the moment, but instead of responding to the urgency of her presence he spied beyond her in a dark corner of an anteroom the big man who had come to his room. The man was hunched awkwardly over as if he were trying not to be noticed in spite of his enormous size and ill-fitting apparel.

"Do you recognize that guy over there?" he asked Madalena Strauss.

She pivoted in her chair—he couldn't tell if she saw him—then she looked back at Harry. "Is it someone you know?"

"We've met."

The improbability of Harry knowing another person in Vienna did not seem to arouse her curiosity.

Harry sat back in his chair. There was a stillness between them that he found unsettling. She was more sinister than he had expected, more attractive than he could have imagined. She had a single-minded need to understand why she wasn't being prosecuted, she showed no empathy for the man she had murdered, and she was comfortable without the chatter that others might have considered a social necessity.

Those sound like symptoms, Harry.

Your doctorate is in the eternal verities, he responded. You're not a real doctor.

Uneasy with his companion's ominous charisma, not comforted by Karen's sardonic wit, he drew himself into focus. "Do you think the police won't lay charges because you're one of them?" he asked.

"No, that is not it."

Harry waited. They both recognized it was time to fill in the details.

After giving the appearance of consulting notes inside her head, Madalena Strauss explained that she worked out of the central detachment at the Polizei Zentralkommando on Herrengasse inside the

Ringstrasse. She was an investigating detective in homicide. When Dietmar Henning floated up in the Danube Canal, his corpse was identified, and she was informed and initially kept apprised of the investigation. As months passed and she heard less and less, she became edgy, then alarmed. She pressed the investigating officers at Polizeiinspektion Donaufelderstrasse across the canal and discovered the case had been filed under *Ungelöst*. Unsolved. They had moved on.

"So you didn't immediately confess?"

"They would have had a stronger case if they solved it on their own. There was lots of evidence but not too much. I am in the profession, Harry. I know how to seed a crime."

"And you wanted them to have the best possible case, of course."

"Of course. You understand."

"It's rather unusual to work for the guilty party. I usually leave that to the defence lawyers, Ms. Strauss."

Harry glanced over into the anteroom. The fat man had slipped away. His coffee accoutrements were still in place on the table beside his empty chair. Harry tried to assimilate conflicting thoughts about the small boy who had trusted his parents, about his own shock and revulsion, about the revised account that had them leaping from the roof, about the absurdity of the bellicose man barging into his room, with the absurdity of the man peeping at him over pastries like a child hiding behind upraised hands.

"Mr. Lindstrom?"

"I'm thinking."

Her lips were red and full but pulled tight against her teeth, slightly open. She was breathing through her mouth.

When her lips relaxed, they were her most sensual feature.

She hasn't stood up yet, Harry. I'm sure you'll find other attributes. What about the extravagant hair? Piercing eyes. Good teeth. Strong nose. Neat bosom. Don't say you're not looking. You are.

Sometimes Karen made Harry uncomfortable. He shifted in his chair, pushing her into one of the darker corridors of his mind where she could amuse herself among shared images and stillborn thoughts.

"Why do you believe your Dietmar Henning deserved to die?"

"He stole a family treasure."

Harry had been expecting a litany of heinous crimes. Theft was not even on his list.

"A treasure worth a human life?"

"A painting." She tilted her head, as if flirting, but she wasn't. She pushed her hair away from her face. "Quite valuable for sentimental reasons."

"Valuable?"

"Twenty million euros."

That's a lot of sentiment, Harry!

"A Klimt," he said without pausing to think.

"Exactly, a Gustav Klimt."

Since arriving three days ago in Vienna, Harry had been in pursuit of that most philosophical of painters. He had toured the Arts building at the Universität Wien, several museums, palaces, galleries, wherever Klimt was on display.

Before the accident, when Harry taught philosophy, when Karen and Matt and Lucy were alive, he had become fascinated by Klimt. A record $135,000,000 was paid for a 1907 portrait and Harry was intrigued by the bizarre correlation between art and value. He published an essay on the subject in an obscure academic journal and explored it in lectures and seminars during his last spring at Huron College. And despite his antipathy to hanging prints of famous paintings at home rather than original works, he had a small Klimt reproduction on the wall of his condo bathroom.

"You own an original Klimt?" he asked.

She gestured to a waiter and to Harry's surprise she ordered a single malt scotch on the rocks. Harry demurred. He preferred the subtlety of wines or the folksy congeniality of a good North American beer.

"Original, yes. It wouldn't be worth stealing if it wasn't. It's the artist's maquette for *The Kiss* in the Österreichische Galerie at the Belvedere Palace."

"I saw it yesterday. It's—" He stopped, at a loss for words. Language in his mind had not yet caught up to his perception of Klimt's dazzling achievement. "What do you mean a maquette? I thought that was a term in sculpture."

"No, mine is on canvas. You forget, English is not my language. It is not a cartoon or sketch. He completed it down to the shimmering gold. It's a relative miniature, the size of a laptop, but it's not quite the same. The one on public display is life-size, perhaps two metres by two metres, six feet by six."

"I'm okay with metric. Is it catalogued?"

"Mine? No."

Harry waited.

"The woman in both paintings is my great-grandmother. Klimt gave her the small one. They were lovers, I assume. I like to think so." Her green eyes blazed in splashes of light from sconces on the panelled walls. "Of course, he had many lovers. Perhaps she did as well. She was very striking, don't you think? You have visited Secession, yes?"

Was that a question, a guess, or an observation?

Harry had been at the Secession building earlier in the day, on Friedrichstrasse off Karlsplatz between the Opera and the Market. It was an art nouveau gem, built in 1897 with an austere white exterior, severe angles, a whimsical facade of owls in conversation, and a gold-leaf dome or cupola cradled in its upper reaches like the sun captured in an architectural vice. Nearly empty inside but the home of Klimt's frieze from 1903 dedicated to Beethoven, with some of the most striking representations of female sexuality ever portrayed. The most erotic of these was a naked woman with electric green eyes, lips full of promise, and a voluptuous mane of copper red hair—a woman who bore an uncanny resemblance to the woman sitting opposite him now.

She obviously expected him to make the connection, as if that would verify the credibility of her claim to owning an unregistered original.

It worked; he believed her.

He asked how they had had such good fortune to keep it in the family.

"Good fortune, oh yes. My great-grandmother was from Mauthausen, a small town near Linz. In Vienna, she lived a bohemian life but retired back to her home town and eventually married a local landowner. After the *Anschluss* in March of 1938, Austria was declared a province of the Third Reich. The painting was hidden. My great-grandmother was Jewish, which meant the picture was Jewish and a dangerous possession. Klimt, on the other hand, was highly prized by the Nazis, who seized many of Austria's treasures. That too made it a dangerous possession."

"Hidden where?"

"Behind another painting in the same frame, an unsigned amateur landscape painted by her daughter, my grandmother. It was given on loan to the Mauthausen Rathaus to hang in the mayor's office just before the *Wehrmacht* took over the building. A beautiful Jew looked down on Nazi proceedings from behind a thin veneer of Austrian scenery. Such irony, yes? And by the end of the war she was forgotten by those of our family who survived, except for my mother, who was determined to leave it hidden, along with her worst memories of the war. She was only eight when she returned home. The painting was part of a fantasy word that was gone forever."

"Until you discovered where it was."

"I did. I stole it back. She was ours."

"You stole it."

"Even the frame. I left an envelope with a thousand euros. That was more than my grandmother's landscape was worth."

Her green eyes flashed as she brushed her hair away from her face. Harry sat straighter in his chair.

"And your grandmother and her mother, what happened to them?"

"*Getötet und gebrannt*, the official ledger declared. There was another sister, my great aunt, who I assume met the same fate. *Killed and burned.*"

"Killed and burned." In those simple words, the horrors of the Holocaust leapt from historical knowledge to personal reality, graphic in their simplicity, terrible in their acceptance.

Harry filled the emptiness with a question, turning their talk back to the painting itself. "You recovered your Klimt quite recently, then?"

"No. No, it was some time ago. My mother told me before she died. She was forty when I was born. I'm not even sure she knew it was anything more than a family story. For me, the actual painting, when I found it, was affirmation. I did have a past—out of the ashes, something beautiful and precious."

"What did you do with it, Madalena? Did Dietmar Henning know where it was."

"My great-grandmother hangs proudly on my living room wall in the Gumpendorfer district beside the reframed landscape by my grandmother. For now, the Klimt is mine to enjoy. Someday it will go to Austria. It belongs to Austria. Dietmar knew *where* it was; he could hardly miss it. But he did not know *what* it was, at least not until the end."

"You never told him?"

"Everyone assumes it's not real. There are many copies of Klimt in the world, some of them very convincing."

"Yet he stole it."

"He stole jewellery—heirlooms recovered when Vienna was an occupied city after the war. I am quite rich."

"And the police, do they know about your Klimt?"

"It is immaterial. They found my jewellery in his abandoned car by the canal. The painting never left my wall. If they had noticed it, they would have thought it a fake, not even a forgery, worth maybe a few hundred euros."

"Fake, not forgery?"

"Forgeries try to replicate the original; that's the point of a forgery. My painting, apart from being smaller, shows a woman with flashing green eyes who looks like she's about to rise up and devour her lover. In the 'official' painting, her eyes are closed, and her arm is draped around her lover's neck. He's not drawn down to her but looming over. She is kneeling and he is standing, and she looks, how do you say, do you know the word, *louche*. It is French. She is not quite so louche as in my version."

Does he know the word! But of course.

Karen.

"Mine does not pretend to imitation."

"And you have the 'chain of evidence' to prove it's authentic."

"My broken family, that is enough."

"And Dietmar Henning figured out it was original."

"Eventually. He was a very bad man, but he was not stupid. I would never have a stupid lover."

"How bad?"

"His trade was extortion and blackmail. His victims were gangsters in the drug trade."

"*That* strikes me as stupid."

"It was profitable. Dangerous, yes, but unlikely to be prosecuted. And without knowing it, as a detective at the Polizei Zentralkommando I provided protection. Eventually colleagues informed me about him—anonymously, of course, for fear of retaliation in case I already knew. When I confronted him, he figured it was time to move on."

"Not quickly enough, it seems."

She apparently saw no humour in Harry's comment. They looked past each other in silence. Then something caught her attention.

"Your friend in the doorway is staring at us," she said. "I wonder, is he watching you or is he watching me?"

"Perhaps both," said Harry, without turning.

"Or perhaps neither," she said. "He's leaving now."

"I thought he had already left," said Harry. The fat man's presence was baffling, although on a minor scale. Far more momentous were the deaths of the Canadian couple and their child. Far more compelling was this woman across from Harry with her unsettling allure and strange determination to be taken for a cold-blooded killer.

"I've often wondered if a work of art is worth dying for?" he mused. "Or killing for?"

"Ah, then you have never owned a Klimt."

"No," said Harry. "I never have."

Madalena Strauss shifted uneasily.

"I think I must go," she said. "Here is my business card."

"Can we meet tomorrow?"

"Yes. I have been very busy, I'm sorry. I had to leave Vienna for a few days. Now we will cooperate. You come to Gumpendorfer, no, is better if we meet at the Café Central. It is very famous and close to my office. At noon. We will have lunch. I will answer your questions."

"Good," said Harry, a little uncertain what his questions would be.

He took her hand as they both stood up, turned it so her fingers briefly rested in his palm. At the same time, he did an inventory as Karen expected, which he completed as she walked away into the main lobby.

Smart skirt, right length, crisp blouse, perfect legs, proud bottom, modest heels. Harry sat down again and toyed with his cup. Curiously, Karen remained noncommittal.

Something moved beside him. He momentarily flinched and turned to catch a spectral image of himself in a polished wood panel. His encounter with Madalena Strauss had left him on edge.

He sat down again and his mind slowly filled with bright colours by Klimt, flat patterns, sensual lines. Copper red hair, full lips, piercing green eyes.

And a killer smile!

He smiled.

You like her, don't you?

Oddly enough, I do.

And maybe her boyfriend deserved his untimely demise.

Brutality doesn't become you.

Well, maybe she didn't do it.

That's a possibility.

But, Harry, just because she's sultry, smart, and deliciously mysterious, that doesn't mean she's innocent.

Nor at fault, just because she wants to be.

That's right out of Citizen Kane, *Harry.*

If I listen carefully, I can hear *The Third Man* theme in my head.

A composer from Vienna called Anton Karas did the music, you know, not Orson Welles. And Welles didn't write the script. Graham Greene did.

That's why it's set in purgatory.

And filled with Catholic guilt and dread.

Esoteric conversations with Karen were often a welcome distraction, but sometimes they were simply depleting. He decided to return to his room for a nap before dining late to accommodate his jet-lagged system. On the elevator, he felt oppressed, as if the boy and his parents had died in his room and not on the street below. Morbidly disoriented, he unlocked his door and stepped into the darkness, sweeping the wall for the switch. Even before the room burst into light, he caught a whiff of cigarette smoke and he knew the fat man was waiting.

2 THE DEVIL EATS STRUDEL

WHEN THE LIGHTS OF THE CHANDELIER FLASHED ON, THE iridescent nightscape of Vienna through the open drapes was instantly erased. The fat man sat in a plush chair, framed by the room's reflection. He motioned at Harry to sit down on the ornate settee and, unable to think of an alternative course of action, Harry complied.

"You wonder why I am here," said the fat man.

"It did cross my mind," said Harry.

"You are famous detective, Mr. Lindstrom."

Vanity vied with humility and Harry said nothing.

"Perhaps after you are dead you will be more famous."

"All in good time," said Harry.

The fat man sat low in his chair, suggesting he would be a cumbersome assailant. He did not appear to be armed, or if he was, his weapon could not likely be drawn before Harry disarmed him. He was undoubtedly strong, in the way very big men often are, but strength wouldn't be of much use if he could not lay hands on his prey. Harry felt irritated, his privacy violated, but he did not feel vulnerable.

"The boy," the man began solemnly, as if placing a topic on the table for discussion. He paused to wipe a thin veneer of sweat from his brow. He took a deep drag on his hand-rolled cigarette. The tip of it glistened and faded. "Ah," he said, after holding a quantity of smoke deep in his lungs, then of necessity exhaling in order to resume breathing. "Is good. You are not smoker? That is too bad. I put cannabis into tobacco. It is medicinal, yes. Makes you forget about cancer."

"The boy?" said Harry.

"He is Albanian. I am Russian. Those people, they travel on Canada passports."

"His parents?"

"Are not his parents. You are Canadian, yes? Once you were teacher of philosophies. Is difficult to understand how you stop thinking as professor."

“For me too,” said Harry. He felt Karen wordlessly concur.

“You are in Vienna on business without license.”

“I don’t need a license.”

“Everyone in Vienna need license.”

“No one is paying me.”

“Not yet, but if you are successful, then you are paid.”

This guy makes me nervous, Harry.

“The boy?” said Harry. “Was he kidnapped?”

“It is complicated.”

The fat man rose awkwardly from the depths of his chair. It took him some time to gather his equilibrium once standing, but when he did he looked as solid as furniture. He turned and gazed out the window. “You see Stephansdom cathedral from here. You see Ferris wheel. Is very famous. You know movie, *Third Man*? Was 1949, when city was occupied international zone.” As he turned back to face Harry, a grimace of pleasure betrayed his nostalgia for times when the world was black and white and espionage was a virulent blood sport.

It still is, for God’s sake.

“Orson Welles makes being despicable interesting.” Harry paused for effect. “Is Harry Lime a role model?”

“Welles was good actor, yes. Very big man like me. Maybe not so big but good actor. Harry Lime, yes, very sinister. He rides on Ferris wheel.”

Harry, why are you talking about films?

Harry rose from the settee and stood beside the Russian. The building opposite, so close in the flaming sunset, loomed far away in the night. Floodlights on the mosaic roof tiles of St. Stephen’s reduced more contemporary edifices to bleak curiosities.

“I’m very sorry about the boy,” said Harry, looking straight ahead.

Sorry doesn’t begin to cover it, Harry.

“Yes,” said the fat man. “Is terrible. You must help, please.”

“Doing what?”

“Many children die unless you and me, we save them.”

“I have no idea what you’re talking about.”

“Ah, but you are witness through glass, Mister Harry.”

“I thought they fell from the roof.” He glanced at the reflection of the room next to his. It was in complete darkness and he could hardly make out the balcony where they had jumped.

"Revisionist history make facts to fit truth. You understand, yes? You see through the glass darkly." The fat man gestured toward the window. "But you and me, we see face to face."

"Saint Paul or Bergman?" said Harry.

"Is from *Book of Corinthians*." The fat man winked conspiratorially.

The same allusion came up on the island of Fårö the previous winter, where Ingmar Bergman had filmed *Through a Glass Darkly.* There are only so many Biblical allusions to go around. "I'm an atheist," said Harry.

"You will be useful."

"To you? I don't even know who you are."

"I am not policeman."

Harry waited.

"My name is Legion. *"Nomen mihi Legio est, quia multi sumus."*

"You speak Latin. Correction: you quote Latin."

"I speak dead language. I speak language of dead people, yes."

Harry wondered, did he himself speak the language of dead people? How much of his relationship with Karen was through old conversations that still echoed in his mind?

Harry! Not now.

"You speak for a legion of demons," said Harry.

"Yes, is in Bible. Many demons."

"Is that meant to set me at ease?"

"Is joke. But I speak for many. You and me, we have same interests, so I ask you to help. Is important we have good talk."

"Perhaps you could speak quickly. I'm hungry and it's getting late."

The fat man took a last deep drag on his cigarette and flicked the butt onto the Persian carpet. For a moment Harry stared at the smoldering detritus, until the smell of burning wool triggered a response. He stooped to retrieve the butt and with the heel of his shoe crushed the dark spot into the carpet's design.

"We will have supper together," said the Russian when Harry returned from flushing the remains of the cigarette. "Come, we go."

With astonishing agility the big man negotiated his way to the door and held it open for Harry.

They progressed rapidly along the Kartner Strasse walkway, around Stephansdom, and down a cobbled alley to a tiny restaurant of the Russian's choosing. Harry had been forced into a limp by the stress on his injured toes, souvenirs of an incident the previous winter when he had nearly frozen to death. They hardly spoke as they each drank a beer and settled into thin golden slabs of *wiener schnitzel* so vast the meat overreached the edges of their plates. Boiled potatoes with parsley in a mild vinaigrette were necessarily served on a side dish.

"So," the fat man said when the course was finished. "My name, yes? Is Yuri Gagarin."

"I doubt that very much."

"You may call me Yuri." The big man dipped a moist finger into *schnitzel* crumbs on his plate and slipped them into his mouth. "Is another joke, yes. Our Yuri is hero of Soviet Union when Soviet Union exist. He die before you were born. Is history, yes."

"A lot happened before I was born."

Harry gazed across the table at his strangely compelling and unattractive dinner companion. The Russian knew too much about Harry, while Harry knew nothing about him. In spite of being expensively dressed, the man was slovenly and vulgar. He had offered no credentials beyond a patently false name but carried himself with enough sinister authority to have made his invitation to dine more like a summons. Not that Harry felt threatened. He had been morbidly curious. And hungry.

"Now we talk," said the Russian, looking sadly down at his empty plate. "Another beer, perhaps?"

"Please," said Harry.

"That woman I see you with in hotel, you know she is bad."

Damn it, Harry, she knew who he was!

He knows her, she may not know him.

"Very, very dangerous," he repeated. "She kill lover, eat his eyeballs."

She didn't mention that part!

"Really, Mister Harry. Is no joke. His corpse had no eyes, no testicles. Your Miss Strauss, I believe she cook them in stew." The big man shifted in his chair, trying to find support for his large bottom. "Or perhaps she eat them raw. Was better that way. If you wish, we not talk until after dessert."

"Yes," said Harry, feeling queasy.

The world suddenly seemed too small for Harry. The unlikely convergence of an Albanian toddler's death, the fat Russian himself, the dead ex-fiancé, the possibility of his various balls being devoured, a killer who looked like she'd stepped from a painting by Klimt, vague allusions to other children dying, and Harry himself, all here in the city of Vienna—how, he wondered, did it all come together?

"Everything connects, Mister Harry," said his unpleasant companion, anticipating the unspoken question. "Your friend, she was not arrested for murder. You are curious why?"

"Perhaps because she didn't do it."

"Or perhaps she did but is best for now she is not made criminal."

"Best for whom? The legion you work for?"

"You think I work for? I am independent man."

"Of course you work for someone," said Harry. "Everyone does, one way or another."

"Ah, you are cynical philosopher, yes. I am idealist, myself. I work only for me. And you, you work for Fräulein Madalena Strauss."

"That depends," said Harry.

"She is, as you say, boss."

"No." Harry was irritated. "If I work for her, it is my choice."

"Is good. Then you may choose also to work for us."

"Really," he said defiantly. "And if I don't?"

"We kill you, yes."

Harry gulped.

"Is also joke. It would be very nice if you work for us. She is treacherous lady, that is no joke. My friends are concerned about what she might do."

"Your friends you don't work for."

"My friends are very shy. Is good word, *shy*. She upsets them. She will destroy many lives if she is not stopped. You will stop her, please."

"Stop her from what, for God's sake?"

"God from atheist. You are angry. Is good."

Harry glowered. "Please get to the point."

"These people, she will expose them for bad scandal."

"That's only a problem if they're innocent."

"Ah, you are philosopher again. Who is innocent in this world, Mister Harry?"

"What exactly are their crimes?"

"She think they do bad things for children. But she also is bad for children; she is worst. And more children suffer if she not stopped by myself and by you."

Harry could not envision the copper-haired woman engaged in the exploitation of children, despite her insistence that she was a killer—

—with an unsavoury appetite for spherical objects.

Harry drew in a deep breath.

A waiter cleared their dishes. Harry's companion ordered strudel with custard. Harry ordered an espresso.

"Mister Harry, you think she bring you all this way to Vienna to prove some crime no one care about? Maybe because you are famous, perhaps?"

"Perhaps."

"She wants to use you and then she will destroy you."

"At least she's clear about what she wants."

"No, she is not. She hides behind murder of lover."

A strange place to seek refuge, you've got to admit.

"I'm listening," said Harry.

The man waggled his finger like the finger of doom and pointed in the direction of the Kressler Hotel.

"She already destroy the nice people from Canada and their little Albanian boy. She is ruthless, yes."

"You're trying to tell me she knew about the jumpers? I don't believe it."

"Believe, Mister Harry. Is no coincidence they die at your hotel. Is no coincidence that she meet you at same hotel."

"And is it a coincidence that you were also there when they died? Is it a coincidence that they are reported having jumped from the roof—after you threatened me, insisting I saw nothing to suggest they had not?"

The other man shrugged. His attention strayed as his strudel was set down in front of him.

"The Viennese, they know how to eat," he observed.

"They know how to cook," said Harry.

Don't be a pedant, Karen whispered.

"Ah yes," said the Russian. "I eat, is good." He cut off a big forkful of pastry and stuffed it into his mouth. "We do not care if she murder Dietmar Henning in lover's quarrel." Flakes of pastry drifted from his lips. "If she make him into stew and serve it to orphans, is okay."

"Come on, Mr. Big, let's get to the bloody point."

Harry, that's an allusion to Sex and the City.

I've never seen it.

Trust me, a man that fat is no Mr. Big.

"We know everything you know," said the Russian. "Is not enough."

"And you want to know what I *don't* know."

"Is very good, yes."

"I take it you've been monitoring my email."

"Your email, Miss Strauss' email. Is not difficult for Russian hacker."

"Then you know as much as I do."

"Yes, Mister Harry. But you are seeker of truth. Like Greek with lantern at noon."

"Diogenes."

"Yes, very good. And when you find truth, you tell us."

"And if I don't?"

"Then you are proud man but dead like Plato."

"Like Socrates."

"Plato, he is also dead. If you don't tell us, we kill you, yes. Is no longer joke."

Harry, let's get the hell out of here!

Harry offered what he hoped was a wry smile and tried not to watch the pastry crumbs slipping from the big man's lips as he chewed.

The Russian continued to speak without swallowing. His eyes had grown dull, his face showed strain, saliva glistened at the corners of his mouth. Hostility he had kept sequestered as affable menace seemed suddenly real.

"We would everyone kill if right circumstance make necessary, yes. Do not make necessary."

He would kill everyone? Or everyone would kill?

Harry had no doubt he would have died to save his kids; he would have embraced his own death or murdered battalions to spare them. He nodded assent.

Harry, please.

Karen didn't, couldn't, try to reason with him, since she was inseparable from the rest of his mind. But he couldn't keep her from feeling, from loving and trying to protect him.

He leaned back and looked at the man opposite. Harry didn't believe in God, so how could he believe in Satan? But here he was, watching the devil eat strudel, wiping flakes from his stubble with nicotine-stained fingers.

"Why would you think I'd betray her?" he asked. In the unreality of the present moment, offensive assumptions about his integrity seemed the most pressing issue.

Why are you having this conversation, Harry?

Harry looked at the fat man's bloodshot eyes, which were focused on a second pastry the waiter had set down in front of him. Harry had not even noticed him order it. Like most gluttons, the Russian took no real pleasure in food. Looking up, he flashed Harry a repulsive smile. And then he began devouring the strudel like it was an adversary.

"You want me to spy on my client. And the rationale is that you'll kill me if I don't and endangered kids will be spared if I do."

"See, you are good detective. Now you think about what I tell you. You must get her to trust you. Betrayal is impossible without trust. Is very important you remember that. But she is suspicious woman. Perhaps you become lovers. That way is best to penetrate defences."

So to speak.

"And how did her last lover fare?"

"Is true. Very dead, no balls."

Asked and answered.

Harry cringed at the absurdity of becoming her lover because it suited the Russian's purpose. Then suddenly he made a macabre and frightening connection.

"Dietmar Henning worked for you, didn't he?"

The man who called himself Yuri shrugged enigmatically, wiped his face with his soiled napkin, and in a great display of bulk rose to his feet.

"You will pay, please. Your boss with repay you. I will be in touch, as you say."

Once moving, the big man edged between tables with surprising agility and with a hand-rolled cigarette already in his mouth disappeared out the door into the cobbled laneway, where a fine rain filled the air.

Harry could hear Karen's words. *Your friend is one very unpleasant character. Why don't we have a nightcap on our way back to the Kressler and think this through?*

As he signed off on the bill, she added, *Harry, no matter how beautiful she is, if you sleep with her, be a gentleman and do it for old-fashioned lust.*

Harry had not been with a woman in the three and a half years since Karen died. She wouldn't have minded. He was still young and he missed sex. But he missed sex with Karen. He couldn't yet dissociate desire from the person desired. Perhaps never. He didn't worry about it.

When he walked out of a side street into the looming shadows of the floodlit cathedral, Harry was surprised to find so many people about, ignoring the drizzle. Instead of following down Gartner Strasse he turned west into the broader reaches of the Graben walkway and progressed slowly through clusters of late-night buskers and vendors and chattering tourists.

The carnivalesque distractions cleared his mind. He had always found it easier to think with distractions, like when the radio was blaring or he was surrounded by a crowd. While he preferred solitude, tranquility allowed him to think too much about himself. I am, therefore I think. That's what philosophers do, and he had been a professional philosopher for most of his adult life. Illusions of objectivity and abstract analysis couldn't obscure the fact that thinking *about* thought began and ended with the thinker thinking. What the mind could not conceive was inconceivable. The mind that always explored the limits was the mind that limited the exploration.

Harry, you've been gazing at your reflection long enough.

He hadn't realized he'd stopped in front of a shop and was staring through diffused light into its murky depths. He tried to bring himself into focus among the handbags and shoes. What he saw was a tall, lean man, close cropped hair prematurely grey, eyes like cracked amber, strong nose and chin, high forehead, clothing indistinguishable from any other well-dressed traveller. He winked without smiling.

He moved along the Graben and past the swank shops and cafés down Kohlmark toward Michaelerplatz, which would then allow him to take Reitschulgasse back to the Kressler. Vienna thrilled him like few other places, but in the bleak night air it was suffocating. He picked up his pace. Overhead the sky was squalid from the lights of the city absorbed in the mist. At street level, shadows loomed in every direction.

Toronto in the summer is looking pretty good about now.

But not until I sort this out.

What? How?

By insinuating myself into Madalena Strauss' good graces, apparently.

Into her pants.

Come on, I need to know if it's true.

If what's true? That she's involved in the exploitation of children or that she's an assassin? Or just that she fucks.

I don't like not understanding.

Even if it kills you.

You know what I mean.

Not always. Trust me, Harry, death is not a viable alternative. You're caught between a guilt-ridden cop with magnificent hair and her creepy adversary. Maybe we should sidestep this one and go home.

"Not likely."

Harry looked around. He had spoken out loud.

"Sorry," he mumbled, as if making amends for his apparent eccentricity to an unseen witness. In fact, there was no one else within hearing range and as he turned into the shadowy narrowness of Reitschulgasse, Harry could smell horses. On his second day in Vienna he had attended a showing of the famed Lipizzaner Stallions at the Spanish Riding School behind these same bleak walls. Not a horseman himself, he marvelled as the horses pawed and hovered like mythical ghost-grey beasts, chillingly robotic yet fiercely primeval. He stopped, hoping to hear them in their stalls. He heard nothing but a single set of footsteps behind him. He glanced around, but the streetscape was empty.

Emerging from the passage through the palace wall, he watched his own distended shadow reach across the street and up the stark façade of buildings opposite. In the chiaroscuro lighting and rain-laden air, an oddly familiar scene appeared bled of all colour, like a black and white film. Surely this was where Harry Lime had lived. Or Anna, his actress girlfriend. On Harry's own side of the street a water fountain loomed in a square that was enclosed on three sides by the stone walls of the Riding School and some civic buildings with which they merged in the mottled gloom.

Harry could hear the footsteps again. He slipped into a niche of darkness by the public entrance to the Lipizzaner exhibition. Following his own long shadow cast across the wet cobbles, the fat Russian emerged through the breach in the wall. Clearly disappointed at losing Harry, he strode off toward the Kressler at a rapid pace, almost breaking into a cumbersome lope as he left the square.

Harry looked up at Harry Lime's apartment.

He was channelling Orson Welles as a kind of interior ghost and, strangely, he felt empowered, as if he were the bad guy himself. He hurried after his shadow, but by the time the Kressler was in sight, the Russian was nowhere to be seen. Just as well, Harry thought. Like the proverbial dog chasing a car, he didn't know what he'd have done if he'd caught him.

3 CAFÉ CENTRAL

HARRY AMBLED THROUGH THE MORNING BENEATH A pastel blue sky and arrived at the Café Central on Herrengasse at the stroke of noon. Madalena Strauss was waiting for him, seated in a booth with red and gold upholstery inspired by Klimt. She was dressed less austerely than the previous evening, with more flow and colour. She smiled when he approached.

"Adolf Hitler used to sit here," she announced, not getting up.

"Really," he said.

"And Tito and Lenin and Stalin."

"Not at the same time, I assume." Harry sat carefully so as not to stir up the dust left behind by such august and murderous patrons.

"Also Sigmund Freud. We will have *kaiserschmarrn*," she announced. "It is famous here."

But only here? She has an interesting mind. She didn't mention that Beethoven and Mahler and Mozart had also been frequent visitors to the Café Central. And Leon Trotsky and Johann Wolfgang von Goethe.

"You will like *kaiserschmarrn.* And coffee, of course. *Mélange*, our version of latte. Did you rest well? You look tired."

Harry wondered if she had any idea about his dinner with the fat man or having been shadowed on his way back to the hotel.

He looked around with admiration. He and Karen had occupied a table closer to the door a dozen years previous, when they travelled from Cambridge while he was completing his doctorate and she was a summer lecturer at Newnham College. He had been interested in Goethe's *Sturm und Drang* phase, she in Freud's sexual dreamscapes.

The building from the outside looked like the opulent stock market it had been until its conversion to a coffeehouse in 1860, with neo-classical statuary perched on stone balusters and intricate fretwork carved around arched windows. Travelling on limited resources back then, they had been daunted, but when they went in, they were mesmerized. Soaring facets of light from the high vaulted ceilings swirled among slender columns. The same windows that had seemed ominous from the street were luminescent with daylight. A pianist played Mozart on a grand piano at eleven in the morning. They had ordered coffees and a luxuriously chocolate Sachertorte to share.

"Let me tell you how they make the *kaiserschmarrn*," said Madalena Strauss, leaning closer as if she were about to share a dark secret. "If a recipe says to work all the ingredients into a thin batter, sprinkle with raisins, or serve when golden brown with cranberry sauce, it is not *kaiserschmarrn*."

She sat back, looking pleased with herself. The light from myriad angles caught in the coils of her hair. Her head moved gently from side to side while she talked, giving her an ethereal yet primal radiance he found disconcerting. Instinct told him she might be a predator. Harry was a rational man; he did not trust instinct.

"You have told me how *not* to make it," he said.

"Indeed," she agreed. "But here is the real thing."

A waiter dressed in black and white set down a serving platter between them piled high with something between a pancake and an omelette that had been randomly sectioned into bite-sized morsels. The morsels gave off a perfume of indescribable richness and delicacy. Cognac? Rum. Butter and sugar and almonds, lemon and vanilla.

He and Karen had seen patrons at other tables eating *kaiserschmarrn* and had returned to the Café Central three times in the following four days to feast on it, skipping proper lunches to justify the extravagance.

"You see," said Madalena Strauss, savouring a bite and speaking delicately, with her mouth full. "It is sometimes better to say what is not than what is."

Harry smiled with lips pursed to keep from embarrassing himself with excessive saliva.

"I will tell you," she continued, knowing she had his attention. "The raisins are stewed in rum. I add a dash of brandy. The egg whites are beaten until very stiff, then folded in carefully. The yolks are blended with other ingredients and allowed to stand for twenty minutes. You must be patient and precise when cooking *kaiserschmarrn*. When only one side is golden, you flip it over, then tear it into pieces quickly and remove from the stove while still cooking in its own heat, so it will be crisp and moist. It is a genius of opposites."

As are you, thought Harry.

Despite the nostalgic power of the situation, Karen had been curiously silent. It was as if she were observing them both, trying to figure out their chemistry. The woman was disturbingly attractive. She was intense and charming and tough. And by her own admission, lethal. If she were involved in the trafficking of children and had actually executed her fiancé with such a diabolical flourish, then Harry was in very big trouble.

Like a moth to a copper red flame.

The pianist played excerpts from Mozart's Piano Concerto No. 21 in C Major. Harry was tone deaf; he heard music as sound but not art. Madalena Strauss told him what they were listening to and he had no reason to doubt her. It was a pleasing arrangement of noises, mixed with the quiet buzz of conversations and the occasional clanking of dishes, an aural complement to the rich textures of light that descended from the pale curves of the vaulted ceilings and filled the vast and intimate spaces with a dream-like atmosphere.

He shut his eyes and listened, then opened his eyes and gazed at the woman across from him. The music faded. "I had a visitor last night after you left," he said.

"The fat man?"

"You knew."

"No, but who else?"

Indeed, he knew no one in Vienna and the fat man had been none too subtle spying on them in the Kressler salon.

"Madalena, do you know what he wanted?"

"With you? Of course not."

"Are you curious?"

Her eyes widened, but she ignored his question, apparently more intent on her own concerns. "I have brought you a file," she said. "It is all I have been able to gather on what the police know of Dietmar Henning's death."

"You refer to him by his full name. A curious formality, given you were about to be married."

"It is how I distance myself from my indiscretion."

Harry took the file from where she had set it on the marble-topped table and tucked it into his shoulder bag.

"Aren't you going to look?" she said.

"Aren't you going to ask what the fat man wanted?"

"What did he want?"

"Ah," said Harry. "He wants me to spy on you."

So much for being covert!

Harry continued, "He feels the murder of Dietmar Henning was not sufficient—"

"Perhaps it was not—"

"—not sufficient to bring me all the way from Toronto."

"Why else would I want you here?"

"His question exactly. And when I figure out the answer I'm supposed to share it with him."

"Or what?"

"Or he kills me, apparently."

"You do not seem alarmed."

"Oh, I am, but mostly I'm baffled. He gave me no indication of when I will know *enough* to merit my death if I don't pass it on."

She looked at him with the same fleeting pity she might have offered a runway model with ill-fitting shoes.

"I suppose you will know when you know," she said.

"He seems to think you were especially cruel in disposing of your ex-fiancé."

"Gouging out his eyes with my thumbs, ripping off his testicles with my bare hands, cooking his parts in a paprika goulash and serving it to the homeless."

"Orphans, I believe. And what about his charges that you are involved in a clandestine operation of some sort."

"Clandestine?"

"A conspiracy with very bad people. He says you are connected to the international trade in children."

"Connected," she murmured. The vaguest hint of a smile crossed her lips. She raised her right hand. It hovered for a moment as if she were going to grasp something out of the air between them, then with the back of her hand she brushed unruly tendrils of hair away from her face and turned her head slightly, so that natural light through the window glistened on her alabaster skin.

"And what do you think?" she asked.

"Is there any truth to what he says?"

"It depends. I have a deep interest in such things."

He waited, shifting uneasily in his chair. With neither an explanation nor denial forthcoming, fascination was fast giving way to revulsion.

"Can you give me details?" he asked.

"No."

He waited. Nothing.

"He says you were involved with the couple who died."

"Involved? You mean the Canadians and the boy?"

"Did you know them?"

"I met them."

Harry had not expected her answer. His nostrils flared. "In the Kressler?" he asked.

"No, in a café at the Imperial Hotel."

"Could I ask why?"

"We had mutual interests. It is not your concern."

"You didn't mention this before."

"It was not relevant. I had a meeting with them in the middle of the day. It was an unhappy meeting. I left. Later, they came to the Kressler. They died. It is unfortunate."

Tragic *might be a more appropriate word.*

"So here you are, enjoying *kaiserschmarrn* with a killer, a woman with *clandestine connections*. You are uncomfortable, Dr. Lindstrom. Feeling guilty, perhaps. Morally compromised? But already, perhaps, you know too much and too little to just walk away."

There's always a choice.

Flee, fight, or submit. Those are options, not choices.

This isn't an exercise in rhetoric, Harry.

Despite the strong possibility Madalena Strauss was a murderer, Harry found she embodied a strange kind of lethal innocence, purring to be admired but ready to wreak havoc if the occasion required—innocence that had nothing to do with passivity or ignorance.

Harry, she's no Mother Teresa.

A woman who doubted the existence of God doing God's holy work? No, probably not. But the analogy hung in his mind as he gaped at the woman across from him, stunned by her casual admission that she was involved with the trafficking of children, sickened by how dismissive she had been of the deaths on the pavement outside the Kressler.

There was something about her that was uncomfortably familiar. Could she be more monstrous than a man who had allowed his wife and children to perish? In a perverse inexplicable way, he identified with her.

Just as he was about to acknowledge that she was right, that he was too deeply involved to back off, she surprised him.

"I think our business is done," she said. She sat back. Her chilling detachment reminded him of a pre-Raphaelite painting by Rossetti, the hauntingly erotic narrative of Pandora, threatening to release her casket of evils on an unsuspecting world. "Send me an account of your costs," she said. "It's the least I can do."

Harry, you're being dismissed!

He stood up, reached into his bag and retrieved a wad of euros, peeled off a couple of notes and dropped them unceremoniously on the table.

"You think I can't walk away, Ms. Strauss. Just watch me."

He turned and strode out the door into the early afternoon sunshine. He glanced back through an arched window and through the glare in the glass saw her sitting preternaturally erect. He glanced up and down Herrengasse, trying to decide whether to go directly back to the Kressler or for a stroll through the oldest parts of Vienna before returning to make travel arrangements for home.

He was unable to book a flight for Toronto until the following day. After a long afternoon circumnavigating the Innere Stadt by following the Ringstrasse counter clockwise on foot, and then clockwise, much as Sigmund Freud used to do between sessions with young women suffering from hysteria (whatever their symptoms), he settled into a good dinner at the Kressler's famed Restaurant Rote Bar. He had managed to get his outrage at being manipulated and his moral confusion both under control by thinking as little as possible. The portentous buildings erected during the glory days of the Austrian Empire had absorbed his interest, drawing him out of himself. The monuments and parks, stonework and stucco, trees and flowers, greys and pastels, had a calming effect. By the time hunger had moved him to return to the hotel, he was feeling the same kind of gnawing disinterest toward the charges against Madalena Strauss that he might have experienced upon reading about typhoon casualties in countries he could hardly imagine. He had separated the agonies of anonymous children from his own unbearable memories.

He might have gone all out and dined in the formal salon but, given his mood, the brilliant emerald decor, green carpet, green walls, green ceiling, and ebony black furniture dulled his appetite. The plush red of the Rote Bar was more to his taste.

The opera crowd had already left for the evening performance and Harry was almost alone in the opulent surroundings. He sat on an upholstered red bench along a red wall beneath a life-size painting of two dogs, a short-haired miniature of indeterminate breeding and, towering above him, what appeared to be a lanky Saint Bernard with a dark head and a thick white coat but no other markings. Harry moved around to a chair so that he could admire the picture, or, rather, admire the dog. Not the toy, the big dog.

The evening was cooling and waiters closed the foldaway windows of the Wintergarten conservatory. With his back to the room, Harry hardly noticed when the other diners had left and he was there by himself. If service people were still around, they were astonishingly discrete, watching him through scarlet shadows.

Rather than feel discomfited by the rare solitude in such an august place, Harry felt emboldened. With only the gilt-framed portraits-of-record of Viennese bourgeois gazing over his head and more in tune with the magnificent dog than his still-life human companions, Harry realized how good it would be to get home. His anger had subsided into annoyance and he did not feel guilty about going.

Perhaps he should get a dog. Not a Saint Bernard. He lived on the twenty-third floor. His aunt owned an Airedale when he was growing up. His name was Davey Jones. Perhaps he'd get an Airedale and call him Davey Jones. Or Beckett, after Samuel Beckett. Not Thomas à Becket. No self-righteous saints in my house, he thought. I'll take the man who wrote, "I can't go on. I'll go on." He understood.

What about Camus: "Should I kill myself, or have a cup of coffee?"

You can't call a dog Camus. "Come, Camus." It doesn't sound right.

Does "Sit, Beckett, stay" sound any better?

Harry was struggling to resist images of the boy on the balcony stepping into the air.

His thoughts returned to Vienna. Like most North Americans of his educational background and ethnic origins, he held the fervent belief that travel was an end in itself. Nothing aroused the sensibilities like a visit to Europe to re-open old memories, whether personal or cultural or historically based. Such was the imperial legacy.

He maundered on about existential dogs and the benefits of travel when a waiter appeared out of nowhere and slid a polished ebony box the size of a briefcase under his gaze. He assumed he was being delivered his bill with peculiar formality, but when the waiter withdrew he discovered the box was sealed by elaborate silver clasps that were only snapped open with considerable ingenuity, something unlikely to induce a good tip.

Lifting the lid carefully, he could see a dark green velvet wrapping surmounted by a faux-vellum envelope with his name imprinted in a bold script that might have been done with India ink and a quill pen. He lifted the envelope carefully from the velvet, but before proceeding he glanced around and with his elbow poised on the white linen tablecloth he raised a hand. Miraculously, a waiter, not the same one, reappeared and topped up his coffee. He took a slow sip as the waiter withdrew. It seemed a point of pride at the Kressler to hurry no one, no matter what the hour.

As he expected, the note was from Madalena Strauss:

Dear Harry, the attached comes with a single proviso, that upon your own death it be returned to the people of Austria. Meanwhile, it is yours for safekeeping. Think of this as an act of kinship, a gift from one troubled spirit to another. Please leave Vienna as soon as you can. Yours sincerely, Lena

So, she's Lena to her intimate friends! And she implies being fired was for your own good.

I wasn't fired. I quit.

He welcomed the return of their chatter. Since he'd left the Café Central, she had been unusually quiescent.

Quiescent? Harry, why not just quiet or withdrawn, subdued, contemplative, reticent, puzzled, confused?

Some words sound better in your head than others.

He closed the box without pulling back the velvet to reveal what it concealed. He paid his bill and returned to his room, where his bag was open on the bed, ready to be packed for an early morning departure. He looked around amidst the overwrought splendour for a setting that would not intrude on his senses when he unveiled the painting. He placed a straight-backed chair in front of the closed drapes; leaning the picture against it, still shrouded, he adjusted the lamplight for optimal illumination. Then he lifted the velvet away.

Harry, my God! It's her!

There was no question about it. Gustav Klimt captured her perfectly. While the public version of *The Kiss* showed a woman who was radiantly submissive, the smaller picture with flashing green eyes, lips parted, and an upward tilt to the chin suggested she was nestling into her own voluptuous cascade of red-brown hair rather than her lover's pallid arms. This was a painting of Madalena Strauss, the woman Harry had met twice over coffee and had not quite seen, before now, not until the artist revealed her.

I know what you're thinking, Harry.

Of course you do, Sailor.

I've never seen a portrait of decadence more seductive, alluring, enticing, provocative, and, I might add, ominously tempting. Harry, it's a painting of the woman's great-grandmother, you do realize that. It's not her.

Ah, but it is; it's just that Klimt didn't know it. He's captured her perfectly.

Beguiling depravity? You can't keep it.

For a while, perhaps? A lifetime at most.

She's trying to ease a guilty conscience.

I can't give absolution.

But you would if you could. Your new acquisition makes you determined to believe she's innocent—and I'm thinking it confirms her guilt.

I'm not even sure of her crimes. I'm thinking I judged her too quickly.

It's on loan, Harry. When you're dead, you lose it.

Harry was mystified by Lena Strauss' conviction that he would do the right thing. He knew he couldn't keep the painting. It would either go back to the donor or in due course he would pass it on to the State. In the argument about value versus worth, this invaluable painting from Harry's perspective was worthless.

Except as collateral. What does she want from you that's worth thirty million dollars?

My soul.

Don't flatter yourself, Dr. Faustus. This woman needs you alive with your soul intact.

Harry read the note again. The vellum seemed warm in his hand. The script made it clear it had been written with deliberation, not tossed off in a moment of panic.

What the hell does she know about your troubled spirit?

He wasn't sure. But her message itself indicated she was desperate. She needed help.

Where does it say that?

It was implicit.

But her warning to get out of Vienna was explicit.

It was.

4 GUMPENDORFER STRASSE

ONCE AGAIN HARRY WAS ON THE STREETS OF VIENNA IN the dead of night. It was warm, so he wore a sports shirt with the sleeves rolled up. The air was oppressively still. He made his way past the looming residence where Harry Lime might have lived and through the dank archway in the Lipizzaner horse palace. He continued across the roundabout at Michaelerplatz and along Herrenstrasse, past the darkened Café Central. Finally, he arrived in front of the stolid Polizei Zentralkommando building, which appeared to be closed. He rattled a door and waited.

Once inside, apologizing for his lack of German, he asked to see someone from Homicide. A stout, middle-aged woman with blue-tinted hair like his late Aunt Beth's led him to a chair beside an oak desk and after he was seated, she sat down behind it, a notepad spread open in front of her. Her teeth glistened with a silver highlight; he avoided looking at her mouth. She was wearing a strand of dark pearls, possibly as consolation for working the late shift.

"Now you wish, yes, to report a murder," she said.

"No," he explained. "I'm looking for a woman in Homicide."

"So, she is dead, perhaps?"

"No, I'm trying to find her."

"She is missing. How do you know she is dead?"

"She is a detective."

"I am detective." She offered a thin-lipped smile. "I am not dead."

"Good," said Harry. "I'm trying to find Madalena Strauss."

The woman's face darkened, her features hardened.

"You think Fräulein Strauss is murdered?"

"No." Harry paused. "I don't know."

It's a possibility, Harry.

"So. You believe she is murderer. I will make notes."

But the woman did not write notes. She leaned forward on her elbows, pressed her fingertips together, and blew air across them as if she were drying her nails. She was waiting for Harry to explain.

"I am also a detective," he said. He didn't add the word *private*; he didn't want to create more confusion. Inexplicably, he added, "I'm staying at the Kressler Hotel."

"And you have credentials?"

"Of course."

"Good." She didn't ask to see them. Perhaps the Kressler was enough.

"I need to find where she lives. I know it's near Gumpendorfer."

"So, American detective, you know Gumpendorfer Strasse. Good." The woman paused.

"Canadian," said Harry.

"I cannot tell you where she is, if she is not here. You will find her yourself, yes. You will excuse me now, please, for one minute. This is my desk, you may use if you like."

She rose rather grandly and walked away. Harry looked around. He looked at the Rolodex sitting amidst bundles of reports and files on her desk. He slid his chair closer and leaned forward. No one was paying any attention. He flipped the Rolodex and found Strauss, Madalena, 23 Marchettigasse, 5.

The woman returned.

"I am sorry," she said. "I cannot help. I am Frau Detektiv Honsberger. It is very nice meeting you. Now, you will excuse, I have much work."

"*Danke schön*," said Harry, rising to his feet.

His chair teetered behind him and he twisted to stop it from falling.

"*Bitte schön*," she responded, apparently not noticing his awkwardness.

"*Danke*," Harry repeated.

She stared at him. Her steely eyes matched the dark lustre of her pearls. He nodded formally and edged away.

Once outside, he took a deep breath.

What was that all about, Harry? She seemed like the gatekeeper on a descent into hell.

She's just an old lady.

Harry. Did you see the silver tooth?

But Harry wasn't in the mood.

He turned west and walked stridently toward the Ringstrasse, which he followed down to the museums and cut west over to Mariahilfer Strasse, passing innumerable plastic mannequins cavorting with static precision behind plate glass windows. He stopped at a bank machine and withdrew 200 euros and bought a surprisingly tasty latte at a vending machine. He sat to drink it on the steps of a church on a small walkway running south and watched a few wary derelicts watching him. Then he proceeded through the night shadows down to Gumpendorfer Strasse. With its modest shops closed at this hour, it seemed more like a small-town street than an urban thoroughfare.

In the quieter sections of the city, the street scenes in Vienna might have been anywhere in eastern Europe. Sporadic lights and drab colours, wrought iron grillwork and no room for grass might have meant Krakow or Prague. Marchettigasse itself, aslant to the moonlight, was even more austere, and he wondered why anyone who could afford better would live in such a bleak setting.

Harry was not used to European domestic architecture. As soon as he stepped through the massive unlocked gate at number 23, he found himself in a passageway opening onto a charming, well-lit courtyard with windows on all sides set into pastel walls covered with vines and ornamental flourishes. Many of the windows were open as a concession to the heat and he could hear quavering strains of a violin as if by consensus the other residents had turned off their sound systems, the better to enjoy their musical neighbour's playing as they drifted to sleep.

This was not the Vienna he had seen as a visitor. He had stepped into the heart of a different city, and he realized that in his travelling over the years he had been a perpetual tourist, looking at façades, whether shiny or in ruins, looking for his own reflection.

Stairs off to one side of the passageway led to a fire barrier on large hinges, a door covered in sheet metal with no locking mechanism, which provided access to a small vestibule and an open elevator shaft encased in wrought iron and surrounded by a spiral staircase of marble and stone. There was sufficient illumination that he decided to walk the five flights, which turned out to be seven because of the peculiar numbering system. On every floor an open stained-glass window let the air flow in. When he reached the right level, there were three apartments, each labelled with a small brass plate.

Madalena Strauss' was closest to the staircase and seemed to span the width of the building, overlooking both the street and the courtyard.

He knocked firmly. He rang the buzzer.

He waited.

He tried the door, but it was locked.

Looking through the stained-glass landing window at what he assumed was the rear window of her apartment at a right angle to him, he saw it was open. There were no lights on. He rang again. He moved back to the window, trying to estimate the distance to her casement.

Don't even think about it, Harry.

I'm pretty sure I could make it.

That's not reassuring. You don't even know she's in there.

It's likely.

You're prepared to leap through the air for a painting?

For a person.

Don't confuse the two. You're re-writing history, Harry. You came to Vienna because you thought she was guilty. You think Klimt proves she's innocent? You need the woman to measure up to her picture.

And what does she need from me?

That's what scares me, Harry. We don't know.

He boosted himself onto his knees on the marble window ledge. Pushing the stained glass open as far as the frame allowed, he leaned out. Far below, the courtyard gleamed like foil. Moving across roof edges above him, an indifferent tabby prowled among silvered shadows. Tremulous strains of the violin slivered the air. Madalena's window was just out of reach. He would have to release his grip on the landing window frame and let himself fall forward with both arms outstretched. He hovered. There would only be one chance at this. If he missed he would fall to an ignominious death. His passport was back at the Kressler, but the ID in his wallet would show who he was.

Karen was silent, allowing him complete concentration.

He teetered and reached out with his left arm, then gradually extended his right, as if moving slowly decreased his chance of making a fatal mistake. For the briefest instant, a ghastly apparition loomed forward and vanished in the dark window. He flinched, trying to comprehend what he had seen while fighting to keep from plunging into the courtyard below. Grasping the frame, rocking on his knees on the marble ledge, he did not take his eyes off the gloomy depths of her window.

Was it only the conjured spectre of his own death, or was something terrible actually there in darkness?

As if in response, the apparition moved out of the shadows into moonlight streaming through the open casement. Harry shuddered. Her eyes rimmed in black were empty, staring out from a mask of striated blood seeping among strands of open flesh. Her copper red hair was lank, plastered against her skull. In the strange muted light of the night, her lips were black battered flesh, the highlighted bridge of her nose was a jagged slash, her chin, her cheeks, the shape of her head were distorted by layers of dried and wet blood. Her moon-white shoulders were stained, her clavicle protruded as if the bone might burst through her skin, her breasts were wretchedly mottled with bruises and abrasions. Blood drained from gashes across her gut down into her pubic area and sheeted like molten ebony over her thighs. Her lower legs were hidden from view. Her arms hung at her sides, smeared in dark blood and as limp as dead meat.

Harry spoke gently, afraid she would fall out into the open air.

"Lena," he whispered urgently. "It's Harry. Lena, Madalena, it's okay. It's okay, it's okay."

He moved slowly back onto the landing, never taking his eyes off her. "Get away from the window, Lena, move back. *Bitte schön, bitte.*"

Harry thought he saw a glimmer of recognition in her eyes, but it might have been moonlight.

"I'm coming in," he said. "Can you open the door? Open the door, Madalena."

She stared ahead, gazing out over the rooftops.

"Lena, I'm breaking in, I'm going to break through the door. Don't move." For God's sake, don't move.

Harry glanced sideways at the door. It looked solid, but most doors are a convention more than an impenetrable barrier.

He looked back into her eyes. They were wounds caught in a moment of stillness.

"Lena," he repeated. "I'm coming in."

Her eyes in the moonlight, tarnished silver discs.

She moved, raising one hand slowly in front of her chest, palm out, strangely commanding, and her unchanging eyes issued a warning. She stood proudly framed in the casement, which gleamed against the night.

My God, Harry, she looks otherworldly. She looks like a nightmare by Klimt's tragic protégé, Egon Schiele.

A nightmare of anatomy, geometry, and passion, a perfect painting of imperious Death wearing robes of ebony and alabaster, encrusted with jewels and shimmering gilt: raw human flesh rendered inhuman, with eyes that saw nothing and everything in the same unfathomable gaze.

Harry stepped away from the window and braced himself against the ornamental iron of the elevator shaft, addressing her door straight on. The key was to *believe* he could break it down. He rocked back and looked out the window, but the angle was off and he couldn't see her. Possibly she had receded into the shadows. Or fallen forward. But there had been no sounds of exploding flesh, only the mournful strains of the lone violin.

Harry breathed deeply three times for a hit of oxygen, crouched into a football stance, then hurled himself at the door as close to the knob as he could without hitting it. The locks burst, the door flew open, and Harry landed with a crash on a blue gabbeh rug. Apart from a single loud crack, there had been almost no noise. The violin paused then started again, picking up a more lively melody.

Gasping from the agonizing pain running through his right shoulder, Harry raised himself onto his hands and knees. Madalena lay still on a larger gabbeh in the room to his left; her body had twisted into a fetal position when she had collapsed or lowered herself to the floor. He crawled close and touched her gently on the forehead where blood was smeared across the taunt flesh.

She moaned at his touch.

The room from outside had seemed impenetrably dark, but inside was filled with the diffused light of the moon and the city sky. She no longer appeared like a painting but like the embodiment of brutalized human flesh.

He could tell in the muted light that whoever had done this knew precisely what he was doing. The cuts had been into her veins, not arteries, so she would not bleed out. She was the victim of torture; death would have been collateral damage.

With the most primal of responses, Harry settled onto his side, easing forward into the curve of her back, and brought his thighs up snug against the back of her drawn up legs. With his lower arm gently under her head he lay his other arm lightly across her body in a motionless caress. He could feel his own heartbeat pick up the rhythm of her pulse and he whispered over and over that it was going to be okay. She moaned several more times and Harry drew her closer, flexing and relaxing his muscles as they picked up the same rhythm.

He was lying in blood.

A part of his mind disengaged, as if he were hovering above a Grand Guignol diorama. He listened for a siren and heard several, but none were close by. No one had reported his break-in. What he observed were two human beings, bonded by incomprehensible horrors.

Harry, Karen urged gently.

The man on the blood-drenched rug holding the battered remains of a living woman smiled into the dark, dank nape of her neck before slowly pulling away. The woman moaned and the man's heartbeat paused in that moment before bursting then resumed. He got up.

Their ungodly embrace had lasted perhaps two or three minutes. He drew the curtains, turned on a light, and shuffled into the hallway. He looked back as she rolled gingerly onto her back. He could see by the bruising and blood between her thighs that she had probably been raped. He closed the door to the landing. The locking apparatus hung from splintered wood, but the door settled securely into its frame. Although it had been locked from inside, he was confident no one else was in the apartment. The intruder, torturer, rapist, had left his victim in darkness. He returned to kneel down beside her. He ran his hands slowly over her body, doing an inventory of the damage, then got up, reached for a pocket, paused, started for the phone on a desk against the wall. He seldom carried a cell phone. Accessibility paradoxically made him feel trapped.

"Don't," she said. Her voice was tremulous but resolute. "No police."

"An ambulance, then," he said, squatting beside her. "You need help."

"No," she repeated emphatically.

Harry rose again, catching himself in the full-length mirror beside the French doors from the hallway. What he saw was the appalling figure of some creature that might have crawled over an abattoir floor standing close to another creature's flayed carcass; as he watched, the other creature rose to her feet and stood beside him, battered, but with a fierce determination. Submission apparently had not been an option. Harry put his arm around her and slowly they walked out of their framed reflection into the hallway.

She guided him to the bathroom on the right. Straight ahead was the kitchen, with a small dining area that looked out over the street and opened on the side onto a living room, with the bedroom hidden from view.

Removing their watches, Harry tested the water in the shower, dancing his hands under the flow until it was tepid. He turned the pressure low and steadied her as she stepped over the tile ledge into the stall. She remained still as the gentle stream soothed her wounds and the pool at her feet turned crimson and swirled down the drain. Harry held the glass door open, ready in case she collapsed.

He tried to hand her a sponge, but she ignored him. He found a bottle of body wash on the granite-topped counter beside the sink, opened it, and created a rich lather on the sponge. Then he leaned through the open door into the stall and began to wash her, hardly making contact with her flesh, pressing just firmly enough to dilute the caked blood until it ran free. He started with her face and worked down.

At her breasts he stopped. He realized a crimson wash was still sheeting down from her hair and he withdrew, found a bottle of shampoo, worked up a lather in his hands, then stepped fully clothed into the stall and ran his fingers through to her scalp, working out the dried blood.

The cuts on her body were deliberate, shallow incisions. He avoided lifting the flaps of skin as he cleaned away the blood. Livid bruises were scattered at random. Numerous welts began to emerge as if poppy blossoms had been smashed on her flesh. What he had taken as stubborn clusters of dried blood seemed to be cigarette burns. Some of them were suppurating as the blood cleared away. For the most part, the burns were on her breasts, around her nipples, but not on them. He expected to see more burns as he squatted down and washed between her legs, but despite the bruising there were no marks nor welts to interfere with the monstrous consummation of her attacker.

He eased her out of the shower and patted her dry with two thick white towels, then dropped the towels on the floor and slid them about with his feet, trying to mop up the reddish pools of water that had drained from their bodies or splattered through the open glass door. She sat down gently on the side of the bathtub and watched him as he stripped off his sodden shirt and pants. Even his underwear was blotched vivid red and he stripped that off too. He stepped into the shower and rinsed thoroughly then towelled off.

He helped her to her feet and examined her closely in the glare of the bathroom lights. Her wrists and ankles showed angry abrasions. There was a gouge deep into the flesh of her left wrist where her watch had been. Her back and buttocks appeared to be untouched—her attacker had wanted her to observe exactly what he was doing. When Harry bent close to examine her scalp for lacerations, he was surprised to find nothing. Her attacker had doused her hair in her own blood, gathered from wounds in her abdomen.

She leaned on him as they walked naked across the living room toward her bedroom. She flinched at the door and when he turned on the light he realized this was the torture chamber. Her bed was sodden with slashes of crimson, drying to brown in air that smelled of iodine and rust, raw like a butcher shop. Tied to each corner post at the foot of the bed were pieces of pale blue silk, pyjama bottoms and a shredded top that had been used to bind her ankles. Tied to one head post was a black brassiere, and another lay on the bloodied sheets in a twist of straps and lace.

She had been left to bleed slowly, to survive her wounds, to remember.

5 THE FORCES OF EVIL

MADALENA STRAUSS PULLED AWAY FROM HARRY AND stepped tentatively into the bedroom then reached back and drew him with her. They moved through to the next room where he had found her. She had turned it into an office of sorts. Essentially, it was less a room than a spacious thoroughfare with bookshelves, a teak desk with a desktop Mac and assorted computer paraphernalia, an office chair from Ikea, an exercise bicycle, and a leather chair with a lamp on a stand for reading. There was a spare cot along the outer wall, and Madalena watched while Harry stripped off the sheets after moving three piles of off-season clothes to the floor.

He wrapped one sheet around Madalena and the other he draped like a toga over his right shoulder and around his waist. With automatic movements, she adjusted hers the way women do, so that the material tucked over on itself above her breasts. She arranged it delicately to stay clear of her wounds. He had to use his left hand to hold his closed. Being naked together had seemed natural, although her nakedness represented extreme violation and his was a consequence of unmitigated compassion. Once they were covered they seemed more exposed.

"Let me get you some juice," he offered with absurd formality. He was concerned about her loss of blood and wanted something to stave off the effects of shock.

"Coffee," she mumbled, true to her Viennese heritage.

He led her to the living room where she settled into the contours of a sleek leather sofa by the window and he went into the kitchen to find coffee. Several times while the water was rising to a boil he looked to see how she was doing. When he returned with a tray carrying two coffee mugs, a pitcher of warm milk, and a plate of biscuits, a thin smile crossed her lips although she didn't look up or bring the room into focus.

"Madalena," he said, his voice was soothing but firm, "this isn't something you can handle alone. You need medical attention, and you need police protection."

Her features froze like a black and white photograph.

Find her, Harry! Look into her eyes.

He called Air Canada to cancel his flight. It was too late, just five hours before take-off, so he'd be charged full fare. Piss off, he thought. Next time I'll fly Air Austria if there is such a thing. He called the Kressler and requested his room for a few more days. They graciously obliged. Then he had the front desk transfer him to the concierge.

"I have a bit of a problem," he explained.

"Yes sir, how can we help?"

"I would like you to send someone to my room." He gave his name and room number. "Have that person pick up my bag; don't forget the toiletries in the bathroom. And there's a black box on the dresser with silver clasps. About the size of a laptop computer. I'll want that as well. Put it inside my bag. If there is no room, dump out some of the clothes."

"Is sir checking out by telephone?"

"No, I'm still registered. I want you to have the bag delivered to the Gumpendorfer district, 23 Marchettigasse, fifth floor."

"I will bring it myself, *Herr Doktor Professor*."

Instinctively, Harry responded, "Harry, please." He did not remember registering with outdated credentials, nor did he like being reminded of a past he eschewed.

"As you wish, Mr. Harry. Is there an apartment number?"

Harry did not want to give Madalena's name.

"No," he said. "I'll hear the elevator."

"Is there anything else, sir?"

"No, thank you. *Danke schön.*"

"Good evening, sir." The concierge spoke as if Harry had made the most normal request in the world.

"Oh," said Harry. "*Was ist*, what is your name?"

"Heinz," he said. "Ichstadt."

"Thank you, Heinz Ichstadt, good evening."

After setting the door with the broken lock ajar so he could hear the elevator, he returned to the living room. Madalena was blowing across her coffee and sipping through swollen lips.

"Thank you," she said without looking up.

He sat down beside her on the leather sofa. For all its Italianate modernity, it was surprisingly comfortable. He turned a little so they faced each other. She stared at her coffee. He wanted to see into her eyes.

After a while, Harry walked into the bathroom and rummaged through an assortment of bottles and jars under the sink until he found a tube with a red cross on it that he assumed was first-aid ointment of some sort. When he showed it to Madalena, she nodded and without being directed swung around on the sofa toward him and loosened her makeshift covering.

Harry gently drew the sheet away from her body. Then he squeezed ointment onto his fingers and delicately worked it across the shallow cuts and into the abrasions. He counted the cigarette burns. There were eleven on the upper sides of her breasts and seven between her navel and pubic mound. He returned to the bathroom and found a packet of bandages. He covered each burn with a dab of ointment and a bandage.

He looked around for a receptacle to dispose of the bandage wrappings. There was no ashtray—of course, she wasn't a smoker. But there were no cigarette butts. Where had her assailant disposed of the crushed cigarettes?

He thought he smelled the scent of honey, of dried flowers, mixed with the lingering scent of fresh paint.

"I need water," she said. It was the first whole sentence she had uttered since he arrived on the scene.

When he heard the elevator, he retrieved his wallet from his blood-soaked pants and went to the door. Heinz Ichstadt stepped out of the steel cage when it came to a jolting stop and bowed slightly from the waist. He handed Harry his suitcase.

"The black box is inside," he said, and then added with just the hint of a smirk, "Have a good evening *Herr* Lindstrom."

Harry realized it must be around three in the morning and he was standing in the doorway wrapped in a sheet. He blushed; he hadn't blushed since he was in his teens. He wanted to explain but realized it would be inappropriate. And in any case, he could not possibly tell Heinz Ichstadt the truth.

"Good evening to you, Mr. Ichstadt," he said, handing the man twenty euros, then thought better of it and added another twenty. "I assume you came by taxi."

"I did. This will certainly cover the cost. *Danke schön.*"

The concierge was staring at Harry's wallet. Did he want more? That was about $60.00. Harry glanced down and saw that his hand was smeared with blood. The euros were bloodied, as well. Heinz folded them carefully, took out a billfold from his inside jacket pocket and placed the bills meticulously between layers of leather, returned the billfold to his pocket, then rubbed his hands vigorously to dry the blood that had transferred onto his fingers.

"If there is nothing else, sir?"

"No," said Harry. "Not at the moment."

"Should I call someone, sir?" He was looking at the damaged locks.

"Goodnight, Heinz. Everything is fine."

"Goodnight, *Herr* Lindstrom." The concierge backed into the elevator cage and drew the wrought-iron door closed without taking his eyes off Harry. The descent mechanism engaged, and the elevator shuddered and began to move. From Harry's perspective, the man's body slowly telescoped into itself until for a brief moment his head appeared to float at floor level, then he vanished amidst the hushed whirring of cables and gears. Harry waited for the whirring to stop and the metallic clang of the cage door as it swung back. He waited until he heard the outer door into the courtyard creak open on its huge hinges and snap shut. Then he turned and went back into the apartment.

What are you thinking, Harry?

I think that was a subtle attempt at extortion, but I'm counting on concierge-client privilege. He won't say a word.

Unless the fat man asks him.

Yeah, maybe.

You're distracted.

I am.

Be careful, Harry. I've never known you to rely so exclusively on instinct. You'd better stop feeling, start thinking.

They're not mutually exclusive.

Sometimes they should be.

Harry nodded in acquiescence. There was no point in arguing.

Closing the door, he walked back into the living room, trundling his suitcase behind him. Madalena looked up and made eye contact; she was coming around.

After thoroughly washing his hands in the kitchen sink, he opened the suitcase, lifted out the box, and snapping open the silver clasps removed the painting from its velvet wrapping. He held it up at arm's length for a moment to ensure that it hadn't been damaged in transit, then seeking a wall that would never be exposed to direct sunlight and spotting the picture hook protruding from the plaster beside a landscape painting only a little bigger, he returned the Klimt to its rightful position. She watched passively, focusing on Harry.

He dressed in a fresh outfit and then asked if she wanted help getting something on. He suggested pyjamas, but she insisted on clothes. She remained in the living room while he went into her bedroom and made selections. He tried not to focus on the bloodied bed or makeshift manacles. He was careful not to touch anything. He didn't want to disturb the crime scene although he accepted that she wouldn't allow him to call the authorities. Hell, he thought, she's one of them. She's a cop. If it's not a crime scene it's not a crime scene. It's her call. She deserves that much out of all this.

Madalena seemed preoccupied as she stepped gingerly into the pale blue panties he had chosen from the lingerie drawer, but when he handed her a lacy bra to match she rejected it and walked determinedly into her room and picked out a wispy affair made of the lightest silk. She quickly returned to the living room where she became temporarily modest, turning her back to him as she leaned over to adjust the weight of her breasts into the cups. Then she turned again and let him help her into the white cotton blouse and beige slacks he had selected.

He got her another glass of water, but she handed it back to him, asking for scotch. In a cupboard above the kitchen sink he found a bottle of Glendronach single malt and poured her two fingers. She downed it and gestured for a refill. He brought it to her. His fears of dehydration were allayed when she took a small sip and then decisively set the glass down on the coffee table.

With her head tilted to the side she offered him a pained smile.

They sat close to each other, turned quarter on, so their knees almost touched.

He wanted to ask if she was all right, but that seemed a ludicrous question. Instead, he tried to distract her by concentrating on something relatively neutral. He shifted his focus to the Klimt and she automatically followed his gaze.

"It is very beautiful," she said. She didn't seem surprised at the painting's return nor immodest that it looked so much like herself.

"Yes," he agreed, as his gaze shifted back and forth from Klimt's picture to his companion until they seemed fused in his mind. Despite her abrasions smeared with ointment, the lividity of the cuts and bruises, she was the same woman the artist had conjured long before she was born.

"His name is Dimitri Sakarov," she said.

"Sorry?"

"The fat Russian. His name is Dimitri Sakarov."

Harry was stunned. He had assumed she wouldn't want to talk about what had happened, but by the fierce tremor in her voice he knew exactly where she was going. She leaned forward and cocked her head to the side again so that her hair folded over and draped across the nape of her neck. They were locked in a gaze like a couple of kids on a roller coaster, revealing fear and exchanging confidence before the ride begins.

"That's why I sent you my Klimt," she said.

Harry waited, putting his desire for logic on hold.

She settled back into the soft contours of the sofa. After a bit, he turned to look at her. He was astounded. She had fallen asleep.

My God, Harry, what do you expect? You should have called the police or taken her to a hospital. The poor woman has struggled through the proverbial Slough of Despond and you're surprised she's exhausted? At least, despite her own prediction, she's not dead. And neither are you, my darling Humphrey. Not yet.

Harry and Karen used to listen to online recordings of a 1950s radio program called *Bold Venture.* It starred Humphrey Bogart and Lauren Bacall as Slate Shannon, soldier of fortune, and his sultry sidekick, Sailor Duval, and took place in the days when murder was something that happened in newspapers and novels. When life was sweet and their academic careers at Huron College were burgeoning with promise, they used to call each other Slate and Sailor in bed, his voice toothy and rough, hers smoky, almost a whisper.

They still talked that way sometimes, but it wasn't the same.

Harry shifted around so his back was against one arm of the sofa and he drew Madalena gently into the protective curve of his body. She stirred slightly as she settled against him. He pushed her glass of scotch back from the edge of the table and drained his own, wincing with satisfaction as it burned his throat.

His mind surged with unanswerable questions. Why did she send him the Klimt? Did she anticipate torture and rape? Was she surprised to survive? Why involve him at all?

Maybe you're the key to what's happening. Keys open locks.

The only unopened lock is my ignorance, Sailor. Your argument circles back on itself.

Keys also provide symbols for reading a map.

In unfamiliar territory, that amounts to the same thing. Look, Lena Strauss didn't just happen on my name in the phone book.

Do they still exist?

So why am I here?

That's an existential question, Harry. You can't expect an answer from me. I'm a ghost.

Ghosts don't exist.

Neither do I.

But Harry was convinced that she did. She was as real to him as he was himself.

He shifted and Lena winced. Her eyes flashed open to see Harry then fell closed again. He eased her head back onto a throw pillow, and then found fresh bedding in the hall closet to make up the cot in her office. He doubted she had many guests. He fluffed up two pillows, then folded the top sheet back. After rolling up the soiled gabbeh and tucking it away in the hall closet, he returned to the living room and, finding she was still asleep, eased her up into his arms, cradling her as carefully as he could. She groaned from the pain. God, he hoped there was no internal damage. He supposed there was not, given the cuts had been meticulously done to release blood but not bleed out and that the cigarette burns were applied with sadistic precision to inflict pain but weren't, of course, lethal.

He lowered her fully clothed onto the clean sheet and pulled the top sheet over her. She tried to smile through swollen lips as she nudged her head against the depths of the pillows and fell back into sleep as he watched.

Harry pulled down the blind and closed the curtains. He turned out the light and, leaving her door open a crack so he could hear any movement, went back into the living room. He sat on the sofa and stared at the Klimt, which seemed radiant as the pale glow of morning ventured through the window to compete with the lamplight off to the side.

Beside it, the alpine landscape painted by Madalena's grandmother and used to disguise her great-grandmother's likeness seemed dull, its mawkish colours and derivative contours eclipsed by Klimt's inspired luminescence. Perhaps sentiment gave it value beyond aesthetics.

You think?

Harry walked over to extinguish the lamp. As he bent to feel for the switch his eye caught an anomaly in the surface texture of the painting. He paused then stood straight and examined it closely. He took the painting down from the wall and walked with it to the window.

In the natural light, it had a peculiar patina. He was no expert, but it seemed like the brush marks revealed an absence of resilience, as if the painting had been applied to a solid surface. Even on the pale washes that were meant to convey flesh, where the weave of the canvas would be expected to bleed through, there seemed to be a hardness beneath the skin.

Clutching the frame firmly with one hand and against all deference to a great work of art he extended the index finger of the other and let it rest gently on the painted surface. It was a wood panel that had been prepared with gesso, a hard compound of plaster of Paris and glue. Nothing surprising in that. But the back of the painting indicated canvas stretched over a wood frame.

He carried the painting into the dining area off the kitchenette where the lighting was better. He placed the painting face down on a newspaper spread out on the table. Small wooden tabs inserted into slots in the larger frame held the stretcher frame in place. These had been varnished over or perhaps it was only the accumulated dust and grime from the office in the Mauthausen town hall where it had resided under the careless eyes of the *Wermacht* administrators, the same men who signed the documents that sent Lena's grandmother and great-grandmother to be killed and burned. *Getötet und gebrannt.*

Trembling with anticipation, he realized there was only one explanation for the differences between the front and the back of Madalena's fabulous Klimt.

Several scrape marks and some lines along the edges of the outer frame suggested Madalena's grandmother had struggled to hide her own mother's Klimt inside the frame for her landscape. She was probably not even aware that more than one painting was being concealed. And Madalena, when she removed the Klimt, had no reason to look for another. One Klimt was more than enough.

Carefully, using the dull edge of a kitchen knife, Harry worked the tabs free, two each from the top and bottom and three from each side. Gently, he inserted the knife into the clefts between the frames. He slowly edged the interior frame upward until it slipped free. Then he gingerly lifted it away.

There was writing on the back of the larger wood panel. It looked like a name and a date. 1902, probably the year it was painted. The name Rachel Damboch meant nothing to him. He turned the hidden canvas to catch the morning light. He gasped.

He had seen the picture before. On Klimt's *Beethoven Frieze* in the Secession Building on Friedrichstrasse. It was breathtakingly erotic, splendid in its nakedness, a detail from the segment of the frieze called *The Forces of Evil.*

In the frieze a woman with a voluptuous cascade of copper red hair poised languidly against the shoulder of a stylized gorilla, the embodiment of depraved bestiality. Beside her was a blissed-out young blonde, and above a pot-bellied woman who seemed oblivious to her own vulgarity. To the left of the gorilla were three world-weary muses with black pubic curls flashing against ghastly pale skin. Over them, a crone with an emaciated body was surrounded by horrified faces as she glared lasciviously across at the woman with the red hair who, alone, looked out of the painting and into the eyes of the onlooker.

The detail Harry held in his hands eliminated everything but the woman with cascading red hair who floated in a swirling mosaic of gilt and shadow. Her right leg was drawn up so her knee touched her cheek, exposing an expanse of pale naked thigh and the underside of her buttocks. The space between her legs was filled with long copper strands of her hair draped to conceal and yet emphasize her genital folds. Waves of hair flowed across the contours of her body, and the swirling vermillion that surrounded her face was embedded with a constellation of flowers.

But it was the face that mesmerized.

In a painting illuminating the salacious forces of evil, it stood out as a contradiction. It was infinitely beguiling, but it was playful, hinting at the profound innocence of open sexuality. Her head bent against her knee, with her chin pushed slightly askew, her broad mouth and parted lips, the narrow bridge of her long nose curving up into bold eyebrows, her eyes, darkly outlined, the blue-green irises aslant to the tilt of her face, looking upward and to the side, with an unrelenting, glamorous, and whimsical gaze, all this promised intimacy, affection, passion, not as sin or vice but as the enthralling allure of forbidden virtue.

It was a portrait of Madalena Strauss.

If the maquette for *The Kiss* caught her worldly appearance, this reached into her soul. And into Harry's, as well. Despite its association with a painting called *The Forces of Evil,* this was so visceral and sensually evocative, it was the closest thing to the spiritual he had ever encountered.

It was an allegory, of course. But haunting and beautiful and terrifying, all at the same time. If I ever write a book, he thought, I'll put this picture on the cover. No matter what the book is about.

6 **CAFÉ SPERL**

HARRY RETRIEVED THEIR WATCHES FROM THE BATHROOM. The crystal on hers was cracked, but it still kept time. On the back, the words *mors certa* were engraved. Death is certain. He left it on the kitchen table and when he went for provisions she put it on. He replenished their liquor supply with another bottle of scotch and a magnum of generic Beaujolais that he drank chilled while Lena drank her scotch neat. She slept a lot on the cot in her darkened office as her body began to heal. After he accepted that she wouldn't submit to police or medical intervention, they had spoken very little. She needed to recuperate. He read from her limited selection of books in English. Although he threw out her bloody bedding and then scrubbed and flipped her mattress, he preferred to sleep on the sofa in the living room.

On the third day he woke at noon to the smell of fresh coffee. Lena had changed into a loose-fitting magenta top over a pale green skirt, both of which flared from her body as she moved with uncomfortable grace and disguised her bruises in a swirl of colour and material. She had applied makeup strategically and brushed her hair.

She passed him a plate of pastries and an outsized cup of coffee.

Instead of joining him, she busied herself rearranging magazines on the shelf under the Klimt, which Harry had replaced on the wall after sliding the detail from *The Forces of Evil* back into its hidden sanctuary behind *The Kiss*. He had decided not to tell her of his discovery until he figured out what it might signify. She moved a pair of brass candlesticks to a side table. With Klimt restored to his proper place, the smoke from tapers made of rolled beeswax posed a hazard. They smelled of honey and flowers.

The pastries were room temperature but had a faint odour of the refrigerator about them. After a few sips of coffee, he focused on Lena as she moved with casual determination around the apartment. He noticed her office curtains had been drawn back and the cot was made up.

After he washed and shaved, Harry sat down across from her at the kitchen table. She gazed at him expectantly and offered a warm crooked smile. He smiled in return.

She appeared fragile and yet more reckless and vital than when they had met at the Kressler or in the Café Central. Damaged but not overwhelmed. Resilient and resolute. Improbably enhanced by the pain she'd endured,

You're thinking in adjectives, Harry. That could be problematic.

Real people don't say *problematic.*

"Madalena," he said gently. "I need you to talk to me. Can you tell me what happened here?"

"Here?"

"Three days ago. Can you talk about it?"

"Sakarov." She spat out his name as if it explained everything.

"Why would he do this to you?"

"I will tell you about the painting," she said, as if that were an appropriate answer. She got up awkwardly, betraying her pain, and poured herself two fingers of Glendronach.

"It's a little early for this, but it helps," she said, waving her glass in his direction. She resumed her place, sitting forward in her chair. "Harry, this painting is my life; it is my great-grandmother and my grandmother and my mother and it is me. They are all dead. I am dead." She glanced at the floor then up again into his eyes. Her expression was almost apologetic. "Do you know about the picture of Dorian Gray?"

"Oscar Wilde."

"Yes, well, this picture in my own attic garret stays the same. It doesn't age like Dorian Gray's. Not in outward appearance. But it has absorbed our lives just the same. When I look at that picture, time collapses. Art Nouveau and the Belle Époque, two World Wars, the Holocaust, the Occupation, the Cold War, the dwindling Détente, they are all swallowed up in that picture. Look in her eyes, Harry. She sees everything and reveals nothing. She is my past and my only future. And that is why I sent it to you. Do you understand?"

Harry rubbed his chin then pressed his fingers together in front of his mouth and blew across them, as the blue-haired gatekeeper at the zentralkommando office had done. Air from inside his own body, warmed by the lifeblood coursing through his veins, was reassuring. He was not in the slightest mystical and yet her account of the picture had made perfect sense. Except for the parts about sending it to him at the Kressler and about herself being already dead.

"Harry, for three days I shadowed you. We scoured Vienna together for Klimts on display. You explored like a determined tourist, visiting old haunts, perhaps, places you'd shared with your wife. You attended a performance of the Lipizzaner stallions, but you didn't enjoy it so much. You toured the ossuary at St. Stephen's Cathedral. I didn't go down to the crypts, but you seemed satisfied when you emerged. You drank *mélange* each morning, drank white wine with spritzer in midafternoon, and *trockenbeerenauslese* as a digestif after good Austrian dinners in several small bistros. You ate *Milchrahmstrudel à la Sacher* at the Sacher Hotel. Twice. And you seem to have brought only one jacket with you. Scandinavian nubuck; quite new I think."

"I have an old and venerable Armani blazer as well."

"In case of unexpected funerals? I've only observed the nubuck."

Observed. It was uncanny how a woman with unruly cascades of red hair could have blended into the scene. Surely he would have noticed her following him. But he didn't. She had been invisible.

Equally unlikely was how, despite her brutalized condition, she could talk as if Harry's comprehension was the only thing in the world that mattered. She spoke with an urgency born out of horror that seemed to defy what she had been through.

"Harry, when you pointed out the fat man while we talked over coffee and biscuits at the Kressler, I knew it was Sakarov. I didn't see him, but I knew it had to be him. When we met at the Café Central and you told me how he had presented himself and that you had dinner together, I realized how easily it would be for you to get drawn in over your head, if you weren't already. You are a philosopher. I believe you are capable of moral outrage. And that has put you in far more danger than you could possibly realize. It is my fault."

Harry didn't argue.

"Could you get me another scotch, please?" She held out her glass. This time he poured one for himself as well.

"Sakarov?" he asked.

"A man to avoid. I really did want you to leave Vienna."

With a priceless painting under your arm.

"I taunted you, challenged you, threatened you at the café. You got up from the table, how do you say, in a huff. That was good. I assumed, after that, that common sense would prevail. I had only to send you my

Klimt. You were to receive the painting and go back to Toronto. I knew you would not be able to sell it—too many awkward questions. I also knew you were sufficiently principled to arrange for its eventual return. That was important. I have no relatives to speak of. I am Jewish by blood, but Austria is my spiritual source, for better or worse. My Klimt is a portrait of Austria. Do you understand?"

She gazed out the window. Despite her wounds and liberal consumption of coffee and scotch, colour had returned to her pale complexion. As Harry watched, her eyes creased at the edges and slowly transformed to limpid green as they filled with tears that began to slide down her cheeks. She made no effort to wipe them away.

He wanted to reach over but didn't.

Madalena shifted her head to the side and looked out across the street and over the rooftops to the hint of green hills on the far horizon. From her elevated vista, Vienna was an infinite panoply of greys and beiges, ochres and reds. Closer, the outside of the window sill was stained with dried raindrops. The metal frame and mullions had been recently painted. Flecks of paint that had been scraped from the glass glinted on the inner sill. Her reflection was distorted in the window closest to her that had been cranked open to let in the fresh morning breeze.

"Harry," she said, letting his name hang in the air. Then she again offered her crooked smile. "I need to tell you so much. I have a daughter." She stopped and looked curiously puzzled, as if she had made a compromising disclosure and feared it might be an imposition. She soothed her mouth with a slow draught of scotch and resumed her story. "I am twenty-nine years old. My daughter turned twelve this spring. I have not seen her since she was four."

Harry shuddered. His Lucy had been five when she died.

"She has beautiful red hair like mine and a resolute chin, a delicate nose and eyes like cracked emeralds."

He knew what she meant—radiant facets of colour shot through with slivers of darkness.

"Her name is Freya. She is gone."

He could feel the depth of her pain as only a person who has lost a child can know it. Although her account was coming out awkwardly, he knew she needed to get it into the open. She needed to connect. To create a context for horrors she was about to describe. To absolve herself for what she had done. Or was about to do.

He saw the terror in his own Lucy's eyes in the instant before her head smashed against rock, the valiant flailing of eight-year-old Matt's powerless limbs as water crushed the life from his body. In Harry's mind, it was happening still. He tried to lose himself in Lena's story, but her words excoriated his wounded soul, a soul he had no reason to believe existed except through the pain that defined him.

When Madalena was sixteen she had fallen in love. She was at school in Salzburg. One day she met a boy while they were strolling in opposite directions along the promenade by the Salzach River. It is so easy to meet when you are young. They caught a premonition of their future in each other's eyes as they passed. They paused and turned around to see if the other had turned. They went for coffee. They laughed. She was from an ancestral town called Hinterbrühl and doing a prep year for university. She intended on going to the Universität Wien. He was on an Erasmus exchange at the Universität Salzburg. He was Norwegian and was doing a degree in cultural studies at university in Oslo.

He didn't speak her language very well and she his not at all. Mostly, they conversed in school-book English.

They became lovers after knowing each other only a few hours. He was her first. She had to con her way into residence that night with a story about being held up at a relative's in Hallstatt, a village in the region renowned for its salt mines and beauty. She was a strange girl and no one thought to check.

He told her his name was Gustav Vigeland and he had a girlfriend in Oslo. That was okay. Madalena was sixteen. She had no intention of getting tied down. They were vigorous lovers, but they never spent an entire night together. On their last evening at the end of the term, she told him she was pregnant. He congratulated her.

She had no expectations, but given the wondrous transformations in her own body and mind, she was bewildered by how detached he had seemed, as if she had announced she got an A in calculus or free tickets to a concert.

She moved to Vienna and took the following year off school. Her mother supplied funds without asking questions. When her daughter was born, Lena named her Freya after the Scandinavian goddess of fertility. She was not without a sense of humour.

When she wrote Gustav to announce the birth, her letter was returned unopened. There was no one by that name at the address she had been given. A handwritten note on the back of the envelope by an anonymous stranger asked, did she mean *the* Gustav Vigeland, the famous sculptor, because, if so, he was dead. She could try reaching his estate at Vigelandsanlegget in Oslo.

Fuck him, she thought.

She had always thought Norway romantic. Now it seemed empty and cold. Not a place she would want to visit. She didn't bother to look up Gustav Vigeland.

Shortly after Freya turned four, Madalena finished her degree in psychology. She was contemplating advanced studies to make the effort already invested worthwhile. Few things have less intrinsic worth, she noted, than an undergraduate degree in psychology.

"What about philosophy?" he parried. "A bachelor's degree in philosophy pretty much precludes a job in the real world." He did not rise to defend education as the prelude to a full life. That he had been a professional philosopher made this clear if implicit.

Only to other philosophers, Harry.

Early in the summer of her graduation, her mother died and Madalena discovered she was quite prosperous. After she liberated the Klimt (she spoke of one painting, not two), she was wealthier than she could ever have imagined. She decided to take a year off from her studies and devote all her attention to Freya, who would be going to school soon, and then it would never be the same between them.

She seldom thought of her lover who had called himself Gustav Vigeland. It was a wonder he hadn't claimed to be Thor Heyerdahl, the most famous Norwegian of all. Even then, she wouldn't have guessed he was lying. People share the same names. There are only so many to go around.

She paused in her narrative before continuing in a lower register, more quietly, painfully. "And then," she said. "The evil thing happened."

Freya was taken from her.

Two men and a woman had come to her door early in the evening. They said they were from Social Services. One man was stocky, middle-aged, well-dressed. The other was younger, taller, with thick black hair plastered close to his skull and eyes that avoided hers by staring at the floor. The woman was attractive, with fair hair cut short and too much makeup. There had been a report of abuse from one of her neighbours in the building. They were not permitted to identify the complainant. Nor were they at liberty to state the exact nature of the complaint. They were very apologetic, but they were required to take the child into custody.

They had several documents with signatures and official stamps of authority. They gave her a slip of paper with an address where she could attend a hearing the next morning and sort all this out.

The situation was the kind of bizarre paradox that had marked so much of Madalena's young life. The men were domineering but gentle and sympathetic; the woman was delicate but very severe. This was for Freya's own good and if everything was in order, she would be back in her own bed the next day. They pulled her door closed when they left, effectively barring Madalena's way. She stared at the back of the door. She had not cried for fear of upsetting Freya.

Eight years later as she talked to Harry, burning tears filled her eyes and rolled down her cheeks and into the corners of her mouth. She told him she had spent the night of Freya's departure in a straight-backed chair, weeping softly. Her tears tasted like salt, like blood. The next morning, she went to the address on the paper. It was a vacant lot where a building had been demolished during the war and ownership of the property was still in dispute.

Fighting hysteria, she went to the police.

A woman at the police station took down all the particulars and that is where the case ended. Hourly, daily, Madalena checked back, and each empty response devastated her more than the one before. Freya had simply vanished. Her disappearance was a matter of record, a police file, an irreversible irreducible tragedy. A statistic.

At the end of the summer, Madalena enrolled in advanced courses in criminology. On the side, she studied computer technology. Two years later, with a Magister diploma in hand, she joined the police force. In spite of being striking in appearance, an attribute she did not try to play down, she progressed through the ranks very rapidly.

She had chosen criminology over law because she needed to understand where the system broke down. She was not interested in justice and social order. She was interested in how the rules that allow society to function can be so easily exploited by those who hold them in contempt.

People working with her often resented her tireless dedication. People above her were daunted by her smile, which was never a shared social gesture; it was always private, as if she were smiling only for herself. People subordinate to her found her work ethic and her poise enviable attributes, although none tried to cultivate her friendship.

She worked on her own time building massive files on child trafficking. No one in the force ever connected her with the teenage girl who reported losing her daughter years earlier, an improbable story that had throbbed through the headlines and quickly expired.

It was assumed she was writing a book. She told Harry this as if she were talking about someone else. Rumour had it she had a graduate degree in criminology and she was generally conceded to be alarmingly bright. She was referred to, offhand, as *Fräulein Magistra*, or *Mag Strauss*. Sometimes, with irony because she did not look bookish, she was called The Professor. She was not discouraged from her private investigation. A well-received study of a universally abhorrent area of criminality would bring credit to her superiors and might give her colleagues a well-needed lift in public esteem.

Madalena became notorious for having no social life. In most people, that would be considered a sad aberration. Because she was beautiful, in her it was considered a tragic flaw, a violation of the natural order, with implications beyond her personal sphere. Over the years, she realized, an aura of suppressed evil developed around her, as if she were inseparable from the terrible things she was bent on exposing. She was a superlative cop, a relentless and methodical researcher, a strange human being.

"Then I met Dietmar Henning."

She paused and looked around for a moment quite frantically, as if she were disoriented by her own disclosures. Her haunted eyes settled on Harry.

"Lena, do you think Freya is still alive?" he asked.

Her eyes darkened.

"Madalena," he said gently.

Her eyes were like mirrors, glazed with tears.

Oh my God, my God.

Harry thought that his heart would burst. He could not begin to fathom the depths of her anguish.

He reached across the table to cover her hands with his own. She pulled away, leaning back in her chair. Her eyes grew wide and she swallowed hard. It was clear she had never talked like this before. She flashed hatred in her eyes, gratitude, fear, but not certainty. Tears slid down her cheeks, into the corners of her mouth.

"I whored myself, Harry."

Harry struggled to keep up.

"With Dietmar Henning," she said.

"Lena?"

"You have to understand."

He was trying to.

"As a homicide detective I work in the field. There is a steady turnover of corpses with grief-stricken survivors, pretty much all the same in their grief. And there are the killers. Every killer is different from every other. Dealing with them is my job and I am good at it. The strange thing is, I seem to communicate with the depraved better than with the bereaved. I haven't been very good handling my own grief, so I wasn't very good with theirs."

Lena smiled her crooked smile. "After I lost Freya, I learned to feel nothing. My research was cerebral. Until Dietmar Henning, I had never met anyone directly involved in the trafficking of children."

"And then everything changed?"

"Everything changed."

She continued her story. The words seemed to come from inside his own head, as if they were listening together.

One evening, walking home from work she had stopped at Café Sperl on the lower end of Gumpendorfer Strasse. It was a little out of the way but one of the best coffee houses in all of Vienna. More low key and intimate than the Central, it was one of her favourite places.

This was a year ago last spring. She had had a good day, closing a particularly gruesome case of domestic violence by arresting the husband, his mistress, and her surprised boyfriend, who had sponsored the affair to extort money but had not counted on murder.

She slid into a booth upholstered in patterned velvet, a comfortably dated floral design of crimson and grey, and ordered *zimtschnecke*, a spiral shaped pastry filled with sweet cheese and crushed nuts. She would skip supper and the calories would average out. She sipped her *mélange* and gazed absentmindedly around the L-shaped room with its dark wainscoting and soft amber walls glowing softly like beeswax from a profusion of congenial chandeliers alight well before sundown. The other customers were reading papers or chatting quietly.

"I've been there," said Harry. She was explaining the scene in such detail, he feared the urgency of her story would get swallowed up in the telling.

"I know," she said.

A shiver ran through him. He nodded. She went on. A man there caught her eye. He was her own age, sitting in a window seat and reading by the light coming from outside. He was handsome and seemed in a world of his own. Her attention moved on, but an odd sense of revulsion made her look back. Why should she feel anything about him at all? She coughed; he looked up. She looked away but not before experiencing another tremor of revulsion.

He went back to his paper and she looked again. He wasn't a known criminal or fugitive. He wasn't someone she had encountered unpleasantly at a social function—she didn't go to parties but occasionally had to attend receptions and funerals. He wasn't a corrupt celebrity, an e-millionaire, or a villain from the movies.

He could be one of a thousand profiles she had put together over the last few years. It was hard to tell. He was not electronic data; he was real. She ran through clusters of faces in her mental inventory, faces associated with different aspects of the child sex trade—abductions for the purpose of illicit adoption, internet pornography, child labour and slavery, prostitution of minors and infants, and the international traffic in snuff films.

She had been fiddling with the pastry flakes remaining on her plate. The waiter asked if she'd like another. No, she insisted, but ordered fresh coffee and with eyes lowered she smiled at the tabletop as the waiter cleared her place. The man by the window glanced over several times. She looked up, caught his eye, she nodded.

He moved to her table like it was the most natural thing in the world. As she acknowledged his conversational gambits with an offhand smile, it was all she could do not to jam a pastry fork into his strangely unthreatening eyes—for unspecified crimes, for the way he made her feel.

He spoke German with an Italian accent. He claimed to be an Albanian refugee, after which he shrugged expansively to let her know he was prospering. He told her he worked for a clothing importer. She said she was a buyer for Pregenzer Fashion on Schleifmuehlgasse, off Karlsplatz, just around the corner and down the street. He modified his credentials to explain he in fact worked for an international security company but had wanted not to seem intimidating. She told him she was not intimidated.

His thick brown hair, worn fashionably unkempt, his boyish features and easy air, combined with clothes from Hugo Boss, hand-tooled Italian loafers, a gold chain around his neck, and a heavy gold ring on the little finger of his right hand, conveyed the kind of mawkish charm of someone who hung out in clubs that had bouncers.

Not her type, not that she had a type. She didn't date. But she was attractive, she knew how to flirt, she was able to transform her revulsion into sultry contempt that made her seem more alluring.

He was pathetic, really. He made no attempt at consistency in his personal revelations, saying whatever came to his mind as he tried to read her responses, and consequently she believed nothing. What might have made him mysterious and even seductive with music booming over loudspeakers and strobe lights flashing, here in the casual elegance of Café Sperl made him seem a handsome buffoon. He had a nice smile, showing lots of teeth, and crinkling about the eyes that suggested a man given to tanning parlours. As he began to anticipate success, he slouched in his chair, conveying a sleazy insouciance Madalena found embarrassing, especially in the Café Sperl where the waiters knew her by name.

"Madalena." Harry's voice intruded.

"Yes."

But he had nothing to say, just wanted her to know she wasn't alone. She acknowledged his need to connect with a pained smile and after a moment continued, "What I've already told you about him was not the whole story. It's true he shook down the criminal class for amusement. The police knew about this and turned a blind eye. What I didn't tell you, and what the police investigating his death don't know, was that he made most of his money from kids. Some from illicit adoptions, but far more from sex, the more degrading the bigger the payoff. It's a billion dollar industry, Harry, and he was deeply involved. Never a kingpin. He wasn't executive material. But as an enforcer and a free agent, he was smart enough to take the initiative when left to his own resources, ruthless enough to do whatever was necessary. That made him a valuable asset and a formidable adversary."

She described having struggled through their initial encounter to quell surges of loathing, even though she knew nothing yet of his actual work. She sensed he was evil. Evil had become her obsession. She needed to penetrate the cheap façade. She was afraid her contempt would scare him off. She used truth as a bait.

She leaned across the table and whispered with all the sensuality she could muster, "I'm a cop."

He flinched then saw she was throwing this in as a challenge. He was in no danger of being apprehended. He obviously felt reckless. She was as beautiful as a painting, but she was a cop, and he held cops in wary esteem.

From there on, it was easy.

Over the next year, she learned all she could learn from Dietmar Henning about his role in the international trade in children. Her accumulated research took on flesh-and-blood reality as depravity became manifest in the actual lives that were touched by her venomous lover.

She learned by listening, by prowling his laptop, by questions that played to his ego. She was able to identify a network of businesses and their numbered accounts, to trace lines of commerce from Tokyo to Toronto, Estonia to Thailand, Athens to New York, lines that seemed almost infinite, like inflamed capillaries spreading through diseased human flesh.

Socially, she introduced him as an international dealer in art and antiques, but he was quite open in private about his extortion sideline, blackmailing the criminal class. During their period of intimacy, never once did she feel anything but disgust for Dietmar Henning; not once did she loathe him any less than the first evening when they had made love and she excused herself afterward to silently retch into the toilet just down the hall from where she now sat talking to Harry.

Before Dietmar Henning, she had no idea what to do with her research. As he came to the end of his usefulness, she developed a plan. She wanted to be absolutely sure of the facts, then she would reveal what she knew in a cyberexplosion of monumental proportions. She would expose the fine people who fucked children, the upstanding citizens who peddled small bodies, the human garbage who adopted kids stolen from their natural parents. She would lay it all out in the open.

She would use the internet but not for anonymity—she would sign her name and supply documents, photographs, links that would back up her revelations. It was the simultaneity of the net that made it the most logical venue for her charges. It would all suddenly be out there. She herself could be eliminated but not silenced.

She was under no illusion that her efforts would close the industry down. But it would provide interference on a massive scale and might even save lives. It would punish, humiliate, possibly destroy. Perhaps in some perverse way it would atone for the terrible guilt of allowing Freya's abduction to occur.

Madalena rose to her feet. "I need to rest, Harry. We'll talk again later."

Harry gazed out the newly glazed window, sickened by the skyline of Vienna, by the world that was the same as before.

7 **PANDORA'S JAR**

EARLY IN THE SPRING, A FEW WEEKS AFTER WHAT WOULD have been Freya's twelfth birthday, Dietmar Henning walked into Madalena's bedroom from the shower with a towel around his waist and his hair plastered flat against his skull. She glanced up and a pain ran though her like a bullet to the heart. With his hair slicked back and his absurdly sympathetic eyes cast down, he was an apparition from the harrowing past. The horror she had felt each time he touched her suddenly coalesced around an unbearable memory. Her mind reeled, she struggled to catch her breath, she squinted. He looked puzzled. It was him, she had no doubt; he was the young man with the black hair who had, along with the dumpy middle-aged man and the woman with too much makeup, stolen Freya eight years ago. Different hair, a nose job, a body filled out, eight years older. But there was absolutely no doubt.

She stared wide-eyed at Harry.

"Lena?"

She raised her head and looked deep into Harry's eyes.

"Lena, you did kill Dietmar Henning, didn't you?"

Unexpectedly, she smiled.

His mind swarmed with the implications. In talking to the Russian, Harry had conceded that virtually anyone was capable of murder if the circumstances warranted. That was the catch. What circumstances warranted murder? Surely she was morally justified in killing the man who had abducted her child. But the gouged-out eyes, the mutilated genitals, that wasn't so easy to reconcile with the smile on Madalena's lips.

"It is Saturday morning," she announced. "I think we should go to the Naschmarkt and buy ourselves a nice lunch."

Harry sucked in his breath. Her revelation had left her curiously euphoric. "Lena," he asked. "Why did the fat man do what he did, and why didn't he kill you?"

She seemed to contemplate his question with wry amusement.

"It was his crude form of communication, Harry. Your presence in Vienna provoked him. He wanted me to know his power over me is absolute. He can't risk killing me—as long as I'm alive, he can force me to suppress what I know about the *business*, as he calls it. If I am dead, he loses control."

"So he's in the business himself?"

"He's an enforcer, a fixer, a dealer. A very unpleasant man."

"And how does he control you?"

"By threatening to kill children—a bomb in a nursery school in Hietzing, the 13th District. It is a fashionable suburb. What might be a back-page story of mindless terrorism in Mogadishu would be catastrophic in Vienna. White European children in expensive clothes, somehow he thinks that would bother me more."

"Would it?"

"Harry, the horrible thing is, I don't know. I don't think so. A child's life is a child's life. But a child like my Freya, flesh of my own bleeding flesh, yes, possibly. Intellectually, morally, it is immaterial. As emotional extortion, yes, it may be that he wields more power by threatening to exterminate my own kind. The very thought of that scares me, that human suffering could be on a relative scale. Such thinking led to my great-grandmother's death."

"At Auschwitz?" Harry named the one Nazi concentration camp that had come to represent over 40,000 others: internment camps, transit camps, slave labour camps, extermination camps, and death camps for children, women, homosexuals, Jews, Gypsies, dissidents, ethnic subversives, and POWs from the Eastern Front. Auschwitz-Birkenau was perhaps the most terrible, if murder can be measured in relative terms.

"Auschwitz is in Poland. She died in Germany. They were taken to the women's camp at Ravensbrück, north of Berlin. My great-grandmother and one of her daughters died there. Her other daughter, my grandmother, was transported back to Mauthausen."

Reduced to explicit details, the past was more coherent than the details of her own life, the horrors more easily accepted.

"My grandmother was transferred from Ravensbrück to the women's sub-camp in Lenzing for work making ersatz wool. Margarete Freinberger, her friend before the war, was *Oberaufseherin*. She returned my grandmother to Mauthasen near Hinterbrühl in the district of Mödling, where she worked making engine parts for the BMW 003 turbojet fighter plane. In the last days of the war she was murdered by the SS, either by gasoline injection or manual strangulation. She died within a few miles of where she was born."

Harry tried to assimilate the atrocities of the Holocaust with Madalena's children's crusade. One was her heritage, the other her legacy.

"You told me you are dead already. But you're telling me Sakarov needs you alive."

"My death is the best protection for those children in the 13th District. There would be no point in killing them if I'm gone."

God, Harry, this woman is psychopathic. Or a genuine martyr.

Perhaps it's a matter of perspective, Sailor.

"You say he needs you alive," he said.

"To control my information, yes. I had hoped my arrest would release me from his power, but I wasn't arrested. I have had to take other measures."

She seemed a guileless innocent in the light streaming through her window. Harry was reminded of the pre-Raphaelite painting she had summoned to mind in the Café Central: Pandora kneeling in front of an ornate box, naked and sensuous as she peered into the future its contents would set loose on the world.

"I don't understand," he said, but he was beginning to. "You thought your files would become a matter of public record if you were convicted of murder, is that it?"

"Exactly. There would be no point in killing me. More significantly, there would be nothing achieved by bombing a nursery school in the 13th District."

"But I gather there are people in authority who might have been exposed. They refused to prosecute. You needed me to help make the case against you, not because you're guilty but to set you free. Are you guilty?"

"Does it matter?"

"Yes, of course."

"No, Harry, it does not."

"Then suppose you are dead."

"Yes, suppose I am."

"Why not set up your files to be released automatically? I'm not a computer whiz, but couldn't there be a floodgate that opens if you don't check in at predetermined times?"

A cryptic smile briefly distorted her features. She said nothing. He tried a different tack.

"Lena, if you have killed already, why not kill again, why not kill Sakarov?"

"Ah, so you do condone murder! It would be good if he were dead, yes, but evil is profligate, Harry. If Dimitri Sakarov dies, ten more will step forward to take his place. The people he works for are not an organization; that's what makes them so difficult to bring down. Their network is vast and discontinuous. And Sakarov himself is very well organized. His death would create a vacuum, and evil abhors a vacuum. His minions would rise to fill the gap. That's what makes him so useful to them and so dangerous to us."

"To us?"

"My files must be released anonymously, simultaneously, in an onslaught of biblical proportions."

"With you playing God."

"I will be dead. It is the only way."

"Then who controls the deluge? How will your files be released, if not by you and not by God?"

Guess, Harry!

"By you, my friend."

Oh shit! Karen's voice, Karen swearing. *Let's get the hell out of here.*

"No," he said, sharing Karen's concern. "No, no, no. No, Lena. Apart from anything else, that would put me in exactly the same position you're in now."

"Not quite, for several reasons. Sakarov will not know you're in control."

"I won't be."

"You don't have a choice."

"There's always a choice," he said, but he knew that wasn't true. Sometimes, the moral imperatives are so clear and the consequences of inaction promise to be so catastrophic, there is no choice but to act.

"Harry…"

Madalena paused, as if for a moment considering the brutality of what she was about to say. "If you could have saved Matthew and Lucy, even if it cost your own life, you would not have hesitated. Am I not correct?"

God, Harry. She's pitiless.

"Yes."

"Exactly. There would have been no choice. Harry, an opportunity will come—not for your own children but for thousands of others. They will depend on you and you will not let them down. It is not in your nature. I have researched you, Harry Lindstrom. I know you."

There's knowing and there's knowing.

"And you realize," said Harry, "Sakarov has researched *you*. He's been reading our email."

"No, he has seen only what I wanted him to see. I am a much better hacker than his accomplices in Saint Petersburg."

"Of course you are," said Harry.

Walking in the direction of the Naschmarkt, Harry felt vulnerable being out in the open, while Madalena seemed carefree, with the morning breeze combing through her long hair. Given her fragile gait, she might have been out for a morning stroll after a night of extravagant love.

They cut between gloomy blocks of apartment complexes hiding charming balconied courtyards behind their walls and came out beside the Wienfluss concrete floodwater bed, at this time of year a meagre tributary to the Danube, which it joined beyond the city limits.

Finally, at the risk of echoing Bogart, Harry slowed his pace a little, and asked, "Of all the people in all the world, why me?"

"Well, let me see," she said with disarming nonchalance. "I needed to enlist a man of intelligence and integrity, cultural awareness, and professional commitment."

That was succinct, Slate, and as vague as an ad in the personals.

But she went on to tell him about the international symposium on "Women in Police Service" held in Berlin the previous April, where she had become friends over dinner and drinks with a Superintendent of Homicide from Toronto, an Inspector with the National Criminal Police from Stockholm, and a Detective Sergeant from Hong Kong.

"I've never been to Hong Kong," said Harry.

"No, but there is a Shirley Zhou there who would love to meet you. You occupied a good deal of our conversation. Miranda Quin and Hannah Arnason made you seem like exactly the man I was after. I asked them questions. They're cops, they enjoy talking about themselves, and they offered what they believed were objective answers about you. For the Swede you were courageous, contemplative, willful, and sexy. And at six feet, you're a little on the short side. For the Canadian, you were tall and handsome, the tragic protagonist in an unfinished story, and a paradox, Harry, an intellectual driven by emotion, a man of smoldering convictions. And sexy."

What the hell are smoldering convictions?

She means I'm a paradox.

And you like that.

Yes, I do.

Madalena's cascading hair caught spirals of the morning sun as she bobbed her head in animated conversation, explaining while they walked how she and Shirley Zhou had encouraged Miranda and Hannah to spin out their revelations.

Miranda Quin was Harry's mentor and closest living friend. They had known each other at summer camp where Miranda was a counsellor and Harry a camper. They had briefly been lovers while he was at Cambridge and she had begun working for the Toronto Police Service after a brief stint with the Mounties. They did not keep in regular touch after that, but when she heard about a young philosophy professor from London, Ontario, who had survived a canoeing accident that had taken the lives of his wife and their two small children, she picked up on his story. At first she felt getting too close would be intrusive, until in anguish and remorse he had burned down his home on the Sanctuary Line near Granton. Then she drove down to London and visited him where he had been hospitalized. As he slowly emerged from the nightmare of still being alive, Miranda helped him in the transition from a job lecturing about the human condition to dealing with it directly as a private detective. He set up briefly on the other side of the continent, in Nanaimo, BC, and then, when his refusal to accept black-and-white justice landed him in trouble with the courts, she insisted he move to Toronto where she could keep an eye on him.

He couldn't tell what Lena knew from Miranda's table-talk and what she knew from research. Miranda might have alluded to family tragedy but would not have turned it into gossip, no matter how eager the audience.

Hannah Arnason was a more recent acquaintance. To call her a friend would not be appropriate, since there was a power differential that had swerved dramatically as their relationship progressed through a murder investigation in Sweden the previous winter. But there was a closeness between them, a shared vulnerability belied by outward appearances. Hannah was six-foot-four and a classic Scandinavian beauty with haunting blue eyes, a slightly upturned nose, full cheekbones, expressive lips, and hair the colour of honey under a harvest moon. She was a cop who bent rules. Harry had suffered as the victim of her unorthodox approach to solving crimes but was also the beneficiary. She had explained to her companions her enduring memory of the two of them trapped inside an ancient burial mound on the island of Fårö in the Baltic Sea when they contemplated having sex but didn't. She had never met anyone so lonely nor anyone who disguised it so well.

"So there you have it, Harry. And of course, I skimmed through your essay in *Philosophy Today*."

"Which one?"

But he knew which one. In a journal that attempted to bridge the gap between an esoteric academic discipline and the educated public at large, he had sometimes fulfilled his professional obligation as "public intellectual" by writing essays dealing with contentious issues. A piece that had come out just before the accident attracted more attention than he had anticipated. It was called "Justifiable Homicide?" The title was rhetorical. He used graphic examples from movies to argue that in certain scenarios the deliberate and unlawful killing of one human by another was morally justified.

The ensuing flurry of notoriety had made Huron College uncomfortable. Even Miranda Quin, who had studied philosophy and semiotics at the University of Toronto before entering police work, found his arguments indicative of a surprisingly facile turn of mind.

If Lena had read it, there was a good chance Sakarov had as well.

"I also read your essay on Klimt."

"In *Thinking*? They don't publish more than three hundred copies an issue!"

"It's online, Harry. There are no secrets anymore."

"I was writing about Klimt as a commodity, about value versus worth."

"An argument provoked by your appreciation of his art."

They approached the bustling forestall area of the market, where scavengers who squatted on cardboard mats were hawking used clothes, old books, discarded knickknacks, vinyl records, the retrieved flotsam and jetsam of a prosperous society. Harry picked his way through the jostling crowd, careful not to let Lena escape from his sight. With her hair aflame in the midday sun, it wasn't difficult and yet he was anxious.

He tripped against a small child on a tether and stumbled forward. Lena caught his arm as he recovered. The child didn't notice the drama and toddled on, stretching her lead to the limit.

"You say you tried to send me away." Harry crooked his neck forward to broadcast his words through the din. "Yet here I am in the thick of things."

"The man I entrusted with my Klimt might have served my needs better from a safe distance. Unfortunately, the same qualities of character apparently ensured you wouldn't leave. Or fortunately, perhaps."

Definitive ambivalence, Harry. She's sufficiently elliptical to be convincing. I'm just not sure what she's convincing about.

"Of course, you must leave," she continued. "You'll know when it's time to go." She had to shout to be heard. "I really do want you to take care of my Klimt for me."

"There's something I need to tell you about your painting." He was tall enough he could speak over the heads of the people foraging between them.

"It's all right, I know."

"You do?"

She moved to his side and looked up at him, her lips tightened, but he couldn't tell if she was suppressing a smile or expressing regret.

"That's a lot of Klimt," he said. He put his arm around her to keep her close. "You need to give them to a museum. I mean, for God's sake, you need to stay alive. Keep your paintings, don't die. There's got to be another way to release your findings."

"No, there is not." Her tone was unequivocal. "You must take Klimt to Toronto, Harry, and then you must think, *Why in the world would Lena Strauss have wanted me to take her Klimts to Toronto?* It is important."

"Fifty million dollars' worth of importance?"

"More important than money."

They crossed a small street and entered into the Naschmarkt proper where the crowd was more orderly.

Strolling among permanent stalls made of brightly painted wood with gold lettering and shutters and canvas awnings and ornamental wrought iron, mostly open to the walkways but a few closed in behind glass walls, they could have been tourists. A cacophony of voices and languages wrapped around the surging crowds, creating a carnival atmosphere. The smells of cooked meats, raw fish, cheeses of every kind, mixed with the odours of flowers in profusion and fruits and vegetables and baked savouries and fudge, gathered in the air like a thick, rich soup.

They found a corner stall with bar stools beside small tables and ordered beer and platters of fat spicy sausages with cold sauerkraut and crisp sesame rolls. Despite the din they tried to pick up their conversation. Her Germanic inflection made hearing and reading her lips easier as she enunciated more clearly than a native speaker. She seemed able to hear him with no problem, although she did most of the talking.

She was telling him how much she liked Miranda Quin and how strangely disturbing she found Hannah Arnason. She was gossiping.

"Lena?" The timbre in his voice telegraphed concern. She was being evasive.

"Let me worry about me, Harry. You worry about you."

"As far as I know, the only person I have to fear is Sakarov."

Surely you're being ironic!

"What about me, Harry. Don't you fear me?"

"Of course, but I'm too polite to say so. I'm Canadian. We're always polite."

"But you've just admitted it."

"Yes I have. Candour by stealth is also Canadian."

"Then let us be candid. I need you to trust me, Harry." Madalena gazed at him with a sly crinkle about the eyes. "I need you. Together we can save lives."

"Or destroy them."

"It's hard to do one without risking the other."

"You think your paintings will entice me? Or that I'll be forced by grief to comply?"

"The Klimts are yours for safekeeping and, for a man like yourself, even briefly possessing them is surely its own reward. As for grief, it may not be an incentive. But guilt—" She left the word hanging. The green of her eyes flashed and her mouth hardened. "I know about guilt and losing a child."

She paused, took a few deep breaths, and continued. "There is no remorse, Harry, no compensation or redemption sufficient, no penance or atonement possible, for what we who have survived must endure."

He swore she was looking into his soul and finding herself in the deepest and most painful recesses. While he did not believe the soul existed, she made it seem real.

"My beloved Freya, my last vision of her green eyes huge with tears and flashing with, oh God, Harry, with disappointment—how could I have been so wretchedly stupid, naïve, gullible, weak, submissive, compliant. But I was. And I will live with that terrible knowledge clutching at my heart until I draw my last breath. I watched my girl wrenched from my arms and did nothing. I did nothing."

Any sense of personal violation he had felt was swallowed in empathy. His own guilt for the deaths of his family had not diminished since the accident. The floodwater conditions of spring had disguised the natural warning signs, made reading the river difficult. But the accident should not have happened. He should not have let it happen. But it did.

The two of them, the investigator from Toronto who thought too much and tried not to, the police officer from Vienna, who felt too deeply, they shared grief in common with all who have lost children, and the guilt felt by all who have survived their children's deaths, no matter how they were taken away.

He thought about the small boy clutching the hand of an adult on either side as they stepped off the balcony at the Kressler Hotel. Harry had been paralyzed, not only by the death of a child he didn't know but by the arbitrary absurdity of his plunging into oblivion because the adults he was forced to trust betrayed him.

Lena had seemed reserved to the point of indifference about the boy's fate. Now, Harry knew she must have been struggling to deal with her own ineffable pain.

He desperately wanted to offer solace.

She toyed with her sauerkraut, lifting strands with the tines of her plastic fork.

"Do you need to talk about the attack?" he asked her in a loud whisper meant to convey privacy yet be heard over the ambient noise.

"No," she said at last. "But I will, if that's what you want."

"Why no police?"

"It was not a police matter, Harry. There are things much more important than my own suffering."

He didn't know how to follow up on that statement, which seemed stoic beyond comprehension.

"Harry. Sakarov and I have one thing in common—I feel no more bound by the law that he does. That is what makes me such a formidable opponent." She mouthed her words to project them clearly. "I have no idea why his own history has driven him to the depths of depravity and I don't care. But what I have endured, losing my child, whoring myself, other things you don't need to know, all this has pushed me to realize the constraints of the law and due process are shit. *Merde. Shite. Scheisse.* Do you understand what I'm saying? Individual rights, Harry, the right to privacy, they offer sanctuary for the vicious and depraved. Those who hide behind the veneer of respectability, behind facile legislation and sleazy lawyers, they must be exposed. Laws only work for those who accept their primacy. For those who hold the law in contempt it is, in fact, contemptible."

Harry drew in a deep breath. There was a circularity to her argument that he found frightening. She condoned subverting the law because others subverted the law. And yet there was enough truth in her indictment of the system he was committed to serving that he felt oppressed, as if the collapse of western civilization were his personal responsibility.

"Let's say I do understand. You're planning to skip the courts—"

"Exactly."

"And if among the dreck, you ruin innocent lives?"

"Wikileaks. Julian Assange."

"That's not an argument."

"I don't need an argument, Harry."

"You're very dangerous."

"I hope so. Believe me, Harry, I have been thorough. No name is in my files that does not belong there. These people are the scum of the earth. Gangsters and pedophiles living among us as politicians and priests, professionals and business executives. We will destroy the scum by exposing it to the open air."

"Not without due diligence to protect the rights of the innocent."

"The children, the innocent, what about them?"

The little boy on the ledge.

He stared at Madalena across the table. He had seen this woman, for her convictions, rendered into bloodied flesh like meat on a butcher's block. She frightened him.

"Do you know about Pandora?" she asked. Despite her relaxed tone, Harry realized she was not changing the topic as radically as it might have seemed.

"Pandora's box, yes."

"It was a jar."

Harry shifted into his bemused professorial mode. "Hesiod wrote about Pandora," he said. "One of the lost plays of Sophocles described the evils she unleashed on the world. Box was a mistranslation by the Renaissance humanist, Erasmus of Rotterdam. It was actually, as you say, an urn or a jar."

"You sound like a scholar trying to obscure a good story with facts."

Karen mumbled, but he couldn't tell whether in defiance or agreement.

"Tell me," he said. He felt an absurdly inappropriate surge of satisfaction, like for a moment he'd slipped back into his former life.

"Pandora was the first woman," Lena continued. "She was created from mud by Zeus to punish Prometheus, who had given away the secrets of fire. She still had the attributes assigned to her by the gods, but now she was mortal. Her only reminder of the world left behind was a jar that contained every evil the gods could imagine, including hope, perhaps the most insidious evil of all. And when out of curiosity she opened the jar, much as Eve had eaten from the Tree of Knowledge, all the evils swarmed out and they infested the newly fallen world."

It's all about fear and loathing of women in the western world. It always is.

Harry concurred.

He was struck by the coincidence of Lena and her exposition with her earlier evocation of Rossetti's Pandora, painted in the likeness of his favourite model, Jane Morris.

"And you are Pandora," he said.

"No, no. I'm here to put the lid back on the jar."

That's quite an undertaking for a mortal and a mere woman at that.

"You're going to confine evil in a single swoop?"

"Not all, but I hope enough to make a difference."

"And hope gets locked away, as well?"

"Hope is an illusion."

"And what if your jar shatters from the strain? What if you release even more evil?"

"It will not happen."

"How can you be so sure?"

"I have a gatekeeper, Harry."

Harry was perplexed. Had the classical analogy descended into gibberish or was she trying to tell him something important?

She responded to his puzzled silence. "With Dietmar Henning, I frightened myself."

"Killing him?"

"Whoring, being with him. My judgment appalled me, Harry. And after I couldn't get arrested for killing the miserable bastard I took precautions."

"You set up a gatekeeper."

"I needed to be held to standards higher than my own."

"That's somewhat illogical, isn't it?"

"Moral equivocation is always illogical, Harry."

"And if, just suppose, you are no longer around and, just suppose, your files are turned over to me—"

"They will not simply be turned over, Harry. Nothing is ever that simple. You know they exist, but you must seek them out. If access were simple, Sakarov would have deleted them already."

So first you decide to take on her project. Then you decide if it's something you want to do. One of you has got this ass-backward, Harry.

But Harry didn't think so. Commitment first, then judgment. A sequence to be avoided, but it did make sense.

"Would I be subject to your gatekeeper's moral authority?" he asked.

"Only if you decide to proceed."

"Then perhaps you should tell me who this person is."

"When I am dead, you will need to find her for yourself. Sakarov does not know she exists."

"It's a woman, then?"

"You will need to find her, Harry."

"If I decide to take up the cause."

"You understand, Harry. Thank you."

"No, I don't understand."

"You will," she said with a smile that struck him as both sinister and seductive. "And Sakarov, he is the face of this scourge. You will bring him down."

Harry wasn't sure where the fat man fit into the structures of evil she described, but her grievously wounded body left him in no doubt that he did. He wanted to move their conversation back to the reality where he was a witness again and not a key player. Before he could speak, she made a declarative statement.

"He had a gun, you know."

She's telling you she wasn't submissive, Harry. She had no choice.

"And he raped you?"

She looked away.

"The torture? Was that after the rape?"

Jesus Christ, Harry.

"First he raped me," Madalena responded.

"My God."

"You say that a lot. You are an atheist. It is odd."

"We live in a world shaped by the God I don't believe in."

"I see." She smiled with bruised lips.

"Are you going to be all right, Lena?"

Slowly her smile fell away as they sat for a while, surrounded by the clamour of the thronging crowd. He needed to bring their conversation back from the moral abyss and away from the diversions of an unregenerate God. He shifted to what seemed like a pertinent but innocuous query.

"Lena, there don't seem to be any men in your family."

"Yes," she said.

Harry waited, then thought perhaps she hadn't heard him. "You have a female genealogy."

"It would seem that way."

"Sorry," he said.

"Sorry for asking? For noticing? For being a man? I do not dislike men, even those who inseminated my mothers before me."

Uh, Harry. Maybe we should move on to another subject.

But Madalena Strauss herself did not seem inclined to pursue the topic. She offered Harry an eerie forgiving smile and lifted the sausage from her plate with fastidious fingers. She sunk her teeth deep into it, breaking the skin and releasing a flow of juices before twisting it to the side and biting off a large mouthful she chewed contemplatively, as if she had not just summoned Freud to dance in a command performance.

Harry winced. He looked away. He watched the crowd, the Viennese shoppers lugging bags of fresh produce and cooked victuals to last them a week, the tourists chewing on handfuls of sugar and fat and salt in mouth-watering combinations. There were surprisingly few children. The Naschmarkt was a serious carnival for adults and for a minute Harry thought he could feel the loathing of myriad people all struggling to hold death at bay as they moved through the stalls searching for sustenance and diversion.

Don't be so bloody morbid, Harry.

He watched Lena devouring her food. Suddenly he wanted to reach across and hold this strange woman in his arms, to protect and comfort them both. He had never met anyone so tough and so vulnerable, so warm and angry and elusive. She had drawn him into some Kafkaesque nightmare devised by her own dreaming mind and he was frightened she'd wake up and he'd lose her. It was confusing and Harry didn't like being confused. But he found the confusion surrounding this woman, menacing as it was, irresistible.

The sun was high enough that the awning now kept only him in the shade. She was in bright sunlight. As she bent to toy with the scraps on her plate, rays gleamed through her mass of copper red hair and caught highlights on her cheekbones and long narrow nose. She did not look allegorical, like the woman in a pre-Raphaelite painting. She looked real and alive, like the woman in the Beethoven frieze.

In a panel called The Forces of Evil, *Harry, don't forget that.*

But Harry wasn't buying Karen's wariness. Beauty surrounded by evil, caught up in a nefarious design, does not make it evil itself.

Nor good, Harry—to stand out amidst evil does not make beauty good.

"I've got to pee."

The radiant vision of wounded beauty at the centre of his metaphysical discourse just announced she had to pee.

"Or do you say piss? I am never sure. In American books they say piss, but usually in films they say pee. In German we say *Pipi* and in French they say *pipi*. I wonder why so many *P*s? It is an interesting subject, yes?"

She had already risen to her feet. She stood beside Harry and leaning close kissed him on the cheek. Her left breast pressed into his arm. He felt her wince from the pressure. Her lips were warm and moist and bruised. He could feel their roughness and he tilted his head back and away so that they could look into each other's eyes.

"Don't worry," she said and slipped past him into the crowd.

Harry waited for an hour, but he knew she wouldn't be back.

8 A DAPPER YOUNG MAN

AS HE STOOD IN THE LINE FOR PASSPORT CONTROL AT Pearson, Harry tried to work out the best strategy for getting through hassle-free. He could reasonably argue he had been in Vienna for pleasure. It wasn't really business, since no one had paid him, but if he had to explain what kind of business he was in he was afraid *murder* might hold him up for a bit. As for the Klimts, he had picked them up from Lena's apartment after she disappeared in the market. When she had kissed him goodbye, he had been distracted by her left breast and didn't notice that she had slipped her keys into his pocket until he stood up and their weight shifted against his thigh. That's when he knew for sure he would never see her again.

She had asserted with cheerless resignation that she was a dead woman already. There was no doubt in Harry's mind that her corpse would turn up with a sufficient flourish to ensure that Sakarov knew of it. There would be no point otherwise.

Since he regarded himself as only the custodian of the paintings, he felt it was reasonable not to declare them. They were inside their ebony box in his Roots shoulder bag and his laptop was in his luggage. They had attracted no attention going through Austrian security before boarding. Lots of North Americans bought copies of great art from street vendors in Europe.

He slipped his passport into the automatic scanner, declared no purchases abroad, which was true, and moved on to the next queue, exhausted after the flight and so busy scheming he hardly paid attention when the agent asked him to reaffirm that he had spent no money and travelled to Vienna for no apparent purpose. He had the usual moment of trepidation because he had no idea what the marks she scrawled on his control card meant, but he was waved through the final barrier with suitcase in tow and a soft leather bag slung from his shoulder worth in excess of fifty million.

When he stepped off the elevator on the 23rd floor and unlocked his door, it pleased him at last to be home. This austere high-rise condo with its Scandinavian furniture and splendid southern exposure overlooking the great freshwater sea of Lake Ontario was his sanctuary. Being away so much over the past year, in Sweden and then Austria, had somehow transformed it from a place he happened to live to the place he was actually from.

He selected a space on the southwest wall of his living room out of direct sunlight and shifted a pair of prints of King's Parade that he and Karen had bought in Cambridge to hang beside the largest of his Blackwood etchings on the opposite wall. One of the prints had been in his office and one in hers at Huron College and both survived when he burned their house to rocks and rubble. The exposed nails weren't quite right, so he dug his hammer out of the hall closet and, holding a copy of *Vanity Fair* between it and the wall so he wouldn't damage the plaster, he pried the nails free. After standing back and envisioning the best locations, he hammered the same nails into place, leaving enough showing that the heads would catch at the back of the picture frames. He tried *The Kiss* to the left and then to the right of *The Forces of Evil*, settling on the left, closer to the window.

He wondered about insuring them but realized that would be impractical, if they were covered for their actual worth, and pointless, if they were not. He decided to upgrade the locks on the entry door and balcony, and to install a security system with a viciously loud alarm. He would enjoy the Klimts in private. Their best protection, as in the past, was to remain unseen.

He ate a light supper from the freezer. It was after midnight in Vienna. He had been away just long enough to bring his internal clock into sync with local time, so he had to adjust all over again, coming home. He cracked open a fresh bottle of Beaujolais, chilled in the fridge. Colder than cellar temperature, but he liked it that way. It smothered the slight candy floss quality of the Gamay grapes.

After eating, he shifted his furniture so that his large teak and leather chair gave him the best possible vantage on the Klimts. Sipping his wine, he sank into exhausted reverie, curiously free of dread or regret. Alive in the moment.

A wonderful phrase, he thought. "Alive in the moment."

Madalena Strauss gazed at him. The piercing green eyes from the Beethoven frieze looked deep into his wandering thoughts, searching, perhaps, for something she had lost. They were haunting, whereas the eyes in *The Kiss* were taunting. And yet they were the same eyes, the same woman, the woman he knew and her great-grandmother who had died at Ravensbrück.

Karen was in the room with him, but they weren't using words. She was in the air and among the familiar objects, the scents and textures and the quiet sounds of his breathing, of his clothing, and of the city outside, filtered through cement and glass.

He got up and reversed the Klimts. They talked to each other in the way paintings do, but their conversation was different, depending on their relative position. When he set *The Kiss* face down on the side table while adjusting the other, he noticed the writing again that had been hidden when the paintings were nested together.

1902 Rachel Damboch

The words were inscribed in India ink but were hardly legible, not so much faded as the result of a pen pressed very lightly.

He assumed Rachel Damboch was Lena's great-grandmother. The year would have been the date Klimt did the painting. There was something infinitely touching being able to connect with such a private and revealing detail from the past. As he walked into the bedroom and stretched out on the bed, he wondered if the writing was in the woman's hand or the artist's.

He woke after a long sleep, sluggish and morose. Back in the living room, he realized his dreams had been thronging with images of Madalena Strauss and Dimitri Sakarov, the repulsive embodiment of all the evils that she had endured. He felt oppressed. He knew Lena was dead. It was her choice. He didn't know how or even where. The details seemed unimportant.

He wished she were there to explain why she wasn't. The more he thought about her, the more despondent he became. And angry. He wasn't grieving; he felt sorrow, but that wasn't the same. Her reckless concession to fate was highly manipulative. He did not believe in fate.

Conflicted, Harry?

Yes, conflicted.

You were a little in love with her, weren't you?

She gouged out a man's eyes.

And cut off his testicles.

Or not, Sailor. Nothing is quite what it seems.

But sometimes it is.

All through the day Harry puttered. He dusted, did laundry, went down to the Harbourfront shops and bought delicatessen groceries.

Madalena stayed in his mind. She had risen above her humiliation only to embrace her demise. He wondered how she had done it.

When her death attracted Sakarov's attention, would the Russian make the connection with Harry Lindstrom in Toronto, Canada?

Hell, Harry could hardly make the connection himself.

Another day passed and then another. A week went by. Then an item from Austria in an online news service caught his attention. A woman's corpse mutilated by passing boats had been pulled from the Danube where it meets with the Wienfluss. He read a brief article in the English language *Vienna Times* online that said a corpse was wearing a watch with a cracked crystal and *mors certa* engraved on the back. Death is certain.

He checked other papers and found something in German, in the *Wiener Zeitung.* Apart from her name, which leapt from the text, a few other words were familiar: *Polizei Zentralkommando, Herrengasse, Gumpendorfer, Marchettigasse*, and *Totschlag*, which he understood to mean "homicide" but didn't know whether it referred to her job or her death. When he used Babel Fish to translate, he still wasn't sure, but the words *kupfernes* and *rotes Haar* came out as "copper red hair." His eyes blurred for a moment and stung from the salt when he pressed them clear.

God, oh my God.

He remembered how she had challenged him on using religious expletives.

And how he glibly responded that the God he had long since abandoned had shaped the world they lived in.

Now she was gone. Sakarov had given her death a strategic purpose. The world felt emptier. In his grief, Harry recognized a seismic shift had occurred in his life. The Klimts were more than collateral; they were a bond transcending death. He was obliged, no, compelled, to take up her cause. His grief was tempered with anxiety and confusion. So much of what she had described were crimes of cultural deviance. He could not take on entire religions, entire nations. Even with criminal adoptions, how would he proceed without hurting the children involved? Or well-meaning parents or misguided social workers? The thought of a single family being humiliated or destroyed, the pain of a child whose life has been thrown irredeemably askew by his anonymous revelations, was enough to tear Harry apart. He needed a gatekeeper as much as Lena had. Perhaps more. Not to bolster his conscience but to override it.

To find the gatekeeper, to find and filter the files, to cause the least harm, he would need help. Harry was not by nature a researcher. As an academic, he had showed little interest in citations and footnotes. He liked to think. Leaps of conjecture thrilled him. The laws of the world paled in relation to being in it. He didn't give a damn about God but was fascinated by the need to believe. He was astonished at being a sentient self-knowing part of the universe, as painful as it sometimes was to be aware of anything at all. As an investigator, what he loved was the revelation, when the pieces of the puzzle fell into place. It was not for nothing that he found such delight in Miss Marple and even more in Poirot, or that redoubtable Canadian, Chief Inspector Gamache. They took little initiative—in fact, the mysteries came to them—but they revelled in their resolution. He resolved to hire a research assistant.

He placed an ad in several of the alternative newspapers. The person he was after wouldn't be a reader of *The Globe and Mail,* the *Toronto Star*, *The National Post*, or that unholy of unholies, the *Toronto Sun.* After wrestling with the wording, he settled on something succinct and sufficiently enigmatic to weed out the dilettantes.

Help Wanted! Salander? Lindstrom.

He was pleased when his ad appeared in print. After three days with no response, he tried again,

Last chance? Come in person! Malone.

If the right person was out there waiting for work, she'd find him at lindstromalone.com. He was looking for Lisbeth Salander. What he got was Simon Wales.

Simon appeared at Harry's apartment door just before midnight. In the crook of his arm he carried a current issue of *Vogue* with Gwyneth Paltrow on the cover. The security door in the lobby had been breached, but that was the least Harry would have expected from a respondent to his advertisement. He didn't anticipate a neatly dressed young man wearing rimless silhouette glasses and a necktie with diagonal stripes. The dark linen suit was a perfect fit. The white shirt was immaculate. His shoes were black, well-polished, with laces.

Simon smiled. He was slight, with perfect teeth. Attractive but not ostentatious. Straight dark hair, dark brown eyes, long thick lashes, high forehead, a smooth, somewhat pale complexion, and an aristocratic nose, whatever the hell that meant. Early twenties.

"I'm here about the ad, Dr. Lindstrom."

So he had done some research already. How much, Harry wondered?

"I understand Lindstrom-Malone is a small agency," said the young man. "And Malone is no longer with us. You are a protégé of Superintendent Quin and a recent associate of the late Madalena Strauss. May I come in?"

Harry was nonplussed. He didn't move.

"Do I get the job, Dr. Lindstrom?"

Harry took in his expensive wardrobe and patrician demeanour.

"Do you need it?" he said.

"Precisely," Simon Wales responded, indicating he had been aware of Harry's assessment. "Quality costs." He flourished his copy of *Vogue* as if no further explanation were necessary.

Harry stood to the side. Simon Wales passed by him and walked into the living room. Although the young man was lithe and of less than medium height, he was not diminutive. He gave the impression of coiled power. He walked to the centre of the room and unbuttoned his suit jacket but made no effort to remove it; briefly surveying his surroundings, he walked to the Klimts, standing first in front of *The Forces of Evil*, then in front of *The Kiss*, before returning to *The Forces of Evil*.

He turned back to Harry, who was amused by his visitor and at the same time disconcerted by his apparent capacity to access information. That's what Harry wanted him for, but was it really so easy to find out the connection between Lena Strauss and himself? If a kid from Toronto could do it, so could Dimitri Sakarov.

"You will pay well, I am sure. But only if I provide the information you need. May I have a drink of Perrier? Chilled. I believe it is in the door of your refrigerator."

Harry shuddered, like a premonition recognized too late. Simon Wales had apparently accessed more than information; he had made a clandestine tour of Harry's apartment. When? While Harry was asleep? Or out? The door was kept locked securely as a concession to Klimt.

There was an awkward silence as Harry opened two Perriers and poured them over ice with a wedge of lime in each.

"Your mayonnaise is past its best before date. I'd suggest you throw it out, Dr. Lindstrom."

"Okay. Sit down."

"Simon Wales."

"Simon Wales. We need to talk."

"Yes, of course, but isn't Elisabeth Bök the most beautiful woman, I mean, ever." It wasn't a question.

"I'm sorry," said Harry. "Elisabeth who?"

"The woman who modelled for Klimt. Your pictures. They are very good."

"Thank you. But who is Elisabeth Bach?"

"Bök," said Simon Wales, modulating the vowel.

"That woman, green eyes, wonderful red hair, she haunts Klimt. She is in many of his paintings under various guises."

"And that's her name."

"Yes."

"And who is Rachel Damboch?"

"I'm sorry Dr. Lindstrom, I have no idea."

"Please stop calling me Dr. Lindstrom. I get it, you've researched me. But I'm Harry now. And you are a student of art history?"

"Not in the formal sense. I have an abiding interest in the visual, the surface appearance of things."

"Art as decoration."

"No, decoration as art. The Austrian symbolist school, Egon Shiele, Gustav Klimt. And *Vogue* magazine."

"God help us."

"Harry?"

"Yes."

"Nothing. Just testing the name, trying it out. It fits quite well."

"It's not an alias." Harry hadn't lost track of how easily Simon Wales had connected him to Lena. He was on edge. "Tell me about yourself, Simon. This is a job interview."

"I'm sorry, I thought the interview was over. I'll tell you whatever I can about you. I've been checking you out since your first ad. Then you pressed, so here I am."

"Perhaps you could tell me about you. You know, the usual—education, aptitudes, character references."

The young man did not smile. He adjusted his posture inside his well-fitting suit. He looked Harry in the eye.

"No criminal record," he said. Then silence.

"That's it?"

"That's it." He paused. "You're quite interesting, Harry. Am I hired?"

"What do you know about my connection with Madalena Strauss? No, hold on, first tell me, how do you know the name of Klimt's model?"

"Elisabeth Bök?"

"And you've never heard of Rachel Damboch?"

"No."

Then what the hell is the name on the back of the painting all about?

"Your paintings are very nice. They must be part of an interesting story." Simon Wales tilted his head in deference to the genius on display. "It is wonderful to see undocumented originals. You are very fortunate."

Harry flinched.

Student of art history? I'd say he's an expert.

There was no point in denying the authenticity of the paintings. His visitor would have already checked their worth. He had had ample opportunity to walk away with them and didn't.

"They belong to Austria," Harry explained.

"The whole country! How expansive. Myself, I prefer the detail from the Beethoven frieze. The woman, Elisabeth Bök, she is not a conventional model. Perhaps that is part of what Klimt loved about painting her. Reminds me of Rossetti's Jane Morris. He was in love with her, you know. You can see it in his Pandora pictures. She was married to William Morris, of course, so they never consummated their passion except through his art, as far as we know."

Harry swirled the ice in his glass.

"I am very interested in models," the young man explained. "That is why I read *Vogue*. I am interested in the correlation between money and taste. And then, of course, the infrangible faces of the models intrigue me."

"Infrangible."

Harry tried not to turn the word into a question. He had an erudite command of English; he knew what *infrangible* meant. But he couldn't recall ever hearing the word in a conversation before, and certainly not by someone barely out of his teens, someone so literal he didn't see irony in confessing an interest in models for their lack of personal presence.

"Yes, 'the unbreakable sum of their parts,' unchanging from one picture to the next, no matter how elaborate the background or exotic the clothing, their faces stay exactly precisely the same. It is uncanny, Dr. Lindstrom. I find it quite haunting." He paused, then corrected himself. "Mr. Lindstrom. I'm sorry." Another pause. "Harry." Seeming satisfied, he continued, "Whereas an actress…" he gestured toward the cover illustration of Gwyneth Paltrow. "Each picture is different. In her face is an implicit refusal to be a commodity. She is not a starlet, she is an actor. Even airbrushed, she appears human."

"And Elisabeth Bök?"

"A born actress. She is the same person and yet always different. Look at her eyes. Here they take in the world and there they keep it at bay. Here her posture is blatantly erotic; she is a proud exhibitionist. And there, in *The Kiss,* despite the relative modesty, the viewer is forced to be a voyeur. And what about you, which do you prefer?"

Who is this guy, Harry? I like him.

He scares me.

Sounds like just the person we need. But who the hell is Rachel Damboch and why is her name imprinted on The Forces of Evil*?*

On *The Kiss*, hidden by *The Forces of Evil.*

How appropriate. And how does he know about Miranda Quin, about Madalena Strauss, about me? I'm sure he knows about me.

Harry and Simon Wales talked deep into the night. When dawn loomed over Lake Ontario they walked up past St. Lawrence Market and found a twenty-four-hour diner for an early breakfast. In the end, Harry learned nothing more about Simon and not much more about how he worked, but he was awestruck by the extent of the young man's formidable accumulation of random facts and his ability to make intuitive connections.

Harry realized his private investigator's application had Miranda Quin's name on it as a guarantor. His credit card account revealed his travel history, his email provided a detailed explanation for why he had gone to Vienna, and the rest was on public record, accessible to anyone inclined to dig deep, draw the lines, connect the dots.

Simon had apparently gleaned details of the accident at the Devil's Cauldron from newspaper accounts, court documents, public records, and guesswork. He knew there had been no funeral service and assumed a private interment; he knew Karen's body had never been recovered and that Harry, disconsolate, ravaged by guilt and loneliness, had burned their stone farmhouse on the Sanctuary Line to rubble; quite remarkably, he knew about Freya's abduction when Lena was twenty-one; he knew about the brutal execution of Lena's fiancé and about her own death. He knew all this from newspapers, legal documents, police reports, and guesswork. Perhaps spurred by an ongoing interest in the visual arts, he had apprised himself of sufficient information about Klimt and his cultural context that he had recognized the paintings on Harry's wall as authentic.

He apparently knew nothing of Lena's work to expose the international trafficking of children or about Harry's involvement. He knew nothing about Dimitri Sakarov.

Harry learned about Simon only from observation. He decided he liked the young man sitting across the grey arborite table, eating bacon, fried eggs, sausages, pancakes, toast, and home-fried potatoes. The Lumberjack Special. Harry did a cholesterol inventory, then looked down at the remains of his own modest repast of dry whole-wheat toast and a single packet of strawberry jam.

He marvelled at how his new employee consumed this gargantuan meal with such fastidious good manners he might have been using a fish-knife to strip away morsels of salmon from tiny gelatinous shards of bone.

Harry wasn't on a diet, just catering to the turmoil in his stomach that this young man had engendered by knowing how to do things through cyberspace Harry could hardly imagine. He liked Simon, but he was wary. How could you trust someone who had no story of his own?

When Harry returned to his apartment, he saw Simon's copy of *Vogue* lying face up on his leather sofa. Gwyneth Paltrow on the cover was wearing a short beige skirt with legs slightly apart but angled to the side, both inviting and resisting the voyeur's gaze. She was staring back at him. Karen occasionally used to read *Vogue*. The sprawling September issue was an annual treat Harry would pick up at the newsstand for her and she would immerse herself among its innumerable ads for hours on end, relishing it in much the way people used to read Thackeray or Trollope or Henry James, for flashes of illumination into lives that refused to run parallel to her own. He turned the magazine over but left it on the sofa for the time being.

He had parted company with Simon Wales in front of the imposing Victorian entrance to the St. Lawrence Market and watched as the young man in his dark linen suit disappeared wraith-like into the crowd of early morning shoppers.

The first assignment Harry had given him was to provide Rachel Damboch with a personal history. Who was she and what was the significance of 1902 in her life? What was her relationship to Madalena Strauss?

As he gazed at the Klimts in the morning light, Harry wondered if the writing on the back of *The Kiss* might have been Lena's. The India ink was similar to the note that accompanied the polished ebony box delivered to him at the Kressler. He lifted the painting from the wall and placed it face down beside Gwyneth Paltrow, then he retrieved the note in the box from the bedroom and held it close to the back of the painting. While the writing looked faded on the painting and bold in the note, it was in the same hand. He had no doubt that he was meant to uncover the connection between Lena and Rachel Damboch.

He replaced *The Kiss* on its nail and stood back. Madalena Strauss was there in the room. In *The Kiss*, the entire painting was in scale, but in the detail from *The Forces of Evil*, although the painting was sufficiently smaller to have nestled inside the frame of the other, her face was more accessible, like someone beckoning from across the room.

His condo was beginning to seem crowded.

It wasn't noon yet but quelling his latent sense of guilt and decorum he opened a cold beer. He went out onto his balcony, curious to know if Karen would follow, but she stayed away. His mind wandered back to Madalena Strauss.

Possibly, his new research assistant would provide some answers to questions he hadn't been able to articulate. The kid had a knack. Meanwhile, he would do some digging of his own.

9 LINGUINI CARBONARA

HARRY HAD DINNER THREE NIGHTS LATER WITH MIRANDA Quin and her former partner, Detective Sergeant David Morgan. They met at Via Veneto, a spaghetti joint on Yonge St. just above Wellesley that had been a hangout for the two detectives when they worked together. Morgan made a crack, obviously meant to be ironic, about the service being slow, but you didn't mind waiting because the food was so bad. Quin grimaced. Harry smiled a little, to be polite.

In fact, it was the best pasta Harry had ever eaten. It was described on the menu as linguini carbonara, but it was made with chunks of roasted salt pork, whole garlic cloves, and just enough flecks of sun-dried tomatoes to turn the cream sauce amber. They divided a huge order among them and ate without speaking, except to exchange a few pleasantries when they paused to enjoy their Brunello di Montalcino—the only Italian wine, Harry argued, to surpass all but the very best Barolo. Morgan concurred, insisting it measured up to a *grand cru* Bordeaux. Miranda avoided the passionate superficiality of their opinions by staying out of the discussion. She told them she was contemplating hockey and the future of the Leafs, if any.

Miranda had arranged the dinner, but she waited until they finished their profiteroles and were sipping coffee before getting down to business. There was no air conditioning; it was a sultry evening. The proprietor had set the front door ajar, which only let in more heat and humidity. Miranda slipped off her jacket.

"So, Harry, weren't you going to call me?"

"About what?"

"About your client being dead."

"You heard?"

"I went to the funeral."

"You what?" Harry was astonished. "In Vienna! Really? I didn't know there was one."

"Of course there was," she said. "An official ceremony."

"Why wouldn't there be a funeral?" This was from Morgan. "There was a body. It's the one time police come together—to bury their own."

"She was my friend." Miranda explained. "There's kind of a global cadre—in oral italics—of *top female cops*. Your buddy Hannah Arnason flew down from Stockholm for the day. Did you know she's been promoted?"

"I thought she was suspended for unorthodox methods in the Ghiberti affair."

"Oh, she was, she was censured. And then she was promoted."

"To obscure the fact that the National Criminal Police of Sweden, including Inspector Arnason, sat on their collective butts while young women died who could have been saved."

"She put in a good word for you."

"Did I need it?"

"We all do, Harry."

"I imagine she looked stunning in black."

"It's the twenty-first century, Harry. She was wearing a summer print."

"At a Jewish service?"

"Lena had already been cremated. It was all very secular. We gathered in a place called *Vereinigung Bildender Künstler Österreichs*. A beautiful example of art nouveau."

"It's also known as the Secession Building."

"Could be."

"Was there any talk about murder? The word kept cropping up when I read about it in the Austrian papers."

"Do you know German, Harry?"

"I know the word for murder. *Totschlag.* It was in the write-up, but it might have been describing her job."

"I don't know German either. I memorized the name of the Secession Building while Madalena was being eulogized by her colleagues."

"You're assuming they were eulogizing."

"What else?"

"Of course," said Harry. "It was a funeral. Was there any suggestion her death wasn't suicide?"

"That's why we're here."

"Having dinner?"

There was an awkward pause before Miranda responded: "You went to the police station, the central command. You were interviewed by

Frau Detektiv Honsberger, blue hair, pearls, silver tooth. You told her you were staying at the Kressler Hotel. Did you realize a Canadian couple died while you were there? Wealthy lawyers from Oakville. Apparently they jumped from the roof."

"So I heard. And the boy?"

"What boy?"

Harry made an intuitive leap to shut up and keep further information to himself until he knew its significance.

"The woman with the blue rinse," he said. "I interviewed her, she didn't interview me."

"And you gave her Rolodex a spin."

"Which she invited."

"Really?"

"Virtually."

"And from the central police station you went to Madalena's apartment in Gumperdorf."

"Gumpendorfer. I did."

"Where there was a lot of blood."

"I cleaned up as much as I could."

"But left evidence that you had been there."

"I never denied it."

"There was an eyewitness, an employee of the Kressler."

"Heinz Ichstadt. So much for patron-concierge privilege."

"Your prints were all over."

"I'm not surprised. How did they know they were mine?"

"Technology, Harry. They're on file from your contempt of court charges in Nanaimo."

"That was a long time ago."

"You broke through her door to get in."

"I had no choice. The blood preceded the break-in. She needed help. Your eyewitness will confirm she was alive when he delivered my things from the Kressler."

"Did he actually see her?"

"Probably not, but she was there. And if you check, she went out three days later, we went to the market together."

"Who would we check that with?"

"Her neighbours, maybe. The point is, she was alive when we went to the Naschmarkt. I flew out the next morning. As far as I know, she wasn't dead when I left."

"You were a very sinister character in Vienna."

"But only in Vienna. And not a killer."

"They asked me to make inquiries."

"Who asked? I doubt it was of pressing interest to most of her colleagues."

"Frau Detektiv Honsberger."

"And otherwise, there wasn't much interest in how she died, was there? She killed herself, Miranda."

"You seem sure of that."

"I am."

"Was she depressed more than usual? Of course, you don't know what her *usual* was."

"But you do, I imagine," he said.

"She was obsessively self-contained, compulsively logical, fixated on her own research project about abused kids, zealously secretive, not given to chatter, liked clothes that played to her complexion and figure, loved her own hair, and she was tough as nails. Vain and vulnerable. I wouldn't have said she was suicidal."

"That sounds like a diagnosis," said Harry. "Not the description of a friend by a friend. The last time I saw, she was on an inexorable course with only one possible outcome. Not all people who commit suicide are suicidal."

"I would have thought it was axiomatic."

"Think of rebels blowing themselves up for a cause they believe more important than themselves."

"You think she's a martyr?"

"Sometimes despair is heroic, that's all I'm saying. It's not the same as depression."

"Thank you, Professor Lindstrom."

"It wasn't murder." Harry needed to believe Lena had been in control of her own death. Otherwise, Sakarov was. He pursed his lips as a gesture of refusal and stood up. "Thanks for the dinner. I figure it's on you. A business expense."

"You're being petulant, Harry."

"Petulance is like paranoia," he said. "Sometimes it's justified."

Morgan rose to his feet and held out his hand.

"Good to see you, Harry. I'm working as liaison with Vienna, with Frau Honsberger. If anything comes to mind about your friend with the flaming red hair, I'd appreciate if you'd pass it on."

So he knows about the hair.

It's a memorable feature, Sailor! She took a course in Toronto, remember?

No, I don't. But she's as hard to forget as she was to know. Right?

"Harry, please sit down."

This was Miranda. She didn't look up, she didn't smile. But her statement was an invitation, not a command. Since she was his only real friend in Toronto, he decided to stay.

"It's awkward being suspected of a murder that never occurred," he said. "Even by a woman with blue hair and a silver tooth."

Morgan waved to the restaurateur, a robust Italian with a pencil-thin moustache, bushy eyebrows, and a flour-smeared apron. With no words exchanged, the man brought a bottle of grappa to the table and four small glasses. He poured one for each of them and one for himself. They tossed back the burning clear liquid, then he poured each another and retired to nurse his alone in the shadows under the latticework with the plastic vines near the kitchen doorway.

"All right," said Harry. "I'll pay my own portion of the bill."

Miranda smiled.

"It's no secret you knew I was going to Vienna," said Harry, addressing Miranda. "How did you know I was back?"

"Because you weren't at the funeral. And because I had a strange visit recently from a young man. We had an odd conversation. He told me he needed to get in touch. I mean, he knew all about you, Harry. He came down to Headquarters in person. I told him you were still in Vienna. No, he insisted you were back. I told him that was too bad, I was on my way there myself."

"Did you mention why?"

"I mentioned a lot of things, Harry. He was very engaging. I didn't tell him anything confidential."

"Or perhaps you did without knowing it."

"Harry, I'm not stupid."

"That's a relief."

"He was a perfectly turned out young man."

"Wearing a dark suit in midsummer."

"It's not midsummer yet," said Morgan. The other two ignored the pedantry.

"It was a linen suit. Grey-blue."

"Not dark? So he has several."

"Say what?'

"He's my researcher, I think."

"You think."

"Sometimes."

"Harry? Why on earth would you need a researcher? What have you got yourself into?"

He forced a grim smile.

"Harry," she continued, "secrets can be dangerous. Is this related to your work for Madalena Strauss?"

"I promise you," he said, including Morgan in a sweeping glance, "her death has already been filed under *ungelöst*."

"*Nein Sprechen sie Deutsch*!"

"*Unsolved*. Look, there's a lot going on. I need time to sort out a few things. I'll get back to you both."

He stood up, nodded in the direction of the restaurateur, and strode out onto Yonge St., turned right and walked south. He had neglected to pay for his share of the meal and didn't remember until he was in the elevator, rising toward his twenty-third story sanctuary overlooking the inland sea.

On what should have been the thirteenth story, the elevator doors slid open. During construction, this floor had been designated the fourteenth as a concession to workers who refused to work on the thirteenth and nobody had thought to renumber when the building was complete. A fit couple in their thirties dressed for a late evening stroll along the waterfront stepped forward, hesitated, then eased back, pressed the down button again, and waved Harry on, to continue his ascension alone. The movement of air as the doors opened and closed stirred up the faint stale odour of dry leaves.

Harry stepped tentatively into the lingering odour in the foyer at his own level. There were only four units on the twenty-third floor. None of his neighbours were smokers. He touched his fingers to the doorknob and twisted. The door opened. The lock had been breached and the red monitor light on the new alarm control panel in his hall was off; the siren was disarmed. He listened, but he could hear nothing. The rank odour of tobacco and sweat hung in the air. Stepping back, he pulled the door shut again very gently, remaining outside.

Leaning against the elevator wall, he dug his cell phone from the depths of his shoulder bag. He hoped the battery was alive. He pressed the only number on autodial.

Morgan answered.

“It’s Harry Lindstrom,” he said.

“I thought it would probably be you. We’re still in the restaurant. Miranda’s in the washroom. I heard her jacket playing ‘Strawberry Fields.’ Why are you whispering? Do you need help?”

“Yeah. I think so.”

“You at home?”

“I am.”

“I’m on my way.”

Harry settled against the wall and waited. He wasn’t sure what he would do if anyone found him there. It would be almost as awkward if it were a neighbour as if it were the intruder. Perhaps not so dangerous; his neighbours weren’t thugs.

Waiting, he had time to think about Simon Wales, who wasn’t the world-class hacker he purported to be. He had interviewed Miranda. Or was it that Harry, with his Salander assumptions, had imposed a particular role on the elegant blank slate the young man provided? He might be a computer whiz, but he was also a people person. He had charmed the Superintendent of Homicide into revealing more about herself and Harry than she had imagined. Who else had he talked to?

When twenty minutes later the elevator doors opened and Morgan stepped out, Harry breathed a sigh of relief.

Morgan, in his early fifties, was reassuringly unkempt, with a crooked smile. He looked like a cop, the same way some surgeons look like a surgeon, some funeral directors like a funeral director. They each have their own way of going.

“Are you armed?”

“I don’t carry unless I have to,” Morgan responded. “No cell phone, no guns. I’m a practising Luddite. Except for Google. I Google a lot.”

“What about Miranda?”

“Yeah, she Googles. And she carries a scaled down Glock. But she isn’t here. I didn’t tell her I was dropping by.”

“Why not?”

“I’ve got a feeling you’re into something big, dangerous, and not for public consumption. She’d be obligated to pass on whatever she knows, so what she doesn’t know won’t compromise either of you, right?”

“What about you?”

Morgan shrugged, then he turned and put his hand on Harry’s door.

“You figure there’s someone in there?”

"Yeah."

"Okay, let's check."

"Unarmed."

"There's less shooting that way," he whispered. "If he wanted to kill you, you'd be dead. It's the smoke, isn't it? Sweet and dry, a blend of pot and tobacco. You know who he is."

Harry shrugged.

"You don't seem like a fearful man, Harry."

"It's not *him* I'm afraid of."

A shadow passed across Morgan's face, coming from the darkness in Harry's eyes.

"Of yourself? You'd kill him?"

"I might."

"Not good. If we're all lucky, he's long since departed."

Harry sniffed the air. If the fat man was gone, why wouldn't he have relocked the door and reset the alarm. If he was savvy enough to break in, he would have been smart enough to cover his tracks when he left.

Harry, you're missing the point. If he's been and gone, it's a warning. He wants to show you how vulnerable you are.

Morgan pushed the door open slowly. Harry followed him in. As they proceeded from the foyer into the hallway, they brushed up against each other. Morgan whispered, "Don't kill him. If he deserves it by definition, he's not worth it."

And Karen whispered her own directive: *Even if you wanted to, Harry, don't do it at home.*

Morgan switched on the lights.

10 **A WARNING**

A SHEET FROM HARRY'S BED WAS CRUMPLED INTO A shapeless lump on the blue linen sofa. There was a half eaten sandwich on the kitchen counter. Cold smoked meat with mayo on rye. Morgan walked through into the bedroom and checked the closet. Harry checked the bathroom and then opened the balcony door to air out the mustiness but closed it again because the breeze forced fumes of the city into his sanctuary.

He and Morgan looked at each other noncommittally. Clearly someone had broken in, but nothing seemed to be damaged or taken. The Klimts were in place. Morgan admired them and wondered if Harry had bought them in Toronto. Harry was just about to offer him a beer when the lump on the sofa moved.

Harry and Morgan both jumped.

The sheet made a whimpering sound and a small hand appeared from the folds, pushing the cotton away. The child did not wake up. She twisted free of her covering and drifted into a deeper sleep.

"My goodness," Morgan observed then added, "She's out like a light."

Harry touched the child's forehead with his fingertips. No fever. He felt for her carotid artery and found a vigorous pulse. He brushed her black hair away from her face. She was generically pretty, the way most children are. Her skin was a translucent brown, her eyes were concealed within a clearly defined crease, and her lips were open, but she was breathing easily through flared nostrils. He guessed she was Korean or possibly northern Chinese. It didn't enter his mind that she might be Canadian.

He said as much to Morgan.

Morgan was the father of a grown son he hardly knew. He wasn't good with children. He stood to the side watching Harry, who seemed lost in thought and offering no explanation for the child's presence. Morgan called Social Services and the police. When an agent, her interpreter, and a lone detective arrived at the same time, there were introductions all around.

The agent called herself Joan DeBrusk. She was in her late twenties, with close-cropped hair with copper red highlights, freckles, and an open smile. She introduced her companion, a young woman called Nguyen Wang, as a linguist. The detective was older. Her name was Frances Dombrowski.

Within a few minutes two paramedics arrived and ignoring the others went straight to the child. While they checked her vital signs, Detective Dombrowski and Morgan talked in the hallway.

"She's been mildly sedated," one of the paramedics explained to Joan DeBrusk. "We'd better take her to Sick Kids."

"No. If she's fine, leave her until morning. I'll stay."

The two detectives came back into the room. Morgan said a few words in private to the social worker, then smiled, nodded goodbye to Harry, and left.

Frances Dombrowski was in charge. She turned to Harry. "You knew someone had broken into your apartment. You called Detective Morgan because you're friends. You came in together and discovered a strange little girl asleep on your sofa. Is that right?"

"That's about it." Were he and Morgan friends? He thought of Morgan as Miranda's friend.

"And you have no idea who she is?"

"No."

"No idea who left her?"

"None."

"Morgan said the alarm system was down and the lock was unlocked. Did you forget to secure the premises when you went out, Mr. Lindstrom?"

Harry looked at the Klimts before answering emphatically, "No, I did not."

He glanced at the child, back at the Klimts, then at Joan DeBrusk, who had returned from walking the medics to the door.

She was very attractive, a restrained version of Madalena Strauss.

"It is perplexing," said Frances Dombrowski. "People abandon infants in dumpsters. Occasionally we get a three- or four-year-old left at the bus station, but this is a first—a B&E to leave something behind."

For Harry's benefit, she clarified. "Break and Enter."

"Got it," said Harry. "I'm a P.I."

"Leaving behind *someone*, not *something*," said Joan DeBrusk.

"Do you want me to take you to Sick Kids?" Frances Dombrowski asked the social worker.

"No," said Joan. "She'll need a thorough examination, but we can look after that in the morning. I told the medics we'll let her sleep it off here." She turned to Harry. "Do you have any coffee?"

Harry hesitated.

"It's for me, Mr. Lindstrom, not the baby."

"Of course. How strong."

She looked over at his Nespresso system.

"Arpeggio," she responded, indicating her familiarity with the pressure sealed capsule system. "She's what, Mr. Lindstrom, maybe four? I call them all *babies*. I grew up near Timmins in a family with twelve kids. Bush Catholic. I was second oldest, so whoever was youngest at any given time was the baby. The most recent baby of the family is thirteen. I'm older than I look."

Harry wondered what the hell a bush Catholic was. Detective Dombrowski asked, "I'm Polish Catholic myself, but I don't know the bush part."

"Well," said Joan, responding to the general air of interest, "I grew up instilled with the fear of God, but we seldom made it to church. We could do pretty much what we wanted and in the end the priest would absolve us. Minimal discipline, doctrine, or dogma; a bit of guilt, some hymns, a few psalms, and infinite absolution."

"Sounds like a license to be wicked," said Dombrowski with the offhand cynicism of the righteous.

Sounds more like running up bills with someone else covering the costs.

Harry and the three women sat drinking coffee. The little girl began to stir as if awakened by the force of their staring. When she opened her eyes, she smiled. Harry felt his heart soar, until he realized it was a defensive smile, not one of joy but of desperation.

"Hello," said Joan DeBrusk, getting down on her knees beside the sofa and caressing the little girl's cheek with the back of her hand. "Can you tell me your name?"

As the social worker kept talking, the girl's eyes filled with tears and her lips quivered as she tried to maintain her smile. She did not understand, but she wanted to please.

Without getting up, Joan DeBrusk beckoned the linguist to settle on the floor beside her. She eased the girl into an upright position so that their faces were on the same level. Harry and Detective Dombrowski faded as much as they could into the background, leaning against the kitchen counter.

Nguyen Wang began playing a sort of word game, quietly tossing sound patterns to the girl, like dangling so many coloured threads for a terrified kitten. The social worker slowly withdrew and joined Harry and Frances Dombrowski without taking her eyes off the girl.

"Has she been brutalized?" Harry asked in a soothing voice.

"Not physically. She doesn't flinch to avoid pain." The social worker used the same reassuring voice, trying to keep the background interference as unthreatening as possible. "But she's been traumatized. Watch her eyes. She's looking for Nguyen's sounds. She's not listening."

When Harry observed the girl's eyes he was astonished. They had the epicanthic folds he associated with Asians, but they were deep dark blue, the colour of night.

The girl cocked her head. The linguist seemed to be offering a range of vocal modulations and tonalities. The girl made a noise, tongue pressed to the roof of her mouth, the linguist responded with oral tremulations, searching for a response. The girl was listening now. She looked like she would cry, then she smiled, not a forced smile but from the heart. These were perhaps the first familiar sounds she had heard in a desperately long time. She held out a tiny hand, palm upward, and let it settle on the linguist's open palm.

"What is it, Dr. Wang?" Joan DeBrusk eased closer to the sofa.

"It's a tough one. At first I laid out a tone palette, I moved through sound patterns favoured in Chinese, then Korean, then through a range of other languages, looking for recognition indicators. A twitch, a smile, flickering of the eyes. I even tried Native American, sounds from the Na-Dené language in the Mackenzie corridor, glottal sounds from Inuktitut. I knew I was trying to penetrate trauma and for a while I thought she might be too damaged to respond. Then I hit on Vietnamese tonalities. There was something! I know she doesn't speak Vietnamese; her reaction was too tentative. And then I had it. Of course, blue eyes, it all fits, she's from the Yenisei River basin of the Krasnoyarsk Krai district of Central Siberia."

Harry had moved close to hear the explanation. "Could you be more precise?" he asked.

Harry, for God's sake!

But Nguyen Wang got the joke.

"How long has she been away from home?" he said.

"Twenty-seven days, six hours, ten minutes, give or take."

Detective Frances Dombrowski was more literal minded and about to say something, but Harry caught her eye. She smiled knowingly, apparently content to have missed the point of their banter.

Without crowding too close, Harry, on bended knees, asked the girl her name.

"She speaks Ket; ask her in Ket. It's vaguely related to Vietnamese. Or try your Athabaskan, Mr. Lindstrom, they're closely related."

Harry looked at Nguyen Wang with a mixture of humility and anticipation.

"You try."

"Oh, I don't speak either, I just recognize the patterns. Only about a thousand people speak Ket."

"In the world?"

"In the world."

"She is a rare gem," said Joan DeBrusk. "She should be easy to trace."

"In Siberia?"

"We'll get her back to her family."

"Unless she was sold," said Harry.

The bubble of congenial good spirits burst. Joan DeBrusk glared. Not because of what he had suggested, it seemed, but because he might be right.

"That is a possibility," she said quite formally.

Dombrowski spoke up. "Work backwards," she said. "Somebody left her, somebody not concerned with being traced because she's been smuggled into the country. She's not officially here. We don't know if she's been abandoned, sold, or stolen. She's in good condition, so she wasn't abandoned. She's been looked after since she was bought or abducted. But before that, she's been loved, you can tell by her eyes. Behind the fear they're full of hope. So, I'm saying she was stolen, not sold. The dark blue eyes, amethyst, I'd call them, they have a touch of violet—she's exotic—there'd be a high price on the street for this little one. Now, let's go back to the beginning. Why abandon her here of all places? Answer: she wasn't, she was left for a purpose. She was left on the twenty-third story of a high-rise condo. So, Harry Lindstrom, where do you fit into all this? And where do *we* fit in? Because if we're doing our jobs, we're all part of the plan. Who are you, Harry? And whose plan is it?"

He decided the best response to Detective Dombrowski was to respond as little as possible. She wasn't interrogating him; she was throwing observations and questions into the air to see where they'd land. Sidestepping, he let them fall unrequited. But he was impressed. The quiet, middle-aged police detective had been observing, thinking, and speculating when he had thought she wasn't even paying attention.

He felt a brief surge of panic, but it subsided quickly. He imagined it would be impossible to connect this foundling girl to the fat Russian menace who loomed so oppressively in the shadows. There was no reason for the Toronto police to associate her with his own role as Madalena Strauss' designated, reluctant, and baffled successor.

"How did you know she couldn't speak English?" Joan DeBrusk asked the linguist.

"How did you know to invite me along?"

"Detective Morgan suggested I'd need you."

"And how did he know?"

"I told him," said Harry.

"Really. And how did you know?"

How did *you know she wouldn't speak English, Harry?*

"Intuition," Harry responded.

"Or is there something you haven't told us?" Detective Dombrowski had sidled around until she stood between him and the child.

"No," he said, as casually as possible. "But her clothes are exactly the right size."

Was that it, Harry? Did you read signs so subtle they escaped the professionals?

He and Karen were thinking like one person.

Lucy was always too big for her clothes or too small, wasn't she? Matt was worse. Remember?

Harry remembered. That was the point. This girl's dress was bought for the occasion. It was a costume.

"Detective Morgan suggested you might know who broke in," said Detective Dombrowski.

"No. I thought I did, but no, I have no idea." He looked at the little girl and thought of the children in Vienna's 13th District and of all the children in jeopardy that Lena believed her death might save.

"Okay," said Joan. "I think it's time we call it a night. It's after three. Dr. Wang, go home. Detective Dombrowski, I take it there's nothing more for you here. I'll call you tomorrow. Harry, could you find yourself a pillow and sleep on the sofa? My little girl and I will take the bedroom—if you have some clean sheets and don't mind."

The interpreter and the police officer left. Harry sat with the girl while Joan DeBrusk made up the bed.

When they were alone, the little girl tugged at Harry's hand and he wrapped it gently around hers. She tilted her head to the side. Her lips moved. He leaned forward to hear her. She whispered the word twice.

"Lucy." She smiled hopefully. "Lu-cy."

Harry lurched back against the sofa. It felt like he'd been thrown across the room. She was not the Russian's messenger. She was the message. A blood-churning, heart-rending threat.

Dimitri Sakarov could kill or he could give new life to the innocent. It was up to Harry.

Oh God, God damn it.

The girl looked frightened at Harry's reaction. She cowered and covered her mouth, as if afraid she had done something terribly wrong.

Harry placed his hands palms up on his lap in a non-threatening gesture and began to speak in the soothing monotone he would have used to settle Matt and Lucy. The point was not the meaning but the sounds of his words. He recited the names of philosophers, quoted passages from Nietzsche, from Heidegger, and finally, as she began to relax, he offered garbled snippets from Lewis Carroll.

"The time has come, the boojum said to the snark … I've believed six impossible things before breakfast … if you don't know where you're going, you can't get back to yesterday … I was a different person then and everything is funny if you can't laugh … and so on and so forth."

The little girl listened intently. When she reached out and placed her hands in his, his heart went out to her. She understood nothing of what he said nor how nonsensical he was being. She had been thrust into a world she couldn't possibly comprehend, where mock turtles and mad hatters were nothing unusual.

But she must have instinctively trusted these new adults in her life to keep her safe, sensing they were different from those who had erased everything familiar. She could have had no idea what she had said to upset Harry, saying the word "Lucy" as she had been instructed.

Harry looked through into the bedroom. He was not used to seeing a woman there. And now, this nice looking young woman with freckles and expressive features could not know her kindly function was inseparable from the most heinous threat. She looked out at him and smiled wanly. She looked tired.

"Bring her in," she called. "Don't carry her. Encourage her to walk."

Harry did as he was directed and immediately backed out of the room. He was surprised when Joan joined him after settling her ward on the bed.

"Don't you need rest?" he said.

"You look apprehensive, Harry. What is it?"

She sat down beside him on the sofa. He could see *The Forces of Evil* over one shoulder, *The Kiss* over the other. In the muted light from the table lamp, her hair had the same copper luminescence that Klimt had captured in the paintings of Elisabeth Bök. The same as Madalena Strauss had displayed with such casual pride in sunlight or shade.

"I'm not sure," he answered. "It's all just a little confusing."

Say nothing or say everything, Harry. I'd suggest nothing.

"Don't worry," Joan DeBrusk responded, "We'll get to the bottom of this. Can you sleep? Would you like me to leave you alone?"

"No," he said. "What did Dombrowski mean by *street* value?" He felt sick, asking the question.

"Probably not sex, Harry. There's more money in adoption. There are people who would pay a very high premium for such an exotic child. Asian features with amethyst eyes. Maybe a hundred thousand, maybe more."

My God, Harry. If Sakarov can afford to throw away a hundred grand to make a point, think of how much is at stake.

"Could I make you another coffee?" he asked.

"A decaf would be nice."

When he returned with their coffee, he settled into the armchair so they were facing diagonally. He wanted to see her without losing sight of the paintings.

"Do you think she'll be okay?" he asked.

"She knows we're the good guys."

"Have you ever heard of Ket?"

"The language or the people?"

"Either."

"Neither. I studied social work. I'm not much of a linguist."

"U of T?"

"London. Ontario."

"Ontario?"

"If you just say London, people in Toronto think you mean England. They're very provincial that way."

"Or intent on making you realize how cosmopolitan they are."

"Which is very provincial."

"I worked there for a while," he said.

"At Huron College, I know."

He looked at her quizzically. "I taught philosophy."

"You and Father Black? I took a course from him."

"Tom Black. Yeah. I was there for twelve years."

"You came in my sophomore year. I nearly switched to philosophy." She had an ingenuous smile. She wasn't flirting, just adding warmth to the conversation. "Do you like this better?"

Her smile meant, being a private investigator, living in a Toronto high-rise, resolving the mysteries of existence on a practical level. She didn't seem surprised by his radically altered life nor did she ask for an explanation.

He shrugged.

"I took American literature from your wife."

What a strange small world it really is!

"Professor Karen Malone," she added in confirmation. She said nothing more, but it was understood that she knew Karen was dead.

Instead of creating a barrier between them, her openness set them at ease. They began to chat the way people do on a first date, revealing and concealing, shaping their stories. All the while they talked, Harry compared her to the pictures behind her. Her appearance echoed Madalena's great-grandmother and Lena herself, yet she was almost their mirror opposite. The same copper red hair but not flamboyant. A dusting of freckles, upturned nose, full cheeks, revealing brown eyes. *Louche* was not a word that came to mind on meeting Joan DeBrusk. Bonny, perhaps. Guileless.

Harry was quite taken with her.

They were relaxed with each other.

The southern skyline began to emerge in the fading darkness.

Joan got up and checked the little girl, then returned to the sofa.

"So, Harry. Are you going to tell me?"

"What?" He knew where this was going.

"I grew up on the outskirts of Timmins. My father worked at a mill and hunted. Mostly small game and moose. My mom grew vegetables and herbs. I wasn't much in the garden, but I've hunted all my life. I still go north and hunt with my brothers. I don't like killing, but sometimes you have to. Sometimes it's necessary."

No, he did not know where this was going after all. He had assumed she would question him about the girl who seemed to have called herself Lucy, about why he thought she was there. What then was she after? Was she offering her own story as an incentive to tell his?

"My dad was a hippy," she said. "Both my mom and my dad."

"Americans?"

"Wannabes. They wished they'd been born in the States so they could have been draft dodgers and left. They were just your regular back-to-the-earth fugitives from a fifties' childhood about ten blocks from here."

"Rosedale?"

"Close but not so rich. The Beach."

"The Beaches?"

"If you live there, it's singular. After they retreated north, they never came south again, not even for funerals. They were born on the same day of the same year. For their fiftieth birthday, they killed themselves. Crashed and burned; a car accident. We split the insurance money among the twelve kids."

"And held their funeral in Toronto."

"Yes, how did you know?"

Irony, narrative inevitability, karma, closure.

"So, now tell me yours," she said.

"My story?"

"What's Harry short for? Henry, I suppose; you're not a Henry. Harold, perhaps."

"Just Harry. What about Joan? Named for the Maid of Orleans or for the first and only female pope."

"No, for Joan Jett."

"And the Runaways?"

"The Blackhearts. My parents loved 'Bad Reputation.'"

Too esoteric for me, Harry.

And suddenly Harry wanted to talk about himself. Over the next hour he told her about his kids, about the accident in Algonquin Park when Matt and Lucy and his wife perished in the Anishnabe River on a family canoe trip, smashed lifeless in The Devil's Cauldron. He talked about his own unbearable survival and the gnawing undiminishing dread of not recovering Karen's body. He described meeting Karen at Cambridge, where she had lectured during the summer he completed his doctoral work in philosophy. He talked about their courtship, about their trip to Vienna. He told her about his older brother who drowned playing pond hockey when they were kids, about his family roots in Waterloo County and about his itinerant parents, about growing up in Nanaimo and Trois Rivières and Fredericton, about his beloved Aunt Beth, about his parents dying, leaving him orphaned in his late twenties.

She asked him about philosophy, about what a philosopher does, apart from trying to lose himself thinking—or find himself. He insisted it often amounted to the same thing. The Buddhists had it right all along.

"And what about God?" she asked.

"What about God?"

"I told you before, I grew up bush Catholic," she said. "I don't really believe in religion, but we went through the motions. I can't quite shake God from my psyche. He's in there, somewhere, lurking in the rafters, watching and waiting."

"Sounds oppressive," said Harry.

She offered a broad grin that he found oddly unnerving. Awareness of mortality? What could be more oppressive than that. He wondered if she had studied Heidegger at Huron College.

"Well?" she said.

"I never really believed in God," he said. "After the accident I thought of God as my adversary, until slowly I came to realize that an abstract deity had become real because I clothed him in the flesh of the loved ones I'd lost. I woke up one morning and declared him extinct."

"One morning?"

"As arbitrary as that. It was liberating. I accepted him, it, or her, as a construct to fulfill human desire, to counter our fears, impose moral order, shore up our dreams, and here I had given him being in the bodies of the dead."

"And what about goodness, Harry? Can you be good without God?"

"I sure as hell hope so."

"Isn't it sometimes hard for you to separate good from evil?"

"Isn't it hard for you?"

"At least I can turn to my confusion for guidance and comfort," she said. "I'm an optimistic agnostic."

That's a phrase people write but don't say, Karen muttered, unless they've been overthinking the subject.

"I suppose like most Catholics," she continued, "I find God is irrevocable in my life, whether I want him to be or not to be."

"And Shakespeare is irrevocable in mine," said Harry.

"So God is dead," she said, missing or ignoring his deference to Hamlet. "That's what you believe?"

"That's what I think; there's a difference. Yes, he is. Although, as Nietzsche observed, in death he casts a long shadow."

"Nietzsche or God?"

"Both," he declared. She was quick. "Well argued," he said. "Let's call it a draw."

Dawn was spreading over Lake Ontario and filling the picture window with a vast play of pale and colourless light.

"A draw," she said. "Do you really imagine the God I'm agnostic about would settle for that. A rhetorical compromise?"

Was this a metaphysical interrogation? he wondered. Or simply killing time.

Or a confrontation with doubt? There can't be many people in her life who'd be willing to talk about these things.

Morgan, perhaps?

He's too wrapped up in an existential quest to prove he himself exists, never mind God.

"For me," Joan continued, "it's quite simple. Only the words are complex. Whether He exists or not, I need him. I want to be a good person, Harry. I think that's what most of us want. Good is good, evil is evil. You've got to choose sides."

"Manichaeism; it makes life more coherent than it really is."

"Unless it really is."

She let the thought dangle. She was beginning to make him uneasy. She sounded like a religious zealot, yet she denied religion. What then? What was the source of her moral serenity? In his experience the kind of peace she projected came through conviction, corruption, or ignorance.

Joan DeBrusk got up from the sofa, glanced at the Klimts, then back at Harry.

"We'll sort all this out," she said as he rose to his feet.

"Where will you take her?"

"Don't worry. She's in the system now. At least this one will be safe."

"This one?"

"You did the right thing, Harry."

"Calling you? It's not like I had a choice."

Her face lit up with a big open smile and she disappeared into the bedroom, coming out in a few minutes with the little girl in tow.

He walked them into the foyer.

“Did you know there’s no thirteenth floor in this building?”

“Yeah,” he said, embarrassed and strangely uneasy.

“That makes you lucky, I guess. You take care, Harry.”

Harry hunkered down to the little girl’s level and looked into her dark blue eyes. He tilted his head and mouthed the words, *Goodbye, Lucy.* He was surprised to feel his eyes welling with tears. He stood up quickly.

The three of them listened to the whirring of the elevator rising on its tether. When the doors opened, Joan DeBrusk took the little girl by the hand and moved partway in, then she turned and tilted her head to kiss Harry on the cheek. It seemed a charming and very spontaneous act.

“Mr. Sakarov will be in touch,” she whispered.

She stepped back into the elevator and the door closed between them.

11 **TAKING STOCK**

HARRY BACKED AWAY FROM THE ELEVATOR. FEELING behind him for the open doorway, he retreated into his apartment. He turned and pressed his forehead against the cool wood of the closed door, trying to quell a surge of revulsion. He banged his head softly against the wood. He felt heartsick for Lucy, enraged at his own naïveté, baffled by Joan DeBrusk.

You're thinking of Shakespeare, Harry.

No, I'm not. Not even remotely.

"O most pernicious woman ... that one may smile, and smile, and be a villain."

Karen, not now.

He was frustrated. There was nowhere to turn, no one to confide in. Morgan was right about Miranda. She would be obligated to deal as a cop with anything Harry might want to tell her. Morgan himself was a good man, but Harry didn't know him that well. Harry needed a confidant who was not bound by legal niceties.

That left Karen.

But Karen was dead and quoting Hamlet.

For the first time in nearly four years, he felt anger toward her, anger because she had left him, anger the living feel for the dead because they've departed, anger that until now he had refused to allow any place in his grieving; anger, which he could not separate from love, from sorrow, from remorse or despair.

Walking back into the living room, *The Forces of Evil* caught his eye.

His anger elevated to fury when he shifted his focus to Lena. How had that woman got him into this maelstrom of—he grasped for the words—this pernicious maelstrom of virulent indeterminacy?

Say what! Talk about sesquipedalian.

I wasn't.

Your thinking is recherché, dear Harry. You're obscuring what you think with big words.

Nothing was what it seemed! Nothing was clear!

The unspeakable exploitation of children was an abomination, but how could he possibly stop it? What sort of an alliance did he have with a dead woman that would empower him to have any impact at all, a woman who invaded his soul and taunted him from the stillness of her likeness on the wall?

Joan's whispering of the Russian's name left no doubt he had to find Lena's files. What he did after that would depend on his capacity for moral compromise.

He broke his gaze from the eyes in *The Forces of Evil*. He looked frantically around the room for a moment, trying to find Karen. Then he stared out over the harbour, knowing he was alone.

The two women who defined Harry's world were both dead. He was angry at them, the woman he knew and the woman he didn't. He started to laugh. He was beginning to see himself as a character in a Robertson Davies novel, fifth business in a literary romance.

If you're too vapid to be the protagonist in your own story, you're in the wrong genre, Harry.

Feeling absurdly elated by Karen's quip, Harry made a breakfast of stale bagels, revitalized in the toaster and lightly buttered, and a glass of orange juice the carton assured him was not made from concentrate. He ate standing up at the counter, then took a coffee onto the balcony and leaned against the rail, gazing over the water. Saturday sailors were out in full force. Dinghies were scurrying in swarms around a course over by Toronto Island. Larger yachts were tacking back and forth, making for the eastern and western gaps. A tall ship was manoeuvring under full sail, trying to catch enough breeze to escape into open water.

Joan DeBrusk fooled you, Harry.

Yes, she did.

Maybe she didn't understand the impact of passing on the Russian's regards.

She saved her message till the last possible minute. It was the delivery that made it so powerful.

The little girl, she'll be safe.

She'll be okay. As Joan said, Lucy is in the system.

Joan DeBrusk is the system.

From Sakarov's point of view, her loss is collateral damage. She's a write-off. She's served her purpose.

To get at you.

Letting me know the extent of his power.

So what's he up to? You don't have Madalena's files.

Maybe I do and don't know it. I'll find them.

Perhaps that's where the gatekeeper comes in.

He agreed. How could he possibly authenticate the charges Lena had taken seven or eight years to accumulate? She must have cached her documents online so they couldn't be erased. Denied but not erased. Once unleashed in cyberspace, they would be there forever.

Lives will be destroyed, Harry. You believe in the rule of law.

Not when it protects the guilty and devastates innocent lives. The law works best for those who hold it in greatest contempt.

You don't believe that.

Maybe not.

He was sickened by the moral dilemma. Was he afraid of mistakes or of repercussions? How far could he trust Lena's research? Fear of the law wouldn't dissuade him. The fear of being wrong might.

There was a polite cough in the balcony doorway behind him. He was momentarily flustered. It was all he could do not to wheel around and strangle the little bugger. But he didn't. He grasped the railing and, without turning, quietly declared, "Simon Wales, one day your habit of transcending the limitations of locks will get you into serious trouble."

Harry settled into one of two Muskoka chairs and indicated Simon should join him. He was wearing a different dark blue linen suit. He set a brown leather briefcase beside his chair. He sat down and pushed his hair away from his eyes, then kept his hand across his forehead to counter the glare from the morning sun.

"What time is it?" Harry asked.

"Elevenish," Simon responded, squinting at Harry's watch that was tilted obliquely to his line of vision.

"Already! And to what do I owe the pleasure?"

"I've found Rachel Damboch."

"Good, well done." Harry was genuinely pleased.

"I'm afraid nothing much turned up about the Findlays."

"Who?"

"The couple who jumped from the roof of the Kressler Hotel." His voice betrayed a slight quiver of emotion, as if they were people he had known in a previous life or had read about in the gossip columns.

"I'm sorry, I don't remember asking."

"But I believe you have an interest," Simon responded.

"Have you been reading my email?" Harry asked.

He hadn't emailed anyone about the incident. He had briefly discussed it with Miranda and Morgan.

"It was in the *Globe*."

"That doesn't answer my question."

"You were staying at the Kressler Hotel when they died. They were Canadians. I assumed you were involved."

"Involved?"

"Curious, then. Their names were Doris and Melvin."

"And the child?"

Simon's silence expressed a moment of confusion before he responded. "There was nothing about a child."

Miranda didn't know about him either. It was as if the little boy never existed.

"And Dimitri Sakarov," said Simon. "I know where he's—"

"Who the hell told you about Dimitri Sakarov? I didn't tell you about Dimitri Sakarov!"

"I thought you'd be interested."

"Bloody hell, of course I'm interested. But you're way ahead of me, here. I wasn't planning on bringing his name into the discussion just yet, not until I gave you a trial run, tracking down Rachel Damboch. You're a scary kid, you know that."

Harry had been Googling Sakarov. Simon Wales was monitoring his computer activities. Okay, that's why he was hired, to do things most people can't.

No one keeps secrets from research assistants, Harry.

"So you want me to start with Damboch?"

Harry adjusted his chair to get a better perspective on Simon Wales, who seemed on the verge of a smile. Two nights ago they had discussed Madalena Strauss and her ongoing investigation. Harry had told Simon that she insisted her files would be passed on to him. He had no idea how or when. He guessed they were out there in cyberspace. Although he told Simon about the murder of Dietmar Henning, he was skimpy on incriminating details, and he had carefully avoided talking about Lena's torture or anything else that might implicate Sakarov. There was no point in casting an aura of fear over their inquiry. That was before the girl who called herself Lucy appeared in the dead of the night.

Simon Wales got up and went into the kitchen, returning a few minutes later with two glasses of Perrier, each with a thin slice of lime. He handed one to Harry.

"You'll make yourself sick," Simon said. "I told you about the mayonnaise."

Harry looked at him quizzically.

"The sandwich in your garbage. I see you had a few bites before you thought better of it."

"You've gone through my bloody garbage?"

"Just now."

If his response was meant to justify snooping by suggesting it was a spontaneous act, it didn't set Harry at ease. But that clearly wasn't the young man's intention. A dark linen suit reinforced by a striped necktie and black lace-up shoes in the midsummer heat was meant to be disconcerting. His way of dressing, like his refusal to smile as a social convention, was a curiously effective instrument of projected power. *Sprung steel* was the expression that crossed Harry's mind.

"So I'll start with the woman."

"Do."

Harry sipped his Perrier. Simon talked.

Rachel Damboch was born in Sudbury, Ontario, in 1928. Her father, Arthur, worked underground in the Falconbridge Nickel Mine from the spring of 1919, following his discharge as a "Stormtrooper" from the Canadian Expeditionary Force, until 1939, when he lied about his age and enlisted again. He died in the Dunkirk retreat on May 25, 1940. Her mother, Edith, worked as a cleaner at Falconbridge until she died on the job in 1948.

When Rachel was two and a half, her parents dropped her off at the Sudbury General Hospital and she was transferred to the Huronia Asylum for Idiots in Orillia. She could not speak and was not toilet trained. She never saw her parents again. Two years later, Rachel's sister arrived at the asylum, which had been renamed a generation before but was still known locally as the Asylum for Idiots. The sister died of pneumonia six months later.

A brother and two more sisters turned up, according to the records, but there was no indication that Rachel knew who they were. The brother, called Arthur after his father, died at age seven. One sister died at age eleven. They were both buried, like their sister before them, in unmarked graves on the institution grounds. The other sister seems to have disappeared from the asylum documents.

Rachel was discharged in 1945 after fifteen years as an inmate. There is no record of what happened to her for the next ten years. In 1955, she was charged by the Toronto Police with soliciting. She was not convicted.

In October of 1962, she turned up in Vienna, travelling on a passport issued in Ottawa the previous June. She worked as a housekeeper for an elderly doctor in the 13th District. She was apparently fluent in French and German and spoke passable Italian. During the next three years, the doctor arranged for her to take courses at the Universität Wien, the University of Vienna. After several years of background work in science and cultural history, she concentrated her studies on the psycho-social development of children, with special interest in Asperger's syndrome and high-functioning autism. She received a Bachelor's degree in 1970 and her Magistra at the age of 45 in 1973.

She wrote her thesis debunking the correlation between Asperger's and a predisposition to violence. Two of her advisors had worked with Dr. Hans Asperger in the 1940s. In 1974, Rachel went to work for Asperger himself at the SOS-Kinderdorf in Hinterbrühl, a town near Mauthausen in the district of Mödling, where he had transferred after being Chair of Paediatrics at the Universität Wien. At his school, she worked as an SOS "mother" with children who had been abandoned by their parents and had special needs.

She left the SOS-Kinderdorf in 1994 and disappeared, but not before writing a book that was never published. In it, she documented conditions at the BMW factory in a satellite of the Mauthausen concentration camp, where engines were assembled for HE 162 jet fighters near the end of the war.

Conducting her research she found that there were no survivors, but from interviews with locals and from public records she was able to put together a devastating picture of barbaric subjugation in the factory, rivalling the Stairs of Death in the stone quarry close by, where Mauthausen slave labourers literally died from exertion as they hoisted heavy stone blocks up 186 steps. A copy of her manuscript, ironically entitled *From Stone to Steel*, was on file at the university but was no longer accessible.

Missing completely was her rumoured manuscript accounting for Dr. Asperger's activities in the early 1940s, working with children in several camps or institutions in Austria and Poland. In it she apparently weighed evidence that might have suggested his devotion to damaged children was inseparable from his work under Hitler's National Socialism. Evidence that this manuscript had existed was uncertain.

There was little doubt that this woman was indeed the woman identified by name on the back of the Klimt painting. She had spent twenty years of her life working with children in Hinterbrühl and in the neighbouring town of Mauthausen, where Madalena Strauss' grandmother had been murdered.

How an abandoned child condemned as irremediably flawed had metamorphosed into a multilingual scholar and devoted caregiver was almost beyond comprehension, but that only enhanced her achievement. Where she had gone after Hinterbrühl, whether back to Canada, which seemed highly unlikely, or into retirement in the mountains of Austria or the suburbs of Vienna, or after an illness into an obscure grave, the rest of her story remained a mystery. And the nature of her connection with Madalena Strauss, signified by nothing more than a date inscribed on an invaluable painting, remained an even bigger mystery, even for Simon Wales.

"You're certainly earning your money," said Harry, when Simon's story was finished.

"I haven't been paid yet. You'll have to decide what I'm worth."

"Probably more than I can pay you, but I'll do my best. What do you suggest?"

"For a thousand dollar retainer, you buy my soul. And then, let's say, five times minimum wage, whatever that is. It's still less than a top ranked caddy."

"I don't play golf, but it's a deal. You've got to stay out of my garbage, though. And let's pretend my locks and alarms actually work. Try knocking."

"Or ringing the buzzer."

"Exactly. Now, what about 1902?"

"It was a vintage year for claret."

"Are you old enough to drink?"

"It was, in fact, a very good year in Bordeaux. Lots of rain early on, lots of sun, cool nights, hot days. A robust vintage, exceptionally long lasting."

"And?"

"The point is, I'm admitting temporary defeat. I've researched 1902 from every conceivable angle and found nothing."

"The Toronto couple, it is said they jumped from the roof. Can you even get onto the roof of the Kressler?"

"Apparently you can."

"So tell me about the Findlays."

"Corporate lawyers, both of them. Large house in Oakville, pseudo-Tudor. Muskoka cottage, Lake Rosseau. Expensive American cars. Tennis and golf. Early fifties, no children to speak of." Simon took a deep breath. "They lost one, apparently."

They lost one. Simon made it sound like the child was misplaced. And then they lost another, the boy who apparently vanished in midair.

Why from the roof and not the balcony next to his room? How did the Findlays connect to the fat man? How did they relate to Madalena Strauss? Why did she meet them at the Imperial Hotel and where was the little boy when they met? How did the Findlays connect with Harry, who had witnessed their deaths?

"I'd like you to find out who was registered in the room beside mine," he said.

"At the Kressler?"

"North-east side. Now let's go back to 1902. Was there something special about that year in the life of Gustav Klimt?"

"Nothing. I followed up the Elisabeth Bök angle. It seems she actually was Madalena Strauss' great-grandmother and she actually did sleep with Klimt. But then so did everyone else. She was the original for the stunning variations of female beauty with unruly red hair and sharp green eyes that hang on the wall behind us. And she probably posed as his principal model in 1902—but the only connection between her and Rachel Damboch is Madalena Strauss and the writing on the back of her painting. I'll keep digging."

Harry leaned in his chair to get a better look at the paintings on his west wall. *The Kiss* was obscured, but *The Forces of Evil* gazed back at him with a suppressed smile, and for all the naked flesh and insouciant lust on display, she seemed remarkably secretive.

He sat forward and gazed at Simon Wales, who was watching the sailboats skittering over or cleaving the waves as dictated by their design. Skimming or ploughing through. Without taking his eyes off the boats, Simon asked, "Did she give them to you or did you steal them?"

"Oh, for God's sake."

"That's not an answer. If you don't want to tell me, you're under no obligation to do so. It's not part of our contract. Did we shake? No, I don't believe we did." The young man reached over and Harry, feeling a little ridiculous, took his hand and shook it.

"We don't have to prick our thumbs and mingle our blood?" he asked.

"No, it's too late for that."

Simon's hand was small, but his grasp was surprisingly firm.

"I've bought your soul, then."

"Good buy. Now, on to Dimitri Sakarov. It is what I didn't find that's most interesting."

Dimitri Sakarov was in his mid-fifties, but like a lot of fat men who survive to middle age, he looked younger. He was a heavy smoker. He did not exist until after the Soviet Union collapsed in 1991. There were indications that he might have originated in the Novosibirsk Oblast of the Siberian Federal District. Nothing to confirm.

He was rumoured to have a sister. He did not have friends. He did not belong to a social circle or play golf. A young woman sometimes accompanied him on his extensive travels but never the same young woman twice.

He was the principal owner of a five star hotel called The Pushkin in Saint Petersburg, which he bought in 1993. There was no record of how much he paid or where the money came from. There was no record of him ever paying personal income tax in Russia, nor in any of the countries of the European Union. He never paid taxes of any sort in the United States or Canada. A passport had been issued in his name in 1993 in Moscow.

The books of the hotel seemed to be in good order. While Sakarov was the Chairman of the Board and Managing Director of Xerxes, the holding company that owned the Pushkin, he drew only a token salary. He had little to do with the day to day operations.

He kept an office on ul. Mikhailovskaja. He had one secretary, a middle-aged woman from Gdansk. She spoke Polish, Swedish, Russian, English, French, and German. He had a long-time personal assistant by the name of Fyodor Blozinski, who likewise had no known history before 1991.

Dimitri Sakarov apparently donated large sums of money to international NGOs that worked with children. He refused tax receipts and always donated in cash.

He had no police record. In the old Soviet Union and in modern-day Russia, it was virtually impossible to have no police or government record.

He was a successful businessman, a philanthropist, and an international traveller, but no one knew who he was.

He was presently in Canada, staying in a private condo he apparently owned in the refurbished King William Hotel.

"He's in Toronto! Now?"

"At the King Willie."

Kids don't call it the King Willie, Harry. That's old school irreverence. Where did that come from?

"Sorry I can't give you more," said Simon Wales. "I'll keep at it."

Harry was rattled to confirm that the smell of pot and tobacco hadn't been in his imagination. At the same time, he was relieved. If he was within reach of Sakarov, Sakarov lived within reach of him.

Harry wrote Simon a cheque for $1000.

"That's your retainer. It's not an advance; it's a bond. Keep track of your time and expenses but don't deduct them."

"No receipts?"

"No bills. Let's just keep this between you and me."

"For sure. With this Sakarov guy, his lack of a public persona is ominous, but it doesn't confirm criminal activity."

"And it doesn't confirm otherwise," Harry responded. He rose to his feet, letting the young man know their session was at an end.

An uneasy feeling lingered for some time that what he did not know about Simon Wales was more important than what he did. And he was certain that what he didn't know about Dimitri Sakarov could be fatal.

12 **COTTAGE LIFE**

HARRY MEANDERED ALONG YONGE STREET AS FAR AS College, picked up a latte at Starbucks on the corner, and sat on a pink granite slab beside the faux stream in front of Police Headquarters. He removed the plastic cover from the coffee and set it beside him. He read the current words of wisdom printed on the cup several times. He sipped. He was undecided about what to do next.

It was late afternoon when Morgan and Miranda approached him from behind. They were on their way out for a coffee and Danish. For fourteen years they had been partners in Homicide and they were still closer than most married couples. They had been through a lot together.

"You waiting for us?" Miranda asked.

"Just passing through." Harry rose to his feet.

"Join us," said Miranda. "Looks like you could do with a refill."

They huddled over a table in Starbucks like conspirators, their mood and their posture determined by Harry. He sat back. The other two sat back. He leaned forward. They leaned forward. Then Miranda spoke in a barely audible whisper, "Morgan told me about the little Siberian girl. The Child Exploitation people at Sex Crimes checked her out. She seems okay."

"I wouldn't think being dumped in some guy's apartment halfway around the world is *okay*," said Harry.

"I thought you'd be relieved to know she wasn't molested."

"She was brought here for black-market adoption."

"How do you know?" Miranda asked, her voice still hushed.

"Have you seen her? People will pay thousands for a prize dog, millions for a stolen painting. There are people out there who'd pay a fortune for a child like her."

"And you know this because?"

"I just know it, Miranda."

"Has this anything to do with your Vienna excursion?"

She was being solicitous. He wanted to explain. But explain what? He said nothing.

"I checked out the power couple who killed themselves," Miranda offered. "Melvin and Doris Findlay from Oakville. You wondered about a little boy. There was no little boy. They had a son, but he would have been grown-up by now."

"What happened to him?"

"He was a runaway. Maybe he's on the street. The parents lost track. They apparently moved on."

How else do you deal with a child's disappearance? You move on. You sure as hell don't accept it, but you have to move on. Or you die.

Harry said nothing. He started to get up.

As he squared his hand on the table to rise, Morgan put his own hand over it. "Joan DeBrusk called me to see how you're doing."

"She's a friend of yours, isn't she?"

"More than a friend," said Miranda.

"She's a friend," said Morgan with emphatic ambiguity.

"And you called her personally when we discovered the girl," said Harry.

"Yes, I did. Is that a problem?"

Miranda looked quizzically from one man to the other. "You called her at home?" she asked.

Morgan seemed irritated, defensive. "She was at the kids' centre when I reached her."

"I need to speak to your Joan DeBrusk," said Harry.

"She's not my Joan DeBrusk. It's going on six. She'll be there by now. You want me to come?"

"I need to talk to her alone."

Morgan was about to protest, but Miranda dropped her hand casually over his arm and gave it a squeeze.

"Yeah, sure. It's on lower Church St. She works as a volunteer five evenings a week at the Zylberman Children's Centre. She's a good person, Harry. I'll call her."

"Please don't. I'll drop in when I get a chance. I'm not trying to cause problems here. There's something I need to clear up."

They talked about other things. Harry left first.

He walked directly across College and along Carleton to Church, then turned south and began looking for the children's centre.

It was one of those mansions looming out of the past that once housed a wealthy merchant family. Now, even the lowliest servants would have felt compromised by the seedy location. With crenelated brick towers and excessive gingerbread trim, flanked by other old houses in varying states of dilapidation, the Zylberman Children's Centre spoke not of grandeur lost but of the squalid present. The verandah was barren. Not a chair or a bicycle. But when Harry opened the wide front door, he was confronted with a riot of colours and raucous activity. It was sad such a sanctuary had to exist, but it was an exuberantly happy place inside.

Amidst the hubbub of children in a furor of unstructured play, Joan DeBrusk stood like a sentinel of serenity. She glanced up at him, smiled, and worked herself away from the free-for-all. She hardly seemed like a harbinger of doom.

"Good to see you, Dr. Lindstrom," she shouted, holding out her hand. "Let's step into the office where we can talk." She led him through to a small windowless room and closed the door. They sat on straight-backed wooden chairs, facing each other.

"Harry," he said. "Not Dr. Lindstrom."

"Joan. I hadn't expected to see you so soon. Lucy is doing just fine."

"You call her Lucy?" The freckles and open smile seemed sinister.

"That's what she calls herself. It's a pretty name, don't you think?"

"It is a pretty name," Harry agreed.

"To what do I owe this pleasure?" asked Joan. "Have you come to offer your services as a volunteer? We always need help. Or a donation? We're desperately poor."

Was she playing him like a cat with a moth, like a terrorist who says "excuse me" when she pushes her way to the centre of a bus before pressing the detonator?

You're escalating your metaphor, Harry, and you're being redundant. That's always a sign of uncertainty. And speaking of redundant, you seem to have developed a thing for dangerous redheads. This one seems guileless, but freckles can be deceiving.

"Harry, I'm sorry. Is there something I can do for you?"

"Last night. Morgan called you at home, right?"

"He called my cell, I was here, working late. I don't stay overnight. Why?"

"But you knew before he called that you'd be coming."

"To your place? No, how could I?"

"You knew that Lucy would be there."

"Morgan told me. He didn't give her a name. Is there a problem, Harry? Where is this going?"

"I'm wondering about your last words on the elevator."

"My last words. I said 'goodbye.'"

"No."

"Oh, I told you Mr. Sakarov sends his regards."

Remember, the most guile is when there appears to be none.

"Is he a friend of yours?"

"Someone I know."

"And he knew about the girl in my apartment?"

"Not at all. How could he?"

"But he knows you know Detective Morgan?"

"He might. It's not a secret."

"That you're dating."

She offered an apologetic smile. "That's none of your business, I'm afraid."

"You passed on a message."

"From Mr. Sakarov? Just that he said he'd be in touch. Is that a problem?"

"When did he tell you?"

"Yesterday, I think. No, the day before. He came in and dropped off a donation."

"Really? A big one?"

"Again, I don't see how that is your business, Dr. Lindstrom. A generous donation. Two thousand in cash."

"He's done this before? Always in cash?"

"Yes he has. And, yes it is."

"I'm confused, Joan. Did he say, if you meet a man by the name of Lindstrom, tell him 'hello.' Or perhaps, if a strange little girl turns up in a condo by the harbour, give the owner my regards."

"Something like that."

Harry waited for an explanation.

"I'm sorry if that's not what you want to hear. There's no conspiracy. He asked quite conversationally if I had ever run into an old friend of his by the name of Harry Lindstrom. I said no, although I recognized the name. He said, 'Well, you move in the same circles. I think he knows your friend, Morgan.'"

"So, he knew about the connection between Morgan and you."

"Like I told you, it isn't a secret. I suppose David was here one time when Mr. Sakarov dropped in."

"David?"

"Morgan."

"Is that his first name? I just know him as Morgan."

"Most people do. So, Mr. Sakarov asked me to look out for you. He's trying to find you."

"He knows where I live."

"Well, whatever. I don't know. You can imagine my surprise when I turned up at your place later the same night."

"And you didn't think to comment on the coincidence."

"No, I did not. I had other things on my mind. Namely, the welfare of a lost little girl who mysteriously appeared on your sofa. Perhaps I should be the one interrogating you."

When Harry left, he went straight to the King William. He was angry. It seemed there were no limits to the Russian's capacity to manipulate the innocent or destroy the righteous. Lena was dead; Joan was compromised; Lucy was the currency of Harry's exchange with the devil.

It was time to look the devil in the eye.

He and Sakarov had been circling each other, both of them wary about closing in for the kill. Harry's defence was Sakarov's ignorance about how much he knew. Sakarov's defence was unmitigated brutality.

Sakarov owned a condo on an upper floor. It was registered in his own name: he clearly felt safe in Toronto. The hotel concierge who doubled as security was helpful. Dimitri Sakarov was away for a few days, visiting friends in Muskoka. For a villain, Sakarov was surprisingly accessible. After a little strategic negotiating, Harry got the name of the cottagers, some people called Fearman, and an address near Port Carling.

It was well past eight but still light. He walked over to Union Station and rented a car. He figured he could be at the cottage before midnight.

Driving up Highway 400 in a Ford Explorer, which far more horsepower than he needed but the only vehicle available, he tried to assimilate his experience with Joan DeBrusk. He found people suspicious who appeared untouched by the world's depravities. She seemed genuine, possibly too genuine. Just past Major Mackenzie Drive, a blue Corvette Sting Ray cut him off. He had to swerve to avoid a collision and almost crashed into a silver BMW Z4 coming up on the inside. He braked and dodged. His heart raced. Adrenalin pumped through his system. Survival response shifted to anger. He speeded up until he could see inside one car a kid, steering with a wrist draped over the wheel, and inside the other, another young driver slouching in the identical posture. They slowed until he was nearly between them, then each gave him the finger and they swerved in, so that he had to brake hard to miss being hit.

They honked derisively and gunning their engines took off. He watched as they wove in and out of traffic, which was surprisingly heavy given how late in the evening it was. They were causing mayhem on the road, endangering lives in a cavalier game of testosterone overkill. Harry increased his speed while telling himself to slow down. When the Corvette and the BMW were just about out of sight, a service centre loomed ahead and he saw them swerve across three lanes and pull in. Harry followed, a few cars behind. They had parked in an open area, putting their cars on display, one in front of the other.

He waited until the young men stepped clear. Then from a few car-lengths away, he gunned his Ford Explorer into the driver's side of the blue Corvette, crushing the door panel against the frame. He squealed into reverse, then forward again into the driver's side of the BMW, collapsing the door into a twisted mass.

He backed away and nonchalantly got out of the Explorer to assess the damage to his own vehicle. Hardly a scratch. Chalk one up for the Ford! The drivers of the damaged cars ran over to him, swearing wildly, but stopped a few paces short. They weren't sure what this deranged idiot might do next.

Harry smiled.

A small cluster of onlookers began to applaud. Harry bowed. The applause grew. An OPP officer sauntered onto the scene.

"Is there a problem, here?" he asked.

"I don't know," said Harry. He turned to the young men. "Is there a problem?"

"Is there a problem?" the cop asked them.

"No," said the fat one with the beer belly.

"Not really," said the one with pimples and a lip-beard. "My dad's going to be pissed off."

"Should we call them?" asked the officer. "We'll call both your fathers."

"No," said the Corvette and BMW drivers simultaneously.

"Looks like you guys sideswiped. Lucky no one was hurt," said the cop.

Sideswiped, both on the driver's side. Harry smiled. Coming from opposite directions.

The OPP officer gazed around at the small crowd that had assembled.

"Is there a problem?" he asked them collectively.

No one stepped forward. Several smiled and gave Harry a thumbs-up.

"Fine, then," he said to Harry. "You have a good evening, sir."

And Harry drove off, pleased with the Explorer. He doubted he'd have to make an insurance claim but, if he did, he'd happily cover the deductible.

Do you feel better, now, Slate?

Yeah, Sailor, I do.

Pavement hummed beneath the tires. His left eye squinted against the glare of the setting sun cutting across the hood. He glanced up at his reflection in the rear view mirror.

Was that an exercise in relieving frustration, Harry?

The best explanation is no explanation at all, he thought.

Maybe I should be applauding a random act of vigilante justice?

I'm not sure it was random. Arbitrary, perhaps. We are defined by arbitrary gestures.

Good grief, you sound like Kierkegaard more than Dirty Harry.

Harry thought about this for a while. He veered off the highway into Bracebridge, then took the turnoff for Port Carling.

It wasn't road rage. He addressed his silent words into the darkness. It was calculated. I was prepared for the consequences. It was necessary.

For whom?

Sometimes you have to fight back, you know. Kicking against the pricks. For the most part, we suffer the insults of daily life and move on. Sometimes we shouldn't.

Aren't you smug!

Yes, I am.

The weathered outcroppings of Precambrian rock gave way to the forced domesticity of lawns and sidewalks and Harry slowed the Explorer to a crawl.

The village of Port Carling rose up from the banks of the Muskoka River around a large lock built for the old steamboats to pass through between the Muskoka Lake side and Lake Rosseau. He knew he was close to the Ghiberti cottage where a girl from Gimli, Manitoba, had been murdered the previous winter. Having resolved the mystery of her death made it no less sickening for Harry to think about, yet the drowning of the oldest Ghiberti daughter two decades earlier seemed more horrifying—the first in a series of family tragedies that only ended when there was no one left to die.

He rolled down into the village to ask directions, but nothing was open, so he followed the highway up the other side until he found a 24-hour Esso station. The night attendant had never heard of the Fearmans, but when Harry said they were on an island you could drive to, he was directed back through Port Carling to a road that would take him past a small Wahta-Mohawk settlement where people traded birchbark trinkets and coloured quills in exchange for hard cash. Beyond that, he would find a signpost with twenty or thirty names posted on a schematic map.

When he arrived at the Fearman turnoff, he doused his lights and let the Explorer roll down the long lane. The Fearman cottage emerged among towering pines against a backdrop of black water glistening from the broken moon. He braked and turned off the ignition. There were lights inside, although the wrap-around verandah was dark. This was a grand summer mansion in the old Muskoka tradition. Stacked fieldstone supported walls of narrow clapboard rising two and a half stories to roof planes slanted in a Victorian riot of geometric patterns and clad in cedar shakes—eight or ten bedrooms, a dining room, an intimate ballroom, a living room with a cavernous fireplace and a sizeable portion of a glass-eyed moose over the mantle, looking like he had burst through from the room behind; a kitchen designed for a chef; four bathrooms, one with a hot tub; a boathouse with an apartment in the loft and three slips to accommodate a classic launch for lake travel, a high-tech outboard for water skiing, and a small outboard for fishing, as well as space for a rowboat, a sailing dinghy, and an old-fashioned cedar strip canoe.

The small boulders marking the drive were not whitewashed. Old money. Aunt Beth always said, the *nouveau riche* paint rocks and plant petunias. Harry was comfortable with old money.

God knows why? Your family were paupers.

Only my parents. The antepenultimate generation were prosperous manufacturers. My great Aunt's generation. She was born with good taste.

I know what antepenultimate *means, Harry—third from the last. But you're not the last.*

I am now, he responded sadly.

Harry, don't. You can't grieve forever.

Of course I can.

He gazed out through the trees, past the cottage, and with his window rolled down, listened to the sounds of the lake.

Harry, why are we here? You're not going in. Either you'll be killed or considered a boor for not calling ahead.

He's come after me. I'm going after him.

Sounds good. Like, he's closing in on you and so you're making yourself available. I like you better when you're logical, not jumping from the gallows to test the strength of the rope.

Harry smiled to himself. Sometimes it was like she was sitting in the darkness beside him.

Let's get a room for the night.

He realized he wasn't sure what to do next. Since he had returned to Toronto he didn't know who was in charge of his life, but it didn't seem to be him. Maybe he really was putting his neck in a noose.

Suddenly he felt the powerful presence of Madalena Strauss. And Harry knew he had no alternative. He was caught up in the deadly struggle between Lena and Dimitri Sakarov. It was too late to step aside.

You can't unknow what you know; you can't undo what's been done.

He opened the car door very slowly and stepped to the ground, which was resilient beneath his weight from generations of dried pine needles. He closed the door gently and pressed the lock button on the key fob. To his astonishment, the headlights flashed, filling the surrounding stand of pines with bolts of illumination.

So what's our next move, Harry?

Floodlights suddenly filled the woods, extinguishing the moonlight. Before he had time to think or flee, he was flanked by two very large men with bulging muscles who didn't smile.

They didn't touch him, but together the three of them walked down to the verandah and around to the lake side where Harry was pushed forward in front of two other men who were sitting in Muskoka chairs, smoking Cuban cigars. Their chairs were at a conversational angle, so they could gaze out over Lake Rosseau while they chatted and see the distant lights of Windermere on the far shore. Harry obscured their view.

"Good to see you again, Mr. Lindstrom," said Dimitri Sakarov. "This is Conrad Fearman." Fearman was a fleshy man, past middle age, with wet eyes, a large nose, a thin mouth, and teeth implants too perfect to be real. "Conrad, this is the private investigator I told you about. Dr.

Professor Harry Lindstrom. We met in Vienna. He gets around a good deal, don't you, Harry?"

"Sakarov," said Harry, ignoring Fearman.

"What can we do for you, Harry?"

Groping for words, Harry snarled like a schoolyard bully. "You are a vicious guttersnipe bastard pervert."

"Is there a particular charge or is that a blanket judgment?"

Sakarov's condescension gave Harry the incentive to collect himself. "You tortured and raped Madalena Strauss." Levelling the charge to the man's face made his crimes seem as horrifically visceral as Lena's own battered flesh. Sakarov smiled.

"Very direct and to the point, Professor Lindstrom. But no, I did not." Sakarov turned slightly in his chair to address Fearman. "Harry was a philosophy professor before certain unfortunate events."

Fearman's eyes darted from one to the other in an expression of detached amusement.

Dimitri Sakarov turned back to Harry, which is to say, he pivoted his head, drawing the folds of fat around his neck into alignment.

"I understand your friend with the flaming red hair has met an unfortunate end. My condolences."

The fat man took a deep drag on his cigar. "My compliments to Fidel, dead though he is," he said to Fearman out of the side of his mouth. "An excellent cigar. Would you like a cigar, Harry? Oswaldo, get Dr. Lindstrom a chair and a cigar."

One of the goons arranged a Muskoka chair in front of the two other men so they could look at Harry or around him at the starlit waters of Lake Rosseau. When he thrust a cigar in front of Harry's face, Harry waved him away.

"Fidel would not be amused," said Fearman. "Would you like a drink? No? Well, then, to what do we owe the pleasure?"

That was the second time Harry had heard that expression the same night. Joan DeBrusk had used it under much different circumstances.

Harry said nothing.

"I gather you received my message?"

"Your threat."

"Hardly a threat, Harry. More of a reminder. She was a sweet little thing, wasn't she? I called her Lucy. I thought you'd appreciate the gesture. I understand she is in the system, now. You have done your good deed. Perhaps it is time to retire."

The Russian used the past tense to describe the little girl. He was finished with her.

Harry realized Sakarov had lost his Russian accent. No doubt he was fluent in Russian, given what Simon Wales had turned up, but he spoke English like a native Canadian. Somehow, that made him more sinister.

"Mr. Fearman is in the hotel business, Harry. As am I, although I'm sure you know that. Your young man will have discovered my business interests by now. All quite legitimate, I assure you."

He knows about Simon Wales. He has access to Joan DeBrusk. He knows your past, Harry. He knows about Lucy and Matt. He knows what your connection is with Madalena Strauss and her project, perhaps more than you do. He knew you were coming here tonight. No wonder the concierge at the King William was so forthcoming. So, now what, Humphrey? We're in a hell of a bind.

She seldom called him Humphrey. It was less ironic than calling him Slate. At the moment, there was no irony at all.

"Will you stay the night?" Sakarov pivoted his head over his neck fat and addressed Fearman. "Conrad, could we set Mr. Lindstrom up with a bed? Perhaps down in the boathouse with Oswaldo and Gregor? I'm sure Harry would accept your kind invitation. He is a gentleman. After six years at Cambridge, one is either a gentleman or exceedingly boring."

"Or both," said Fearman. "I spent a few years there, myself. King's College."

As if in response to his congenial tone, two little girls of about six and eight appeared at his side.

"What are you doing up so late, my darlings? Where's Nanny? You should have been in bed hours ago."

"We couldn't sleep, Grandpa," said the older of the two girls with a lilting cadence that struck Harry as vaguely Irish. "Nanny's gone off somewhere. I think she's skinny dipping with cook." She smiled. "Will you please come and read us a story and tuck us in?"

"And snuggle us, please," said the younger girl. "I'm scared. There's an owl outside my window."

"Is there really?" Fearman said, reaching out his arm and pulled them close, one against the other. "Listen," he whispered. "You can hear an owl from here. Maybe it's your owl's friend. Listen."

On cue, the owl hooted.

"See," said Fearman. "My owl is calling your owl. They're sisters, I think. Their names are Marissa and Colleen."

"Grandpa," the younger one squealed. "That's our names, too. I'm Colleen."

"Then you must be Marissa," he said, drawing the older girl down to kiss her on the forehead. "Off you go. We have grown-up business to do. I'll read you an extra-long story tomorrow."

The girls went off hand in hand, disappearing through the French doors into the cottage.

Harry realized he had been monitoring their relationship with Fearman, looking for indicators of abuse. They seemed to be happy kids. He seemed to be a warm and attentive grandfather. Harry felt oddly relieved, if a little surprised. He had assumed, by the company he kept, that Fearman must be a monster.

"Now then, Harry," said Sakarov, "I think all of us could do with a good night's sleep. You go along with the boys. They'll see to it you're taken care of. Good night."

The Russian dismissed Harry with a peremptory wave of his hand, which brought the two goons to Harry's side. He rose and walked with them down the steep path to the boathouse. Neither man touched him, but he might as well have been caught in the jaws of an ineluctable vice. The vague scent of body odour pressed from either side.

Whatever Harry had hoped to do by confronting Sakarov, there was no catharsis at hand.

What did you expect?

Nothing, he thought, as they entered the boathouse.

13 THE MESSAGE

WHEN HARRY WOKE UP FOR AN EARLY MORNING PEE over the rail at the front of the boathouse loft, he discovered one of the goons sitting in a chair reading Tolstoy by lamplight. *Anna Karenina*.

"You read English?" said Harry, cringing a little as he heard pee splatter on the deck below.

Now that *was boorish.*

"Is good," said Gregor.

Harry sat on the edge of his bed.

"Of course," said Gregor. "Is better in English. In Russian, too much words."

Harry smiled, uncertain what he meant.

"Bullshit," said Oswaldo, rising out of his sleep and bracing on one elbow. "You read lazy in Russian. No more words, longer words. Is better. In English, best is Stieg Larsson, better than Tolstoy."

"Idiot," said Gregor. "I read in Swedish Stieg Larsson. In English, is not so good. I read both. But he is like Tolstoy, yes. Great social vision. Strong character. Story move fast. Very complex. You agree, Mr. Lindstrom?"

Harry looked from one Russian to the other. Had he followed Alice down the rabbit hole? Had they slipped him acid? Was he still asleep?

"Mister, he ask you," said Oswaldo.

"I hadn't thought about Larsson as the new Tolstoy," said Harry. "Maybe the new Dashiell Hammett or Agatha Christie."

"Ha!" Gregor exclaimed. "You read like sissy."

What on earth does that mean?

"Now you get dressed," said Oswaldo. "Mr. Fearman, he will call soon to see you."

Harry had slept in his clothes. He stood up, slipped on his shoes, and waited, warily curious about what would happen next. Perhaps a lecture on Renaissance art over breakfast.

With his wardens beside him, he descended to the boat level of the dock. He avoided the Rorschach splotch on the darkened cedar and splashed lake water on his face, while Gregor and Oswaldo attended to more conventional ablutions using the small bathroom. Then the three of them climbed the hillside path to the verandah. Fearman was sitting in his Muskoka chair, smoking a cigar. He had changed his clothes, so it seemed he had not spent the entire night there. He appeared older in the cruel light of day. He waved at Harry to sit down in the chair beside him that had been occupied by Dimitri Sakarov the night before.

"Mr. Sakarov had to leave early. He sent his regards. He will be in touch."

"He has a habit of sending his regards," said Harry. "And of staying in touch."

So, Oswaldo and Gregor were employed by his host, not by the repulsive Russian.

Harry rose to his feet. "I think I'll grab some breakfast in Port Carling. Thank you for the use of the bed and my charming companions to watch over me."

"I do not think you will leave just yet," said Fearman, nodding to Gregor, who placed both huge hands on Harry's shoulders from behind and pushed him down with excruciating force.

"Would you like coffee? Yes, Oswaldo, please bring coffee for our guest. Thank you. Now Harry, we need to talk."

"I don't even know who you are," said Harry. "And I don't much care. I came for the fat man."

"You do not like Mr. Sakarov."

"Do you?"

"I have never thought about it. No, I suppose I do not. But it makes no difference. We are business associates. We do not play golf together."

Oswaldo drew up a small table beside the arm of Harry's chair and set down a tray with a bone china cup, a silver pot of coffee, a silver bowl of white and brown sugar cubes with silver tongs, and a silver pitcher of thick cream.

Harry passed on the sugar and cream. The coffee by itself was superb.

"Could you clear something up for me?" said Harry, blowing steam across the top of his cup.

"Of course?"

"Am I a prisoner or a guest?"

"Whichever you think. I would like to have a conversation with you. Since you might not want to have a conversation with me, then I suppose you are my guest until I am finished."

"It's always good to know where you stand."

"Now, then, to business. You have access to certain files."

"I don't know what the hell you're talking about."

"Please do not swear. We do not swear in this house. My girls, you know."

"Fuck you," said Harry.

He momentarily lost consciousness. His cup shattered on the floor. He wasn't aware of letting it slip from his hands, but he heard it break into pieces. He blinked trying to clear his head. Gregor had walloped him across the back of the skull. So much for Tolstoy.

"The files, Harry." Fearman spoke as if nothing had happened. "Some of them might incriminate me. You will find them and you will delete them before doing whatever you must do with the rest."

"And what must I do?"

"Whatever you think best, of course."

Muskoka chairs are designed to relinquish their grip on your buttocks only with a great deal of effort, but Harry eased slowly forward. He had no interest in alarming Oswaldo or Gregor. When he was seated upright on the front edge of the chair, he felt more in control.

"Let me say this as clearly as I can, Mr. Fearman. I do not have in my possession files of any sort that could possibly be of interest to you. Or to Dimitri Sakarov. If I did, I would not be able to release them. My problem with Sakarov is that he tortured and raped my friend in Vienna and probably had her murdered."

"Ah, well, whatever your quarrel with Sakarov, it is no concern of mine. But he assures me, you have access to incriminating information of the worst sort. If you do not have it now, he assures me you will. Before you do with it whatever you have to do, you will see there is nothing left that can be traced back to me. Do you know, the Fearmans have had this cottage for five generations? We are an old family and we are fiercely proud. We do not take kindly to scandal. Am I clear?"

"And what sort of scandalous material should I be looking for?"

"Oh, Harry," he chuckled. "I'm sure you know the sort of thing I mean. Start with my granddaughters. Leave them out of this. My interest in trying to help childless couples with adoption procedures, leave that out of this. My own travels to Thailand for personal reasons, leave that out as well. The investments I have in companies employing children, I know nothing about them. I am old-school Church of England, Harry. In business, however, I do not discriminate. I would not like my support, let us say, of Imams in this country who encourage female circumcision to be known. I protect them, they pay me. It is a growing industry in our larger cities. Experts are brought in from Saudi Arabia. A moral cesspool, Saudi Arabia. But a strong economy. Most of the countries I deal with are Muslim. Did you know rape is a punishment in Pakistan? A curious situation. It is purely a business necessity, I assure you—dealing with Muslims, not rape. But you get the idea, Harry. In Somalia a couple of years ago, a thirteen-year-old girl was stoned to death in a football stadium for reporting she'd been raped. Now what kind of people do that, I ask you? But deal with them I must. So, Harry, if you find anything that might prove an embarrassment to me by old-fashioned Canadian standards, in one word, *delete*. As for anyone else, I don't give a good God damn. Am I clear?"

"You really are a nasty son of a bitch." Harry steeled himself for a brutal blow to the head, but a smile broke across Fearman's face as the two little girls he called his granddaughters came through the French doors and trundled in their thin cotton nighties over to the old man and crawled up on his lap. He cuddled them then pulled away and addressed Harry.

"You see, Mr. Sakarov and I are not exactly on the same side, Harry. I would prefer you proceed with the Viennese files. It would be good for business. Dimitri, of course, wishes to protect himself and many others your files will embarrass. It is not for me to say, but I suggest it might be to your advantage to eliminate him."

So much for honour among the degenerate.

"I will do my best to arrange protection for you, if you'd like." Fearman snuggled his girls. "I have many friends."

"I'm sure you are legion," said Harry. "I'll manage on my own."

"Good. As you wish. I think we understand each other. The boys will look after you now."

Gregor and Oswaldo walked Harry up to the parking space. When they reached the Explorer, each placed a hand on one of his shoulders. They squeezed in what could have been taken as an amiable gesture but was clearly meant to intimidate.

"Goodbye, Harry. It was nice meeting you," said Gregor as they walked away. Oswaldo said nothing.

Harry stood heavily on the pine needles, feeling their pungent aroma sing through his veins. As he looked through the towering trees past the cottage, he was overwhelmed by the beauty of Lake Rosseau shimmering in the morning light. He felt strangely disoriented; the tranquility of the scene was thrown askew by the atrocities it obscured. The image of a woman's face hovered on the edge of his mind. He tried to focus. Karen, Lena, other women in his life, lovers, friends, passing strangers, all morphed into the image of a diminutive, indomitable Joan DeBrusk.

Intuition, Harry?

She's not one of the bad guys.

She's not necessarily one of the good guys either. You're taken by her resonant beauty and worried by what it conceals.

Resonant beauty?

It echoes Madalena and reminds you of Klimt.

The two Russian goons who read widely and practised a modified version of Tolstoy's pacifism disappeared around the corner of the verandah. He'd have to ask them about Dostoevsky some time, especially *Crime and Punishment*.

Or The Idiot, *Karen whispered. Forget about those guys, Harry.*

Duly forgotten.

Fearman might be right about eliminating Sakarov. Harry's life was precarious as long as the fat man was alive, but at least with Sakarov the enemy had a face. Terminated—Harry let the words roll through his mind; the enemy would be anonymous, amorphous, ubiquitous, assiduous, inexorable—

Karen interrupted. *You're being pedantic, Harry, and missing the point. You're not a killer.*

He didn't try to respond. He had been hiding behind words. Of course, he wasn't a killer. Of course. He slid behind the wheel, started the SUV and backed out the long drive, swinging onto the gravel road that led out to the route to Toronto.

Driving down Highway 11 onto the 400, he tried to keep from thinking. He needed to let the myriad feelings and thoughts crowding his mind sort themselves out, find their own levels of significance. Sometimes the most logical behaviour was to keep logic at bay. By the time he got home, he was exhausted. It was only midafternoon, but after a cooling shower he crawled between the sheets and fell into a deep sleep.

He woke up with fingers digging into his shoulder. Without opening his eyes, he knew who it was—by the slight but talon-like grip and because, who else? An assailant would have already assailed him. No one besides Harry had a key. That left Simon Wales.

"Good morning, Simon," he said, rolling away and pulling a pillow over his head. He felt like he had a wretched hangover but he hadn't had a drink.

"It's eight o'clock, Harry."

"Go away. It's too early."

"In the evening."

"Oh," said Harry, rolling back and opening his eyes. "And you're here why?"

"Well, I checked out Joan DeBrusk. She's straight as they come."

"How the hell do you know about Joan DeBrusk?" Harry sat upright. He couldn't remember mentioning her name.

"I was sitting behind you at Starbucks yesterday."

"No, you were not."

"You had a latte and a carrot-bran muffin."

"Corn meal."

Actually, Harry recalled he had traded muffins with Miranda. He had ordered corn meal but eaten carrot-bran.

"I think Dimitri Sakarov has a spy working at the Zylberman Children's Centre," Simon continued. "It's not her."

"You're sure?"

"I interviewed her."

"Did she know you were working for me?"

"Of course not. She's very attractive for a redhead."

"Don't you like redheads?"

"I do, actually. My expression was to indicate I personally am not interested in Miss Joan DeBrusk. It was a form of self-definition, not meant as an insult. I think she's having an affair with your detective friend."

"Morgan?"

"Not Miranda. She's your other friend."

"You're making me sound pathetic."

"Friends are not all they're cracked up to be."

"How old are you? Never mind? You can wait for me out there." Harry got up and put on some casual clothes. When he walked into the living room, Simon Wales was sitting in the armchair. Harry lowered himself carefully onto the sofa.

"What else have you been up to?"

"Well, the room on one side of yours at the Kressler was occupied by an American businessman. Middle-aged, gay, a recluse. From Oklahoma, in textiles. The room on the other side was registered to Dimitri Sakarov."

"Not Melvin and Doris Findlay."

"Apparently not. The curious thing is that Sakarov phoned from Saint Petersburg the day before your friends died to say he would not be coming to Vienna."

"The Findlays weren't friends. I never met them."

"But apparently Sakarov insisted on holding the room in case he came later in the week. He has an account there. He also has an account at the Imperial."

"He was in Vienna the night they died. He paid me a visit. We had *wiener schnitzel* together near St. Stephen's Cathedral. What else did you find out about him?"

"Nothing. And a great deal. He travels a lot. He has many business connections, apparently in relation to his hotel. His past remains inaccessible. It's like he imagined himself into being as a fully formed, middle-aged adult. I'll get to the bottom of it, find out who he is, but I need time."

"What sort of business dealings? *In relation to his hotel* seems rather vague."

"Of course. That's what he intends. He lives in Toronto part of the year. He meets with major tycoons, establishment lawyers, and powerful gangsters. They talk behind closed doors. There's no paper trail, and not much of a cyber trail. Mostly, whatever his business, it's done person to person, over scotch and a handshake."

"Do you know anything about Conrad Fearman? Anything come up in your prowlings?"

"Old manufacturing money, Upper Canada College, Queen's University. Two years at King's College, Cambridge. Home in Rosedale, cottage in Muskoka. Never married."

"No grandchildren, then?" Harry felt a chill run down his spine. "Has he ever been convicted?"

"Investigated twice as a sex tourist to Thailand. Never indicted. He does business there. Electronic parts. Assembly needing small fingers. A major contributor to the Conservative Party of Canada, a benefactor of Princess Margaret Hospital, the Children's Wish

Foundation, the Art Gallery of Ontario, the Canadian Opera Company. Received an honorary doctorate from Queen's University two years ago."

"You tracked him through Dimitri Sakarov."

"No. I already knew about Conrad Fearman. But yes, there is a connection."

Simon Wales was turning out to be a very big mystery, himself. He seemed a genius at ferreting out connections, at violating personal and private space. Yet he was more elusive than Dimitri Sakarov. He had no history, but he knew about Fearman. Did he have a life, however secret? He was an invaluable asset but, Harry worried, with so much knowledge might he also be a liability?

Simon was staring at the picture of Madalena Strauss, *The Forces of Evil*. In *The Kiss*, her face was wrapped in the larger narrative, inseparable from Klimt's design. But in the excerpt from the Beethoven frieze, she loomed large, her face was a portrait of wanton allure, tilted against her updrawn knee above the expanse of her naked thigh, her features framed by a whorl of burning red hair that flowed down over her breasts and coiled between her legs. A few stray tendrils were caught up with erotic abandon in fingers that clasped her ankles.

Simon Wales seemed to be mesmerized. What did he see that evoked such interest? Had he only guessed that the paintings were authentic? Had Simon himself become Harry's link with Lena and her story? Was he like Faithful in *Pilgrim's Progress*? He had clearly taken on Harry's cause as his own, even if Harry's cause was fraught with danger and confusion. He was neither a servant nor a friend but a companion and fellow traveller devoted to getting Harry through to wherever he was going. It was not Simon's journey. He was vain and wore invisibility like a costume—he would be swallowed up in the *Vanity Fair*, even as he urged Harry through to the other side.

Oh for God's sake, Harry. He's just a weird kid who dresses too well and is paid too much.

How much is too much?

Depends what he turns up, I suppose. Get off the literary kick, Humphrey. You're a philosopher, not a critic. And right now you're a detective, so let's get detecting.

Sailor, sail on. But thanks for the cautionary note.

Don't lose yourself in abstractions, Slate. It's too easy.

"Nothing's easy," Harry whispered.

"Pardon?" said Simon Wales.

"Nothing," said Harry, resenting the intrusion.

"Sorry."

"No, not at all. Can I get you some Perrier? Okay, I see you've already got one. Fine. What else have you found for me?" Harry squinted at Simon. Light from the falling sun glinting off the lake flickered across his features. For a brief moment, Harry thought he saw Madalena Strauss in his face, in his posture, poised in the big leather chair. He was both relaxed and ready to spring, like a cat resting in the evening light, relaxed, lethal, strangely content.

Simon shifted his gaze from *The Forces of Evil*.

"I've found what you're looking for, Harry."

"You've found Rachel Damboch?"

"In your email."

"What are you talking about."

"You don't empty your Junk file."

"Not very often. Does anyone?"

"I do. But it's a good thing you're a bad housekeeper. You have an important bit of junk addressed to Dearest Beloved."

"Buried among letters offering eternal love, a bigger penis, and/or thirteen million dollars if I provide my personal particulars. It's e-pollution. No one is dumb enough to respond."

"Wrong. Some people do. Greed makes people stupid, the same people who buy lottery tickets. Do you realize, statistically, you're more likely to be shot by a sniper on Yonge Street between ten and eleven a.m. on a Thursday in October than you are to win the jackpot?"

"So what's the big discovery?"

"There actually is a letter from Rachel Damboch."

"You've got to be kidding."

"Well, someone is using her name. Probably your dead friend from Vienna."

Harry flipped open his laptop on the table in front of him.

"Here's a printout," said Simon. He waved a single page document in Harry's direction. Harry closed the laptop, got up, took the document, and settled back on the sofa to read. It was the usual claptrap nonsense, under the subject heading, *Your Noble Commitment Required.*

Dearest Beloved, How are you this day? I believe you to be highly respected personality, considering the fact I source your profile from human resources database of your country of domestic life.

I am Barrister Damboch, legal personal attorney to Mr. Abel Canaan, who recently passed off, on summer excursion to northern part of our beaudiful Country in Nigeria.

Mr. Abel Canaan left in Security with me Consignment Luggage in funds totalling $7,420,234.03 calculated in United States funds.

Since I am recently unsuccessful in acquiring known relatives to Mr. Abel Canaan, you must now become aware I have legal protocol to make you next of his kin.

All required from you is sincere corporation as appropriate. We will divide money as follows: 60% to you and 40% for my own. If you are quick this will not take me time. We will not be breach of soever law in your country or mine.

Be sincere to provide four digit code number for appropriate transaction. I will be sincere also.

Send to email address above only your number as Security.

Your beloved

Barrister Rachel Damboch

Harry grimaced. He smashed a fist into the paper against his open hand then it into a ball and threw it at Simon, who smiled his rare elliptical smile.

"We are not amused," said Harry.

Oh but we are. Come on, Harry, it's so bad it's got to be good.

"It's her," said Simon.

"Rachel Damboch?"

"I doubt it. If she's still alive, she'd be at least in her eighties or more, too old for computers. I mean, this is a sophisticated way of hiding in plain sight. I'd say it must be Madalena Strauss."

"Who is dead," Harry observed.

"In that case, you'd expect her to sound more biblical."

"Simon, she has been autopsied, cremated, and mourned by her colleagues and friends."

"Or she's hiding behind a shroud of pure kitsch."

Can kitsch be pure? Just asking.

Harry ignored Karen's glib response to death. She had the right to an attitude, if anyone had. He found it more difficult to penetrate Simon's derisive contempt. Then he realized the young man was cutting through sentiment to get at the message from beyond.

Harry retrieved the document and smoothed it out on the sofa.

"Do you think it's in code? What's the date?"

"No, it's not in code," said Simon with an authority that suggested he knew about codes. "Unless being sent a few days after Madalena Strauss killed herself is a code."

"I think she was murdered."

"Sorry. I thought you told me she did herself in."

"Sakarov virtually confessed. He was gloating."

"You've seen Sakarov."

"So you don't know everything about me?"

"I lost you when you took off in that SUV gas-guzzler."

"Yeah, well, Sakarov and I had an encounter against the backdrop of beautiful Lake Rosseau."

"Muskoka. I take it the encounter was satisfactory."

"Satisfactory?"

"You survived."

"Yes."

"And that's a good thing."

"I suppose it is."

"Now, to work."

"Yes?"

Simon reached down and took his MacBook Air, identical to Harry's, out of his Roots shoulder bag, which was also identical to Harry's—burnished natural leather, an accessory to complement the masculine essence of the man carrying it. A perfect accessory for Simon Wales. For Harry, it was just a bag.

Simon walked around the table and sat down beside Harry on the sofa. He slid Harry's laptop to the side and opening his own began typing.

Harry noticed Simon's computer had a few dints and scuff marks. While Simon let his fingers race over the keyboard, he gazed absentmindedly at the Klimts.

"Where'd you learn touch typing?" Harry asked.

"Just something I picked up along the way."

There was no point asking for further explanation.

Simon abruptly tilted his screen so Harry could see it.

"There," said Simon. "I've sent notes to myself."

"Yourself?"

"My home computer. Now let's answer Frau Damboch. Or whoever is buried inside her name."

"Come off it, Simon. First of all, you don't answer garbage. Second, if it's from Lena, she's dead. Third, I'm not sure I want to connect just yet."

"Of course you do."

"She set herself up as judge and jury, but I'm the intended executioner."

"You told me there's a court of last resort."

"A gatekeeper. Yes."

"Rachel Damboch?"

"Possibly."

"Then let's move forward, Harry. If Fräulein Strauss' appointed conscience hasn't released the files yet, I don't think she will do it now just because you connect. Surely, she needs you to evaluate."

"That could take years."

"Not the files, Harry. The consequences. That might take no more than a second or two. You do want to bring down the Fearmans of the world, don't you?"

"Desperately."

"Then let's make a beginning. We have the four digit number."

"1902?"

Simon typed in the number.

There was an immediate return.

"Not good," said Simon. "An automatic response."

"Read it," said Harry.

They read together; under the subject line, *Your Noble Commitment Admired*, a terse message.

Dearest Beloved,

I know you could not avoid connection.

Barrister Rachel Damboch

"It's her, Simon."

"Rachel?"

"No, Lena. Look at the subject line. *Your Noble Commitment Admired.* The first one said *Required.* She's playing games, but it's her."

"No, it's pre-packaged," Simon explained. "I'm afraid Rachel Damboch won't get us anywhere after all."

Why the sudden reversal? Harry felt his heart sink. The name *Rachel Damboch* wasn't floating around in the ether. It didn't just materialize in cyberspace, teleported from the back of a painting or from random records in Vienna of a mysterious woman who worked in a group home for damaged children and created a selfless life from the leavings of others.

He could hear Karen whispering: *"to create a selfless life" seems almost a contradiction in terms, Harry. There's more than that to Rachel Damboch.*

And there was.

To Simon's apparent surprise, a new message appeared on his screen.

Subject line: *Lazarus.*

Harry pushed past Simon to open the message.

It was terse and to the point:

Hello Harry. It took you a while.

Prepare for the onslaught.

Lena

14 A WOMAN WITH COPPER RED HAIR

OVER THE NEXT HOUR AND A HALF, THOUSANDS OF documents flashed on Harry's desktop and immediately disappeared. Sometimes their residual images allowed him to guess their content. Others left only a fleeting impression. But there was no doubt they promised vile revelations of child exploitation on an unimaginable scale, ranging from illicit adoptions to the most sickening depravities. At 11:20 p.m., the document fragments stopped coming.

Simon emailed Rachel Damboch, asking if the transmission was complete. No answer. He tried addressing Madalena Strauss. No answer.

"That's it," he said. "You see what she's done."

"Yeah, she's set me up royally. She knows my computer's being monitored by Sakarov."

"No, no. She's given you insurance against Sakarov. He may want you roughed up a little, but he won't kill you. She's confirmed that you are the heir to her files, but she's also confirmed that you don't have access to them. At least, not yet. Until you do, he has to let you live. She's protecting you."

"She's protecting herself."

"Too late, since you've assured me she's dead. At this point, you could just let the whole thing drop, you know. Walk away from it. Enjoy your Klimts."

"Too late. He knows Rachel Damboch is my contact."

"He knows you've accessed junk mail. He wouldn't be able to hack into the deluge. I mean, it's like grasping water. If *we* can't hold onto it, how could *he*?"

"He knows her name."

"The phone book's full of names. It won't mean anything to him. But we've got to find her, Harry."

"You think so, do you?"

"We're morally obligated."

Harry, this kid is impressive.

Or delusional.

"Harry, we can't get full access to the files without the gatekeeper."

He's using "we," Harry. He's Faithful to a fault.

Harry avoided a response. He'd never actually read John Bunyan's awkwardly engaging tale of conversion, but *Pilgrim's Progress* was part of his culture; he felt like he had.

"Simon. You don't have to be a part of this," he said.

"I rather enjoy the adventure. Let me find Rachel Damboch, Harry. Let me get onto it. I'll drop around in the morning and tell you what I've come up with. Do you have a gun?"

"Unfortunately, I do. Do you want it?"

"For you, Harry. I'm fine."

Simon got up to leave, but Harry motioned him to wait while he looked for his gun. He found a metal pistol case in the bedroom behind a box of the thirteen volume *Oxford English Dictionary,* the 1933 edition reprinted in 1961. The online version made it not only dated but perpetually redundant. He brought the case out into the living room and set it on the table, snapped open the clasps, and gazed at his pistol that had never seen open air since he bought it three years ago.

"Glock Gen 4," said Simon Wales, picking up the gun and weighing it in his hands. "Nice. Nine by nineteen calibre, magazine capacity seventeen, barrel with a right hand twist. Very nice."

Why shouldn't he know about guns, Harry? He knows damned near everything else. And you won't touch the fool thing.

I don't like guns.

"Is this registered, Harry?"

"Of course. I'm a private eye."

"Where's the ammunition?"

Harry, do you own ammunition?

Simon Wales passed the pistol from hand to hand, then announced with a conspiratorial air, "You can always throw it at your attackers."

Suddenly a tremendous crash signalled the door bursting from its hinges. Gregor and Oswaldo lumbered through the hall into the living room. They didn't seem worried that the noise might attract attention. They obviously didn't intend staying long.

Gregor was carrying his own Glock, a larger model. He swiped Harry's gun from Simon's grasp and it clattered to the floor.

Oswaldo went straight for Harry's laptop. Harry tried to stop him. Oswaldo shoved him backward onto the antique Persian carpet and then walked out onto the balcony and dropped Harry's laptop over the rail. Simon tried to slip his own laptop behind the cushions of the sofa. Oswaldo lifted Simon into the air with one hand and dropped him on the coffee table. Simon cracked his head as the table tilted and spilled him onto the floor. Then Oswaldo carried Simon's laptop out to the balcony and tossed it into the air.

Gregor watched, holding his pistol casually but with his finger on the trigger.

"You finished?" Harry demanded. It was hard to be righteously indignant, sprawled on a kamseh rug on the floor.

"Check for other computers," Gregor commanded.

Oswaldo disappeared into the bedroom, which Harry sometimes used as an office. He had an old Mac on the desk that he hadn't used in two years. From the crashing sounds, he assumed he would never use it again.

A cell phone chimed the opening chords of "A Hard Day's Night" from Gregor's breast pocket. He clicked it off without bothering to answer.

A neighbour must have heard the door being smashed and called 911. The police had arrived in the lobby. A lookout was warning them. Harry wondered if it was the fat man himself.

Gregor and Oswaldo took Russian leave, descending a few flights on the stairs beside the elevator shaft as the cops went up, then presumably taking the other elevator down to the lobby. Harry knew this because that's what he would have done.

Meanwhile, he struggled to his feet and Simon twisted away from the table remnants and stood up as well. Both were still disoriented when a team of cops in flak jackets stormed into the room with guns drawn.

"Hands up, high, higher," one cop yelled and slammed Harry against the wall between the Klimts. Another cop dropped Simon to his knees then pushed him face down into the carpet.

The bruiser handling Harry swung him around.

"What's going on?" he demanded.

"You might have asked that first," Simon said without looking up.

"It that your Glock?" the bruiser demanded, seeing Harry's gun on the floor.

"I live here," said Harry, gasping for breath. "I'm a private investigator."

"Someone came through your door without knocking. It's flat to the floor."

"Weak hinges," said Harry. "Cheap lock. Can I put my hands down?"

The bruiser jabbed him in the ribs with his pistol.

"Don't move a muscle till we prove who you are."

"I didn't say who I am, you moron. My name is Harry Lindstrom and you got here too bloody late."

The bruiser holstered his gun.

"Well, now, then, you're the one stupid enough to call a man with a gun unpleasant names, Harry Lindstrom. Who's the moron now?"

Harry, Karen whispered, *it's time to name-drop, if ever there was one.*

"Superintendent Quin," Harry said. "Detective David Morgan."

"Yeah?" said the bruiser. "What about them?"

"Friends."

"Of yours?"

"Yes," said Harry with as much conviction as possible.

"And what happened here?"

"Nothing."

"Nothing?"

"Nothing," Harry repeated. "The door broke."

"Really?"

"Really. I'll have to get it fixed."

"Quin and Morgan? Nothing happened? You want us to leave?"

"Please," said Simon.

The bruiser held up his hands palms outward in mock submission, nodded to the other cop, and they left.

"How was that for adventure?" said Harry.

"They didn't kill us," said Simon. He got to his feet and seemed disappointed when he reached around to feel the back of his neck for blood and came up with nothing but a few beads of sweat.

"Sorry about the table," he said.

"George Jensen, secondhand, mid-century modern, solid teak," said Harry. "You just loosened the joints."

"Loosened," said Simon. Then added deferentially, "Sorry."

"You said that,' said Harry.

Simon brushed imaginary flecks from his linen suit with the back of one hand. "I'll see you in the a.m.," he announced, and before Harry could say anything he was gone, then he returned to explain that the police had stood the door upright in its frame, but Harry should get it seen to as it wasn't secure and might fall on an intruder, who could sue for damages. Simon was curiously ebullient, considering he'd been manhandled and his computer destroyed.

Harry settled back on the sofa, but at some point in the middle of the night he rose and struggled through cursory ablutions before stripping to the buff and stretching out on his side of the bed.

By mid-morning when Simon returned, Harry was already on his third coffee.

Simon looked remarkably fit, particularly when he admitted to having spent most of the night on his home computer. He was wearing a fresh suit that Harry hadn't seen before, with a purple tie.

"I had a revelation," Simon announced.

"Me too," said Harry. "Life is dangerous. What's yours?"

"Elisabeth Bök, Madalena Strauss' great-grandmother."

"What about her?"

"I knew a poet by that name. He pronounced it Book. I scanned for Elisabeth Book, Elisabeth with an s, then with a z like the Queen. Elizabeth Book. Deceased, Toronto, 1986."

"Couldn't be the same person. If she modelled for Klimt, that would make her well over a hundred when she died."

"Exactly. Elizabeth Book with a z was the daughter of Elisabeth Bök. Follow me, Harry. She was Lena Strauss' great aunt, her grandmother's sister. The sisters were shipped to Ravensbrück in 1943 with their mother, who had been Klimt's mistress and model. The mother died there in '44. Lena's grandmother was transported back to Mauthausen in Austria where she died. Elizabeth, Lena's great aunt, was barely alive when Ravensbrück fell to the Allies. Her mind was gone. She was nursed back to physical health by Canadian Army nurses. When they sorted out her mental problems sufficiently, she was sent to Canada as a Displaced Person. That was in 1947. Once she reached Toronto, she was indentured as a maid for a year, then she picked up work as a freelance translator and eventually a major Canadian publisher hired her as their international editor. She was fluent in five languages, but she refused to travel. She lived on her own in an apartment on Avenue Road. Until."

Simon paused for breath or dramatic effect.

"Until?" Harry demanded. "Don't be coy, Simon. Go on."

"Until in 1955 she encountered a damaged young woman being held by police for soliciting. Elizabeth was at the Don Jail on a translation job. I'm not sure of the details, but she ended up taking the young woman home."

"The young woman being Rachel Damboch."

"Right, yes, it was Rachel Damboch, formerly of the Huronia Asylum for Idiots in Orillia and then with no fixed address until rescued from the streets by Lena Strauss' great aunt. The details make a very tidy story, don't you agree? Of course they leave out the emotional trauma of two tortured souls, one haunted by the fiendish dementia of her Nazi countrymen and the other by being locked up as a mental defective."

"And how could you possibly know all this?"

"Ha! That's the simple part. I told you that Rachel had written a book while she was a house-mother at Asperger's SOS-Kinderdorf in Hinterbrühl. Her book was about Mauthausen slave labourers building prototype jet engines for BMW and hauling stone blocks from a quarry by hand. She apparently drafted another book on Dr. Hans Asperger's wartime activities. Both are in manuscript and held at the University of Vienna."

"You told me you couldn't get access to them."

"Yes, but I figured, correctly, if Rachel wrote books, chances were good that her mentor did too. Elizabeth Book wrote a memoir! It wasn't about surviving Ravensbrück, it was about her years in Canadian exile. It was never published, but she did significant work as a translator and editor so her employers kept her private papers with her work projects and the whole shebang is presently being scanned by a PhD student from U of T. It's all there, relatively available, and fortunately written in English."

"So how did Rachel end up in Austria?"

"Back to the ancestral homeland, I suppose. By proxy. Elizabeth was so traumatized by her wartime experience she couldn't bear to return. Rachel, her education well underway, went in her place, liked it, and stayed. You know the rest."

"Not quite," said Harry. "You told me last night you were sure there's a closer connection between Rachel and Lena Strauss."

"That part's not quite clear. We're looking through a glass darkly, here."

The last time Harry had heard that expression, it was from the slovenly lips of Dimitri Sakarov.

"Once Rachel left Toronto," Simon continued, "I don't think she and her mentor ever saw each other again. Austria never purged itself of its Nazi past the way Germany did. Claiming to be a victim of the *Anschluss,* it allowed fascism to fester. Elizabeth was horrified, mesmerized. She kept tabs on the political activities of the extreme right wing *Freiheitliche Partei Österreichs*, the so-called Freedom Party of Austria. She fulminates in her memoirs about the insult to humanity of their existence. She writes about her mother, Elisabeth Bök, almost as if she were a myth. She writes about Ravensbrück but not from memory. She writes more about Rachel; she writes about Rachel's retrospective books on the Nazi era. She was afraid for Rachel, afraid she was stirring up a vipers' nest."

"Simon, please. Tell me about Rachel and Lena."

"I'm sorry, Harry, but you need background. There's a lot to assimilate."

"You told me last night the connection was obvious. Lena's gatekeeper has to be Rachel."

"Lena, yes. Lena's mother was raped. Is that direct enough?" Simon struggled to catch up emotionally with his own revelations. "I'm not trying to obfuscate, Harry. You gave me a job. I'm trying to do it."

Patience was never your defining virtue, Harry. Let's hear him out, shall we?

The veins stood out on Simon's temples. He seemed under progressively more strain as his narrative developed. Harry offered a grimace of sympathy and sat back. Instead of continuing, Simon gazed across the harbour. He seemed to be distracted by the squadrons of dinghy sails billowing in the freshening breeze.

"You have a lovely spot, here, Harry. Do you sail?"

"Never," said Harry. "Please, Simon. I need to understand about Lena."

"Of course you do." Simon rose to his feet and walked out onto the balcony, then turned and faced Harry framed through the open doorway. "Parentage can be a nasty business," he announced. He moved back into the room almost serenely, like he had shared a great burden. He resumed his seat.

Harry couldn't help wondering if Simon was extending his account to include Harry's situation and the deaths of his children. Or if he was connecting to his own situation, about which Harry knew nothing at all.

"Lena's mother was gang-raped by neo-Nazis," Simon continued. "Retaliation for being a red-haired Jew. She was devastated. No charges were laid. She was pregnant. She found her way to the Kinderdorf in Hinterbrühl. I suppose there had been letters between her aunt in Toronto and Rachel, maybe between her aunt and herself. Lena was born at the school in 1982. Her mother relocated to Vienna. However, Lena lived under Rachel's care in the Kinderdorf until moving to Salzburg at sixteen for her university preparation."

"The school was for children with Asperger's, wasn't it?"

"Primarily. Founded by Hans Asperger and Asperger's was Rachel's specialty. She may have had an autism spectrum disorder herself, although it's much rarer in girls. Or it may be that the Asylum for Idiots created conditions where simulated autism was a survival technique."

"Simon, I wonder if Lena Strauss also suffered from Asperger's."

Simon gazed at Harry with an expression of curious affection. "Tell me," he said.

Harry's entire experience of Madalena Strauss coalesced in his mind, from grand tragic gestures to nuances caught in the flick of her hair, the fixed gaze, intonations carried on the edges of conversation, the urgency of confessions and explanations that had drawn him into her world.

"Pathologically focused, difficulty with small talk, literal-mindedness, chronic anxiety, inappropriate movements, lack of empathy."

Think about it, Harry. Every one of those symptoms could also be a natural human response to particular horrors in the woman's life.

Are you recanting, Sailor?

Not recanting, reassessing. She grew up in an Asperger's environment, raised by a woman who possibly had Asperger's herself. What you saw was most likely imitative behaviour. From infancy, she saw those symptoms as being the norm.

Her mother was traumatized as a child by her wartime experience, then raped by neo-Nazi thugs too numerous to establish Lena's parentage (had anyone been inclined), and retreated into solitude in the heart of Vienna, where she eventually died, leaving Lena a modest fortune in recovered assets.

Her other mother was Rachel Damboch.

And Lena herself, with her own child stolen, exchanged intimacy for information that drove her to murder. She was brutalized by the fat man and ended up a mutilated corpse in the Danube.

Harry, look at Simon. He's here, he's waiting for you to process what he's told you. Speak to him, Harry.

"So," Harry said, breaking the heavy silence between them. "Now all we have to do is track down Rachel Damboch before Sakarov does."

"Good. You intend to release her files."

"Which are accessible through your computer at home."

"Yes," said Simon.

"I have to check them out, I owe Lena that much."

"If Sakarov figures out that Rachel is the gatekeeper, he'll kill her."

"You assured me he wouldn't."

"That was last night, this is now. I hadn't realized the intimate connection."

"Then I've got to reach her before he does."

"Harry."

"Yes?"

"There's more. I've kept the most perplexing part until last."

"Perplexing?"

"Confusing, disturbing, amazing."

"I can't wait."

"Last night when I left, someone was waiting outside your building."

"Dimitri Sakarov?"

"No. I think it was Madalena Strauss."

Harry gave no indication he had heard. A huge black chasm opened inside. He felt nothing, he thought nothing. It was like those brief flashes of consciousness following his rescue from the Devil's Cauldron when he realized that his family was dead.

"Harry! Harry, I'm sorry, I thought it was her. Maybe it wasn't."

Harry slowly swung his head to the side so that he could look out over the islands and across the open expanse of Lake Ontario.

"Harry. I recognized her from the paintings. Maybe. I don't know. It was raining. I couldn't be sure. There was a heavy mist. She was highlighted in copper and gold. It was an illusion; sleep deprivation; a concussion; my jumpy imagination. Harry? Maybe it was her."

Simon Wales was thrown off his style, not by the sighting of a dead woman but by telling Harry she was alive.

Harry drew back from the abyss. He spoke in a soft voice. "Of course it was her," he said. "I should have known. Perhaps I've known all along."

"Really," said Simon in affirmation, not disbelief.

"No dye job, no disguise," said Harry.

"Hair like burnished copper. Like Klimt."

"Of course. Why would she bother to hide it? There are only three other people in Toronto who'd recognize her. Miranda, Morgan, and Dimitri Sakarov. She's a master of blending in, in Vienna, at least. Maybe not so much, here."

Simon offered a grim smile.

"So it was suicide, not murder," said Harry, as he tried to gather the explosion of thoughts set off by Simon's announcement into a revised narrative.

"Assuming I saw her last night, there's a good chance it was neither." Simon gave his chin a sagacious rub.

Harry offered his own grim smile.

"If her death was a set-up," Simon noted, "wouldn't she have had to come up with a body?"

"It was decomposed, mutilated by river traffic. She was a cop. She'd know where to find a corpse if the occasion required. It took careful planning, of course. When we had lunch together at the market she would have already planted her dead doppelgänger in a storm sewer along the Wienfluss. It was a pleasant lunch, though."

Harry, wit is the refuge of wise men, sarcasm the refuge of fools.

Just scrambling to catch up, Sailor. By the time the Russian tortured her, her scheme was already in motion.

Corpses and cadavers aren't that easy to come by, you know, even for a cop.

A street person, an overdosed drug addict. Her friend Frau Detektiv Honsberger might have assisted. The little old lady with the blue rinse and silver tooth.

You don't think Honsberger is the gatekeeper, do you?

If she helped find Lena a superfluous corpse, she'd hardly qualify as her conscience. She was just a sympathetic ally.

Is, not was. Your friend is alive, unless Simon made a ghoulish mistake.

Simon doesn't make mistakes.

Simon had been watching Harry thinking.

"Harry," said Simon, "what's it all about? Why would she do this?"

"Death gives her impunity."

"Impunity?"

"It makes her lethal."

"She's here to kill Sakarov."

"Exactly, Simon. She's here for revenge."

Harry rose to his feet, restless. Simon stood up when Harry did and sat down again when Harry did. Harry had never had such a faithful companion. It was annoying.

"Simon," he said. "Go home, get some sleep."

Simon rose again, straightened his linen suit jacket and started to walk toward the door, then paused and turned around.

"She wasn't downstairs spying on us. She was waiting for the fat man, wasn't she? After we got through to her online, she knew he'd turn up here."

"And I'm sure he did. He was the lookout for Fearman's thugs."

"Those two work for Conrad Fearman?" Simon asked, not surprised.

"Our slovenly pot-smoking Russian acquaintance works alone. He uses other people's muscle to do his dirty work. And yes, I think Lena used me to find him last night."

"Why not just go to the King Willie?"

Harry got up and walked Simon to the door, which leaned clumsily in its shattered frame.

"Because you're not the only one who experiences revelations, Simon. Mine was false; Sakarov's wasn't."

"I'm sorry, but I have no idea what you're talking about."

"His indifference to Lena's death when we talked at Fearman's cottage told me he'd murdered her. It seemed reasonable given he'd already raped and tortured her. But he knew he hadn't killed her. And since I was no longer buying the suicide thing, he reasoned that she might still be alive. And if she were alive, he reasoned she might be out to kill him. And since he was in Toronto, he figured she might be here. So he went low profile and stayed away from the King William. But he couldn't afford to stay away from us, Simon. Not after he realized we'd connected with the dead woman who was no longer dead."

"Ah," said Simon as they stood in the hallway. He pressed the elevator button. The door opened immediately. The elevator hadn't moved since he'd arrived. In the short time Simon had been there, Harry's world had changed.

Lena was alive and Sakarov was a dead man but for the killing. After Simon's revelations, Harry both knew more, and understood less, about the dark world Lena inhabited.

15 FINDING LENA

AFTER SIMON LEFT, HARRY'S CONDO SEEMED ESPECIALLY empty. He was getting used to having the kid around. Simon was unnervingly prescient about Harry's needs, but his methods were frightening. Harry did not like having someone so close who understood what he didn't. He realized that was the modern condition. We're all surrounded by people who know more than we do. He should have been a Renaissance man, Erasmus or Leonardo; a lesser version, perhaps, but alive when it was still possible for one person to know everything.

You'd be long dead by now, Harry. Make the most of your faithful companion. He won't be around forever.

Sounds ominous.

Just realistic. One way or another, he'll move on.

I'll miss him.

Meanwhile, what about your red haired friend?

Lena or Joan?

The one who murdered her ex-fiancé. And is planning to kill again.

If Sakarov knows she's alive he'll do his damnedest to kill her first. It's all very Darwinian.

So find Sakarov and you'll find her.

Harry stepped out into the sunshine at street level feeling apprehensive. He made his way north through the grotty catacombs under the Gardiner Expressway and emerged into the daylight beside Union Station. Women were dressed in shorts and summer dresses. He realized it must still be the weekend.

At the King William the concierge informed him that Mr. Sakarov had not been available for several days. Harry gazed around the refurbished lobby. He wondered how much of the Edwardian decor was original and how much was reproduction. The fact that he couldn't tell affirmed his appreciation for what had been done. There was a lovely accessible decadence about the place that would have made the original Elisabeth Bök feel quite at home. Klimt might have designed the upholstery.

There was no security to speak of, so after checking the registry Harry slipped onto a service elevator unnoticed and got off on Sakarov's floor.

You would have drawn less attention using the regular elevator, Harry.

It was probably monitored. This way, if he's here he's in for a surprise.

And if he isn't?

But he is.

Gut feeling?

Logic.

Are you going to knock on the door and say you're here to save a life but you don't know whose?

He rang the buzzer under a brass nameplate with Dimitri Sakarov's name etched in cursive script, waited, and rang again.

The door opened and the fat Russian squinted against the light of the hallway and offered a cruel smile.

"You're here sooner than I expected. Come in."

Sakarov turned away from Harry and lumbered back into his apartment, which was emotionally austere in spite of the opulence. Expensive shiny things from different eras and cultures with little relationship to each other, set against darkly embossed wallpaper and lit with a strange plethora of light fixtures ranging from Tiffany to Waterford. Much like a higher-end antique shop, Harry thought, as he glanced around, looking for evidence of Lena's presence.

"She is here, yes," Sakarov announced. They both understood he meant Lena. "In the spare bedroom. You might say she accompanied me home from a chance encounter down by the harbour." The Russian turned to face Harry. He was holding a small semi-automatic that was dwarfed by his stubby fingers. He waved the gun. "She came willingly, of course. Now, please," he said with exaggerated courtesy. "Put your cell phone, your keys, and your gun on the table. And your wallet, of course."

Harry placed his wallet and keys on a burled walnut table cut down to coffee-table height. It might once have been in the foyer of a Jarvis Street mansion.

"Your gun?"

"I forgot to bring it."

"Cell?"

"Never carry one. Someone might call."

Sakarov moved close and patted Harry down then shrugged.

"You will please join her." He indicated with a wave of his pistol where he wanted Harry to go. "I did not think it would be so easy."

"It's not over yet," said Harry.

"Just about, my friend."

With Sakarov prodding him from behind, Harry stepped gingerly over an antique akstafa rug and moved down a corridor walled with expensive paintings and hangings until he came to the door at the end.

"Go in," said Sakarov.

Harry hesitated.

"She is alive."

Harry turned the knob and the door swung open into a room with the lights out and velvet drapes drawn tightly closed. From behind him, Sakarov spoke to the shadows.

"You see, Fräulein Strauss, your rescuer has arrived." He pushed Harry forward into the room. "I will leave you to become acquainted once again."

Sakarov locked the door from outside. Harry could hear breathing. He groped for a light switch, but failing to find one he felt for the draw-cord and opened the curtains. Sunlight flooded the room. Turning, he saw the bed was made up and empty. As his eyes adjusted, he discerned a figure cowering on the sofa with a blanket drawn around her.

"Lena," he said. He approached cautiously. "Lena, it's me."

"Harry?" Her voice trembled as she stirred and looked up. "Go away," she said.

"It isn't an option at the moment. What happened?"

"Help me sit up. Oh God, I hurt."

It must be bad, Harry. She's not a complainer.

He was relieved to have Karen in the room.

"Did Sakarov do this?"

What difference does it make?

"Those two men. He watched."

So their Tolstovian pacifism doesn't extend to women.

"At least you're alive," he said, realizing immediately how foolish that sounded.

"Small consolation," she whispered, as if she were sharing a secret.

Harry moved around the room turning on lamps. Damask wallpaper the colour of dried blood absorbed the illumination. The day was bright enough, but Harry wanted more light. There were no pictures, no mirrors, no objets d'art, little furniture, nothing that could be used as a weapon. It seemed to Harry he had stumbled into a medieval torture chamber, a room that was serenely elegant and yet reeked of brutality, where the Inquisition could foster the illusion of Godliness as it tormented the souls of the blessed and the damned.

"What can I do?" he asked, squatting down beside her.

"Nothing. I hurt."

Harry gingerly pulled the blanket back. At first he could see no wounds apart from the ones already inflicted by Sakarov in Vienna. Then he realized contours of her naked body were glistening as if lit from beneath the skin. A luminescence of smashed blood vessels indicated bruising from an upholstered weapon, perhaps small sandbags wrapped in silk to inflict maximum pain with minimal mess.

He drew the blanket up again and tucked the upper edge around her shoulders so that she seemed inside a cocoon of the finest wool. She settled back for a few minutes, actually relaxing enough to extend her body out of its fetal clinch. Then, while Harry was walking around, doing a reconnaissance of their elegant cell, she suddenly sat up. A few involuntary groans issued from her pursed lips, but she rose to her feet.

"Hand me my clothes, Harry."

Harry was dumbfounded. How much pain could this woman endure? He searched the room with his eyes. There was a small neat pile on the floor by the bed. Gregor or Oswaldo, true to their capacity for the unexpected, had folded her clothes after beating her. Or before.

For the second time, Harry helped Madalena Strauss ease her injured body into her clothing with a mixture of shyness and admiration. She said nothing as he helped her dress, but a few inarticulate sounds emerged as expressions of her extreme discomfort.

In underwear and a skirt but no blouse, she pulled away and went into the bathroom on her own. He could hear water splashing and then silence. After ten minutes she emerged. Her hair had somehow been teased into order by fingers run through its copper cascades. Or commanded into order. Her face, which had no bruises, looked radiant from being immersed in ice-cold tap water. Her lips without makeup glistened red and her green eyes flashed with wicked irony. She knew she looked ravishingly beautiful, like a painting by Klimt.

Of course.

"Now, Harry, we must focus on how to get out of here."

What about accounting for how we got here in the first place, sweetheart? Karen sounded like Lauren Bacall doing a Bogie impersonation.

Easy, Sailor, he cautioned. We'll deal with last things first. There's time for thinking later.

You've mastered the "thinking later" thing. You do know the guy in the other room, not to sound like a comic book narrator, is your mortal enemy, yes?

"Harry, are you okay?"

He peered into Lena's deep emerald eyes. Karen was right. He wanted answers. Before he could start with the questions, she asked, "Why are you here?"

"I figured you were," he said.

"And how did you know that?"

"My friend saw you last night."

"The boy in the suit. And he followed me?"

"No, he had other things on his mind. But this morning he told me he'd seen you. And, once I adjusted to your resurrection, I figured the only reason you'd be in Toronto was Sakarov. So the best place to start looking was here."

"But he seems to have caught you off-guard, Harry."

"And you."

"He was armed. I was not. I came quite prepared to kill him with my bare hands."

Harry balked, then realized it might actually be something her police training had prepared her to do, and he shuddered.

"I was happy to accompany him home. I was prepared to disarm him. A fat man with a small gun. It didn't seem daunting. However, I wasn't expecting his Russian friends. They were watching TV when we got here. I was outmanned, so to speak. They argued with Sakarov. I understand a little Russian. They told him no killing. They would rough me up, nothing more. They did their job, locked me in here, and left. And here you are."

Yes, Harry. Here you are. Now what?

Lena was obviously wondering the same thing.

Harry gazed at her with righteous anger. This woman, who had drawn him into her crusade to save children, had compromised the entire project for private revenge. She had turned her outrage into a blood feud, a vendetta, against one man. No matter how vicious Sakarov was, no matter what horrors he had personally inflicted on her, no matter how large his corpulent bulk loomed in the exploitation they were bent to expose, bringing him down on his own was not worth the compromise.

So now it's your project, Harry. You're annoyed it might have been compromised. But what about you? You're here.

When he and Simon determined that Rachel Damboch was the gatekeeper, Harry realized he should have pursued the old woman, cutting out Lena from the process, and he should have forgotten about the fat Russian. Sakarov was an unpleasant distraction. Lena had made herself expendable.

By turning up dead?

But she's not.

And you're angry.

Yes. No. She's my friend.

Harry, you've got a lot to learn about death.

"You're not dead yet," he said out loud, shifting his focus to Lena.

"But I did die, didn't I?" Lena responded as if he'd been speaking to her. "It was very authentic."

"It was," Harry agreed. "And the living and the dead, we both pursued Sakarov. And here we are; he's caught us."

She smiled a tight, crooked smile.

"Listen!" he said. "Do you hear something?"

Scuffling sounds, followed by silence. Then a pistol shot cracked the air. Harry and Madalena Strauss exchanged looks of startled alarm.

"Maybe it wasn't," he said.

"It was," she responded. "With no silencer."

He took her word for it. She was more an authority on guns than Harry. But neither of them knew who had fired the shot or at what.

After an interminable wait where the air hung thick in their chamber there was a tentative knock on the door.

It had to be Simon Wales. Only Simon could have figured out where they were. Simon had borrowed Harry's gun and bought ammunition. Simon had shot Sakarov.

The lock clicked and the door was pushed open deliberately, as if Simon was unsure of what macabre scene awaited on the other side.

"Simon, for God's sake, come in," said Harry.

It wasn't Simon. Joan DeBrusk stepped into the room. Her clothing was dishevelled. She looked frightened. She held out Sakarov's diminutive weapon, which appeared huge in her hands. Harry took it from her and handed it to Lena. He did not like guns, particularly ones still warm from being fired.

"Joan, where's Simon? Is Morgan with you?"

She shook her head in bewilderment and sat down with Harry's assistance on the edge of the bed. He left her with Lena and started into the corridor, then came back for the gun before walking out to the living room.

Sakarov wasn't dead as Harry expected. He was slumped on a large Victorian sofa, bleeding from a flesh wound in his side. Being a fat man, he was a difficult target to miss. Being a fat man, his vitals were difficult for a bullet to find.

"Hand me a cigarette, Harry."

Harry glanced down at a silver cigarette case on the burled walnut coffee table. Why not, he thought. He pocketed his keys and wallet, then removed a well-rolled cigarette from the case and handed it to Sakarov. He flicked on a butane tabletop lighter and the big Russian took a few deep drags. Despite his wound, he seemed to relax.

"Good," he said. "Thank you, Harry. A little marijuana, it helps. Given the circumstances, you are free to go. Take Fräulein Strauss with you. And my assassin, Miss DeBrusk. On your way out, would you ask the concierge to arrange for medical assistance. I'll need a doctor who makes discreet house calls. I think we all want this to play out as quietly as possible. Please, Harry, I seem to be bleeding on my sofa."

"Lucky for you it's only a slip cover," said Harry. "If you get up, avoid the antique carpets. Bleed on the hardwood."

"The akstafa, yes. It is tribal from Caucasian Mountains, like me."

"You're not really Russian," said Harry.

"Not that it matters at the moment, but I'm from Saskatchewan. Russian parents, intellectual bourgeois turned hardscrabble farmers."

"And you reinvented yourself after the USSR collapsed."

"In 1991, yes. Harry, please go now."

Harry went back to the room where he had been prisoner before Joan liberated them. The two women were sitting close, as if proximity offered mutual consolation—to Madalena for the brutality she had endured, to Joan for having shot a benefactor of the Zylberman Children's Centre.

Benefactor?

She's here; she would have known where to find him. But why? That's another question entirely.

Ask her, Harry. The fat bugger won't bleed to death. And if he does, it's poetic justice.

Nothing poetic about it if Joan DeBrusk gets charged with murder.

Keep an eye on Lena. She might take the opportunity to finish him off and let Joan take the blame.

It's not Lena's kill. And it won't be Joan's. She's in shock. I don't think she's ever shot anyone before.

Just Bambi's mother and the occasional moose.

Hunting and shooting are different.

Tell that to Bambi.

Joan helped Lena get into her blouse and buttoned it up for her. They went out through the living room and passed Sakarov smoking uncomfortably on the sofa without acknowledging his presence. It obviously wasn't the appropriate time for Lena to kill him; Joan didn't want to see what damage she'd done; Harry was determinedly indifferent to the man's level of discomfort.

Steadying Lena between them, Harry and Joan made their way down the elevator and into the airy opulence of the lobby. Suddenly, they were confronted by the immovable mass of Gregor and Oswaldo standing in front of them.

"Gentlemen," said Harry. "Mr. Sakarov needs your assistance upstairs."

Harry urged his small cohort to move directly ahead. The two Russian thugs looked puzzled but stepped aside and Harry, arm-in-arm with two striking redheads, moved with conspicuous grace across to the entry and, after awkward realignment, out the revolving door.

They flagged a taxi for the short distance to Harry's condo, to the annoyance of the driver who lost his place in the rank. Harry tipped him well to make up for it. They didn't talk until they reached the twenty-third floor and were inside his apartment. Only then did it occur to Harry that introductions were in order.

"You are the woman in the pictures," said Joan.

"No," Lena responded. She seemed alarmed that the connection had been made, then smiled as if flattered that it had.

"Why don't you two get yourselves cleaned up in there?" Harry pointed to his bedroom. "There are a few women's clothes in the cupboard."

Harry, you should never have brought them here. The clothes, not the women. They're morbid souvenirs. What they don't put on, throw out.

The bedroom curtains were drawn. Joan walked in, without turning on the lights. Lena followed her into the darkness, closing the door behind her.

16 **SIMON SAYS**

AFTER THE LIVES OF KAREN AND MATT AND LUCY WERE extinguished in the thundering waters of the Anishnabe River, after being distraught with grief and setting ablaze their lovingly restored stone farmhouse on the Sanctuary Line outside London, Harry collected the few things left in the world that reminded him of his family and gave them to the Salvation Army. There were Matt and Lucy's outgrown clothes in plastic boxes stored away in the old drive shed, there were bicycles and toys, Christmas ornaments and ice skates, odd and ends. He found nothing but grief in souvenirs of the dead.

And yet he kept a few things of Karen's. Her body was never recovered; her death wasn't absolute in the same way as Matt and Lucy's. There were two silk blouses, a professional suit and a cashmere sweater that had been at the dry cleaners following a conference where she gave the keynote address, along with a small leather zip bag of makeup she kept in her office. As Harry's anguish assimilated, they became dark reminders of her physical absence. She urged him to throw them out as demeaning talismans and he promised her he would, eventually.

He rustled around in the kitchen and put together a favourite recipe of udon soup made with fresh noodles, miso, tamari, porcini mushrooms, and baby bok choi. When the women came out of the bedroom he had the table by the window set with a steaming tureen and a plate of Ontario cheddar and biscuits. He poured a crisp cool sauvignon blanc for each of them.

Both women looked like they'd just returned from a spa. Their copper hair—Lena's shimmering in luxurious rebellion as she moved; Joan's casually controlled—was exactly the same colour and texture, yet made them look utterly different and each breathtakingly attractive.

He could almost forget the ordeal they had just been through.

Neither of them had used Karen's clothes or makeup.

They wouldn't, Harry. Not the makeup. And their clothes just needed brushing out. Joan shot Sakarov, she didn't wash her hands in his blood. And Lena was considerately relieved of her clothing before *she was beaten.*

They looked terrible, now they look great.

Such is the way of the world, Harry.

"Aren't you worried his men will come here?" Joan asked. "This soup is terrific."

"Thank you," said Harry. He was teaching himself to cook smart and appreciated the compliment. "It's not like they don't know the way. But no, I'd say they'll go back to Conrad Fearman and cast Sakarov to the wolves. They're thugs, not killers. They'll steer clear of him for now. They don't want to blow their permanent resident status. You realize Zakarov was intending to kill us until you showed up? It was a missed opportunity."

"Sorry," she said. "No, of course I'm not sorry. Who's Fearman?"

"Just a guy, a pervert with money."

"He is a bad man," said Lena. "Mr. Sakarov associates with very bad men. Conrad Fearman is one of them, one of the worst because he is rich and well respected. He keeps a series of so-called granddaughters on hand, before turning them out on the street when they reach puberty."

Joan turned ghastly pale, which highlighted her freckles, making her eerily like a gamine in a pre-Raphaelite painting.

That's what you thought your Viennese friend looked like, Harry. A painting by Rossetti. You're either a very casual connoisseur or exceptionally fickle.

Harry wanted to remind her that paintings were tropes for the viewer's own sensibility—they weren't real in themselves—but he let it go.

"Joan," said Lena, turning to the other woman, "exactly where do you fit in, in all of this?"

Lena took Joan's hesitancy for confusion and proceeded to clarify. "Who are you? How do you know Harry? How do you know the repulsive Mr. Sakarov? How did you end up coming to save us? And shooting him?"

Harry knew Joan was trying to assimilate what had happened to her, to process the weird and terrifying turn of events in her life. She seemed a genuinely open person, ingenuous to a fault, and he imagined she was uncertain how to respond to the woman who looked like paintings by

Klimt, who seemed unfazed by violence, and whom she seemed to have rescued from imminent death. Joan lived as an innocent in a fallen world, but this must have been more than she could grasp. Only an hour ago, they had been in a chamber of horrors. Now they were eating a light and elegant lunch, overlooking Toronto harbour filled with sailboats crisscrossing like insects prepared to take flight.

"Simon told me," she said in a resolute voice. Clearly she had simply been gathering her thoughts.

"Told you what?" Harry asked.

"I had been thinking about little Lucy. Our linguist Nguyen Wang tracked down someone in Greenwich Village who understands the Ket language."

"Ket!" Lena exclaimed. "Very unusual, yes. From the Yenisei River basin of Central Siberia."

"Amazing," said Harry.

"Yes," said Lena. "There are not many left."

"No," said Harry. "Amazing that you know about them."

"I know things, Harry. That is what makes me interesting. It also makes me dangerous. Especially for Dimitri Sakarov. So, Joan, how do you know Sakarov?"

"He is a donor at the children's centre where I do volunteer work."

"You volunteer. No one pays you to work."

"I am also a social worker. I am paid well."

"And how did you disarm him?"

"I shot him with his own gun."

"Yes, but how did you do that?"

"He tried to feel me up."

"I do not understand 'feel up.'"

"He groped her," said Harry. "He had us in custody. He was pleased with himself. Self-pleasure made him randy."

"Yes it did," said Joan. "He is a disgusting man. A terrible, terrible man. When he grabbed me, I struggled. His thing fell out."

"His 'thing?'" Lena seemed amused.

"His pistol. It fell. He is a very fat man. When he bent down to pick it up, I pushed him over. He tumbled, crash. He was spitting mad. He got onto his feet and came after me. I warned him. He kept coming."

"So you shot him."

"Yes, I did. I hope he won't die."

"No," said Lena. "He won't die. That would be too simple and he is a very complicated man in a very complex world. He will die soon, however. I will kill him. But he will not die now."

"You will kill him?"

"Yes."

"Okay, I can live with that," said Joan, blushing, apparently shocked at her wicked disclosure of approval. "What about the police? Will I be arrested?"

"No, he will not tell them."

"Why not?"

"It is complicated."

"Will you tell them?"

"No, I won't say a thing. Now, who is this Simon Wales to you?"

"He is an old friend."

This took Harry by surprise. Simon had intimated he had only encountered Joan in the course of his research. "You and Simon, really?"

"Just a minute," she said. "I'll lose my place. I'm telling you about Lucy. When we found the linguist in New York, she got Lucy to tell her on the phone about how she ended up here in your apartment."

"Stop, stop, stop," Lena muttered. "Explain to me about Lucy."

"The little girl with blue eyes, she was left here."

"As a warning," Harry explained.

"And it turned out Mr. Sakarov did it," Joan continued. "When Simon came to see me this morning, my goodness, was that only this morning, he told me Mr. Sakarov is a nasty, twisted, degenerate pervert. What Simon says seemed so improbable, I needed to confront Mr. Sakarov myself."

"To do what?" asked Lena, disarmed by Joan's courageous naïveté.

"To make him confess."

"And then you would give him absolution?"

"No," said Joan, her abrupt response suggesting that she hadn't thought through her next step. She was obviously distressed by the possibility of accepting money for the Centre from such a degenerate source.

"Okay," said Harry, pouring them each another glass of wine. "Joan, you and Simon? How do you know Simon Wales?"

"He came to the Centre as a volunteer when he was in his mid-teens. Really, he came as a kid who needed help but wouldn't admit it; he wouldn't tell us anything about himself. He was frighteningly brilliant.

We registered him in the system, but we couldn't force him to talk about himself. He studied art on his own and he was incredibly good with computers. We arranged for him to go to school and picked up his costs. I suppose Mr. Sakarov picked up his costs. But we could not track down his origins. He was a boy without a story."

"But that *is* his story," Harry observed.

"Yes," she said. "He wears invisibility like one of his linen suits. Things changed, though, after he met you, Harry. He discovered his parents were dead. They were from Oakville and they died in Vienna."

Harry sat back abruptly on his chair and stared at Lena. She was gazing out over the water and seemed not to have heard.

"You knew about this," he demanded, reaching out and placing his hand on her forearm to command her attention. "Lena?"

"I do not know Simon Wales."

"But his story, you knew it."

"That depends. Tell us more about what he told you, Joan." Lena Strauss was a homicide detective; she knew when to ask questions and when to listen.

"He totally opened up," Joan replied. "He wouldn't tell me his parents' names, but he said they were lawyers. He had plucked the name Wales from a map. He liked the name Simon; it means 'the listener.' His parents had called him Peter. He told me they had adopted him when he was a toddler. A private adoption. They bought him. When he was old enough, he became a day student at Ridley College. He said he was originally from Romania on the Black Sea. He said they paid a lot for him because he was very smart and could talk before he was a year old. In his teens he mastered the internet. He discovered his birth mother's identity. He told me she was a virgin who had been raped by a Russian sex tourist, kept in confinement during her pregnancy, and turned out on the streets after she stopped nursing him. When Simon confronted his adoptive Canadian parents about his background, they disowned him and turned him out. They went back to their contact in Vienna for a replacement. That's where they died. I believe he discovered you while doing research on himself, Harry."

You didn't find him, Harry. He found you. You just provided the opportunity with your Salander advertisement.

"I assume their contact person was Dimitri Sakarov," Harry observed. "Or at least Sakarov made the arrangements. They jumped from his balcony in the Kressler Hotel with a young boy from Albania."

He was reviewing the facts in his mind but speaking out loud. Joan realized she had ventured into something the other two understood more than she did. She stopped talking. There was an awkward silence.

Harry got up and made three Nespressos. Strong. He served them without offering milk or sugar. Then he turned to Madalena Strauss.

"You met with Doris and Melvin Findlay the morning they died. What happened?"

"We talked." She grimaced from her bruises as she shifted in her chair to peer directly into his eyes. "I told them their new little boy was not an orphan. His father was a Russian pimp who murdered the mother and sold the boy and his infant sister for drug money. They were disgusted, Harry. They were sickened to find their child had come from such a sordid background. They had been promised an abandoned love-child from a good family."

"And you threatened to expose them. Don't you see, Lena? That's the impact of going public."

"I made no threats. I simply told them what I knew. They met with Sakarov in his room at the Kressler later the same day. Either by threat or force, he compelled them to jump."

"Compelled?" Harry said. "You pushed them to the limit. They were desperate."

"Sakarov pushed them."

"Their lives were destroyed. They took the boy with them."

"Parents kill children when their own lives seem hopeless; you'd be surprised how often it happens."

"They weren't his parents."

"But they were desperate."

"And you knew all along they jumped from Sakarov's balcony, not the roof."

"I stayed out of it, Harry It was not time to go public. Whatever happened, it was still Sakarov's show."

"And my being there and watching them fall, that was a nasty coincidence?"

"You were not there by accident. You happened to be looking out your window at just the right time."

"The wrong time."

"Of course."

"And by then you had a submerged corpse on hand, ready to cut free as a floater."

Joan DeBrusk emitted an involuntary gagging sound but said nothing.

"Details, Harry. It does not matter."

"I have said this before, Madalena. You are a very scary person."

"I shall take that as a compliment."

"That's not how it was intended."

A loud crashing noise shattered the air. All three took sharp intakes of breath. Another crash, and another, then swearing, then Simon Wales lurched into the room. He was dishevelled, his dark linen suit rumpled, his hair strangely askew. He was clutching his abdomen. There was a trickle of blood oozing between his fingers.

"Sorry about the door." Simon's pale complexion was ashen grey. He shuffled to keep his balance as Harry rushed to support him. "Should get it fixed." He tried to focus on Harry's guests. "Joan," he nodded. "Ms. Strauss. Striking resemblance." He glanced at the Klimts. "Elisabeth Bök."

Harry eased Simon onto the sofa and gently revealed Simon's wound.

Joan scurried into the bathroom. She returned with a damp washcloth and a white hand towel which she folded into a rectangle. She directed Harry to remove Simon's jacket and to undo the necktie that Simon had used to bind a wadded handkerchief against the lacerations in his gut. She cleaned around the wound, which seemed flensed on the surface like dead meat, and pressed the towel into him. Slowly the white towel revealed veins of red, then gradually turned scarlet as the blood from deep inside his abdomen soaked through.

"Thank you," Simon muttered with a grimace that passed for a smile. "It was a bad day."

"It's not over," said Harry, shifting Joan's drenched towel aside with a clean one. "Call 911."

Joan wiped her hands on a dish cloth and reached for the phone.

Lena had not moved from the table. She observed keenly but displayed no emotion.

"No," Simon commanded with a quavering voice.

"Make the call," said Harry.

"My decision, Harry," Simon declared.

"Simon." Harry felt a tremendous surge of affection for his wounded protégé.

"S'okay," said Simon.

"What happened?" Harry took hold of Simon's hand. "Was it Sakarov?"

Simon suddenly shifted on the sofa and pushed Harry back so he could see into his eyes. His voice came from deep inside as he struggled against the pain.

"My bag," he said. "Please."

Harry nodded to Joan and she went out into the hall and retrieved Simon's shoulder bag by the open doorway. The door was lying flat on the floor.

"New computer," said Simon. The words were distinct but uttering them drained him. He slumped back.

Joan opened his bag and pulled out a Mac Air in pristine condition.

Simon reached for it and Joan slid into place beside him to hold a fresh towel against his gut. Harry helped him open the computer and boot up, then positioned Simon's fingers on the keyboard. Harry realized this would be easier for him than speaking.

Simon settled against Joan as she watched the new towel grow heavy with a fresh flow of blood. Harry steadied the Mac. Simon closed his eyes, but his eyelids flickered as he seemed to be searching inside his skull and he began to type. His fingers raced across the keys with lives of their own, delivering their letter-perfect message.

Harry, I went to the King Willie to find you. I was worried. For Joan too. I was afraid she'd confront Sakarov by herself. S. was alone, shot, sprawled on the sofa. He asked for a drink and I got him a tumbler of water. He grabbed my arm, pulled me off balance, smashed the water glass on the table, plunged the jagged end into my gut, twisted deep, and smirked before he passed out from the effort. I left and took a taxi here. The driver noticed blood and took off before I could pay.

Joan started reciting the 23rd Psalm, falling back on her bush Catholic reserves.

"For God's sake, Joan. Not now." Simon's eyes flashed open. Despite the urgency, his voice seemed to come from a long way off.

Joan fell silent.

Lena finally got up and walked over. She squatted beside the sofa and lifted the blood-drenched towel away, then pressed it back against Simon's body.

"It is very bad inside," she said, smiling sweetly at Simon to confirm what he already knew.

Simon's eyes closed again and his blind fingers groped for the keyboard, then he began to type, this time with slow deliberation.

Joan, I liked being Simon Wales. You'll miss me, Harry. I like that. Cremation, please scatter me free. Thank you for everything. It has been interesting.

Simon squeezed Harry's hand and drew in a slow deep breath. His eyes opened and he gazed into Harry's eyes and tried to smile. The pain seemed to have left his face and a beatific calm settled over his boyish features. His eyes fluttered as he glanced in the direction of the Klimts, then he closed them deliberately.

He lay ghastly still for a minute, then shuddered briefly, and Harry could feel through his hand the life going out of Simon Wales as he quietly died.

17 **FORTY-EIGHT HOURS**

THREE DAYS AFTER SIMON'S DEATH, HARRY GATHERED A small group of their mutual friends for a dinner at Via Veneto on Yonge Street. Joan DeBrusk and Madalena Strauss flanked Harry on one side of the table, facing a wall mirror set between fake Corinthian columns, in front of which sat Miranda Quinn, David Morgan, and two volunteers from the Zylberman Children's Centre. Harry had pre-ordered a heaping platter of linguini carbonara for seven p.m., along with a trough of Caesar salad and four bottles of Brunello.

Harry arrived first with Joan and Lena. The two women had become unlikely friends in the last few days. While Lena stayed with Harry (he slept on the sofa), she spent most of her time with Joan. Harry had been occupied with making arrangements for Simon's cremation and the dispersal of his ashes from a spit of land near the Eastern Gap, with only the three of them in attendance. He would have looked after Simon's personal effects, but no one knew where he lived.

Morgan and Miranda arrived together. Morgan did a wry double take when he recognized Lena.

"Harry hadn't told me you're alive again," he declared.

Miranda paled when she saw Lena and then smiled.

"You look quite good," she said.

"For a dead woman, yes. Thank you."

"I attended your funeral."

"Again, thank you."

"At great effort and expense."

"But Vienna is lovely in the summer, don't you agree?"

"Lovely. Especially the *Vereinigung Bildender Künstler Österreichs.*"

"Your German is not so good. The Secession Building, yes. I wonder, I hope, Miranda, I'd prefer to remain dead, if you don't mind."

"I'm sure you have your reasons. I had expected to meet someone called Elizabeth Book. That's how the investigating officers looking into Simon's death identified you. An innocent bystander, a friend of Miss DeBrusk's."

"It is a family name."

"Good," said Miranda. "We'll leave it at that."

The volunteers from the Children's Centre were no more confused by the incomprehensible conversation going over their heads than by any other aspect of Simon's passing. They were there because they had liked him and wanted to share the sadness.

Morgan and Joan greeted each other with warm cordiality. Their cursory kiss on both cheeks seemed nothing more than an amiable display of affection between friends with a full generation between them. Miranda nodded in Joan's direction without smiling. It occurred to Harry that those other rumours, dating back to when Miranda and Morgan were partners, might actually be true.

There was minimal small talk as they ate. No one mentioned Simon until after the table was cleared, when the proprietor with his pencil-thin moustache and bushy eyebrows produced a bottle of grappa, before warm zabaglione and steaming hot coffee were served.

Harry toasted Simon. He felt uncomfortable. Simon would not have wanted to be toasted. It was not his style and Simon had style. That's how he had re-invented himself, a young man with style. Peter who called himself Simon would have preferred an earnest discussion about anything other than himself. He had consciously designed his life to be solitary and the world seemed awesomely undiminished by his absence. No one wanted to talk about him. Only Harry and Joan mourned him. None had stories to share. He was on their minds. And perhaps that, thought Harry, was enough.

The two volunteers left before the zabaglione was served. Morgan left before the espresso. Harry regarded himself in the mirror, seated between two women with copper red hair. Miranda, in front of the mirror, smiled as if she knew what he was thinking and pushed a loop of her own hair away from her face. Auburn, not copper, highlighted with grey. His own had been blonde and turned prematurely white after the accident, curiously showing a scattering of silver that falsely suggested it had once been dark, even black.

You're developing a hair fetish, Harry.

Ah, he thought, I'm glad you're here. It wouldn't be a wake without you.

The three women and Harry sipped their coffees in silence. For Miranda this was a brief and solemn interlude, for Joan a way of sharing her sorrow. If Harry had intended their dinner to be a celebration, Simon's carefully maintained isolation made it difficult. For Madalena, her grief was not for a young man with whom she had only a fleeting acquaintance but for all the damaged children his brief sad life represented.

Simon's death had been deemed first-degree murder, but no charges were laid. Although Dimitri Sakarov's name came up, it seemed he had been staying in Muskoka at the time as the guest of a distinguished citizen by the name of Fearman. The antique akstafa in his condo was missing, according to Morgan, who also informed Harry there was no slip cover on Sakarov's sofa.

Morgan had driven to the Port Carling cottage to interview Sakarov. The big man had been affable and obtuse. Suffering from gout, he declared, accounting for his invalid status on a sturdy chaise longue on the cottage verandah. Sakarov's alibi pleased Joan. She could not be held accountable for shooting him if he hadn't been shot.

No one offered an alternative explanation for Simon's death. He had apparently appeared at Harry's condo and bled out before he could account for what happened. The case would remain open, Miranda explained. He was a well-dressed street kid, but with no witnesses, no forensic evidence, and no plausible alterative scenarios, it was likely to remain unresolved.

Neither Lena nor Harry had any desire to pursue the matter of their confinement at the King William. The police accepted Harry's explanation that his door had been battered down during a failed break-in attempt and he gave the names of the investigating officers. He was told to get it fixed and have his security system upgraded.

The bruises on Simon's neck had clearly preceded being gutted by a shattered drinking glass and were acknowledged in the police report as evidence of an earlier altercation. They thought perhaps he'd been assaulted in a bar-room brawl. Simon! Neither Joan nor Harry could tell the authorities much about him. They didn't know his real name. They said nothing about his infancy on the Black Sea, nor about his being a Findlay from Oakville. When he died he was Simon Wales.

Over the next few days Harry got used to seeing Madalena Strauss wandering around his condo in casual dishabille. Her sexuality was enhanced by the erotic hauteur of her great-grandmother's pictures on the wall, but Harry felt certain the intimacy was not an invitation. She made no advances toward him and he assumed none toward her. They settled into a comfortable arrangement. Sometimes he talked to her about Simon, who had been an incomprehensible phenomenon in his life—he had appeared fully formed. For a brief time he had been Harry's closest living friend. Then he ceased to exist. From *being* he disappeared into Heidegger's *nothingness.*

Talk of Heidegger made Lena physically ill. If it was meaninglessness he wanted to discuss, she insisted they look to Sartre. At least he wasn't a Nazi. She quoted Schopenhauer. "We can regard our life as a uselessly disturbing episode in the blissful repose of nothingness." Sometimes she quoted Nietzsche. You can always fall back on Nietzsche, she said, for pointlessness and dread. Simon's death was usually the agent of their discourse that took Harry back to the days, the life, before the incident on the Anishnabe when everything changed. Often, Simon got swallowed up in their talk. Esoteric words subsumed the reality that he had ever been. These exchanges, more than existential despair, made Harry uneasy. Then, especially, he wanted to hold this strange woman in his arms. But he didn't."

And then one day, after about two weeks, she disappeared.

He had been out shopping for a few groceries and when he returned she was gone. Her small travelling case was missing. The only evidence that she had been there was the lingering indefinable feminine scent that reminded him of Karen. And he discovered she had left him a magnum of Dom Pérignon in the fridge. And the Klimts on the wall.

In retrospect, he realized, they had spoken very little. She was recuperating from her bruises and wounds. She refused to discuss her files, telling him they would talk, all in good time. They watched television together, ate their meals together, mostly prepared by Harry, and took long quiet walks along the waterfront in the early evenings. Sometimes Joan dropped in and the three of them chatted about nothing. They read a lot, occasionally aloud to each other. They might have been a married couple in their sixties, not two strangers decades younger who were bound by the suppression of terrible secrets.

Toward the end of August, when the nights were getting cooler, Harry spent a lot of time on his balcony in the evenings, letting the chill of the onshore breeze sweep over him while he drank coffee or cognac and tried not to think.

Karen had been largely absent during Lena's stay and after she'd gone Karen remained deep inside his mind, hardly a presence at all. He needed his solitude and she left him to it.

He wasn't worried about Lena. Madalena Strauss could look after herself. She would do what she had to do. As far as he was concerned, he had been removed from the equation. He would enjoy the Klimts. Another case would come along. He was prepared to move on. In spite of explosive revelations that might come from her in the future, Lena was history.

Sometimes the past is prologue; sometimes it is simply the past.

Quoth the raven.

Ah, the voice of doom and gloom. Where have you been, Sailor?

You had other distractions.

Which made me realize how much I missed you.

No, Harry. You're getting used to it.

Never.

You figure she's returned to Vienna?

Back to Austria, for sure. Probably not Vienna. Not if she planned to stay dead.

It's a big city.

Not old Vienna, not with flaming red hair.

She'll dye it.

Never, Karen. That would be like erasing her identity. It's her genetic connection with the women of her past.

Or a fetish. Do you think Sakarov will go after her?

He knows she wants him dead. It's a Mexican standoff. Back to where they were before I came into the picture.

You miss her, don't you?

Of course.

You've always got Joan.

Much too young. Too sweet.

She wasn't too young for David Morgan and he's ten years older than you.

Apparently. But I'm not looking.

Maybe you should be.

Karen, go away.

And strangely, she went.

Harry walked out onto the balcony, swirling his cognac and drinking in its generous aroma while his eyes scanned the distant horizon where Lake Ontario merged with the late evening sky.

Being alone suited him at the moment.

He sipped his cognac.

Beethoven's Fifth struck up in the room behind him.

Harry didn't hear music as anything other than the arbitrary arrangement of noise. He could never figure out what moved others to ecstasy or despair that for him seemed random and vaguely intrusive. To sceptics, who insisted he just needed proper training, he used the analogy of trying to make a person who was blind since birth imagine the colour purple. But he insistent opening of Beethoven's Fifth was one of the few chords of music he recognized. It was his default ringtone.

He picked up:

"Harry? Is that you?"

"It must be. What can I do for you, Morgan?"

"Have either of you seen Joan?"

"Lena's not here. She left a week ago. And no, I haven't seen Joan."

"She's not in her apartment. She didn't report for work at Social Services and she hasn't turned up at the Children's Centre."

"How long?"

"Two days. She's disappeared."

"If she turns up I'll give you a call."

"You miss the point, Harry. I want to hire you."

"You're kidding." Silence. "Sorry, you're serious."

"I think she might be in trouble. I checked out your big Russian friend at the King William. He wasn't there. He's the only enemy she has in the world and that's just because, rumour has it, she shot him. She's a sweet kid, Harry. That's her fatal flaw. She's too nice. To everyone."

"Is that what happened with your romance?"

"What the hell are you talking about?"

"If you've hired me, I get to ask questions."

"Mind your own fucking business."

Harry had never heard Morgan swear. He had never even heard of an instance where Morgan was said to have sworn. He smiled to himself and mumbled into the phone a few expletives about swearing.

"That's okay," Morgan said. He seemed flustered.

"I wasn't apologizing. Your relationship actually is my business—unless I've already been fired."

"It didn't last. I had lived a full lifetime before she was born. She told me it didn't matter. That's when I knew we were wrong for each other. It didn't matter to her. It mattered to me."

"How so?"

"I remembered the moon landing. She read about it in books. I was just little, but I remembered Neil Armstrong screwing up his lines. That confirmed he was like the rest of us and that made him a hero. By the time she came along he was mythic. He'd already become as unreal as Columbus. I remembered the Manson murders that same summer. She thought Manson was a gender-baffled rock star. And so on. There was a fundamental gap in our cultural experience. That's more than you want to know, right?"

"Just enough. I'll get onto it in the morning. Does she have a passport?"

"Yeah, we went diving in Bonaire last year."

"One last question. Why me? You're a cop."

"That's why. Because I'm a cop. I just want to know she's okay. She lives in a very sordid world, Harry."

"Dealing with messed up kids?"

"Yeah."

"I'll let you know as soon as I have something. You relax. I'm sure she's okay."

"I'm not. I won't. Call me." Morgan clicked off.

Well then there now.

Yeah. Glad you're back.

What have we got?

Hard to say. He's worried.

She couldn't have gone with your friend from Vienna, could she?

Not together. Morgan would have noticed if Joan had been away for a week.

He keeps a pretty close eye on her.

The niceness that ended their romance puts her in jeopardy in a fallen world. He's concerned for a nice friend.

Don't kid yourself, Harry.

Maybe there's a bit of residual longing.

The way you love me.

Karen, don't.

Only she's alive, Harry.

Let's hope so.

Harry slept well. He wasn't worried about Joan DeBrusk. She was an incidental participant in the heinous affairs of Dimitri Sakarov and even less compromised than himself by the poisonous relationship between Madalena Strauss and the Russian from rural Saskatchewan. She probably wanted to be alone for a while. Her innocence had been tainted and she needed time to re-purify.

He wakened to Billy Joel's song from the seventies running through his head: "Only the Good Die Young." He couldn't capture the music, of course, and the irony evaded him. He noticed an unusual odour hanging in the air.

He smelled pot and tobacco. Sakarov had let himself in.

God, Harry. Why didn't you get deadbolts installed when they repaired the door?

I did, I forgot to use them.

Nobody seems to knock anymore.

Or bother to buzz from the lobby!

You might as well get dressed. He'll wait. Lord knows how long he's been out there.

Harry got dressed and even took time to shave, then he walked out into the living room. Sakarov was sitting in the big easy chair.

"Good morning, Harry."

Harry made himself a cup of Nespresso. He didn't offer one to his visitor.

"Now, Harry, sit down. You will be pleased to see I have recovered quite nicely. So, we need to talk about your friend, Miss DeBrusk. She is a lovely young woman. I hope she does not worry too much about shooting me. It was a misunderstanding."

"What do you want?" Harry demanded.

"It is what *you* want that brings me here."

"Really? What do I want?"

"Miss Joan DeBrusk. She has disappeared," said Sakarov.

"Has she?"

"You know that, of course. Her friend Detective Sergeant Morgan is looking for her. I imagine he has hired you to find her for him. Yes?"

"I'm listening."

"Good. She has gone to Austria, I believe."

"You kidnapped her?"

"Oh no, Harry. She kidnapped herself."

Harry refused to respond.

"She has gone to Vienna. She will die in exactly two days. It will be a merciful death. Torture would serve no purpose."

Harry refused to bite, although his guts were churning. He waited.

"Unless," said Sakarov. "Of course, there is an *unless*. You see, I have an advantage over people like you and Miss DeBrusk. I am a man quite comfortable with the consequences of bad behaviour. All I had to do was tell the young lady her charity centre would be incinerated with children inside if she did not go to Vienna. Or if she informed Detective Morgan of where she would be. And just like that she is there! Now, I must direct you to do the same thing."

"You have a limited imagination. Killing innocent kids is the same threat you used with Madalena."

"I do not need imagination, Harry. You know about the nursery school in the 13th District? That is good. You will track down Madalena Strauss for me, Harry. You have forty-eight hours. If you do, Miss DeBrusk will be free to come home. If not, she dies."

"Why send Joan to Vienna if you're threatening her children here?"

"Because that is where you will start looking for Fräulein Strauss. That is where Miss DeBrusk is far from her friends in the Toronto Police Service. Vienna is a beautiful city in case she gets bored while waiting for her expiration date to fall due. She can visit the museums and shop in the Graben."

"Does she know there's a time limit on her life?"

"We all have time limits, Harry. Hers is predetermined and depends on the efficiency of a mutual acquaintance—that would be you." Harry was struck by how his Russian accent kept creeping into his voice although his syntax was North American. "No, she does not know. There was no point in making the situation more complex than it is. She has enough to worry about."

"And what makes you think I'll exchange Lena's life for Joan DeBrusk's?"

"You have no alternative. Trust me, Harry. If Fräulein Strauss survives, Miss DeBrusk and her children at the Zylberman Centre will die. On the other hand, if we kill Fräulein Strauss, the children in Hietzing will survive as will Miss DeBrusk and her children here. We will all be happy."

"Except, of course, Madalena Strauss, who will be dead."

"She is already dead, Harry."

"You are a miserable scum-sucking tub of guts."

"Ah, Harry. You are channelling Marlon Brando. I am flattered. But do not let things get personal. Our differences are purely business; we should keep it that way."

"I don't kill people."

"Really? I have heard otherwise." He paused, apparently to let the ironic cruelty sink in. "No matter. You find her for me, and I will kill her."

"Why didn't you kill her when you had the chance?"

"When was that?"

"In her apartment on Marchettigrasse."

"You are very naïve, Harry. I have never been to her apartment."

"I witnessed the damage you inflicted firsthand."

"Well then, there is no telling you otherwise. I had no reason to kill her. When she arranged her own death in order to assassinate me, then it became personal. Everything changed."

"You were not her primary target. She wanted her files released."

"She came to kill me at the King William."

"How? You had the gun."

"No, she had the gun."

"I beg your pardon?"

"It was her gun. The weapon I used to subdue you, Harry. The weapon Miss DeBrusk used to attack me. It belongs to Madalena Strauss. You did not know that? I am surprised."

"Where would she get a gun in Toronto?"

"Where would she get a corpse in Vienna? She is a resourceful woman. She lost her gun when my associates, I suppose you would say, rescued me. It was hers. Do not trust her, my friend."

"We are not friends."

"Perhaps you are right. Do you know she grew up in an institution for mental defectives? She does not think like other people."

"It was a school for autistic children."

"So you know things about her. Good. You will find her for me. You have forty-eight hours. That is two days. That should be enough. You had better get moving. It is already past noon in Vienna."

Harry rose from his chair and walked into the kitchen. He made himself another coffee, moving up in strength from Roma to Arpeggio. He returned to the sofa, setting his cup gingerly on the table, still rickety after Simon collapsed it.

"I admire your paintings, Harry. They are excellent likenesses of Fräulein Strauss. In the manner of Gustav Klimt but not so good, I think. Well, to business. We had an arrangement, you and I. You were to keep me informed of her activities. You did not do a good job, but now you will find her, yes? You have two days. Otherwise, Miss DeBrusk will be exterminated. Perhaps raped. Perhaps not. We shall see."

18 FAST TRAIN TO SALZBURG

THE QUICKEST ROUTE TO VIENNA WAS A DAYTIME FLIGHT through Frankfurt. Waiting at Pearson for take-off, Harry could measure the wasted time by the thudding of his heartbeat. He had decided not to tell Morgan what was happening. The last thing he needed was an enraged cop as a sidekick. When he reached Frankfurt, he felt icily calm. The terminal stank of stale tobacco smoke. He was relieved the stopover was brief. In Vienna he checked into the Kressler Hotel. The night concierge, Heinz Ichstadt, recognized him and looked flustered. Harry ignored him. It was Friday evening. He had thirty-six hours to go.

He grabbed a quick bite along the Kartner Strasse pedestrian walk and went directly to the Polizei Zentralkommando on Herrengasse. Frau Detektiv Honsberger was on duty. Her blue hair had been modified to a purple that in the artificial light of the police station looked like a potpourri of dried crocus petals. Her silver tooth gleamed as she explained to Harry that Madalena was dead.

"Well, if she wasn't, where would she be?"

"With Elvis Presley, I expect."

"Frau Honsberger, this is extremely important. Please help me."

"Mr. Lindstrom, I was the person who identified her mutilated corpse. Even Pope Retzinger—no, it is Pope Francis now—he could not bring Madalena back to us. The ashes have been scattered."

"Where?"

"This is a windy country; you will never find them."

Harry explained that he did not want to collect Lena's ashes. He just wanted to know where she had arranged to have them dispersed.

"I sent them to a school in Hinterbrühl."

"Good, good, do you have a name?"

"Honsberger, yes."

"No," he said. "Who did you send her ashes to in Hinterbrühl?"

"To a woman, let me see, her name is written down." Frau Honsberger rummaged through slips of yellow paper piled neatly in the top drawer of her desk, found the one she was looking for, smoothed it on the desktop to make its inscription legible, and copied the name on a fresh yellow slip that she slid across to Harry.

The name was so precisely printed it looked like the work of a machine.

"Rachel Damboch. Are you sure?"

"Fräulein Strauss left instructions. I do not think the lady, this Rachel Damboch, is at the school. She is in retirement, I think perhaps into the country near Salzburg. Perhaps it is to Hallstatt she went. The Kinderdorf in Hinterbrühl, they will have her address. The package was to be sent forward. You must write down the school. Here. I shall do that."

She took the yellow slip from Harry and wrote down the rest of the information.

"There, that is all I know about where she is buried, yes. Do we say *buried* for ashes? Where she is disposed, yes. There was nothing to bury. She is disposed."

"Thank you," said Harry, rising to his feet. Salzburg, then. Hinterbrühl and possibly Hallstatt. "*Danke schön*, Frau Honsberger."

Harry stopped at the Café Central for a quick *mélange.* Its rich bitter genius was wasted on him in the rush. He didn't take time for *kaiserschmarrn.* Then he cut over to Stephansdom, forced himself to slow down, and ambled along the pedestrian walkway, trying to sort out his next move. He'd need sleep before going to Salzburg. If he found Rachel Damboch he was convinced he'd find Madalena Strauss.

But do you really want to find her, Harry?

Do I have a choice?

You can't just turn her over to Sakarov?

If I don't, kids die. Most likely, I die. And Joan too, I assume.

It would be a matter of good housekeeping for Sakarov.

He breathed deeply and exhaled audibly.

Between rocks and hard places, Harry, devils and the deep blue sea. Let's think.

As he walked slowly back to the Kressler, Harry abandoned emotive clichés and resorted to pure logic, which left him grasping at nothing.

He bought a hot doughnut confection from a street vendor, but a single bite flooded his mouth with sugar, salt, and grease. He dumped the remainder in a trash bin and wiped his fingers on the insides of his pants pockets.

That's disgusting.

I know.

There's always a third option, Harry. When the choice is impossible, choose neither!

I can hardly walk away.

There's a fourth. Choose both.

He was searching for the wrong person! He needed to track down Joan first then keep her close while he found Lena.

What about the children?

Until Sakarov finds Lena, they're safe.

He regretted the mouthful of doughnut and the late evening coffee. He went into a bar at the Kressler and asked for a double cognac, XO. He was exhausted and fine brandy was the best route to a good sleep. He remembered Madalena had ordered single malt scotch. Cognac was more subtle, but she was mercurial and elusive, not subtle. He had no idea what time it was back in Toronto. It didn't matter. He had thirty-three hours to go.

From his hotel room, he could see the reflection of the Kressler in the sheer façade of the building opposite. He turned out his lights and traced with his eyes a deliberate pattern until he found the balcony where the Findlays had jumped to their deaths, no doubt feeling righteous to the end. That would have been Sakarov's room, next door to the one Harry had occupied. But the Findlays were staying at the Imperial. Lena had met them there, where she informed them she would make their private transgressions a public scandal. In speaking on the child's behalf she condemned him to death.

Joan would be at the Imperial. Sakarov would have sent her there on his personal account. He would have conceived of no reason to hide her or forcibly hold her captive. He was indifferent to Harry finding her. Harry had to find Lena. His moral commitment would keep him under control.

Harry lost himself in the shimmering dimensions of the window glass—seeing the boy, seeing himself, seeing the lights of Vienna, and seeing the shadowy room behind him. For a brief and vivid moment, Simon Wales appeared in the mêlée of images, as real as if his ghost had replaced Harry's own reflection. Harry turned away and at that moment consigned Simon to the same dark regions of his psyche where Matt and Lucy resided—ageless and immutable beyond thought or grief or memory. Simon was simply a part of him, totally absorbed.

In the morning, after a rough night and with twenty-four hours to go, Harry logged onto the Western University mainframe. He had never cancelled his Huron College account and as a Western affiliate it provided access to university files around the world. What he needed was entry into the shadowy stacks of the Universität Wien, not more than a short ride on a Ringstrasse trolley from his hotel.

He tracked down Rachel Damboch. He found her manuscripts. They were itemized but had not been scanned into the system. Signing as Professor Harry Lindstrom, Department of Philosophy, Huron College University, London, Ontario, he sought out an archivist by email and explained that he would shortly be arriving Austria to do research and would need permission to view the Damboch papers. Did Universität Wien have an address where Frau Damboch could be reached?

He received a cordial response immediately from an assistant librarian telling him Rachel Damdoch's last known address was in care of a school in Hinterbrühl. The librarian told him she was familiar with Harry's work and assured him the university would be most accommodating when he arrived in Vienna. She also informed him that, before her employment at the library, she had worked on early iron-age funeral rites. If she could be of any assistance, she would be happy to help.

She attached a copy of a paper she had recently published in an American academic journal. It was entitled "From Bronze Age to Iron, Shifting Burial Practices through Central Europe, from 1000 to 500 BCE." She didn't question the authenticity of Harry's unusual non-institutional email address: *lindstromalone.com.*

This was the first time Harry had actively participated in academia since the accident. It was a nostalgic reminder of how intimate and expansive that world had been, for both Karen and himself, until it was suddenly swallowed up in a tumult of water and razed in a fiery inferno.

He felt good as he made his way to the Imperial. He would take Joan with him to Hinterbrühl. Once he located Rachel Damboch, he would find Lena. And then, and then. He became distracted as he approached the hotel, an imposing stately edifice just past the Staatsoper across the Ringstrasse. He was being followed. Stopping to gaze into the reflection in the angled window of a high-end clothing store, he could see who it was. He was dismayed but not surprised.

Dimitri Sakarov paused to look into another shop window. He didn't seem to care if he was seen. Perhaps he preferred it that way.

But clearly he had no desire to connect. It was more threatening just to be there, to be watching.

Harry found Joan DeBrusk in a comfortable suite, registered under her own name. She was virtually a prisoner of fear. No one was guarding her. She was alarmed to see Harry. Vienna was a city of strangers and, despite the pleasantness of the hotel staff, reassuringly remote. A familiar face could only mean trouble.

"Did Sakarov tell you why you're here, Joan?"

"No." Her face was flushed with colour. "But he gave me no option."

"I know." He tried to sound reassuring.

"People will miss me. I didn't show up for work. The Centre will miss me. I don't mean to whine, but I would much rather be home."

"Joan, have you any idea where Lena is?"

"Isn't she still in Toronto?"

Lena hadn't let Joan know when she slipped away. Joan had assumed Lena wanted privacy and not tried to reach her.

He explained his mission and told Joan to pack nothing more than she could carry in her purse, which conveniently was a large Roots bag with lots of pockets. She resisted.

"Where are you going?" You, not we, she said.

"Salzburg. A school in Hinterbrühl. We're looking for Rachel Damboch, the woman who raised her."

"It is too dangerous to leave," she said. "Mr. Sakarov told me I am being watched. If I do not do what he says, they will set fire to the Zylberman Centre. He told me they will lock the doors from outside and kill children, Harry; he will burn them to death. He did not seem angry that I had shot him. I had better stay here unless he allows me to go."

"Joan, don't you understand?"

"Yes, you must find Lena, of course. But..." But there was nothing more to say.

Her face showed the strain of her situation, but terror was oddly becoming. The pallor of innocence had fallen away and she looked almost wanton, despite her Walmart apparel and modest demeanour. Her hair caught the sunlight filtering through linden trees outside the hotel window. It shimmered like burnished copper. Her lips were full and glowing vermillion, her high cheeks gleamed and a scattering of freckles enhanced her delicate features. She did not look at all like Madalena Strauss, but it struck Harry, in this frightening situation, she looked very beautiful. It was as if she had at last come into her own.

Damn it, Harry. This is the most exciting thing that has happened in her entire life.

"Joan, if we don't find Lena, you will end up floating in the Danube. Countless children will die."

Joan was pondering. She was confused. He didn't believe there was a moral dilemma. Joan DeBrusk was a good person. She was afraid. She appeared not to trust her own judgment. She appeared not to trust Harry. The only thing she seemed sure of was Sakarov. She had shot him. He would kill her.

Harry moved around the suite, gathering a few toiletries, a change of lingerie, an extra pair of walking shoes, stuffing it all into her bag.

"Now," he declared, taking her hand firmly in his. "We're leaving." She resisted. He pulled firmly. "We're leaving," he repeated.

She moved robotically at first, but by the time they got to the emergency exit, she mumbled, "I'm sorry, forgive me," and picked up the pace. "Where are we going?"

"We're trying to get out of here without Sakarov seeing us."

"Oh my goodness, my God. Is Mr. Sakarov actually in Vienna?" She wrenched herself free of Harry's grip. "I think I had better stay here," she declared, grasping the stair rail with both hands.

Fear as a moral imperative, Harry! Maybe she's right.

Joan was standing on the step above him. He reached out to her gently. She stared at his hand like it was holding open the gates of hell. Then, with what Harry took as an act of astonishing whimsy, she crossed herself, stepped down and thrust her own hand into his.

"Let's go, then," she said. "He's fat, but he's fast."

They descended the stairs to the basement and slipped out a service entrance past garbage containers into a laneway that led to a knoll beside open water. Once they were safely beyond the sight range of the hotel, Harry paused to look back. Sakarov was nowhere in sight.

They moved with the strolling pedestrians toward the U-Bahn at Karlsplatz. Harry knew they stood out as North Americans. He wasn't sure whether it was the clothes or their way of moving. When they descended underground, he tried to sort out the intricate network of subway systems to find the best way to the train station for Salzburg.

Once seated on an IC high speed train, they both relaxed.

Joan fell asleep before the train pulled away from the station. Harry realized she probably hadn't slept much in the last couple of days.

Looking at her, he felt pangs of sadness. She was like a fish out of water, he thought—scales glistening in the open air before it expired.

The train surged into motion. He looked down at his watch then glanced up. Sakarov was standing on the platform outside their window. The big man looked directly at him and cocked his thumb and forefinger like a pistol. With a grotesquely explosive shuddering of his lips and a recoiling of his fist, he simulated firing. Harry instinctively ducked. When he looked out again, the train had picked up speed. He leaned forward but couldn't see Sakarov.

About halfway to Salzburg, Harry relaxed enough to enjoy the spectacular scenery. Joan stirred several times. Harry covered her with his nubuck jacket. She slept the rest of the way.

After just over three hours they disembarked. Outside the station, they saw the back end of a trolley as it pulled away toward the town centre. Annoyed at missing it, he took Joan by the hand until she picked up his pace. They walked along a bustling road through an area that had been devastated by American bombs during World War II and rebuilt in a perfunctory fashion with American money. When they reached the lee of a forested hill the architecture and ambience transformed into a Tyrolean movie set. From nondescript grey, the buildings turned cream and ochre with symmetrical rows of small windows set flush to the wall, each whimsically backed by lace curtains and fronted with a meticulously tended flowerbox.

They cut down into the old town straddling the Salzach River. They had wasted precious time not taking the trolley. Crossing the riverside promenade, Harry was reminded that this was precisely where sixteen year old Lena had met her Norwegian boyfriend, Freya's father, who used another man's name.

The looming baroque profile of Hohensalzburg Castle passed out of sight as they turned down the venerable Getreidegasse with its invitingly ominous passageways and its profusion of iconic signs made of sheet metal and gilt. They ducked into The Von Trapp Family Establishment Restaurant, featuring portraits in its windows of Christopher Plummer and Julie Andrews. Harry chose a seat by the window on the theory that they'd see anyone following them before being seen.

"What's our next move, Harry?"

He looked down at his plate with a single large Bavarian sausage slung across it, dividing the diced potato salad on one side from the lank clump of sauerkraut on the other. Harry had chosen the least impressive restaurant in a town famed for elevating honest German cooking to a culinary art. He should have known better. The sign was in English.

Joan had already begun digging in. She was famished from her voluntary captivity in the Imperial. She should have used room service. It was Sakarov's nickel.

"I saw Sakarov in the Westbanhof station in Vienna," he said.

"Oh my God." She instinctively slunk down lower in her chair and bent her head forward, but didn't stop slicing off grey discs of sausage and scooping up forkfuls of sauerkraut and oily potatoes.

"We need to rent a car," he explained, sitting forward to gaze at the late summer tourists streaming along the Getreidegasse, many of them filtering in and out of the passageway in the building opposite lined with expensive shops. "We've got to get to the school in Hinterbrühl."

"Why?"

"That's where Lena spent her childhood."

"Do you think she'll be there?" Joan sat straight again, her attention piqued.

"I'm sure she won't be, but they'll be able to tell us where to find the person who does know. Eat up. Let's go."

"I'm eating as fast as I can," said Joan, pressing her lips closed with her fingers, as if the pressure would make her chewing go faster. She swallowed then spoke: "Harry, I'm sorry about my behaviour at the hotel. Hesitating like that was selfish. Of course we must save Lena. Morality is not intuitive, you know." She pressed her lips again, trying to chew faster. "But since I'm with you, there's not so much rush, is there?"

Harry looked puzzled. She tried to explain: "I mean, why would Mr. Sakarov want to murder me and the children now? It would accomplish nothing. He got what he wanted."

"What's that?"

"You. You're tracking down Lena. He doesn't need me anymore."

Harry gazed across the table at her. He tried to swallow a forkful of potato salad. He wondered if they'd both be better off just putting Joan on a plane to Toronto. Let Morgan and Miranda look after her.

She smiled around a mouthful of food. Not elegant, he thought, but unnervingly sweet.

And still at risk.

You think?

Doesn't she get it, Harry? She's your incentive to keep going. You stop and she dies.

He glanced at his watch and did a brief calculation. He'd been on the move for a full day. Her execution was set for eighteen hours from now—unless Sakarov and Lena connected, or unless Lena was rescued and the three of them managed to escape together.

So, there's an escape *clause! You're not going to give up Lena.*

Not if I can help it.

That probably means leaving Sakarov dead. Otherwise he'll murder children on two continents.

"Harry, if you know we can find Madalena through this school, then why wouldn't Mr. Sakarov know the same thing?"

"Because she's not a schoolgirl anymore," he responded, pushing his plate to the side. He took a deep breath. She would cooperate more efficiently if she understood and his explanation had plausible simplicity.

"Sakarov deals in kids. He works with adults. He doesn't make the connection that we were all kids, even his customers, even the woman who wants to bring him down. He knows all about her work as a renegade cop in Vienna. I doubt he knows anything of her life growing up. It doesn't interest him. But she's taken refuge in her own childhood, and that's where we're going."

"Umphh, I'm finished. Aren't you going to eat anything more? Here, let me." She picked up the untouched sausage from Harry's plate, wrapped it in a wad of serviettes and stuffed it into her Roots handbag. "We may need it later."

The cashier told them the best place to rent a car was on the other side of Festungsberg mountain. They could walk through the passage carved in solid rock under the Hohensalzburg Castle in twenty minutes.

Walking through the bowels of the mountain made Harry nervous. He expected Sakarov to be waiting in any of the innumerable pockets of shadow. When they safely emerged into daylight on the far side, he sighed audibly. Joan looked at him and smiled.

Harry showed the man behind the car rental desk the slip of yellow paper from Detektiv Honsberger with the school address.

The man looked puzzled then grinned apologetically. "Mister, I understand," he said. "You want to drive to Hinterbrühl. That is good. But first you should take the train to Vienna, yes."

Harry was baffled. The rental agent walked him to a wall map and traced the route to Vienna, then dropped his finger slightly and tapped on the map.

"There is Hinterbrühl, yes. You must rent my car and drive here for a few days through Tirol district. It is most beautiful. Then you take a train to Vienna and rent a car from my colleague. We both make money and it is cheaper for you. You want a large American car? I have a very good Ford sedan, almost new. Also a BMW if you like German."

Harry grabbed Joan's hand and strode out into the sunlight.

"What's the matter, Harry?"

He was sick to his stomach. Only a few other times in his life had he been so certain about what he was doing that it simply didn't occur to him he could be dead wrong. When he made the choice to paddle the Anishnabe River with his family, it had not entered his mind he would not read the moving water. He and Karen were experienced canoeists. In summertime. Not during the spring run-off. Karen and Matt and Lucy died.

Hallstatt was a fixture in Harry's mind. Even before his librarian contact in Vienna had told him about her research, he knew the area was a centre of iron-age culture. It was renowned for its prehistoric cemetery with over a thousand burial sites, one for every resident in the contemporary village. It was famous for being picturesque and it was an important part of Lena's narrative.

When he had put together her life story from things she told him and from Simon's research, history distorted geography. Her grandmother had died as a slave labourer in the Mauthausen concentration camp. She had mentioned relatives in the village of Hallstatt, which he knew was in the Salzkammergut region. In his mind, he had correctly situated the camp near their ancestral home in Hinterbrühl, where Lena lived at the Kinderdorf with Rachel Damboch, but he had incorrectly placed Hinterbrühl in the vicinity of Salzburg where she did her prep year before university. To find Rachel, to find Lena, he had to get to Hinterbrühl.

Like so many North Americans, Harry envisioned Europe as a network of places famous in history. The landscape between was filler. It had never occurred to him to check an actual map.

He felt like a complete and utter fool.

And with good reason. But don't panic.

I don't panic. I'm not. But damn it, damn, damn.

There's still almost a day to go.

Despite the urgency, Harry walked slowly with Joan back through the passageway carved under the Festungsberg mountain. She had no idea why they were backtracking or why he seemed so despondent.

"Do you realize we're right below that big palace?" she said, apparently trying to cheer him up.

"It's not a palace—it's the Hohensalzburg Castle."

"Why isn't it a palace?"

"I don't know. Joan, I've screwed up. Let's just walk."

"Where?"

He didn't answer her. At the train station he bought two tickets on the next fast train to Vienna. They had a couple of anxious hours to kill. The clock was running down. They stepped outside and sat on a bench in the open, under a spread of linden trees. Joan only spoke when she found herself irrepressibly compelled to and expected no answers. After a while she began to cry. Not sobbing, just a few tears and a suppressed sniffle.

"I'm sorry, Harry. I don't understand what's happening."

"I made a stupid mistake and brought us halfway across Europe because it didn't occur to me I should look at a map."

"It's only a three hour trip. Plus waiting time. We'll make it up."

She was trying to comfort him. That made him feel worse.

"I got us into this, didn't I?" she lamented.

"God no!" He reached out and put his arm around her, drawing her closer. "Joan, I'm the one who messed up."

"No," she said emphatically, followed by a thoughtful pause. "It is Mr. Sakarov's fault. He used Lucy as a lure and I bit, you bit, and we're here together. Darn it, Harry. Let's go and rescue Lena. She's innocent in all this."

Harry hugged her then pushed her away so that he could peer into her eyes as he explained as much as he could about Lena. Joan seemed to accept she was in the midst of a world beyond understanding, It was her religious set of mind. But she had had no idea about Lena's reckless immersion in goodness and evil.

"My Lord, my God," she finally exclaimed. "She has lived a very bad life."

"Yes she has."

"And that has put her in danger and made her dangerous."

"Yes it has."

"Then we had certainly better find her. She needs our help."

They both sat back on the bench, feet thrust in front of them, and stared at the cobblestones dappled in sunlight that filtered through the linden branches.

It felt strange to Harry to be loitering while a killer was in pursuit. When they roused themselves to re-enter the station, he couldn't help feeling relieved that the deadly chase was about to resume.

Walking along the platform to find their car, Joan observed in an off-hand way, "She was very young when she had her first lover."

Harry mumbled. Hooking up at sixteen didn't strike him as rare. Joan worked with street kids in social services and at the Zylberman Centre where he assumed by mid-teens sex was the norm. What was she getting at?

Maybe the comparison was personal, Harry. She was measuring against her own experience. Different as they are, she seems to identify with the woman you're after.

"She was quite devious, wasn't she? You told me that sometimes she would stay out all night and tell the school she was with relatives in that village called Hallstatt."

"I think it was only the one time."

They clambered onto the train and found their seats.

"The school authorities believed her, didn't they?"

"Apparently they did."

"Then doesn't that mean Hallstatt is close to Salzburg. Otherwise, you know, it would be a pretty lame excuse."

"It does mean that, yes. It's in the Salzkammergut region."

"But since she was only sixteen, whoever her relatives were, the school already knew about them. They had to be her guardians."

"Not they," he said. "She." Rachel Damboch.

What purported to be Lena's ashes were forwarded to Rachel Damboch. She was Lena's guardian. She had retired to somewhere near Hallstatt according to Frau Honsberger. Hinterbrühl was a diversion, simply to confirm an address!

Harry jumped to his feet. It was like he heard the messenger's approaching footsteps with a last-minute reprieve as the gallows' trapdoor creaked before springing open.

He grabbed Joan's hand and bolted for the door. The train lurched. The door was locked. The train was moving. He looked around frantically, saw an emergency alarm, and pulled it. The train shunted to an abrupt stop, sirens wailed, the doors clicked open. Drawing Joan with him, he leapt onto the platform and ran at breakneck speed out onto the street.

With any luck, Sakarov would still be on the train.

19 **SCOTCH AND GOSSIP**

AS HARRY AND JOAN MADE THEIR WAY FROM THE BAHNHOF back to the tunnel through Festungsberg mountain, he was convinced Dimitri Sakarov was in hot pursuit, yet every time he glanced around he saw only sunlight glistening from immaculate windows and creamy plaster, dappled with an amiable carnival of shadows. Very Rodgers and Hammerstein. Cloying and sinister. The Nazi *Anschluss* derided by the sounds of music. Harry wasn't musical.

He could hear heavy footsteps behind them. He darted into an alcove, pulling Joan along with him. The footsteps stopped, then resumed.

"Harry?"

"Shhh."

The footsteps got closer. Then Sakarov rushed past them.

Joan whispered almost inaudibly, "Harry, I'm frightened."

Harry nodded.

They retreated back into the sunlight on the near side of the mountain and found a different car rental agency.

As soon as they passed the edge of town, Harry pulled their sky blue Fiesta onto the narrow shoulder and they both got out.

"Check your bag," he explained as he emptied his pockets onto the car hood. "Check your clothes, the seams, everything."

"What are we looking for, Harry? Do you think we're bugged with a tracking device?"

"Something like that."

"Maybe he's just smart."

"Yeah," said Harry. "He is."

"No bugs," she announced after they'd done a thorough search. "Maybe he's *preternatural.*" She mouthed the word like it was a new flavour.

If you can believe in holy ghosts and that Mary conceived in her sixth month, I guess nothing seems impossible.

"Damn it," said Harry. "How the hell does he keep track of us?"

"It's an unholy mystery," Joan cheerfully proclaimed.

She's enjoying this.

What could be more exciting for a good Catholic girl than being at the centre of an unholy mystery? I think it was Christopher Hitchens who said that faith causes people to be mean, selfish, and stupid.

She's not mean. Judgement hovered in the air with her unfinished sentence.

"Most of the time, he's invisible," Joan said as they clambered back into the car.

"Sometimes the best way to blend in is to stand out just enough to be part of the scene," said Harry. "The clinical term for not seeing him is 'selective discernment.'"

"You just made that up!"

"I did, but that's what it is. I used to be a professor. We make things up."

Glad to see you're chipper again, professor.

As they drove into looming shadows of landscape, Harry began to have second thoughts. He wondered if his certainty about Lena's whereabouts was compensating for the stupidity of misplacing Hinterbrühl. He had a map now. They were on the right route, but was Hallstatt the right destination? He wondered how much of what he believed was based on fact and how much on willful desire.

Saint Augustine, Harry. Faith over reason.

He felt strangely reassured, but as they drove, the unrestrained beauty of the Alpine terrain made him uneasy. The sheer grandeur of mountains inspired awe tinged with fear—a perfect definition of the sublime. Mountains were emotionally remote. They could only be viewed from a distance. Thundering waterfalls were frightening close up, but mountains close up were nothing but rock.

And waterfalls are nothing but water, Harry.

Mountains are mass. Water is energy.

It's all a matter of perspective, Einstein.

What is?

Everything.

Still a master of the meaningless.

I was a literature specialist, Harry. What do you expect?

You're a cultural theorist.

He used the present tense.

He glanced over at Joan. She seemed lost in private thoughts as she gazed at the passing scene.

What if Madalena isn't in Hallstatt? You only have fourteen hours left.

We're almost there.

"Harry, are we looking for Lena or the woman who raised her?" Joan interrupted his reverie. Before he could respond, she shifted her query. "Are we on a quest or in flight?"

"They amount to the same thing. We're in a race and if we don't get to the finish on time, people die."

"What if we don't find her?"

"Lena? We will."

"But if we don't? Will he kill me?"

"He'll try."

"Harry."

"Yes."

"If we do find her, what if we were, just hypothetically, to turn her over to Sakarov?"

"He would execute her. And then he'd murder us if he could. And he might kill the kids anyway, to round out some perverted equation."

"So when we find her, why don't we escape together?"

"Then the children die for sure. Grim retribution."

"Well, we have no option, do we?"

"Joan?"

"The only solution is to kill Mr. Sakarov."

She has an interesting mind, Harry.

They drove quietly until the premature darkness of the valley closed around them. It was eerie because the sky directly overhead was shot with sunlight. Harry turned on the car lights and at the same time noticed the lights of a car behind them. He slowed, then the other car slowed.

Rounding a sharp bend, he wheeled the Fiesta down a lane cut into the brush on the uphill side and doused his lights. Twisting in his seat he watched a black BMW sedan cruise by.

"You don't think he knows why we're here?"

"He assumes we're tracking down Lena."

"But does he know we're looking for Rachel Damboch?"

"I don't know what he knows," said Harry. He backed the car out onto the road and resumed driving. After a while, he noticed headlights in his rearview mirror.

"Good," he said. "He's behind us again."

"Crafty bugger."

"Uh, yeah. It confirms he doesn't know where we're going."

When they arrived at the darkened village of Hallstatt along a narrow road blasted into the mountainside, Harry felt strangely relieved. Given his previous blunder with geography, he half expected the village to vanish as they approached.

It was still tourist season, but they found a single room in a rustic Gasthaus. The *patron* looked like a dead ringer for the most recent actor to play Inspector Poirot. He acknowledged that his guests were travelling without luggage but seemed to shrug off the implied slovenliness as foreign eccentricity. He set out a late supper of cold *wienerschnitzel*, chopped cabbage, and a nondescript white wine and then went to bed, leaving them by the fire he had lit to counter the evening chill.

"Do you think Mr. Sakarov knows we're here?" Joan asked.

"I'm sure he does," said Harry.

She drew her chair a little closer to the fire.

"Why don't you go up?" Harry offered. "You'll be warmer."

"Not likely, Harry. I'm staying with you."

"I imagine he's sleeping in his car unless he called ahead for a reservation somewhere. He probably did, but he'll be outside at the crack of dawn."

"That's comforting. Come on, then, let's both get some rest. It's a big bed, Harry. There's enough room for two."

"I'll be up in a minute."

You sure you should be sleeping, Harry?

With her?

No, just sleeping. You're working to a deadline.

I won't be much good if I don't. In real life, people sleep.

Then eat your veggies, get lots of rest, and don't forget to floss.

He smiled. This was her Sailor Duval persona.

When he got to the room, Joan was sound asleep with a grey blanket pulled up to her shoulders but folded back on his side so he could get under it too. He tucked the blanket close around her; he found another in an armoire and pulled it over himself, stretching out on his back like a corpse. He ruminated through the night while Joan slept soundly beside him.

At the first blush of morning light, Harry slipped from the bed and pulled back the gingham curtain. His blue Fiesta looked sullen and seemed to be cowering. As the sky grew brighter, he saw the black BMW sedan parked farther along the narrow street carved into the side of the mountain. Gradually, he could make out the entire village of one thousand souls perched precariously on ridges and in niches carved out of the rock. Below him were rooftops of buildings the colours of cream and dried blood, mostly clustered close to a small stone church with a squared tower surmounted by a slate-grey spire. On a small spit of land jutting into the deep dark waters of the Hallstätter See, a ferry terminal and a few boats hauled close to the shore were a reminder of days when access to the village was only by water.

He thought of going down and accosting Sakarov in his car, but he realized from Sakarov's perspective everything was going as it should—Harry's apparent abduction of Joan was a fortuitous deviation. It made it easier for Sakarov to keep track of his enemies.

So what's your plan, Harry?

The next part's a bit fuzzy.

Remember, once you and your copper-haired friends subdue Sakarov, you still have to deal with those files.

Depends on how permanently he is, as you call it, "subdued."

I suspect either it will be permanent or not at all.

If it is, then, the release of the files will be up to Lena and Rachel Damboch. Joan and I will head back to Toronto.

A lot of innocent people are going to be exposed to scandal. Lives will be destroyed.

And if she doesn't release them?

Lives will be destroyed.

He thought he saw movement in the black sedan. He drew back from the window and pulled the curtains closed. He stripped to the waist and began washing at the cold-water sink in the corner. Joan mumbled "good morning" and rummaged around behind him, digging into her bag beside the bed, then slid a disposable razor across the floor in his general direction.

"Thanks," he said. "You sleep well?"

"Absolutely. Where's the toilet?"

"Down the hall."

"At least it's not out in the yard."

"We're in Austria, not Lower Slobovia."

"Or the outskirts of Timmins," she said. "I grew up with a privy. It's cold on the bottom in winter, tacky in summer. The best thing about busing to school in town was flush toilets." She yawned. "Listen to me, I'm nostalgic. It seems like we drove forever."

Harry made eye contact in the little mirror over the sink, then he returned to working up an insipid lather with hand soap and cold water. Suddenly, Joan sprang from the bed. She was naked. She had been saving the fresh underwear he'd put in her bag until morning. It was morning.

If he had been aware she was stripped to the buff beneath the blanket beside him, he might have got more sleep, just knowing how absurdly trusting she was.

Or openly available, Harry.

Watching her in the mirror as she tugged the gingham curtains open and stretched in the sunlight, Harry refused to believe that. She was slight and supple and there was something so wholly pristine about her nakedness, he was disturbed by his visceral response. She was a child utterly unaware of her own vulnerable beauty. He looked back at his own reflection, but he could still see hers in the background.

He started to turn.

"No, don't."

Being an image in the mirror allowed her an illusion of innocence that direct confrontation destroyed. He resumed shaving.

She addressed his reflection. "Do you think I'm attractive, Harry?"

She was asking a serious question. Slowly, he turned to face her directly.

"I think you should get dressed."

She looked mildly annoyed but quickly rallied. Gathering her lingerie from her bag and the rest of her clothes that were neatly piled on a chair, she stepped naked into the hallway. The last thing Harry saw was her bottom as she pulled the door closed behind her.

Over breakfast, Harry asked the *patron* where he could find Rachel Damboch.

"I know of no such lady," said the man, stroking his waxed moustache. "I grew up in our village, but I have been away in Vienna for almost forty years. I have only come back since two years, while my father was dying."

"I'm sorry," said Harry.

"He is dead now, it is okay."

"You've never heard of Rachel Damboch?"

"You eat. I will ask my neighbours. Perhaps someone knows her."

He went out the door, walking in his best Poirot style like a wounded penguin, and was gone before Harry could protest that he'd rather ask around on his own so he could take in the layout of the village and check on the whereabouts of Dimitri Sakarov.

Before they finished their coffees, the *patron* returned.

"I am sorry to tell you, your friend was dead since three months. She is in our cemetery. We do not dig people up as we used to, to pile their bones in the ossuary. She is still in her grave."

Dead end, Harry!

He felt like he had been struck in the solar plexus. His breathing was shallow and rapid. Then he realized he couldn't hear Joan breathing at all. Suddenly she exhaled. She was bewildered. Harry reached out and touched her pallid cheek with the back of his hand.

"It's okay," he assured her. He wished he felt the same confidence he was trying to express.

"I am sorry for your loss," said the *patron*. "She was family, yes? That is sad. It is very bad when close people die, even when very ancient. I nursed my father, but he dropped dead in this room. Sometimes it is better to die quickly like Frau Damboch."

Harry needed to get into the open air. He needed to think. Checking out of the Gasthaus was simple, since they had no luggage. They climbed into the sky blue Fiesta and sat there, gazing along the narrow street at the cluster of buildings down by the ferry landing.

"We can't do it, Harry."

"Do what?"

"You're thinking that if we catch the ferry at the last minute we could leave Mr. Sakarov behind."

"No, actually I wasn't thinking that at all."

"Well, we can't leave without rescuing Lena. How much time do we have?"

He glanced at his watch. "Four hours. Damn it."

"Could we negotiate for more time?"

"I doubt that's an option. We might have to deal with Sakarov before we find her."

Deal with, as in kill? You're not a killer, Harry.

There's always a first time.

There doesn't have to be. That cliché collapses under its own weight.

She's got to be here.

"If this is where her surrogate mother lived, she'll be here." Joan spoke with total conviction.

Harry nodded agreement. He hoped she was right. "So we ask around," he said. "Someone has to have seen her."

"You don't think she'll blend in?"

Harry turned to her and smiled broadly.

"No, I don't think 'selective discernment' applies in Hallstatt."

They got out of the car and walked through the village. Harry was struck by the strange feelings of ambivalence it offered, cramped tightly against sheer rock on one side but open to the dark lake and distant landscape on the other. Intimate and expansive, a nice combination. There was no sign of Sakarov. His BMW was still there, empty and ominous.

They dropped into several shops and failed to find anyone who knew either Lena or Rachel. Finally, in a shop built into the front of a house on a short side street they found an old woman who had known Rachel Damboch. The woman's body was bent and gnarled, but her face was serene. She told them Rachel was her friend. The woman's English was limited, but they managed to figure out that Rachel had lived on a high precipice overlooking the lake, in an ancient chalet with electricity from its own generator but no running water and no road access.

"The scenery, yes, is *wunderbar*," said the old woman, smiling. "I have not been to chalet since we were young. Rachel lived there much time after retirement. Even before retirement. She preferred to come visit me here. She would arrive at holidays and a few bottles of scotch we would share and talk very serious and laugh. It was pleasant, those times, but she became old. She is better off dead."

"Oh no," Joan exclaimed.

"Oh yes," said the woman and grinned with satisfaction for having outlived her friend. She talked for a while about Rachel and about her decrepit chalet, then hobbled with them to the door and as they were going out she added, "You tourist people, you come to our beautiful village and you look for exotic women. It is very strange."

Harry stopped short, letting Joan slip by onto the street.

"Someone else was looking for Rachel Damboch?"

"Not Rachel, no. Fat Russian, he look for beautiful red-haired woman. Perhaps Madalena Strauss, Rachel's girl. After she became policewoman, I never saw her again. I have been told she is dead, now, since after Rachel is dead. Her body in the Danube floated up. I think her friend lives in the cabin, now. Very secret, no one sees who. This person, I think very beautiful, she gets deliveries. She gets scotch whiskey and groceries. Sometimes other things. But maybe the Russian looks for your wife. She has red hair like Madalena, only not so wild. Mister, I nothing tell him. I did not like him, like the pig he smelled, like he sleep in his clothes."

"Fräulein DeBrusk is not my wife," said Harry, seeing Joan from a different perspective. "*Auf wiedersehenn*, thank you."

"Good bye. Good bye, Fräulein DeBrusk. *Danke schön*."

The old woman handed Harry her card as they left.

"You come back sometime to visit," she said.

"So," Harry exclaimed to Joan, handing her the woman's business card to put in her bag. "Our Mr. Sakarov has been here looking for Madalena. That means he doesn't know about Rachel."

"Which doesn't give us much of an advantage since the poor old soul is dead." She smiled. "We still have two hours, Harry."

They scrambled along a narrow laneway, following the bent old woman's directions, until they came to a path etched diagonally by the feet of countless generations into the steep incline. They worked their way past ancient shrubs that clung to small pockets of earth scattered amidst rocky outcroppings and came to a smaller path veering upward even more steeply. They had moved around the mountainside, out of sight of the village. Sometimes they used their hands to pull themselves ahead. Harry's toes hurt, the missing bits more than the ones that survived. He wasn't sure what they would find at Rachel's cabin, but he relished the notion that the big Russian would have to negotiate the same difficult landscape to follow them.

Since he had returned to Austria, Harry had been thinking of Sakarov as a Russian again. In Canada he was a second generation Canadian from Saskatchewan with a ludicrous accent. In Europe, he was a member of the Russian new-capitalist amoral elite.

More than an hour had passed since they began their climb when suddenly they broke out into open space. Harry turned and looked back, but there was no sign of Sakarov. Off to the side, a weather-beaten log chalet was perched precariously on a rocky ledge. It had a steep roof with wood shingles covered in lichen and moss and overhanging eaves to cope with heavy snow. There were a few shambling outbuildings and straight ahead some abandoned mining carts close to a large ironclad door blocking entry into the mountainside.

"Who knew she'd been living next to a salt mine?" Joan said. "God, it reminds me of Timmins."

"Do you realize every last thing in this place was hauled up here on somebody's back?"

"I know. Some of these salt mines are thousands of years old." Joan gazed around her, taking in the details of the ragged terrain. Then she declared with uncharacteristic authority, "Four hundred years ago Hallstatters built a pipeline forty kilometres long. It carried brine to be dried for the salt market and they used more than 12,000 hollowed-out trees."

"Are you making that up?"

"I read a brochure at the tourist office down by the ferry."

"When, for God's sake? You haven't been out of my sight."

"The last time I was here."

"You've been here before!"

"Seven years ago. After I graduated, the summer before I started my M.S.W., a girlfriend and I travelled by Eurorail and auto-stop."

"You hitchhiked! You really are an odd one, Joan. I'd never have guessed that you'd bummed around Europe. Does Morgan know?"

"He never asked."

Harry was not really surprised.

"It was a long time ago," she said.

"Seven years is not a long time."

"It's all relative, isn't it, Harry? I've seen a lot more than you'd think."

"Have you been up here before? Did you tour the mines?"

"We visited ossuaries, saw lots of bones. But one salt mine looks much like another. The big iron door isn't familiar. Of course, it would have been open, wouldn't it?"

Now didn't seem the time to pursue her story, but she had one after all. They were leaning on each other like siblings who knew everything and nothing about each other. Her copper red hair, damp from sweat, caught the sunlight as she shook it away from her head. Harry pushed his own back, although it was cut so short it stood almost straight off his skull.

As they moved up onto the weathered porch, he reached out and gave her hand a squeeze. In another life they might have been lovers and in another he might have been her professor and she the kind of student he'd look forward to seeing in the second row from the front and be disappointed the days she skipped class.

Despite the derelict condition of the logs and frame, the chalet door was solid. It was unlocked. He pushed it open. They gasped. She grasped his arm so tightly he winced. There was zero consistency between the disrepair of the exterior and the high-tech modernist hideaway they encountered inside. It could have been an executive sanctuary in Scarborough or the Vienna suburbs. There was not a soul in sight, but the air was filled with that same indefinable feminine scent he had noticed in his apartment after Lena had left.

He called gently, afraid the illusion might collapse from the sound of his voice.

They stepped inside and pushed the door shut behind them. A hush filled the air as the outside world disappeared. Small dots of green, orange, and red glowed from computer components along an exterior wall below a thermal Venetian blind that glowed from the light outside but admitted no image. Several blank monitor screens reflected the room imperfectly and one live monitor with the sound turned off featured Wolf Blitzer in pantomime on CNN. There was a sealed urn beside one of the monitors, a plain metal cylinder of the kind used to transport human remains.

I wonder if they're her own?

More likely they're Rachel's.

Harry surveyed the sleek ambience with all the amenities. The furniture was much like his, mainly teak and leather. Along the back wall was a fully equipped kitchen with stainless steel appliances and to the right an open door led into an extension that from the outside had seemed nothing more than the remnants of a board and batten shed.

Clearly, much had changed since the gnarled old woman in town had visited her friend's ramshackle retreat for their evenings of gossip and scotch.

As his ears adjusted to the quietness, Harry could make out the soft rush of a shower coming through from the wing where the bedroom and bath must be. He spoke to Joan in a low voice, expressing satisfaction.

"She's in there," he said.

"Lena?"

"Who else could it be?"

"And we've lost Mr. Sakarov, haven't we?"

"For the time being."

"Harry," she whispered. "If Rachel Damboch is dead, who is this gatekeeper you told me about?"

"The keeper of Lena's conscience? Good question. Maybe there isn't one."

The latch of the front door clicked inordinately loudly in the silence behind them. Mountain air swirled in from outside and before they could turn, there was another metallic click. Harry and Joan both knew intuitively it was the sound of a gun. From having seen too many cop shows they automatically froze with their hands in the air.

"Joan DeBrusk! How good to see you," said Madalena Strauss. "You too, Harry. Please turn around slowly. You can both put your hands down. I'm sure neither of you is armed. I see the Russian isn't with you. I expect he will be along shortly."

The first thing Harry saw when he faced her was the muzzle of a semi-automatic. The second thing was that the woman holding the gun was wrapped casually in a bath towel, with a few locks of copper red hair escaping the confines of a matching towel bound around her head. Bare feet, no makeup, perfect complexion, eyes flashing. She was radiant.

She looked like a study by Klimt, of course.

Not a painting. More like one of his disturbing and luminous pencil sketches of women exposing themselves, masturbating with their crotches exposed, their unknowable faces ecstatic.

20 THE HARROWING OF HELL

HARRY FELT A SURGE OF VERTIGO, AS IF HE'D CLOSED HIS eyes then opened them to find he was in a different room, a stranger in a different world. He had trekked up the mountainside hoping to find Madalena Strauss. He had found her in the flesh and to his astonishment she was apparently expecting him. She was holding a lethal weapon trained on his heart.

He was angry at himself for not understanding the situation. He glanced over at Joan. She looked bewildered but oddly serene.

"Lena," said Joan. "I don't think you realize why we're here."

"No," Lena responded. "I don't think *you* do." She fired her pistol; Joan reeled and crumpled to the floor.

"For God's sake," Harry shouted. The sharp retort of the gun blast rang in his ears as he wheeled away from Lena and her gun to kneel beside Joan, who was trembling, her eyes huge and unblinking. He ran his hands gently over her body, ruffling her clothes, searching for the wound. There was no blood.

"You stupid, stupid woman," he declared over his shoulder, aiming his words at Madalena as he dropped his voice to a quiet curse.

"Harry, if I'd wanted to kill your friend she'd be dead. My first bullet was a wax slug—I like to avoid gratuitous killing when a warning will do. But I promise you the second is lethal. She'll be fine once she realizes she's still alive."

From his kneeling position, he pivoted to glare at Madalena Strauss. "You are absolutely," he searched for a word, "*unreal*."

"I expect I am."

"Why her, for God's sake? Why not shoot me?"

"You're not the enemy, Harry. Nor is Joan. I like you both. But I need to be in control now."

"Control what you want. You don't need the gun."

"Yes, I think maybe I do."

By the time Harry had arranged Joan comfortably on the sofa, she was in command of her faculties, but she lay quiet, waiting for Harry to work out the Kafkaesque complexities of their situation or, perhaps, trying to work them out for herself. Harry, meanwhile, felt very protective. He had got her into this.

No, Harry. Sakarov got her into this. You came like a knight errant to her rescue.

By betraying Lena—that's what Lena thinks.

It's only betrayal if you don't get her help to take out Sakarov together. But, Harry.

But?

How does she know Sakarov is on his way?

Lena interrupted. "I'm so glad you're here, Harry. We've got work to do."

"You do realize Sakarov is intending to kill you."

"So I understand. But my research project, it's time."

"Perhaps we should talk strategy first. Like how to deal with Sakarov."

"Forget him, Harry. We are about to create a deluge. Wikileaks only leaked—we're going to create a flood to rival God's first holocaust. We'll drown the bastards in their own evil effluent."

"And hope the innocent rise to the surface."

Perhaps she was right. When Sakarov got there, if he was able to negotiate the climb, Lena's future was in her own hands. She had the gun. Harry shifted around on the edge of the sofa. He could feel the warmth of Joan's thigh press against him as he scanned the computer wall with the opaque window-blind in the centre. Lena had set her pistol on the desktop in front of her computers, disarming herself but keeping it within easy reach.

He knew her approach to the horrors of child exploitation would have horrendous repercussions. The Findlays' leap from the Kressler balcony with the little boy, driven by her revelations, was proof of that.

What about Simon's death, Harry? They lost two kids, the one they discarded and the one they didn't know.

Lena began busying herself among the electronics.

He had to slow her down, to stop her if possible.

"Why now? What about your gatekeeper?"

"I know you have reservations about this, Harry."

"What about Rachel Damboch?"

"What about her? We worked on my research together. Do you realize everything here had to be lugged up by hand? From computer components to groceries. Rachel loved this place, but it's actually mine; it's been in my family for generations. We used to mine salt."

"I thought Rachel was your conscience."

"I don't have a conscience."

"And that's why she wanted to keep you in check."

"You are partly right, Harry. Rachel worried about what she called my 'moral judgment.' Especially after the Dietmar Henning incident."

"You did kill him?"

"I did."

"And removed his testicles?"

"And gouged out his eyes. I used surgical instruments. He was unconscious."

"Before or after you cut him?"

"Does it matter? When I told Rachel what had happened—"

"What you did."

"When I told her about the incident, she insisted on setting up a gatekeeper to guide me on how I should deal with our findings, should she not be here when the right time came. And she isn't here, Harry."

"Then who's the gatekeeper? You obviously need one."

"I thought you would have realized. It's you, of course."

Like a drowning man reviewing his entire life in a kaleidoscopic instant of time, every moment of his relationship with Madalena Strauss compressed into a startled blink of his eyes.

Karen was silent.

Madalena rose from her swivel chair. She leaned over casually and picked up her pistol, holding it cradled in the flat of her hand as if it were an injured bird and she had to decide whether to save it or to put it out of its misery. Then she did a totally surprising thing. She handed the gun to Harry.

"You take it. I need to get dressed."

She walked out into the wing where her bedroom was, closing the door behind her. They heard an exterior door shut—that's how she must have got out to come at them from behind. But she was still inside; they heard her rummaging around, getting dressed.

Harry looked down at the diminutive semi-automatic in his hand. He emptied the magazine and dropped the bullets into his pocket, then he set the gun down on the coffee table.

Lena obviously felt coercion was no longer necessary. Somehow, without the weapon, she seemed more dreadful. What unspeakable powers did she have more powerful than gunpowder?

"Harry, what in the Lord's name is going on?" said Joan, pushing against him to sit up. "This woman is a lunatic."

"A brilliant lunatic."

"Looking around here, I'd say the old lady was the brilliant one."

"I think they complemented each other. They worked on child exploitation as a joint venture."

"Until your friend Lena went viral."

"Until she discovered she was sleeping with the man who abducted her daughter."

"My God, my goodness."

"Exactly," said Harry.

"So Rachel reined her in. But here's what I don't get—well, there's a lot I don't get—but especially, I mean, she as much as said you can stop her. If I've understood what you told me in Salzburg, she's about to unleash Armageddon. But only if you'll agree to it. Does she think she's going to debate you? I mean, you've got the gun."

"Unloaded. She still seems to be in charge."

"Then reload, Harry."

"It's not about guns. It's about control. Whoever knows the most holds the reins."

Spoken like a true philosopher, Harry.

"So how can you be her conscience if we don't know what's happening?"

Lena walked back into the room. Her outfit—a scooped-neck blouse printed with geometric patterns, a bejewelled choker, a dirndl skirt with a broad leather belt, and black slippers—seemed like an Alpine costume. The subtle application of eyeshadow below her eyes as well as above them gave her a haunted appearance. She looked less like an Tyrolean peasant than an Edwardian courtesan painted by Klimt's morbid young protégé, Egon Schiele.

Lena sat down in the easy chair facing Harry and Joan, who were still side by side on the sofa. She crossed her legs with elegant precision and tossed her head to shift a cascade of copper red hair away from her face.

"I see you two are quite comfortable," she said. "So, Harry, we should resume our conversation. Rachel gave you powers you didn't know you had, and now we must use them to our best advantage."

I think you're supposed to say shazam, *Harry.*

Joan was thinking along the same lines. "Well, Peter Parker, it seems you've been bitten by a nuclear spider."

A deep full-throated laugh issued from Lena as she waited to hear what Harry's response would be.

"I didn't even know Rachel Damboch existed until a few weeks ago," he said.

"But she knew you, Harry. She knew your writing. The paper on Klimt, yes. But more importantly, she had come across your essay on necessary murder in *Philosophy Today.* I think you called it 'Justifiable Homicide.'"

"It was 'Justifiable Homicide?' with *a question mark.* An interrogation, not a declaration."

"But very thoughtful, very wise. Rachel ran across your writing during her work on Hans Asperger. It was your moral civility that made her decide to abandon her research into his possible Nazi activities. She shifted her focus to the concentration camp at Mauthasen where slave labourers worked on the BMW turbojet fighter. That is where my grandmother died."

"I'm so sorry," Joan interjected. "Are you Jewish?" She seemed flustered by not knowing. "How did she die?"

Lena glowered without bothering to shift her gaze from Harry. "By gasoline injection. Or strangulation. Possibly from malnutrition or exhaustion." She paused. "Once she got involved in my project, Rachel was never able to finish her own study. A single camp, my grandmother's death, seemed inconsequential in comparison."

"It sounds terrible," said Joan.

"It *was* terrible. You cannot possibly imagine." Lena paused again and then resumed her account of Rachel's research projects. "She had studied with Dr. Asperger and spent a great deal of time in the libraries of Vienna when she lived in Hinterbrühl. That's where she was my surrogate mother and guardian, at his SOS-Kinderdorf school in the district of Mödling and then, after she retired, here. Even before, she would spend months at a time in this place. Her computer brought the libraries of the world to Hallstatt. So, Harry, she researched you. She knew about your accident on the river. That distressed her. She had grown up in a place called Sudberry."

"Sudbury. Northern Ontario," said Harry.

"Me too," said Joan. "Near Timmins."

"I don't know if you'd call it growing up," said Harry. He felt the need to show he was not entirely in the dark by reminding himself what he knew while bringing Joan up to speed. "Rachel was a ward in the Huronia Asylum for Idiots in Orillia; that's how it was known back then. She was turned out on the streets as a misfit and eventually came under the care of Elizabeth Book in Toronto, Lena's aunt, and the daughter of Elisabeth Bök, Klimt's model and Lena's great-grandmother and prototype; red hair, green eyes, wicked ways."

"Ah yes," said Madalena. "You are a researcher too."

"Not at all. I hate research. I hired Simon Wales to do it for me. Did you know he was the boy that couple from Oakville bought and discarded?"

"Of course. He ran away."

"Did he have a choice?"

"It is not my concern, Harry. Listen, you need to know how we brought you into the picture. We researched your background as a scholar; we knew about the deaths of your family and that you had become a private investigator. We knew you had a connection with Superintendent Quin of Toronto Homicide. We discovered you had been locked out in the extreme cold last winter. We hacked into your medical information."

"You can't do that."

"We did it, Harry. You'd be surprised how brilliant Rachel was with computers. A little old lady, a *cybersavant,* you might say."

He recalled both his own and Simon's dismissive judgment of the old woman's computer savvy.

"Rachel had a rare and special mind, Harry. It was her blessing and her curse."

His silence was taken as an invitation to elaborate. "Rachel appeared slow, below normal, until she was ten, when she received a severe blow to the left side of her head from a fellow inmate at the asylum. She nearly died, but after she recovered she was different. There are other cases recorded like hers. She had gained access to hidden parts of her brain. Suddenly, she could remember everything that was spoken to her, every word, and repeat every conversation *verbatim*. She picked up languages she'd never heard before in a few weeks. There are other documented cases of such a radical explosion of intelligence. No one thought to document Rachel. Going from one extreme to the other, she tried to learn how to be normal and tried to teach herself normal behaviour, but she was strange. They didn't know what to do with her at the asylum so they set her free. The next decade was very troubled as she tried to adjust to life on the streets of Toronto. Why am I telling you this, Harry?"

He felt like a Pirandello character lost in a play, in search of the author.

"Perhaps it doesn't matter anymore," she said.

But Harry knew it did. She was describing aspects of herself. She had been strange as a child and was taken in by Rachel, who recognized a kindred spirit. Life for Lena was a sequence of conscious decisions. Perhaps she wasn't autistic, but she displayed obsessive-compulsive behaviour and, he realized, she was never spontaneous. Even now, she was only simulating impulsiveness in her revelations about Rachel. She needed Harry to know things about her. She did not care if he liked her or agreed with her. She needed him to understand.

"Please," he said. "Keep on. You were talking about computers and how you hacked into my medical records."

"Rachel did. A couple of years before Bill Gates and Paul Allen created Microsoft, she was writing programs in Austria. She mastered Fortran before its limitations and special applications were known. Computers were not mathematical machines for Rachel; they were geometric landscapes. She had an extremely rare form of synaesthesia. Everything that happened inside a computer she visualized in terms of colours and textures and shapes. She knew computers, Harry. There was nothing they could do that she could not envision."

Joan spoke up. The attraction of ideas seemed to have erased her fears. "I studied savants in psychology. They used low frequency impulses to temporarily impede functioning on the left side of the brain and that gave people's minds astonishing abilities. But only in spurts, nothing long lasting."

"Well," said Lena, "the effects of Rachel's blow to the skull seems to have lasted her whole life."

"So she read my medical files?" Harry wanted to get back to the fundamental question of why he was here.

"She was enthralled by computers, but she was old-fashioned and preferred to read books. She could read two pages at once, the left eye taking in one page, the right eye taking in the other, with virtually total recall. Dr. Asperger wanted to study her. She refused. She preferred caring for damaged children. When she retired to Hallstatt, an infinite library was available online. She read everything. But she loved to gossip, of course. It took her mind off her mind."

"She gossiped with the old lady in town."

"And with me. She hated being different. She loved Russian novels."

"And digging into my records."

"Yes, you were hospitalized for hypothermia. They had to do a *lavage*, washing your guts with warm water. You lost a couple of toes."

"Parts of toes."

"Parts. And there were detailed copies of your electrocardiogram readings. That's what we were after."

"What bloody use were ECG stats?" He felt violated, as if they had tapped into his innermost secrets.

"Everyone's readings are a signature, Harry, as different as fingerprints. Actually, you only have to isolate the five phases of one single heartbeat to make positive identification. We have your heartbeat on record. And now, we have you. That is, I have you. Rachel is gone. But so, we match the two heartbeats, your living heartbeat and the one from Toronto embedded in our security system. Bang! We unlock my files. Thank you very much."

"And you need me to be here in person?"

"That's how Rachel insisted we do it."

"And you were fine with all this restraint?"

"Rachel died a natural death, if that's what you're getting at."

"It never crossed my mind."

"I would not have hurt her, for goodness sake. I loved Rachel. She helped me realize the need to keep certain of my impulses under control. Revenge must not consume the avenger's soul, she would say. And now she's here again, acting through you. Not in a creepy way. It's not about ghosts and the supernatural. But you do see, I need you here for your heart."

"For the harrowing of hell."

"*Ikh bin dokh a yid.* We have *sheol*. Jews don't believe in hell."

"And I'm an atheist, which means hell is what we make it."

"It's part of the Apostles' Creed," said Joan.

Lena turned to Harry for an explanation.

"Between death and resurrection, Christ descended among the dead and redeemed the souls of the righteous who had lived during the millennia before he was born. I don't know how far back he went, I don't know if he included Neanderthals."

"Retroactive salvation," she said. "A rather facile bit of religiosity."

"What seems facile," said Joan, "is that you believe you're the redeemer."

"Hardly. I have no desire to absolve the damned."

"No," said Harry. "But you're intending to descend among them and pass absolute judgment."

"Yes, if that is what *harrowing* means."

"Close enough," said Harry. He regretted he'd got them into the arcane machinations of theology. "It's one thing to judge when you know all the facts. It's another to judge when you don't."

"I think I shall enjoy the harrowing of hell, Harry. It's more interesting than *sheol*. Now let us proceed to your heartbeat. We'll need to take an electronic reading."

"And why would I cooperate? I'm not at all sure what you're doing is right."

"But you think I could be."

"Not without filtering your files very carefully first."

"Harry, your heartbeat. Come over here."

Harry stood up as if under an inexorable compulsion.

Harry, sit down.

He fingered the bullets in his pocket.

Madalena proceeded to arrange wires and electrodes attached to a machine the size of a printer.

"This is still in development; it takes time-delineated readings, then we make a representative selection. It doesn't hurt, of course. Sit there."

Harry, don't sit.

He chose to remain standing. He watched Lena sort out her equipment for a while, then repeated his question, hoping the answer would be different this time.

"Why do you think I'd let you do this, Lena? I'm not prepared to open Pandora's box, not until we've sorted through what sort of evil might fly out. So far, it's all pretty vague."

"You forget, we're restuffing the jar. There's nothing vague about what we're doing, not for the children involved. Where do you want me to start—infants sold for adoption, children sold for sex, child slave labour in fields and factories, death squads of child soldiers, children as toys, expendable children, children as commodities. An obscene and savage economy. You want facts and figures? They're all in here."

She gestured to indicate her computer set-up. She seemed to be suppressing frustration.

Harry gazed at her with a mixture of horror and admiration.

She had become the righteously decadent courtesan of Egon Shiele's haunted imagination. Apart from the gorgeously unruly hair, it was difficult to recall the sly provocative images by Klimt.

"Who do you want to protect, Harry? Conrad Fearman? He has had two granddaughters, as he calls them, for decades. When one set of girls reaches puberty, they are replaced with another. He likes them in pairs. The discards are sold to pimps if they're lucky. Not by himself, of course. By a broker. Some are loaned out to be raped and eventually snuffed. Their little bodies are buried in your endless and majestic Canadian wilderness."

Harry felt sick. He remembered their names, Marissa and Colleen. Did each pair have the same names? They had their own nanny. They summered in a luxurious cottage on Lake Rosseau.

"Fearman's girls are from Ireland, Harry, not China, not India, not Papua New Guinea or Lesotho. Born as punishment to Catholic girls who strayed. Their Albanian nurse has been with them from birth. She will be there until they no longer meet Mr. Fearman's requirements. Then she will return to Ireland and be given a new assignment. Yes, women are involved in this too."

Joan listened intently. She said nothing. Harry realized the revealed horrors of hell she had learned as a child from nuns and priests had never been so graphic as what she must be envisioning now.

"You mentioned the Findlays from Oakville," Lena said. "They bought a replacement child after the boy called Peter, you knew him as Simon, was banished. I told them they would soon be exposed," Lena continued. "They tried to buy my silence with money and with tears. They went back to their dealer, Dimitri Sakarov. I suppose he explained that he couldn't stop me. They were humiliated—no, *mortified* would be the right word. They were respected members of their community. Death was their only option. I didn't expect they would take the little boy with them. But it's as well they did. Sakarov would simply have sold him all over again."

Joan ignored the cruelty of Madalena's judgment, asking instead, "What about your own daughter, Lena? Harry told me you have a daughter. Is she alive?"

Lena glared, then her lips pulled into a smile while her eyes narrowed to a pained squint. "She is dead. My ex-fiancé Dietmar Henning told me how she died."

"How did he know?"

Harry realized Joan did not know the details of Dietmar Henning's death.

"After a certain amount of coaxing, he confessed to killing her."

"Oh my God!"

"Your God, not mine," Lena declared bitterly. "My Freya would not cooperate with her captors. He was one of them. So he raped her."

"Oh God!"

"She was four years old."

"Jesus!" Harry exclaimed.

"Dietmar was humiliated by pride, not shame. He did not regret that he had done such heinous things to a child. He had done them before, and sometimes they died. He was very disturbed that I knew what he'd done. I was his betrothed, his one true love, he insisted that to the end."

"But he told you!"

"As I explained, Joan. I coaxed him. His dying words were a confession."

"With no absolution!" Joan's voice quavered.

Harry knew Joan believed in a ferocious God who could only be mollified through priestly intervention. She seemed more disturbed by Dietmar's death without the confessional sacrament and remission of his sins than by how he had died or whether he might have deserved eternal damnation.

Dominus noster Jesus Christus te absolvat! Karen murmured. *Exclude the bastard from the communion of saints. Cast him forever into the darkness.*

Harry recoiled from Karen's bitterness.

Freya and Lucy would have been the same age.

For himself, he was utterly repulsed by Lena's admission of brutality but profoundly moved, knowing the terrors her daughter had endured and the shock Lena must have experienced on discovering what her fiancé had done. He wanted to hold her and share her pain. He had a great capacity for pain. He wanted to throttle her for the cruelty of her response.

Lena had gone back to sorting through her paraphernalia, preparing for Harry's electrocardiogram.

"If you will just settle back on this mat on the floor, Harry. It would be better than sitting. Remove your shirt and your socks." She nodded to a fine Persian prayer rug on the floor between them.

"And if I don't?"

"I thought you understood, Harry. If you do not, I shall be forced to hurt Miss DeBrusk. Very badly if necessary. That is why she is here."

21 **PATHETIC FALLACY**

KAREN'S VOICE REVERBERATED INSIDE HARRY'S SKULL. He could hear the urgency and confusion. She was trying to speak in real time. He couldn't make out her words, but the panic was clear. He glanced at the pistol lying on the coffee table. He glanced at Lena. She seemed so certain of her dominance that the gun was superfluous. He glanced at Joan. She appeared distressingly indifferent to the threat on her life. Could it be she didn't understand?

There was a lot Harry didn't understand himself.

"Lena," he said, trying to suppress his frustration, to stifle his outrage. "We're here because Sakarov gave us no choice. We've come to bloody well help you."

"Mr. Sakarov is going to kill you if you don't kill him first," Joan added in a quiet voice she might have used to refuse cream in her coffee.

Lena turned away from her bank of equipment and smiled. The smile was unnerving. She could have been a deranged Dr. Frankenstein about to jolt his experiment into motion. Yet there was something beguiling in her smile, as if she had discovered herself to be the scientist's awakening monster, robust and bewildered in a baffling world.

"Listen, Harry. Listen! You can hear his footsteps."

She's bloody demented, Harry.

But Harry could hear heavy shuffling outside.

For an interminable moment, nothing happened. Then the door pushed open and Dimitri Sakarov filled the frame. The big man braced himself on both sides of the doorway, his chest heaving as he tried to catch his breath.

Well then there now. Everything's changed now, Harry. You're off the hook for your moral authority, but your life is seriously at risk.

Madalena Strauss seemed relieved by the fat man's arrival. Harry found this perplexing. Either she didn't understand why Sakarov was here. Or he didn't.

Or both do. Or neither does. The permutations are intriguing.

Sakarov tried to grin, but it came across as a grimace. The thick roll of fat between his shoulders and bulbous head was shot through with red striations. His cheeks showed a bloodless pallor as they pushed up into his eyes, reducing them to painful slits. He was wearing city shoes. Italian leather scuffed beyond redemption. His suit jacket was drenched with sweat; his pants had a rip in one knee, stained brown from dried blood. He glowered at Harry and ignored Joan.

Okay, Slate, if you're going to take him down, now's the time.

But Harry didn't move. He was too busy trying to read whatever was passing between the fat man and Madalena. As random ideas swarmed toward clarity, it was all beginning to make sense. He glanced at Joan. She offered him a heroic glimmer of solidarity. He glanced at Lena. Her voluptuous masses of hair absorbed sunlight diffused through the insulated blind. It looked matte black, with only a few hints of scarlet.

"So, Mr. Harry. You are not surprised to see me, yes?" Sakarov had resumed his Russian inflection.

"Not really. You've been following us for the last two days."

"Ah no, I was chasing you, don't you see? I was urging you on, making sure you were going in the right direction."

That's a different way of seeing things.

Sakarov glanced at Lena then aggressively back at Harry. He lifted a bulky arm and made a show of looking at his watch.

"You have less than one hour to go. You are very lucky I am here. You have saved many lives, perhaps. Of course, I am sure you thought when you found her, together you would gang up on Sakarov. Poor Harry."

Harry caught Joan's eye. He couldn't make out her expression.

Demure confusion, Harry? She's fifth business, crucial to the plot but extraneous as a character.

Her allusion to a Robertson Davies novel heartened him, but Sakarov's contempt and his confidence were disconcerting. As the big man trundled slowly across the room and eased himself into the largest chair, Harry forced himself to make a huge leap in logic. "You've been working with Lena all along," he said. The words spoken aloud seemed absurd.

"Not working *with* me, Harry, he was working *for* me."

Reality collapsed like a house of cards, the same way it had when he discovered she was no longer dead. Lena picked them up and began to reshuffle the deck.

"His options were limited," she explained. "They had been for some time." She stepped closer to Sakarov and placed a hand on his shoulder. He cringed almost imperceptibly and smiled. "You've done a good job, Dimitri. A little clumsy, perhaps. The death of those Findlay boys was unnecessary, especially the one who called himself Simon Wales. He was Harry's friend."

"I was angry. There was a weapon at hand."

"A water glass," said Harry.

"I was out of sorts. I had been shot by Miss DeBrusk and I was bleeding to death."

"My God, imagine if you really were," Lena observed. "There must be vast quantities of blood in that body of yours." She turned her attention back to Harry. "You see, I needed you here. That is what Rachel insisted. Dimitri made it happen. Joan was a means to an end. She is so wonderfully untouched by the world. I knew if you believed she was in danger, you would be compelled to rescue her. It's in your nature."

"Kidnapping Joan was your idea?" Harry was incredulous but not surprised.

"I arranged for Mr. Sakarov to insist Joan come to Vienna. I knew you'd take it from there."

"And just how did you force him to comply?"

"By killing his sister."

Oh God, Harry. Don't say anything. Just listen.

"He didn't like her," Lena declared. "Ask him. She was a manager at his Pushkin Hotel in Saint Petersburg. She was stealing from him and having an affair with his personal assistant, one Fyodor Blozinski. I did not go to Russia. I don't like Russia. I met her in Toronto."

"You met her, yes. You strangle her in Canada," Sakarov offered. "I did not like my sister so much, but Fräulein Strauss also promised she would murder my grandchildren unless I do what she says."

There seems to be an epidemic of threatening children, Harry. Who even knew the fat bugger had children of his own, never mind grandchildren.

Real grandchildren, I wonder?

Yes, real, or he wouldn't care if she destroyed them.

"Why didn't you just kill her?" said Harry to Sakarov with brutal logic. "And why the hell don't you speak the English you were born with?"

"Is my parent's English. I am Saskatchewan Russian."

"You're pathetic."

"You ask why I didn't kill Fräulein Strauss? Is not so simple, Harry. I tell you when we meet in Vienna how much power she has for control of lives. Information, you know, is most powerful weapon. Was better I cooperate."

"Better for whom?"

"If I do what she says, she promise the record of my criminal dealings is gone like wind, my grandchildren are okay, and I keep my Pushkin Hotel. Is very good business."

"When you first turned up at the Kressler, you were already working for her then?"

"Oh yes, from beginning."

"Drop the goddamned fake Russian."

"I am not fake Russian. Fake Canadian, maybe. I grow up in Saskatchewan and never play hockey. I never curl. I do not drink double-doubles. I like Timbit doughnut holes but not so much as *vatruska*. Is ancient pastry, very sweet. I never collect funny money at Canadian Tire. I go to agricultural college but never graduate." He seemed amused by his litany of Canadian traits.

Harry tuned Sakarov out as he scrutinized Lena's face for an indication of denial or remorse. She had settled into a desk chair with her back to the computer system and seemed to enjoy seeing her nefarious powers on open display. The opaque window behind her had turned sullen grey. The sky must have clouded over; a storm was building up and hiding the sun.

Pathetic fallacy; nature reflecting the human situation.

He ignored her. She was being willfully cheerful.

"This was all so that I would lend you my heartbeat, Lena? Why not just ask?"

"Because you would have refused."

"Your mentor was a very wise woman."

"Yes, she was."

"And you are self-consciously devious."

"Self-consciously? Yes, I am."

Harry scrolled through the details in his mind of their entire relationship. Since she had first contacted him by email she had been manipulating to get him to come to Hallstatt but more significantly to control his mind. She had played Sakarov like a pawn, and Sakarov had played Harry.

"Lena, did you plan for me to return to Toronto after you died the first time?"

"With my gift in the black box, yes."

"Your Klimts."

She looked dismayed that he had revealed the contents of the box.

"Just poor imitations, Harry."

"Oh really."

She stood up and walked over to him. He backed away and sat down on the sofa beside Joan. The natural light in the room had turned gloomy. She stood between Harry and the opaque window. In silhouette, she looked familiar again. She leaned close and spoke in a barely audible whisper.

"That part is between you and me. Whatever else happens, it is important that Elisabeth Bök remains safe and eventually returns to her homeland. Please, you will honour the terms of my gift."

"You have strangled Sakarov's sister, you have murdered Dietmar Henning, you have dumped a woman's body in the Danube Canal, and you have led me around Europe like a puppy on a leash. Now you are threatening the life of this woman beside me who has done nothing but good her entire life, and you are about to open a flood of accusations that could destroy the lives of thousands—but you ask me to honour your trust?"

"Yes, I do."

"It's that simple?"

"That simple, yes. I have avenged myself on the man who murdered my four-year-old daughter, Harry. I have eliminated the vicious sister of a man whose crimes are monstrous in scope and brutality. I have deceived you, perhaps, but you are here and unharmed, and I have threatened Miss DeBrusk but only because you might refuse to play your part in exposing inestimable decadence. And the woman in the canal, she was a derelict, her body was useful. She achieved more in death than in life, I expect. In the moral balance, I am perhaps not so bad."

"Why did you send me away after I just got here?"

"It's very simple, really. I brought you to Austria to help me. I needed your heart, yes. I needed your moral authority. Mr. Sakarov and I, we tested you, Harry. Over *wienerschnitzel* and *kaiserschmarrn.* For my purposes, you were suitable."

"And for Sakarov's?"

"He doesn't matter. You were much as Rachel thought you would be. You would do the right thing at the right time. Meanwhile, I needed you to take care of my personal property. So I made sure you were sympathetic to me, if not my cause, and sent you home."

"You sent me! Was that before or after you turned up dead?"

"Death was my disguise. I needed to disappear because Mr. Sakarov's very powerful and infinitely cruel colleagues were closing in. I needed us both to be safe."

Harry turned to Sakarov. "You warned her about your friends?"

"I had my grandchildren and my hotel to protect."

"But not your sister?"

"It was too late."

Harry turned back to Madalena.

"If Sakarov was your reluctant ally," he cast a withering glare in the Russian's direction then looked back to Lena, "if he was under your control, how could he have tortured you? Why would you allow him to rape you?"

"If I allowed him, it would not be rape. But look at him, Harry. He is a pig. He would not get near my body unless I was dead."

"But he did."

"Harry, there was no torture," Lena declared emphatically.

"I saw you, for God's sake. You were brutalized."

"I wanted to make sure you were totally committed before you went back to Toronto. How better than to share my suffering."

Harry was bewildered. He had washed away blood from her wounds, he had cleansed ash from her burns, he had soothed her bruises with ointment.

"It's impossible," he protested.

"Unlikely, perhaps. Not impossible."

Listen to her, Harry. She's proud of herself.

He was thinking. The cuts were surface wounds. The burns were hideous but superficial. The bruises were only in places she could reach.

But wouldn't an autonomic survival mechanism kick in?

Apparently not.

He could not conceive of motivation strong enough to override the pain she must have endured. "You have a monstrous imagination, Lena."

"You're here, aren't you?"

Harry sat forward on the sofa and tried to stare into the depths of Madalena's haunted eyes, but he could only see his own image reflected from their surface sheen.

"I could smell wildflower honey and fresh paint," he said. "You burned yourself with beeswax tapers and cut yourself with a window-glass paint scraper. You beat yourself with bare fists. You also burned yourself with cigarettes, knowing I'd connect them to Sakarov. You probably used his brand and you flushed the butts. You were never raped. That's why you refused to permit medical treatment."

"You noticed my windows had been painted. You are very observant."

The woman's resolute courage conflicted with her depraved commitment. He searched for clarity. "What about your beating in Toronto?"

"In the King William? That was real, of course. Oswaldo refused to cooperate, but Gregor was willing."

"He was willing? You invited the beating."

"They knew their employer would approve."

"Conrad Fearman?"

"Yes. They knew he was disturbed by my project. Oswaldo could not bring himself around to beating a woman, but Gregor complied. He used a dishtowel, he wrapped it around his hand, he hit me as I directed. I bruise quite easily. It is the pale skin, I think."

"Why, for God's sake?"

"I knew you were coming to my rescue, I had to make it worth your while. I needed you, Harry. But you are a thinking man—for me, that was your strength, but it was also your flaw. I had to be sure you would be ruled by what you felt, not what you thought."

It worked, Harry thought.

"I enjoyed our interlude while I stayed as your houseguest. It was pleasant spending time with you as well, Joan, and so easy, with you, to remain an unknown commodity. I was happy. But Mr. Sakarov became anxious. He was afraid Fearman's thugs might realize their folly in cooperating with me. They might return and eliminate me. The beating was a contentious issue. Murder would simply be work. Sakarov worried this might happen before I had time to remove evidence of his own criminal activities from our files. He worried that if I was eliminated you would release them yourself, although I explained that you couldn't. Rachel had made sure we must work together."

Sakarov shifted his gigantic bulk in his chair. He was looking uneasy. Harry suspected the fat man was only beginning to realize the extent of Lena's Machiavellian powers. He had assumed in doing what she ordered he had remained in control of his own destiny. Now he apparently wasn't so sure.

"I must admit," Lena said, addressing Harry as if the others weren't there, "I was disappointed when you left Vienna quite so suddenly. I thought you might have stayed for the funeral."

"You didn't float to the surface for another week."

"But Vienna has so much to offer."

"You told me about your Pandora's hoard of iniquity and at that point I wanted nothing to do with it."

"I also told you about my gatekeeper. You didn't know it was you, of course. When you returned to Canada, you chose art over life, Harry—trinkets on a golden bough; my Klimts over the lives of innumerable suffering children."

That's not how it was, he thought, but he couldn't be certain.

"So," she said, "the threat to Joan got you back on track."

Harry rose to his feet and walked behind Sakarov to the window. He reached past Lena to raise the blind. The sky over the Hallstätter See had turned an angry grey. The lake water itself was virtually black. Lena tilted her head. Her hair radiated in waves away from her face which in the softened illumination looked strangely serene, as if everything was happening according to a plan that only she understood.

Harry glanced at the pistol on the table. He felt the weight of the bullets loose in his pocket. Sakarov shifted in his chair and Harry remembered how fast he could be despite his bulk. Harry wondered if Sakarov was armed.

As Harry surveyed the room, Joan watched him with an expression of sustained fascination, like a pedestrian caught in the headlights of an oncoming car. He gave her a nod of encouragement.

He wasn't sure what he was going to do next, but he needed her to be engaged, needed to be able to count on her.

"Joan," he said, "what do you make of all this?"

She brightened, as if until now she had felt excluded.

"I think we are in a hell of a mess." She paused, apparently adrift in her own thoughts for a moment. "Harry, why wouldn't Mr. Sakarov's friends follow him when he was following us? It would have been in their best interests to do so, don't you think?"

She gave her hair an abrupt toss away from her forehead.

"I think you're right," said Harry. "Unless they're counting on Sakarov."

"To do what? Perhaps they know you and Lena must both be present for the release of her files. And here you are."

"I don't even think Sakarov knew that."

Sakarov shifted his weight but said nothing.

Joan smiled with inexplicable satisfaction. "I hate to use a hackneyed term, but this is ground zero for the bad guys, isn't it? If biometric identification breaks down, or if Lena changes her mind, they are free to carry on as they have been."

Where's she going with this, Harry?

Lena spoke up, unaware of Karen's misgivings. "Rachel counted on my powers of persuasion and Harry's philosophical acumen to harmonize. There is no going back. We will release my files; you will be our witness. Mr. Sakarov is free to go."

"And if you are both dead?" Joan asked, still smiling.

"Then the files die and countless children continue to suffer."

"Would the files be irretrievable?" Joan asked.

"Lost in a cyberspace cache for eternity."

"And what if you remain alive, but your computer system breaks down?"

"It won't."

"But if it did?"

"The files would no longer be accessible. Rachel established this as our access point. We might as well be dead."

"That would be a shame," said Joan with a guileless smile. She reached into her large handbag and withdrew a tissue and blew her nose. She reached in again and pulled out a scaled down Glock semi-automatic, brandishing it like an outsized tube of lip gloss. The others stared at her in wide-eyed amazement. Harry expected to hear the rumblings of pathetic fallacy from thunder outside.

"Oops," said Joan with cloying cheerfulness. "It seems Mr. Sakarov's business associates are represented after all."

Joan flourished her weapon with a dexterity that surprised Harry.

She was a hunter, remember. She's used to killing big things.

Sakarov started to rise from his easy chair.

"Sit!" Joan commanded, slipping the safety catch. "Mr. Sakarov, you and I are not allies. I shot you once, I look forward to doing so again. Did you really think you could hurt my friend Simon and not pay the price? And you should not have groped me. That was not at all nice."

"But I didn't."

"You did. In the King William."

"Oh that," he sneered. "I had forgotten. I suppose I did."

"You deserve this," she said, shifting her gun from one hand to the other.

"*Morituri te salutamus.*" He offered a mock salute as he settled against the back of his chair.

With a startled look in her eyes, Joan fired in Sakarov's direction. His head lurched slightly within the collar of fat around his neck. His eyes widened and his pupils rolled upward trying to focus on what looked like a housefly that had settled on his forehead. A thin wisp of blood escaped from a small crater as the fly disappeared into Sakarov's skull. Behind him, a fine spray of blood and viscera hung in the air. His mouth formed a gasping hole and his eyes went perfectly still.

22 THE SALT MINE

SAKAROV SANK INTO HIS OWN BULK, A PYRAMIDAL MOUND of immovable flesh. Harry felt strangely dissociated from the death scene. He listened for Karen's voice, but she had burrowed deep into his mind and refused to be heard. Madalena Strauss looked curiously amused. She seemed indifferent to arbitrary death and was apparently impressed by Joan's surprising metamorphosis. Joan herself was a picture of composure with the same sweet smile and soulful eyes, the same aura of injured innocence, that had endeared her to Harry when she had first appeared to take charge of the foundling girl in his apartment.

Joan gazed out the window, assessing the weather. "We're in for a good storm," she announced.

"Were you expecting your friends?" Lena asked.

"Oh no, I am here on my own. Look, you can see the rain clouds sweeping up the mountainside. Lena, Harry, we had better get moving. Please, on your feet."

Sakarov was evidence of what happened with non-compliance. Harry and Lena moved in the direction Joan indicated. The three of them stepped through to the shed and then outside into a different world altogether of battered wood, rusted iron, shattered rock, and mounded tailings. As they moved amid what seemed like a primitive industrial wasteland, moisture-laden air turned to lashing rain. Its elemental force drove them more quickly toward the great iron door into the mine.

At Joan's direction, Harry removed a heavy crossbar and struggled to pull the door open. Rusted hinges shrieked against the din of the storm as he worked them loose. He turned to the two women behind him when the door was open enough for them to squeeze through. He was under a slight overhang of rock and his jacket was relatively dry, but they were both drenched.

Observing Joan, Harry was reminded of canoe trippers he'd met as a kid who seemed oblivious to weather extremes. Her russet hair was plastered close to her skull and rain water smoothed the flesh of her face into sculptural contours. It was as if she enjoyed being caught in the storm. Lena had appeared less in her element, but once under shelter, when she violently shook her head, her hair glistened like a halo and she seemed like a woman who had just stepped from the shower prepared for a night of debauchery.

Joan motioned with her Glock. Harry and Lena slipped deeper into the dank confines of the darkened mine. Water sloshed at their feet as Joan followed them in.

"Puddles, good. You will have water. I'll leave you now. But Harry, the car keys, please. Thank you. I'm sorry about the cabin, Lena, but as soon as the rain stops, I must cremate Mr. Sakarov. Then I'm off for home. My friend David Morgan must be worried."

"You're not going to burn down my house?" Lena challenged. "My computers! Please, Joan, do not do this."

"It would not be possible to move Mr. Sakarov, even if both of you helped me. And where would we put him? Not in here with you. That would be very unpleasant."

"Don't you dare destroy Rachel's computers!" Lena screamed.

Harry had never heard her so desperate.

"Rachel's computers? Your files. Yes, I'm afraid I must. There will be a fire, then there will be nothing left of Mr. Sakarov but ashes among ashes."

"Apart from his monstrous legacy of grief and perversion," Lena snarled.

"Ah, don't you see? The harrowing of hell is impossible. We have long since fallen from grace. There will be an endless succession of Dimitri Sakarovs in this middling world of ours. If there were no hell, then what's a heaven for, as they say. I'm sorry to leave you like this, with no possibility of closure."

"I'd say trapped in a salt mine is closure enough."

"I meant for your daughter."

Lena Strauss slipped into silence. Harry felt her presence at his side. She had become no more substantial in the darkness than Karen. Except Karen made sense to him and Lena's Machiavellian obsessions put her beyond comprehension.

Joan stood in silhouette against the ragged landscape visible through the entryway door.

"Joan, why?" Harry asked.

"No reason, Harry."

She scrounged for something in her Roots bag and came up with a wilted Bavarian sausage.

"Here," she said. "You might as well have this. And thanks for packing my other shoes. I'll need them once I get back to Hallstatt."

He couldn't see her features, but her voice sounded eerily calm. She started to back out through the partially closed iron door, then paused.

"I know you'd like to understand, Harry, but there's not much I can say. I'm not driven by existential angst or childhood trauma. I was never abused or subject to bouts of depression. I had a reasonably happy childhood, a good education, a modest but satisfying love life, an engaging job, the prospect of contentment through a long middle age, and the genetic predisposition for a relatively brief dotage and satisfactory passing. When Mr. Fearman approached me to do what Mr. Sakarov wanted, it seemed so out of the ordinary, I was easily won over. His offer to donate a million dollars to the Zylberman Centre helped. His friends in Vienna gave me the gun. Then you turned up as predicted. And that is my story—there is no story. Amen."

"What about Simon?"

"Simon was my friend. His killer is dead."

Harry felt a surge of grief before letting Simon Wales slip into the black hole where he suppressed his inconsolable losses. Joan DeBrusk backed out into the dusk.

"For God's sake, Joan, you can't just leave us here to die," Harry protested.

"There's another way out; there's always another way out. I've been here before, remember. There are miles and miles of passageways. This mountain is riddled with tunnels and shafts. It'll take you a couple of days, but you'll find the exit. I'm sure Lena knows where it is. You may have to improvise a bit. But you're very resourceful, both of you. I'm sure you'll be okay."

"Joan," Lena spoke in a quiet voice. "The tunnel is blocked."

Joan pushed the door shut with a reverberating clang, followed by a loud grating sound as she slid the iron crossbar into place, leaving Harry and Madalena Strauss locked in total darkness. Instinctively, they moved closer. The sense of the other's presence was reassuring. Neither of them spoke. Harry reached out and took Lena's hand. Together they edged away from the door onto a slight rise above the pooled water.

Harry couldn't remember ever experiencing such an absolute absence of light. There was paradoxically more brightness when he closed his eyes tight than when they were open. With even the tiniest sound reverberating against the rock walls, he felt absurdly disoriented. He took a step, but his knees threatened to give out as he tried to compensate for the absence of sensory cues. He crouched down to steady himself.

"Are you all right, Harry?"

"Yes, keep talking. I need to connect."

"Me too. It's better with voices."

"You know your way around?" he asked hopefully.

"I wasn't allowed to come in here when I was a kid."

"So you didn't?"

"I certainly did. And yes, there used to be another exit. I'm not sure I could find it, but it doesn't much matter. Five years ago a gigantic rock slide completely blocked it off."

"Completely?"

"Sorry."

"This isn't good." Harry had lowered his voice to an echoing whisper.

"Harry, did she mean us to die here?"

"No, her job was to erase the files. Fearman convinced her they would destroy innocent people. I suspect the elimination of Sakarov was moral outrage she couldn't otherwise bring into focus. And revenge, which I'm sure she'd deny."

"She's a strange one, Harry. I kind of liked her."

"Yeah, she's likeable. Nice hair."

"Of course," said Lena. "Beautiful hair."

"We've got to get moving."

"Where, Harry? The tunnel is blocked."

"We need to explore."

"There's nowhere to go."

"We need heat. We need light. We need to think."

"We have plenty of time to think."

"We're not giving up."

"No Harry, we're not. But perhaps we need to accept the grim reality. There is no way out of this terrible place."

Harry stared into the darkness. He moved his head, but nothing changed.

"Do you think there's anything in here that will burn?" he asked.

"There might be some branches and boards. Kids dragged stuff in to make forts over the years. I once even slept here when Rachel thought I had run away."

"Did you run away often?"

"A few times."

Harry hitched his pants to pull the damp material away from his skin. He reached into his pocket. The bullets were still there. He grasped a single bullet and pulled it out. He squatted and felt for rocks smaller than his fist. Then he manoeuvred around until he found a dry flat surface of packed rubble. Lena stayed close as he moved.

Using the rocks as a vice and pliers, he carefully worked the slug away from the casing.

"Lena, stay very still. I'm going to dump gunpowder on the ground. If I can get a spark, we'll have a brief flare of light. Look around you. Memorize what you see. We need wood and we need something to elevate us off the ground. We need water to drink."

He tapped the bullet casing against stone, spilling its contents into a small pile. Then he took a rock in each hand and struck them together over the pile. No sparks. He needed steel. He felt for his belt buckle. It was brass.

"I need your belt," he said.

Her broad leather belt had a steel buckle. He felt the surface of his rocks and chose the one with hard smooth facets that he hoped meant it was flint or quartz. He struck the stone and buckle sharply together. Sparks. He kneeled down close to his pile of gunpowder and struck his makeshift lighter again and again. Suddenly there was a blinding flare. Harry saw nothing but white light that burned into his retinas and then flickered to black.

"Okay," said Lena in a muffled voice. She was facing away from him as she spoke. "It's all familiar. There's a bunch of wood. I'm going to crawl over." She must have been pointing. He understood her need to crawl. Moving in an upright posture in the absolute darkness induced vertigo. "Keep talking. Your voice will tell me I'm going in a straight line. This part of the mine is an antechamber about the size of the chalet with an ungodly deep hole off to one side, an air shaft to a tunnel way down underneath us. Okay, when I've found the wood, I'll let you know. Do another bullet, I'll gather whatever I can."

"I'll come too."

"I need your voice there. Anyway, you're the light source, Harry. I'm a creature of darkness."

You see, symbolism is hard to resist.

Harry talked as he listened to Lena slither over the coarse earth and through puddles. He described what he was doing as he prepared to explode the powder from the second bullet. When she was ready, he lit the gunpowder. It flared, again blinding him.

"Keep talking, Harry. I've got some good stuff."

Over the sound of his own voice, he could hear boards and branches being dragged across the cavern floor.

"Okay, you're nearly here," he said. He reached out and his hand sank into her bedraggled hair. "Good. Are there any twigs? What about pine needles?"

"It's all too big. Have you got your wallet?"

Harry removed a small cluster of euros from his wallet. He set up another flare with the third bullet and handed Lena a euro to hold an edge into the combusted powder when it flared. After this, he had one bullet left.

"Ready," he said. "Here we go."

The euro caught, flickered, and went out.

"The damned thing is damp," Lena said.

"This is our last bullet," Harry explained. "Try blowing."

"It'll just get damp from my breath."

"Okay, let's try it again."

What about bills or receipts, Harry? I'll bet they're more flammable than money. And doesn't your friend carry a lipstick? That's grease!

Hearing Karen at this point made him feel like a scared kid who'd wandered from home only to discover his parents knew where he was all along.

"Bills," he said out loud.

"Pardon?" said Lena.

"Have you got any pockets in that outfit?" he asked. "Have you got any lipstick?"

"Lip gloss. There's a little still left in the tube."

"That'll do."

He found a couple of folded receipts in his wallet and handed them to Lena, directing her to coat them with lip gloss.

"Okay," he said. "Let's get some wood ready in case this works."

Together they broke off some shards from the weathered boards and gathered a few branches small enough to break with their hands. Then they crouched to the task, the gunpowder flared, the greasy paper caught fire, the pyre of wood ignited.

"Thank you, Karen," he said out loud.

"Thank you, Cairn," said Lena, mimicking his homage to an unknown deity.

"Let's get some rest, then we'll get to it."

"To what?"

He didn't answer. He wasn't sure.

Shadows danced across the walls like frightened spirits as the fire roared and then quieted down as the flames faded to a soporific glow. It had been a long day. It was probably nighttime by now. They arranged a few boards by the fire and curled close to each other on top of them, drawing his soiled nubuck jacket over like a blanket.

They dozed fitfully. Several times, Harry woke up and shoved charred ends of wood deeper into the embers to keep the fire alight. Eventually he couldn't sleep. He got up, walked into the shadows and relieved himself. When he returned to the fire, Lena's eyes gleamed green in the flickering light as she shifted to give him more room on the boards.

"Good morning," she said.

He could not decide if she was forcing her cheerfulness or if good cheer was the product of hopelessness.

"I wonder if the sun's up?" she said. "Has Joan turned my chalet into a funeral pyre? She's a very strange girl, you know."

"You said that before."

"She is. Her primary motive seems to be a kind of innocent curiosity. She's pathological, Harry."

"No, she's religious. There's no need for moral responsibility when you're convinced you're right."

You're an anarchist to the end—but you're right on, Slate. The girl's bush Catholic?

Both of you insist on calling her *a girl.* As if executing a man in cold blood and consigning us to death in a salt mine is cute.

"You figure we slept through the night," he said, addressing the only other living person present. "I couldn't tell you whether I've had two hours sleep or ten. I still feel depleted."

Lena didn't respond.

"I'm going hunting," he said.

He drew a small root with a flaming end from the fire and, holding his torch at arm's length, set out to explore their prison. First he went to the door. The puddle in front of it had soaked into the packed rubble. Off to the side, a rock wall glistened and felt damp to the touch. By digging down with his hands, he cleared a depression the size of a basin which slowly filled with water. He took a sip. It tasted brackish but was drinkable. He beckoned Lena to come over and she crouched on her knees and drank.

He tested the door. It was unyielding. They turned and walked hand in hand, exploring the limits of their confinement. To one side, there was the vertical air shaft big enough for a man to fall through. On the other side the rock wall was rough with the marks of prehistoric miners scrabbling for rock salt to preserve their meats and trade with their neighbours. At the farthest end of the cavern, the actual mine tunnelled into solid rock.

He blew on his smouldering torch to revitalize the flame.

"You stay here," he said. "I'm going in."

"It's blocked, Harry. The rockslide."

"Yeah, I know. Joan was here before it happened."

"You are not making excuses for her?"

He wondered if he was. He moved forward. The glare of his torch nearly blinded him as one foot reached tentatively in front of the other, feeling for a purchase in the stifling gloom. He gasped as his foot struck an impediment. He held his torch to the side so he could see ahead.

The beginning of the slide.

He looked back, startled to find Lena only a few paces behind. She moved up beside him. He put his arm around her for a moment, then they both turned and retreated back into the quavering light of the antechamber.

"Not much fuel," he announced. They picked up stray bits of wood as they made their way to the fire. "We'll have to burn our bed-boards. It's amazingly dry in here." Residual salt in the rock leached moisture from the air.

Natural mummification has already begun, even before you've expired.

Thanks, I needed to know that. You're unnaturally chipper.

I'm dead.

He realized once they had dried off they weren't cold. The ambient temperature was comfortable. They needed the fire to fend off the oppressive darkness.

"Sit down and rest, Harry. Don't use up your energy. Sleep for a bit."

When they woke again, Harry fished around for the limp sausage staining the pocket of his nubuck jacket. He stuck a small branch through it and warmed it over the fire. They ate it slowly. He was aware of how salty it was, but the grease felt good hitting his gut.

After a while, they dozed. When they woke they took deep drinks of brackish rainwater. The level in the basin was diminishing.

Harry walked over to the air shaft and dropped a precious stick of burning wood into the depths. It exploded into brilliance from the rush of fresh air as it fell, then as it tumbled against rocks the light shattered into sparks and the shaft returned to a menacing black. To confirm his estimation of its depth he tossed a couple of small rocks into the darkness and listened for them to hit bottom. He retreated to the fire.

They talked. Their lips were cracking. The lip gloss was gone. Their throats were raw but the company of words was worth the discomfort. They tried to talk about Joan, about destructive innocence. They moved on to Klimt and Egon Shiele for a while and shared their impressions of the Secession building and the Beethoven frieze. They drifted into an exchange on the voluptuous evil of Orson Welles in *The Third Man*. She hummed a few bars of the theme but, without the otherworldly drone of the zither, Harry couldn't connect.

When they woke again, the fire had burned down to embers. Lena squirmed around and poked it until an array of sparks lit the air with flashes of red and orange. They gazed at the colourful shower, then in a rasping voice Lena asked, "Harry, are you afraid of dying?"

"No."

"Me neither. I've done it before."

Me too, Karen whispered.

They crawled over to the water supply and strained a few mouthfuls through teeth clenched to catch the grit. Returning to the remains of their fire, they leaned against each other for a while in the flickering darkness.

Harry went back to the air shaft. He dropped another shard of burning wood into the hole. He edged forward, bracing his weight against the rock wall, and stretched across until he could touch the far side.

"Lena," he called. "I'm going down. I need light."

Silently, she crawled over to him. She seemed to assess his plan, then returned to their meagre supply of wood by the fire and brought the entire small pile back to him.

He lit a gnarled root from his flare and once it was blinding bright he dropped it into the darkness. After a brief shower of sparks when it landed, the root continued to glow, filling the shaft with a flicker of light. Still, after all his calculations, he wasn't sure of the depth. He didn't like not knowing. He reached behind him and his fingers found Lena's thigh. He gave it a squeeze, then edged forward until he was braced sideways between the rock walls.

He had put his jacket back on to diminish abrasions, but as he inched his way down the rock gouged into him. A foothold gave way. He lurched, plunged a full body length, extended, twisted, jammed himself between the walls, caught his breath, worked his way down, slipped into air, and sprawled across the smouldering root.

"Damn it," he called. "Lena, we've made it."

He looked up. It was only a three storey drop, maybe four. Her hair flared against the flickering light from the fire in the antechamber.

"Come on," he shouted. "Drop the wood to me. We'll need light."

Suddenly pieces of board and branches plummeted down and he had to duck to the side.

"Now you," he called.

"No, Harry. I can't."

You waited too long, she hasn't got the strength.

Oh God.

On the other hand, if you hadn't waited so long you wouldn't have been desperate or foolish enough to try. Do you really believe this will lead to another way out?

Gotta believe in something.

Said the atheist.

"Lena, I'll catch you," he called.

That would be bloody absurd.

But in the twisted logic of terror, it seemed plausible.

As he watched with his heart thudding against the inside of his chest and his stomach knotted, she edged forward, blocking out the flickering light overhead, then slowly she descended. When she finally reached the top of the chamber he was standing in, Harry reached up. He touched her thigh, the last place he'd touched before he left her. She released her muscles and fell. Together they toppled onto the rubble and lay tangled in each other's arms, both gasping for breath.

The first thing Harry noticed when he rose to his feet, after helping Lena to sit upright, was the burning root. Tiny flares popped here and there on its gnarled surface. There was fresh air nurturing the flames back to life.

Harry picked it up and surveyed their surroundings. The tunnels on either side of them, large enough to permit human entry, led into absolute darkness. But one tunnel held only dead air. The other came alive with the flickering of his torch as he moved into it.

He gathered their wood in a bundle, then reached out for Lena.

"Harry, I can't move."

He tried to lift her to her feet. She screamed.

"Your muscles have seized," he whispered.

"Leave me, go on. See what you can find."

A flush of terror swept through him as he stood over her. He could not bear the thought of getting lost and dying alone. Or of returning and finding her dead. He squatted beside her and began to massage her limbs.

"Here?" he asked.

"Yes."

"And here? Here?"

License my roving hands, and let them go
Behind, before, above, between, below.

Dear God, he thought, addressing the deity of the impious cleric John Donne as he added more appropriate words from Donne's famous sermon, "Never send to know for whom the bell tolls; it tolls for thee."

Too soon for the death knell, Harry. Rage with Dylan Thomas against the dying of the light.

Lines from innumerable half-remembered poems clashed in his mind. Enough, he mutely declared, staring into the shadows. Enough!

"Come on," he said, addressing Lena. "Let's go, let's give it a try."

Slowly they rose together; taking up their torch and bundle of wood they shuffled into the darkness.

Other small tunnels led off to the sides, but they followed the flimsy current of fresh air until they came to an impasse of boulders that had tumbled down from another shaft. There was no possibility of moving forward.

Simple as that, Harry. It's over.

Nothing dramatic, merely rubble and rock. Air seeping through between immovable boulders. As simple as that. Their hoard of wood was nearly consumed. With no words between them, they turned back. They stopped to rest as little as possible to make the most of their diminishing light. At one point they heard the clanging of steel.

"The door, Harry!" Her voice cracked from the strain.

He tried to shout. Nothing intelligible came out, only the guttural sounds of a stricken animal. He tried to lick his lips, his tongue scraping over the calloused raw flesh. He whispered, "It's nothing."

They moved ahead.

When they reached the spot below the shaft, Harry tried to make sounds by smashing rocks together, but the sounds echoed like a taunt and there was no response from the darkness above.

He gathered the few bits of wood that still littered on the rubble floor and created a small fire. They settled close together on his shredded jacket and disappeared into sleep.

23 ABSOLUTE DARKNESS

TIME THICKENED AND BECAME IMMEASURABLE. THEY dozed, stirred, drifted at the edge of consciousness. Finally, saturated with sleep, Harry rose and in the dying light explored the dead end tunnel and finally found a trickle of water. He drew in a slow mouthful and took it to Lena, letting it drain from his mouth into hers. After a few draughts, they both felt better. They talked, despite the discomfort. They discussed their dreams.

"Mine are loaded with symbolism," Harry declared. The pain made him smile.

"Can you interpret the symbols?"

He thought she was smiling as well. "When I wake up they shatter."

"Dreams do that, don't they?"

They both experienced severe stomach cramps and massaged each other's bellies. At least they had water.

Time simply became a context for each separate moment. The agonies of making themselves talk were affirming. They talked about the impossibility of Nazi atrocities, they talked about the impossibility of crimes against children, they talked about the impossibility of evil.

Eventually, talking became more painful than silence. They listened to the quiet, interrupted by the feeble crackling of their diminutive fire and the raw sounds of their own parched breathing. Each appeared spectral in the flickering light. Then the light flared and turned into darkness. All they had left were their voices, their touch, their imagination.

"It would be nice to believe in God," Harry murmured.

"Why? I can die without God."

"I know what you mean."

A few times, when he hovered between wakefulness and sleep, Karen whispered to him. He knew she was nowhere except in his mind. He knew his mind was closing down. Yet strangely it gave him comfort to know she was there.

"Harry?"

"Yes?"

"What do you think about drinking blood?" Lena's voice was surprisingly clear, but the strength had gone out of it.

"Not while the bleeder's alive."

"I suppose there's no point, anyway." After a few moments of contemplation, she said, "What about eating flesh?"

"Maybe," he said. "It would have to be cooked."

"Fire's gone."

"Maybe raw."

"But only after the other one dies."

"If it isn't too late."

"Too late?"

"It just might not seem worth it."

"I'd rather we go at the same time," she said.

"You can't wish yourself dead."

God knows there were times when he'd have liked to. On the banks of the Anishnabe River when he realized Karen and Matt and Lucy were gone—the horror when he realized he was alive, and later when he realized Karen's body had been consumed by the river. For Lena, there must have been times after Freya was abducted and again when she knew how Freya died—when death offered the respite of oblivion but would not come on its own.

"Do you want to talk about the files?" he asked.

"It's over, Harry. My research was solace. Vengeance was, was," she faltered, "was knowing I tried. We cannot change anything. We can tame the cat and call it domestic, but it is still a tiger inside. It will kill what it can. We are fallen, Harry, we can only weep."

"I'm sorry."

"It's over."

She nestled close to him, making herself small. "I don't want to talk anymore," she said in a brittle voice.

Harry closed his eyes against the unutterable darkness and flickering apparitions danced in his skull against the rock all around them.

Later she mumbled about Freya in German or perhaps Yiddish, repeating the word *Freya* over and over.

She didn't speak after that.

Karen had lapsed into silence as well. She had settled in, waiting.

He slowly released his hold on Lena's body and laid her out beside him on the dry rubble and covered her with the remains of his jacket.

He waited. Time spread around him like a vast, dense emptiness.

Sometimes he crawled to the trickle of water. Each time, he returned to Lena's side, pressing against her, touching her, sometimes whispering, sometimes dreaming, awake and asleep. Sometimes ravaged by familiar images, sometimes aware only of the swollen blackness surrounding them. Sometimes impatient.

He felt Karen's presence, but she remained silent.

He thought about Joan, mostly in images where she merged with Lena, where her radiant smile turned into a gaping maw that swallowed him whole into the darkness inside her. He thought about the destructiveness of innocence, about Joan's childhood where absolution displaced rules and God was awesome but indifferent and faith was a facile convenience.

She was named after a rock star, Joan Jett. Snippets of of her lyrics floated through his mind.

Gradually hell closed over him and he remembered the red canoe hovering, plummeting into thundering impossible turbulence, his children's smashed and twisted bodies, Karen hurtling among rocks. He felt himself falling into welcome unconsciousness.

But he wasn't unconscious. He snapped to, sat upright, alive. Hope is the worst evil of all, Nietzsche whispered inside his head. Hope prolongs torment.

Hope conjures the future, he answered. He rose unsteadily to his feet. He moved around his small cell, scraping at the walls with his fingers until they bled, finding holds to grasp in the rock face, pulling himself upward, falling, getting up, discarding his shoes, climbing, seizing a purchase with his fingers, with his toes, bracing, climbing, jamming himself against the walls of the shaft, furiously, calmly, frantically, slowly, working his way upward, eventually up over the edge onto the floor of the antechamber.

He crawled to where he knew their fire had been.

He could smell the odour of their bodies and sweat, the odour of lip gloss, of burnt wood, of fear and of courage. He slipped into unconsciousness. He dreamed empty dreams. Blackness swarmed. He couldn't tell if he was awake or asleep.

Startled by the piercing clang of the iron door, he scrambled onto all fours. Blinded by the flooding light, he rose to his feet and staggered toward it. He tried to speak, but no sounds came out. He coughed.

"Hello, hello," said an ancient voice in the light.

Harry closed his eyes and stepped through.

"*Ach, mein Gott in Himmel.*"

The old woman from the village struggled as she put her arms around Harry to steady herself.

"Your friend, Fräulein DeBrusk, by herself she take your car, I think."

Harry struggled to bring his rescuer into focus, to make sense of her voice. The old woman held both his hands in hers. They steadied each other.

"She call last week to see where you were. So I came looking for you, but Rachel's chalet to the ground had burnt. The person who lived there took the Russian away, I think. A man from Salzburg very angry he came and drove away his BMW auto."

The old woman was depleted from opening the door, from climbing the mountain, from finding Harry. She reached into a small rucksack and pulled out a water bottle. While he took deep sips, she unwrapped a mint and handed it to him, nestled against its wrapper so her skin wouldn't touch it.

"So, Mister," she continued. "A few days ago, your Fräulein DeBrusk, she call me again. So I come back. I even look into the mine like she said, but you are not here, only some pieces of burnt wood. Then today, since I think about that fire it was fresh, I come again and *mein Gott* you are here now. You stink very much like death. But, *ist gut*, better than if you are dead."

Back in Toronto, when Harry stepped off the elevator on the twenty-third floor, he felt a surge of relief, but only after he walked into his living room and gazed out at the magnificent vista, taking in the harbour, the islands in full autumn colour, and the cold open blue of the lake rising to meet the horizon, only then did he relax.

It's good to be home, Harry.

It was. And yet he felt an uneasy distance had grown between them, like she wasn't quite there.

It's called "getting used to it." Life intervenes. Sooner or later you'll need to move on. It's what we both need.

For God's sake, he wanted to protest. Stay with me, Sailor. You're the only one I can count on.

That's an illusion, Harry. I'm dead.

No response seemed adequate.

Harry poured himself a single malt scotch from the bottle he bought duty free in Vienna and stood with his back to the Klimts, gazing at the malevolently grinning whale in his Blackwood etching. Then he slowly turned and examined the paintings, picking out the brush strokes and tracing with his eyes where the hard edges and soft contours merged, trying vainly to reduce art to technique and design. The woman in *The Kiss* was ecstatic. He could easily imagine Gustav Klimt locked with his beloved Elisabeth Bök in eternal submission. The detail from *The Forces of Evil* was not so allusive. It did not deliver a narrative or allegory. Removed from an imponderable story and painted with exquisite precision, it seemed to animate the most elusive blending of innocence and desire that anyone could ever envision. Apocryphal, perhaps, but it was a perfect and haunting portrait of the model's great granddaughter, Madalena Strauss.

It hadn't been until he and the old woman had descended the mountainside to the village and he had eaten, cleaned up, and changed into clothes she went out and bought for him that he felt confident there would be no one looking for Madalena. She had died in early July in Vienna. Her funeral had been held in the Secession Building. As Frau Honsberger had assured him on his circuitous way through to Toronto, giving her thin hair streaked with fresh green strands a knowing shake, it was a worthy place to celebrate the life of an exquisitely beautiful woman.

No one at all would be looking for Dimitri Sakarov.

Harry looked back to the Klimts with bittersweet nostalgia. He knew he'd have to return them to Austria where they belonged. If he negotiated with sufficient finesse, he might get a finder's fee to cover his costs.

He wandered restlessly from room to room then picked up his phone. There were several messages. He decided he needed ice in his scotch and paused to admire the untouched Dom Pérignon in the fridge before skimming through until he came to David Morgan's voice. He listened as he sipped his drink.

Harry, call me when you get back. I talked to Detective Honsberger. She said you'd been staying with an old woman in a village near Salzburg. Thanks for sending Joan home safely. She was elated when she got back. She said you and Madalena had been very kind in getting her through a rough time. You helped her to find herself, Harry, which at her age is apparently more important than losing herself. But she's done the strangest thing. When I went over to let her know you were on your way back, she told me some damning things about Conrad Fearman, and then she told me that she'd been contemplating taking vows for some time and had made her final decision. As of this moment, she's a novitiate with The Sisters of Perpetual Grace, somewhere near Brockville. I gather our mutual friend, Madalena Strauss, has gone into necessary seclusion of a different sort, being officially dead—but I hardly expected Joan to give up the ghost. Let's have a drink. Call me.

Harry jumped as the security buzzer from the lobby reverberated through the apartment. He had come straight from the airport. No one knew he was back. A few minutes later, a delivery man handed him a wrapped bouquet at the door. Inside were three stems of white orchids with a blush of scarlet at their centres. After he carefully removed the little tubes on their cut ends and settled the flowers into a vase he opened the envelope and read the card.

Welcome Home, Harry,

I'm glad everything worked out for the best!

Mr. Fearman's anonymous donation to the Children's Centre is a Godsend. I've given Morgan evidence to prosecute him without our involvement. And you'll be relieved to know I've retired from the world.

Love, Joan

P.S. Our Lucy is back with her parents in Central Siberia.

For the best? Was it for the best that Lena died? Could she possibly have lived in a world beyond redemption? Did Joan know she was dead? Did it matter if she knew? Joan believed in salvation, if only for herself. Let her be disengaged, he thought. Let her be.

He picked up the orchids and walked out to the trash chute beside his front door. He opened the chute but hesitated before releasing his grip. He held up the flowers to the fluorescent light, smiled, and gently closing the chute he carried the bouquet back into his condo.

"We deserve, these, Sailor. The nights are getting cool and autumn's coming on. Flowers are good. And people, people always … aren't."

Aren't always, she said, cheerfully adjusting his grammar.

www.ingramcontent.com/pod-product-compliance
Ingram Content Group UK Ltd.
Pitfield, Milton Keynes, MK11 3LW, UK
UKHW041643190726
13854UKWH00006B/2673